I0606631

WORLD OF MIRRORS

Judith Copek

A Wings ePress, Inc.
Romantic Suspense Novel

Wings ePress, Inc.

Edited by: Camille Netherton
Copy Edited by: Joan Powell
Senior Editor: Anita York
Executive Editor: Marilyn Kapp
Cover Artist: Pat Evans
Photo: Hans Copek

All rights reserved

Wings ePress Books
www.wingsepress.com

Published In the United States Of America

Wings ePress Inc.
3000 N. Rock Road
Newton, KS 67114

Dedication

To my husband and "first reader" Hans, who never fails to encourage me, and to my long-time writing group who always challenge me to make the scene better. To the friendly people on Rügen who answered a curious author's questions. In the intervening years, this jewel box island has become a huge tourist destination with new hotels and accommodations. The decaying buildings of the early nineties have been rehabbed, but there are still thatched roof cottages and hidden harbors as well as beautiful sailing waters.

* * *

Author's Note

Background of the East German political situation in June 1990.

At the end of World War II, the Allies divided Germany into four zones of occupation. The Soviets received the Eastern part of the country and the Eastern half of Berlin. The French, English and American zones became the German Federal Republic in 1949, while the Soviets formed the German Democratic Republic. Due to better living conditions, a steady migration began from East to West. In 1961, to stop the flight of its citizens, the East German government sealed its borders and constructed the infamous Berlin Wall.

In October 1989, the East Germans celebrated forty years of the GDR, followed immediately by peaceful demonstrations and relaxations of the borders of other Eastern-Bloc countries. These acts led to a bloodless revolution once the East German government understood that the Russians would not come to their aid in this "domestic dispute." A month later, East German citizens were allowed to travel to the West. Soon, mass demonstrations called for a total re-unification of East and West. In March 1990, the first elections were held. The vote for a complete reunification passed. In May, a treaty established the basis for monetary, economic and social unions. In July of 1990, the western D-Mark became the currencies for both countries. The Unification treaty went into effect in October. It was the Year of Miracles. *World of Mirrors* begins in June 1990.

Prologue

Stralsund, East Germany, June, 1990

All this cloak and dagger stuff was stupid. Bruss put on his windbreaker and stepped out of the tavern into the damp night. A murky darkness hung over the empty harbor. He left the *Goldener Anker* and walked toward the abandoned grain elevators, wondering if he'd nursed one too many beers as he waited for night to fall. His footsteps echoed down the wooden platform alongside the elevators. Lonely sound. Not a soul around.

Eintritt Verboten signs were plastered on the bricks and the boarded windows. "No Trespassing." If the police patrol came along, how would he explain his presence?

Wanting a cigarette, he waited in the shadows, away from the streetlight's halo in the fog. After this interview, which was bound to go badly, he would visit his sister in Hildesheim. He hadn't been back since their mother died. Ten years. He would walk around town like a tourist, admiring the half-timbered houses. The ancient white rosebush growing on the cathedral would be blooming. They called it the Millennium Rose. More than a thousand years of blossoms. Now that was something technology couldn't produce.

Even in the gloom, Bruss recognized the man walking to meet him, the "Back Office" as he insisted on being called. The code names were even stupider than the rendezvous spots. He was "the Go-Getter." Goodborn was "the AWOL." That at least fit.

Back Office didn't shake hands, but flicked on a small flashlight for an instant, right into his eyes. Typical of his rude manners. Back Office muttered, "In here," and pushed open a heavy door into a chill black space.

Inside, a stale blend of grain dust and old brick and dank harbor assaulted his nose; probably full of rats. Somewhere up in the cavernous ceiling, faint moonlight filtered down through a grilled window, illuminating a small patch of floor.

"Where is he?" Back Office's voice echoed in the vast dark space.

"We met in Sassnitz, but he wouldn't say where he was living."

"So what did he say?" Back Office never included small talk.

"He won't come home. He certainly won't give it back. He called me a 'weaselly asshole,' and told me to get lost. Said his new friends would kick my butt all the way back to the States." Bruss took a deep breath and braced himself for unpleasantness, hoping he would still be paid.

Back Office paced in the dark. "Is that all?"

"It's enough for me. He sounded very determined."

"And the woman?"

"She wasn't mentioned. I didn't ask."

Back Office paced around in a circle, his tread soft on old floorboards.

Bruss experienced a pang of fear when he heard the man's pacing stop behind him.

A rough hand yanked him by the hair and he felt a stab of pain in his throat. He flailed and grabbed at his neck, realizing with horror that the wet substance was his blood. In the moment before his death he did not think of Hildesheim and the cathedral with the white roses sprawling against the apse, but of the treachery and betrayal of those he had trusted.

One

Two days later

Through the plate glass window, I watched the juggernaut of Monday morning traffic on the Edens Expressway with envious eyes. With every fiber of being, I longed to be in one of those cars heading into Chicago, but instead, I stood in the suburban Northfield office of Coppola & Henry, staring at my boss in mute disbelief.

He waved my letter of resignation like a semaphore. "One last trip, Zara. To Germany—rather East Germany. The Wall is down now, so no problemo."

One last trip was the last thing I wanted.

"Your contract specifies that you'll give three weeks' notice. Did you forget?" Still brandishing my letter of resignation, he produced a smarmy, trying-to-be sympathetic smile, but I knew he was gloating.

He sat while I stood, which is never the position of power. I made a major attempt to look cool, but inside I seethed and boiled. You bastards. *What part of "I quit" don't you understand?*

"Why couldn't we reach you this weekend?" he asked. "What the hell were you doing in Colorado? It's not even ski season. While you were off the grid, this assignment fell into our laps. Unorthodox, perhaps, but...lucrative. A piece of cake. David says you'll love it." He smiled again.

While I fantasized ripping off his glasses, punching him in the eye and hurling him into the traffic, he blathered on.

"Very lucrative. For us and for you, naturally, as there is a generous bonus involved. The whole business has to be wrapped up by the end of the month." He cast an exaggerated glance at the calendar. "Three weeks will take us to the end of June. Fortuitous, wouldn't you say? Of course, you may be home in two weeks, maybe less."

I didn't trust my voice, and my hands were balled into fists. Time to ditch the angry woman persona. I sat down in the chair across from him. "Why can't you understand? My family situation has changed." In a calm reasoning voice. "My divorce is final and my daughter needs me. I resign effective immediately, with accrued personal time and vacation." The anger came ripping through me again. "I'm through traveling, so find someone else. You'll have to sooner or later." I stood up and smoothed my skirt over my thighs.

"Oh Zara, Zara! Why the sudden B.S.? With all that money you make, you can afford excellent housekeepers and nannies. You are going. Let me make this very clear. If you ever want to find another job in this town, you are going. I have not forgotten that business last year when you refused to recommend the software we were pushing."

"It was a piece of crap."

"We don't pay you to make unilateral decisions." He hesitated and issued a faux smile. "And besides, it wouldn't look good if word got out that you slept with a client."

Unbelievable. The nadir of threats. "I married him for God's sake! You know that!"

"Nevertheless..." He tented his fingers and narrowed his eyes. "You didn't marry the other one, since you were already married." He cleared his throat.

I wanted to kill him. I could not believe they were actually going to make me go.

David, the other partner in the business, strolled into Dennis's office.

"Good morning, Zara," he said, with that weasel smile. "We've got a great assignment brewing. Has Dennis briefed you?"

David Coppola and Dennis Henry are the principals of Coppola & Henry Enterprise Integrations, Ltd. The staff calls the company "Dungeons and Dragons," but not in earshot of the principals. I'm a computer integration specialist, which involves recommending off-the-shelf hardware and software components to build or upgrade complex computer systems. I come on site, analyze the business needs and make my recommendations. I'm good at what I do, and it used to be a power trip to realize that blockbuster companies all over the world heeded Zara Gray of Coppola & Henry.

But now six-year-old Chloe comes first, ahead of ego and big paychecks, far ahead of constant travel and missed birthdays. The knowledge that I had a child who needed more than a weekend mother had actually sunk into my geek-prone head.

David's brow wrinkled as he looked from me to Dennis and back. "Zara doesn't look very happy."

David plays good cop to Dennis's bad cop. I used to like David until I caught on to their game.

Dennis straightened his collar and ran his hand through his curly hair.

"Zara wants to leave us," he said, waving my resignation at David. His eyes bored into me. "But she has one more commitment, which she doesn't seem to understand. This is so tedious. Take her next door and explain the assignment and her obligations." He stood and handed my resignation to David.

I felt stubborn as a bulldog with a rag between its teeth. "You owe me five days vacation and five comp days," I said. "I plan to take them before I leave."

"I never figured you for the Mommy Track," he said, with a sour face.

"I always figured you for the dickhead track." *Touché.*

Dennis lowered his head and began flipping through a stack of paper. I had really pissed him off. David took my elbow and tried to lead me into his office, but I yanked my arm away.

"Jesus," he said. "Calm down. You're going to love this assignment."

In his big office, David sat behind his sleek cherry wood desk and I slumped in a chair in front of it.

While the pause grew ever more pregnant, he seemed to consider what he wanted to say. Then he cleared his throat in an exaggerated way.

"Your old friend, T.K. Drummond, called Thursday with an interesting proposition."

Another pregnant pause. I didn't like it already.

Months ago in a bar in San Francisco after too many Cosmos, I had confided to David about a client I met in Germany last summer. Back then; I was down in the dumps about the up-coming divorce. David had seemed sympathetic, but I got the impression that he had shared my confidence with Dennis, because Dennis started to regard me with a lecherous gleam in his eye. I gave him the iciest of shoulders until the gleam faded.

My antennae bristled. T.K. had been the guy I'd confided about to David.

"Most of T.K.'s propositions," I said, trying to sound off-handed, "had nothing to do with business."

He paid no attention. "The, ah, project, is a little unusual, but the price is considerably above the rate we bill for you. And all you have to do is validate some software."

I smelled a rat already. One of T.K.'s endless machinations from the sound of it. "How could that possibly take three weeks? Three hours is more like it."

~ * ~

David's brown eyes met mine with such faux sincerity that I wanted to head for the hills.

"The software has to be located first," he said. "The validation would be brief. And Dmitri in our lab has already cobbled up a CD-ROM reader for your laptop." David clasped his hands in front of him.

He was always a fashion plate with the latest Armani suit, Italian shoes and 18-carat gold cuff links. Dennis was the opposite in rumpled suits and clunky wing tips with grease stains on his ties.

"Perhaps the best way to initiate you into the details of the assignment is to let you listen to the tape of Drummond's phone call."

"What did you mean the software has to be 'found' first?"

"Drummond says the software is in Germany; East Germany, actually." He made a sound between a snort and a chuckle. "He thinks."

He glanced at my face. Men hate dealing with an angry woman: *fishwife, termagant, shrew, bitch, scold, virago, harridan, harpy.* What shall it be today? Virago seemed right.

"Listen, go get some coffee. Better make it decaf with your nerves. I'll have the phone tape ready in ten minutes."

I glowered at him.

"And Zara, don't even think of leaving. Okay?" His jaw had that stubborn pugnacious thrust that meant he was digging in his heels. I stormed from his office to the break room where I poured myself a twelve-ounce mug of high test. This could not be happening. I wanted to howl and scream and set my hair on fire.

T.K. Drummond. Odysseus in a Brooks Brothers suit: troubleshooter, hard-nosed negotiator, jackanapes of all trades, who had specialized in "finding people and fixing situations." He had a knack for mild disasters, and could add failed spy to his resume. Knowing his bizarre espionage background, there were likely to be a few old spooks involved in some half-assed impossible scheme.

Oh God, what was I going to do?

~ * ~

Fifteen minutes later, I was back in David's office with my coffee and even more attitude, but I felt queasy inside. They were going to derail the plan for my new life with Chloe. The custody agreement made it mandatory that my ex and I both remain in Chicago. The problem was between them, David and Dennis had served on every technical committee and belonged to every techie organization in town. It was almost a joke, how they knew everyone in IT management.

I had gone out on a limb by refusing to recommend some useless software a friend of theirs had developed. It got ugly. The threat that I would never work in Chicago again was not a bluff.

Exhaling a long sigh, I thought about T.K. We had been friends, then rivals in an ill-fated venture, and for one weekend last summer, lovers. We had exchanged jubilant phone calls in November when the Berlin Wall came down, but I hadn't talked to him for months. Whatever we had was not a relationship.

As a math geek, "relationship" in the conventional sense is a term I despise. Geometry and trigonometry describe relationships. The Pythagorean Theorem has nothing in common with the untidiness of human interactions.

Coppola & Henry, CYA to the max, taped all outside calls on the company line as a matter of course. David flicked on the tape and settled back into his chair with a look of anticipation on his face, like he was going to hear a fantastic sonata. I knew better. He was thinking of all that money rolling in.

As the tape played, I recognized T.K.'s Midwestern voice, expounding on the new political realities.

"...with no death strip and empty guard towers. An East Germany with unification in its future, a Communist-free East Germany."

T.K.'s mother had been a war bride, and a united Germany would mean a lot to him.

He continued, "I've been entrusted to find an AWOL American software pirate and get my hands on the CD-ROM he's made off with. I've got until the end of the month. Three weeks and money's no object. The backers will pay big bucks to get the CD-ROM back to the owners."

What software was that valuable? And why would the thief abscond to East Germany with it instead of say, Brazil?

T.K.'s voice had a higher than normal timber, as if he was nervous. Afraid of being turned down.

"I need Zara as a technical resource to validate that we've got the right CD-ROM and answer any questions I might have. She knows I'm not Joe Technology."

That was on target. T.K. wasn't a Luddite, but I wouldn't let him anywhere near *my* laptop.

"With Zara's looks, we should be able to get close to the thief. He'd never suspect her of coming after him. Our cover will be a married couple on vacation."

I dropped the f-bomb and gave David a harpy glare. "A married couple? Are you out of your mind?"

He had the decency to blush. "Well, er, ah, after what you told me about you and him, I didn't think you would object. Actually, I thought you might be happy, you know, after the divorce and all..." His voice dropped into total lameness as he polished his cufflink with a monogrammed handkerchief.

"I don't need you pimping for me!" Each new outrage topped the last one.

"Ah hell, Zara. You said you liked the guy. And how was I to know you were going to resign? It's easy money."

"No."

"We'll throw in a new laptop you can keep when you leave."

I shook my head.

"A satellite phone to keep in touch? I understand the phone system in East Germany is like, something the Russians invented. And then denied." He chuckled.

"Satellite phones won't be on the market for another six months."

"God, you know everything! We'll give you a big bonus, just to show no hard feelings."

I felt myself waver. Starting my new life with a financial cushion would be a good thing, especially if a job didn't materialize right away.

"How big?"

"A month's salary."

"Chicken feed." I crossed my arms and narrowed my eyes.

"I guess you heard what Dennis said. We could make it tough for you. Of course, we don't want to, but business is business. We would be losing a bundle if you don't go." He hesitated, brushing an imaginary crumb off his tie. "They need you right away. Like, in a couple days."

My mind was running through a maze, and coming up against dead-ends at every turn. I had arranged to spend the rest of June in Chicago looking for a new position. Chloe was already in Colorado with my sister and her family.

T.K. was an intriguing, infuriating man with whom I'd had good chemistry, but this might turn into one of his debacles. And what I had never told David or anyone is that in our business dealings, I'd inadvertently done something which had resulted in T.K.'s losing his job. I wasn't sure he knew, but if he did, he would have no reason to feel kindly toward me. Something about this assignment didn't seem right.

Time for kick-ass bargaining.

"I get an over-the-moon recommendation."

"You know you will." A relieved smile.

"And a bonus equal to three months pay."

A slight hesitation. "Two months."

"Three."

"Okay, dammit."

"And a first class ticket."

"Business Class."

"Then upgrade me with your million plus frequent flyer miles." I paused to think what else I could cadge out of this deal. "And I'll need the fastest and lightest new laptop."

"Done." Wearing a pleased half-smile he didn't look hangdog and defeated as I'd hoped. Cripes. The gravy must be sloshing out of their boat.

"Everything in writing. With signatures. Today."

"Okay, sure. By noon."

"This sounds like a meatball deal from the get-go. What makes this software so valuable? Drummond didn't even mention what it does. Or who makes it."

"That's another conversation. On Dennis' tape. You can listen later. How soon can you get going?"

"Tomorrow evening." I could polish my resume tonight and contact a first-rate headhunter in the morning. I knew several Chicago corporations with sprawling, complex computer systems. There had to be a place for me at one of them.

"Then you'll want to stop over in Portland, Maine. Maine Mining Software's home office. You can spec up there."

David continued, "They've developed a new wrinkle for a data warehouse. Drummond didn't explain it very well, but it sounds like a system our customers would go for. When you find out the details, pass them on to the home office. And stay in touch with us, Okay?"

I nodded, only half-listening.

Portland Maine and East Germany. One last trip. Before I left for the day, I bopped in to see my pal Mark in accounting. He knew all about the new "project."

"We already have the down payment. Everything else goes into an escrow account until you come back with the CD-ROM. Or not." His crooked smile betrayed his doubt.

"How much are Coppola & Henry raking in on this?" I asked.

"I hear two hundred thou." His smile broadened.

"Criminy, if I'm gone for two weeks, that's $2500.00 an hour."

Still grinning, he said, "Mind like a steel trap."

"I was always good at math."

It was one of those embarrassing talents that as a teenager, I hoped no one, especially boys, would notice. In college, I stopped bothering about who noticed and majored in computer science. For me, math and computers were like love and marriage should be.

Mark cocked his head. "This venture sounds cockamamie weird."

"You're right. I have a bad feeling about the whole business." I bent my head toward him, and lowered my voice. "I need eyes and ears on this side of the pond. Will you be my lifeline? We'll have a steak dinner and some vintage wine at Gene & Georgetti's when I come back."

"My girlfriend would love that." He grinned. "Call me anytime."

He gave me his home and cell phone numbers.

~ * ~

Monday night I called my sister in Colorado and told her the news. "You're crazy," she said. "Tell them, no way."

I didn't argue, but asked for Chloe. She seemed happy on the farm with a litter of kittens and her cousins.

After the call, I wiped away a stray tear, promising myself I would attend every play, concert and parent event in the entire second grade. I would even bake brownies and volunteer for homeroom. These resolutions didn't patch the anguish that had settled in my heart. All those negotiations today? Was I still monetizing motherhood?

~ * ~

The offices of Maine Mining Software in Portland were on the second floor of an old brick building in a rehabbed part of town. In spite of the appointment I made late yesterday, they weren't expecting me. The middle-aged receptionist, in white jeans and a T- shirt, seemed flustered as she tried one extension after another. "Oh dear, Mr. Standish is in Europe, I believe, and Mr. Chen is out of the office."

Her eyes looked red from crying.

"I'll page Mr. Wohlauer. What exactly are you here for?"

"A confidential matter that I can only discuss with one of the principals." I passed her my business card. She turned and left the lobby.

Moments later, she reappeared with a tall, dark-haired man, graying at the temples. He wore khakis and a green polo shirt, and introduced himself as Barry Wohlauer. The bags under his eyes gave him the look of exhaustion, even defeat. When I mentioned validating the software, he cast an apprehensive glance at the receptionist and said, "We'll talk in my office."

Instead, he ushered me into a small conference room with walls of painted white brick and watercolor paintings of America's Cup yachts on the walls. We sat at a long narrow table blanketed with disorderly piles of paper. Wohlauer rubbed his hands together as if chilled. There was a giant computer monitor with a keyboard at one end of the table and a black "spider" phone in the middle of the mess.

I explained why I was here.

Wohlauer's face blanched. "I'm, ah, not really in the know about the, er, the recovery process. Edgar, Mr. Standish is making those arrangements." He paused. "You'll have to forgive us. We've had an unexpected shock. A long-time colleague died yesterday." He rubbed his hands again.

"I'm so sorry. Now is a bad time to talk?"

He opened his hands. "Tell me how I can help."

"I need to know enough about your Aristotle product so that I can make an informed decision as to its validity when we retrieve the CD-ROM."

He stared out the window while I explained that as an integration specialist, I would be in a position to recommend your company's Aristotle software to various companies if I understood what the product did.

Wohlauer nodded, and called somebody named George.

"Don't refer to Germany or the missing copy. Those are confidential matters."

A few moments later, a young guy with long hair and granny glasses came into the room.

"Please give Ms. Gray an introduction to Aristotle." Wohlauer eyed me. "George will take care of you." We shook hands. "Good luck and be careful."

He said "careful" under his breath, and emphasized, "luck" with such fervid sincerity that I turned to watch him leave the room. Good luck, of course, applied to finding the software. *Be careful.* What the hell did that mean? Careful of what? I didn't know whether the warning was specific or generic, but it left me with an uneasy feeling.

I put my worries away for the time being, and sat next to George, the Aristotle guru who signed onto the system and put the programs through their paces.

"We've created a robust data warehouse," he explained, "but the cool stuff is the data mining."

Data mining is the adaptation of machine learning techniques to business applications. I knew a dozen corporations that would kill to get their hands on this product. George and I had a wonderful geekout. Behind the little round glasses, his eyes gleamed with pride. Maine Mining had leapfrogged generations ahead in data warehousing, but the data mining made me sit up and take notice. Not only did George answer my questions, he handed me a demo copy of Aristotle. "The copy expires on June 30th," he said.

I could see Coppola & Henry drooling over these technical goodies and now I understood why money was no object in getting the missing CD-ROM back to Maine Mining. I left them psyched about the software, but with a head bursting with worry and questions about the admonition to "be careful."

~ * ~

Hours later, sprawled in the wide leather seat, wrapped in a soft blanket, hurtling through the night on a wide body en route to Germany I woke up with a powerful thirst from too much wine and the humming drone of jet engines in my ears. I raised the window shade. Neither dark nor dawn. Faint light played in the eastern sky. Suspended between night and day, we flew over a thick layer of cloud. My eyes opened wider. Pools of blood lay in declivities atop the clouds. This eerie sight had to be an illusion from the light of the not-yet-risen sun, but the gory clouds looked so real. An omen? My heart hammered as I stared at the crimson lakes.

"Get a grip," I told myself and found my Evian bottle and gulped down some water.

This trip to Germany? Just another job to do. Find, validate and go.

I recalled my weekend trip to Colorado. It had been wrenching to leave Chloe, sobbing and clutching my waist with her thin little arms. Explanations about a new job and a new life just hadn't cut it, making me feel like a first-class shit. Why was I on this damned plane instead of home with my daughter?

A few minutes later, the 747 hit a pocket of rough air that bumped me out of my guilty thoughts.

Another glance out the porthole revealed a rising sun, with only a pink blush daubed on the cloud tops. A good omen. I slept again.

The jet descended through a thick gray ceiling in a hellish crosswind, landing with the wheels bumping and the fuselage bouncing. As we taxied to the gate at Berlin's Tegel Airport, strong gusts drove fat raindrops against the windows, and splashed watery waves along the tarmac. In tones of pewter, tin, gunmetal and old tarnished silver, Tegel glistened in the rain. Berlin on a cold June morning. I'd taken enough trips here to pick up some German.

The flight attendant returned my navy blazer from the wardrobe. Waiting to disembark, I opened my passport. The photo wasn't bad. The woman with the slightly quizzical expression and the faint smile was not glamorous, but appeared self-assured. I wore my hair shorter in the photo, but then as now, the medium auburn color was jazzed up with burgundy highlights. Subtle makeup made my eyes bigger, my lips fuller, and my cheekbones sculpted. Making the best of good features. Vainly, I decided that I could easily pass for twenty-something.

In my passport photo, I wore the same thin white cashmere sweater and navy blazer that I had on today. Even the identical nautical patterned red, white, blue and gold silk scarf. The image didn't reveal the soft denim jeans and suede loafers. Toronto or Tampa, Los Angeles or London, unless I had a business appointment, I never arrived wearing anything else.

T.K. didn't meet me, but the rain had let up, so I dived into a taxi.

"Hotel Kempinski, *bitte*," I told the driver.

The doorman greeted me with a giant umbrella. Walking through the chic lobby, I admired the fat teak pillars, red sofas and thick modern carpets on green marble floors. A spare-no-expense floral arrangement graced a polished wood table. The welcoming comfort of money.

T.K. had already checked in, and I was expected, so they handed me an extra key and delivered my bags to the room. T.K. had only booked one room, but I was too tired to care.

The fact was I still had no idea how this thing with T.K. would unfold, but I eyed the queen-sized bed, thinking how typical of T.K. to make that assumption. Mostly I felt ambivalent, but any feeling at all after a night flight was only a step above numbness. T.K. had left a note in the middle of the bed, scrawled on the hotel stationary, "Running errands. Back soon. xoxo."

The word 'hare-brained' etched itself into my consciousness as the best adjective for my situation.

A long sybaritic bath would ease my tired bones as well as my psyche. Under a mountain of fragrant bubbles, I lapsed into a pleasant reverie in the bathtub. I woke to a low voice from the bedroom singing "Louie Louie." How long had I been napping?

A light tap on the door. "Zara, are you up for a welcoming glass of champagne?"

"Just a moment!" Naturally the drinking would begin.

With iridescent puffs and spumey wisps of the *bain moussant* still clinging to me, I slipped on the thick white robe and knotted the belt. Time for a lucid conversation about this project and to start laying down some of the ground rules.

When I emerged from the bathroom, T.K., in a charcoal gray suit with his tie askew, was leaning over the laptop I had unpacked and set up on the desk. He held a brimming champagne glass in each hand, and his brow puckered in a frown as he stared at my laptop.

"Hey," I said. He looked up at me, and he seemed different than I remembered. I could never decide if he was handsome or not, but his self-possession was so absolute that good looks seemed a given. His face was a series of flat planes that merged smoothly into an interesting masculine appearance. Neither chiseled nor polished. He had exchanged his horn-rimmed glasses for contacts, and his dark blue eyes assessed his surroundings with an edgy new alertness.

"Even wet and slippery as a seal, you're a wonderful sight."

A wonderful half-naked sight.

He smiled in his careless way and put the champagne glasses on the coffee table, but instead of bestowing the friendly kiss I expected, he grabbed my bathrobe sash and pulled me toward him. The sash came undone and the robe fell open.

"What's the matter with you?" I asked, wrapping myself up again.

He took a step backward. "Off on the wrong foot already."

"Don't mistake me for your comfort woman." I knotted the sash twice.

"Comfort is a word I rarely associate with women," he muttered, picking up the champagne glasses. He chugged one glass and nodded grumpily in the direction of the laptop. "What's with the computer?"

"State of the art and bleeding edge. But the best thing is that my company's hardware guy cobbled up a CD-ROM reader attachment. I can verify the data warehouse when you find it. It's so...so James Bond."

My voice trailed off as his brows again contracted into a scowl. I stood with the bath water running down my ankles and feet, into the rug.

"You can't take that thing where we're going. It would attract too much attention."

"I certainly will take 'that thing.' Do you think I can validate software with an...an ouija board?"

T.K. had omitted even the most elementary pleasantries. Like hello, how are you? Like, sorry I didn't meet your plane.

A white-hot fire stoked by too little sleep and this rude reception raced along my nerves. *You bastard! Job or no job, I'm not going anywhere with you.*

In my iciest voice, I said, "If they gave out medals for boorishness, you'd walk away with the gold! There's not enough money on this planet to keep me on this project. I'm out of here on the next plane. Find some ditsy bimbo with mush for brains to do your validation."

I swept across the room and turned off the laptop. His scowl had metamorphosed into nonplussed disbelief as he gaped at me. Someone knocked softly. T.K. hesitated, put down the glasses, and opened the door.

A bellhop bearing a vase filled with pink and white roses took a few steps into the room. Sensing some tension, he glanced uncertainly from T.K. to me. Acting as if we had been interrupted while sipping tea, T.K. exchanged the flowers for a big tip. The bellhop threw him a curious look and left. T.K. put the vase on a table and extracted one half-opened bud. Muttering something about a "peace offering," he sauntered across the room, bowed and offered the perfect pink rose with a courtly flourish. "Sweetie," he said, "you're cute when you're mad, but can we cut this whole scene and start the cameras rolling again at the moment when you stepped out of the bath?"

<h1 style="text-align:center">Two</h1>

While I stood dumbfounded, holding the rose, T.K. took a boom box out of a carton, popped in a tape and Vivaldi's guitar concerto filled the room. He bustled around, picking up cardboard and plastic bags and stuffing them into the wastebasket. Making amends.

Maybe I had rushed to judgment; maybe the bathrobe had been an accident. Maybe. I stuck the rose back into the vase and picked up the champagne flute.

"To the burial of the hatchet," I hesitated a moment, and raised my glass.

"Amen," he said. "Best friends forever?"

I gave a half-nod. Not quite so fast. "What's with you?" I asked. "I'll need my laptop when you find the CD-ROM."

"Oh shit, I'm sorry. But—don't you think it's totally out of character?" He gestured at the computer. "How many wives lug a laptop around on vacation?"

"This is no vacation. And anything could be in that case."

We sat side by side on the edge on the brocade loveseat and drank champagne. T.K. exasperated me, but I could never stay angry for long. I looked through the collection of tapes. Vivaldi, Bach and the Beatles. All the music he knew I liked.

"You're on probation," I said.

~ * ~

A little before three, we left the hotel and walked along the Kurfürstendamm, the famous shopping, strolling, making-the-scene-in-Berlin street. I was collapsing with jet lag and yearning for a power nap, but T.K. insisted that we had an important meeting with his associates who had an office around the corner from the Europa Center.

My goal was to get through the meeting without yawning in everyone's face. Finding out about how we would locate the software would be a plus

"I didn't know you had colleagues," I said. "Are they more technical resources?"

"No, sweetie, you're the technical resources."

"Then who...?"

"The guy who hired me and one of his tiresome bureaucrats. Not important to our operation."

Probably his spooky old friends, trying to make a few Deutschmarks.

"I need some background information before I meet your colleagues. Who is this software thief you're going after?"

He gave me a sideways look and cleared his throat. "Charles Goodborn, late of Maine Mining Software in Portland, Maine, is a bad apple. He's also a marketing genius. The gossip mill says he was one jump ahead of the IRS, the alimony demands of two ex-wives and the 'Deadbeat Dad of the Year' award."

T.K. took my arm as we crossed the street. "A month ago he took off with his German girlfriend, an ice cream habit for cocaine and a CD-ROM containing Aristotle." T.K.'s eyes met mine. "Our assignment is to lay our hands on that CD and return it to Maine Mining."

"How conversant are you with the Aristotle software?" I asked.

He stared at the sky. Men always hate to admit they don't know everything.

"I read their marketing propaganda on the plane," I said, not mentioning my little side trip to Portland. It hadn't been easy to read with a big "confidential" stamped on every page. "This is killer software. If it does what it's supposed to, Maine Mining should be kicking up their collective heels all the way to the bank. When this Goodborn ripped off their new product, Maine Mining must have panicked."

"It was a seven alarm fire. They were hoping for a sweet deal for Aristotle when Goodborn took off."

I stifled another yawn, as T.K. stopped to admire a pricey raincoat in a display window.

"Maine Mining's suitor is an outfit called Software Umbrella," he said.

Everyone knew about Software Umbrella, a behemoth that bought up classy little high-techs by the gross. Aristotle's dating mining would be right in their sweet spot.

"Software Umbrella wants to close the deal before the end of the quarter. Megabucks are at stake. Maine Mining has their reputation to say nothing of their life savings on the line."

We crossed another street, passing the towering ruin of the Gedächtniskirche, a blackened spire, the war memorial in the midst of the economic miracle.

T.K. continued. "We've got to find Aristotle ASAP."

So now it's 'we'.

"If Goodborn stole the software a month ago, why did it take them so long to go after him?"

"Nobody knew where the hell he was. It took all month to track him down."

"And who did that?" I asked.

A man dressed in white stood on the sidewalk behind his colorful barrel organ. A wind-up toy monkey perched on top wistfully clapping his plush paws together next to the donation box. With a pang, I thought of Chloe's delight in such a sight. The jaunty tune, instead of cheering me up, reminded me of the carnivals that came through little eastern Colorado towns in the summer. The mechanical music brought back all the rigged games, saccharine cotton candy and hokey sideshows.

As I dropped some coins into the open chest next to the monkey, T.K. said, "My associates don't know anything about you and so I, uh, exaggerated your professional experience a tad in certain matters."

"What?" I looked at him. He hadn't answered my question about who tracked Goodborn down.

He thrust his hands deep into his jacket pockets.

"They, ah, my associates, think you have specific credentials for, um, this line of work."

"What are you saying?" I asked, dense with fatigue. Straight ahead was the busy plaza in front of the Europa Center. In the reflection of a shop window, I saw T.K. frown, but he didn't answer. "If I don't have the right credentials, then why did you ask for me?" He was so exasperating. "I select software for a living. I can certainly identify and validate Aristotle. So I don't know what you have exaggerated."

"Hold that thought," he said. "Here we are." T.K. pulled open a plate glass door, motioning me inside the foyer of a modest office building. We trod along a drab hall and he pushed the elevator button. T.K. stuck his hands back into his pockets, and stared impassively at the elevator. I caught his mood. My anxiety molecules were swarming.

We rode to the fourth floor in silence.

At T.K.'s knock, a man with a blue blazer admitted us.

"Ah, Drummond!" He gave me a careless nod and said, "Hello, luv," as if I were his favorite barmaid. I would expect an Englishman to be a bit more formal, but before I could react he asked, "Where's the technical bloke?"

"She's right here!" T.K. said in an off-hand way, gesturing in my direction.

The man stared at me with cold eyes. He was expecting Bill Gates?

T.K. introduced William Putnam, who shook hands without a shred of cordiality. His ramrod posture signaled a military background, a spit and polish Brit with sharp eyes, and a nose that zigzagged below the bridge; the nose of a fighter and the jacket of a gentleman.

The office was furnished entirely in teakwood except for a Haitian cotton sofa against the far wall. A second man sitting at the desk stood when we entered. His getting up was a prolonged process; all six and a half feet of him had to unfold. In a laconic accent I immediately placed as Midwestern, he shook my hand while identifying himself as Jesse Smith.

Smith indicated that T.K. and I should be seated. I chose the sofa and T.K. slouched down next to me. No one seemed inclined to chitchat.

Putnam retrieved a piece of fax paper from an in-basket, and handed it to T.K. He said it had arrived last night from Portland Maine. T.K. swore under his breath while he read the fax, and before he had finished, our hosts began a difficult-to-follow conversation.

"Bloody well changes everything," muttered Putnam.

"We'll have to scramble." This from Smith.

Putnam spoke again, his voice bitter. "That's what comes from sending in the amateurs. They blow the operation, wind up dead, and the pros have hell to pay."

T.K. grimaced.

"I don't think it can be a coincidence that he was killed." Smith again.

I sat up straighter. *Killed?*

Putnam narrowed his eyes. "Those software boyos had no business sending this Bruss chap over here—somebody Goodborn knew."

After a disquieting moment, it dawned on me. This was the dead colleague everyone at Maine Mining had been so distraught over. "That Bruss chap" had been sent over here to find Charles Goodborn. Like T.K. and me. And now he was dead. Murdered. Yet T.K. and I had been hired before anyone knew the first mission had become a train wreck. What kind of asinine scheme was this? Wohlauer's advice yesterday to "be careful" was a drastic understatement.

I looked at T.K., who handed me the fax. The East German authorities in the port city of Stralsund had discovered a male body in a grain elevator. The West German passport of Helmut Bruss of Portland, Maine was in his pocket. His throat had been slashed.

No wonder the employees in Portland had been teary-eyed.

While Smith spoke of regrouping and contingencies, and taking the plan to the next level, Putnam kept repeating, "I don't like it. This fairly well changes everything," which echoed my thoughts exactly.

I could still hear the faint music of the barrel organ down in the plaza, but now the tune sounded sinister. I realized all three men were looking at me expectantly. T.K. gave me a little nudge. Lost in my thoughts, I hadn't heard the question directed at me.

"Oh sorry, I was thinking about poor Bruss."

T.K. nodded toward Putnam.

"Bill would like a rundown of your professional credentials."

"Your technical qualifications." Putnam stared at me with narrow eyes and a thin mouth.

I ignored him and addressed Jesse Smith. "I know the underlying technology that Maine Mining is using, and I can outline the business reasons driving the development of Aristotle."

They were all listening now, so I continued more confidently, "And this whole scheme doesn't make any sense from the viewpoint of a computer analyst.

"As I understand the situation, Goodborn walked off with the specifications and the code to an extremely complicated system that is ahead of the curve in the West, and totally unknown in Eastern Europe. It's part of this new technology known as data warehousing and data mining. The Maine Mining product needs a sophisticated network, a network management system, a graphical user interface, a state of the art RDBMS, a server that can accommodate lots of gig, and a clutch of add-ons. High-powered hardware. Security. Artificial Intelligence software to scrub the data. Maybe some fuzzy logic. And middleware to glue it all together."

I had reeled off the futuristic laundry list, practically licking my chops at the cool technology.

Putnam's eyes glazed over; Smith uttered, "technical." T.K. made a wry face and asked, "Any chance of your translating that into English?"

I debated apologizing for talking over their heads and decided not to. "What I tried to say is that you wouldn't peddle an ICBM to Attila the Hun."

"Couldn't Goodborn market his product in Western Europe?" asked Smith, rubbing his chin.

"That would be tricky if the software wasn't purchased legitimately," I said, standing and walking around the room. "There would be no licensing agreement or support going forward. "I paused and addressed Smith again. "Initially these big systems need loads of support. Database administrators. Network jockeys. That's why the deal Maine Mining made with Software Umbrella is so good. Software Umbrella would have the troops to maintain complex products. Goodborn would know that Aristotle needs experts to do the technical handholding." I sat again. "Then it would seem that Goodborn is looking for a payoff." Smith said, still pulling on his chin.

"That would be my guess." T.K. said. "But why shoot the messenger?"

"We can't be sure Goodborn even knows the messenger has been shot," Smith said.

T.K. scowled again, and Putnam disappeared into a back room. Smith stood slowly, like a robot, and walked around his desk. He pulled a wilted rose out of a vase on a side table and dumped it into a wastebasket. He sat down again.

"Did you know that this Bruss had come to look for the software, too?" I whispered to T.K. Before he could answer, Putnam returned with a tray, which held four glasses, a wine bottle and a corkscrew. "Edgar says, 'no payoffs.'"

"Who's Edgar?" I asked. Smith and Putnam turned and looked at T.K. "And why no payoffs?"

"Edgar is the man with the money, the one who's been financing the project," T.K. said quickly. He added, "Edgar thinks sending Bruss after Goodborn verged on idiocy."

Putnam poured four glasses of Mosel. We each took one.

"Edgar is in charge now?" I asked.

"Yes, Edgar is calling the shots," said Smith.

I wasn't positive, but I thought Wohlauer had mentioned the name "Edgar" yesterday in Portland.

T.K. stretched his legs out in front of him, and grimaced, like he was in pain. The news hadn't improved his temperament. He lit a cigarette, and offered one to Putnam, who busied himself lighting it. He inhaled greedily.

"Edgar is intent on protecting his investment." Spoken in a cloud of smoke.

"Then what I can't visualize is how this whole business is going to work," I said. "In the first place, I don't understand why we were hired if this Bruss was expected to talk Goodborn into returning. The second thing is Goodborn's not likely to relinquish his CD-ROM with all those technical goodies. Not without a wad of cash. If this Edgar refuses to deal, and somebody is shooting messengers—"

"Bloody hell!" interrupted Putnam, jumping to his feet. His face had gone magenta. "What we don't need is a nervous Nellie Prima Donna making a bottle of things." He was looking at T.K. while he spoke in clipped sentences. "Drummond, you said you could assemble a 'team.' Blokes who could work together." He nodded at me. "She's one of these bloody clueless technical types!"

I had blown it with the messenger remark and the techno talk. If I was on my way out the door, I wanted to leave on my terms.

"You bloody well need to keep your mind on the business of getting Goodborn's CD," Putnam barked, hooking his thumb in my direction. "And she's only good for one thing."

Was Putnam insinuating that T.K. wanted me along only for sex? That scenario had crossed my mind, but I was appalled to think of it as a topic for group discussion.

Smith twiddled his thumbs and stared at his desk blotter.

T.K. glowered at Putnam. "We are perfectly capable of retrieving that god-damned CD!"

He stood and Putnam stood. Before I knew what was happening, Smith jumped up and grabbed my handbag and me. With a firm hand he practically frog marched me out of the office, down the hall, out of the building. In the elevator, I could hear T.K. and Putnam bellowing at each other. Smith deposited me at an umbrella-shaded table in the plaza.

This was worse than anything I had imagined. Putnam's crude sexism, these crazy spooks and now a murder. Not with any old victim, but the man sent here to do our job. How creepy was that? I needed an exit strategy. I waited at the table in the plaza I saw T.K. approach with his jaunty walk, just like everything was hunky-dory. Men!

~ * ~

Afterward, when I had asked the outcome of his set-to with Putnam, T.K. had blown me off with a cryptic, "Just keep a low profile and let me deal with him." God knows, I didn't want to deal.

Now T.K. and I were eating sauerbraten, dumplings and red cabbage washed down with beer and wine in the cozy pub-like atmosphere of a restaurant tucked away in a corner of the glitzy Grand Hotel. The Grand Hotel lacked that comradely feeling. Built with Japanese yen, the hotel, an East Berlin showplace of the "People's Republic," sat solidly in capitalist splendor off Unter den Linden, the boulevard between Alexanderplatz and the Brandenburg Gate. East and West. Then and now. Night and day. Everything changed with the toppling of the wall last November, but mental gears, in their habitual grinding, shift slowly.

Compared to the cacophony and bustle of a Chicago restaurant, our corner table in this wood-paneled room felt quiet, almost isolated. Nevertheless, T.K. lowered his voice to a confidential pitch and said, "Before the old regime collapsed, these walls witnessed all kinds of Cold War shenanigans."

"Like what?"

"Like some of the rooms were outfitted with interes-ting... hardware."

"Along with robes and hair-dryers?"

"Hidden cameras and listening devices. My dear, what big eyes and ears you have," he quipped with a leer.

"And was the mini-bar stocked with Mickey Finns?"

"In every flavor."

The waiter came by, and I watched T.K. as they conferred. In the last year, his brown hair had become thatched with white, but all six feet of him still slouched, leaned and tilted, feet up whenever possible, hands moving in lazy casual gestures, like the careless sweep of his arm now as he discussed the virtues of various local beers in accent-free, idiomatic German.

With his gestures and jokes and easy manner, he acted like a man who had been pardoned.

Why do I even like T.K.? I asked myself, not for the first time. I'd met him on an assignment last summer. He was on a project as a negotiator between two companies and he passed the unconscious screening tests—age, deportment, manners, intelligence and even humor. He squired me around the city, introducing me to food and drink typical to Berlin, and drank Campari Orange with me at the Kempinski Sidewalk Café.

We had commiserated about my disintegrated marriage and his rootless life. He was fun, romantic and had even seemed a little vulnerable. We shared crazy adventures on the Berlin project, and fell into bed in Bremen. In the uncertainty and chaos of the project last summer, I had overlooked his lack of candor.

Before we got back to the hotel, I would have to walk a tightrope over the morass of the great sexual swamp. Negotiate the ground rules. Negotiating was T.K.'s forte. He kept up a gossipy chitchat through dinner, shunning all shoptalk.

Time to take the bull by the horns. I took a deep breath. "Putnam will likely give me the bum's rush tomorrow, but just in case he doesn't, tell me how we will find Goodborn. Where is he? My management said East Germany."

T.K. flashed his careless smile. "We're going to rent a conspicuous car and drive up to the Baltic, to a beautiful little island with thatched roof cottages and hidden harbors. I'll look for real estate bargains and investments, and you can visit the spa and play with your laptop. How does that sound?"

"Like a vacation. Now tell me what's really going on, without the spin. Who is this creep Putnam and why does he hate me? Why didn't you tell him you would have a female technical analyst?"

"Long, long story," said T.K. with a lazy smile. "Billy Boy and I go way back."

I tried another tack.

"What about this woman that Goodborn decamped with?"

"Cherchez la femme," he said, with a wicked grin. "Romy Motte."

T.K. told me that German-born Ms. Motte was the Maine Mining administrative assistant who spoke excellent English. He crossed his fork over his knife to signal he had finished his entrée and continued his story. "Right after Chuck and Romy left, the company hired a private detective to find them. The detective traced them first to Berlin and then to the island—this based on Romy's place of birth on a three-jobs-ago employment application. She had a different date and German town of birth at every job.

"The Baltic island was a perfect hiding place—until the wall was chipped into souvenir pieces. With the two Germanys voting to unite, hiding places will disappear quicker than the old regime."

T.K. said that Chuck had been friendly with a Maine Mining technician named Herbert Bruss, a German national. Maine Mining Software executives begged Bruss to go to East Germany and try to talk Chuck into giving back the CD. They told Bruss that Chuck would get his share of the money when the sale went through. They would cough up a little extra, because they knew about Chuck's financial troubles. Bruss had telephoned Portland that he had located Chuck and would make contact. And then Bruss dropped off the map.

T.K. repeated that Maine Mining should have sent a professional after Chuck, someone Chuck couldn't bamboozle.

Had Chuck "bamboozled" Bruss by killing him? Didn't sound right to me.

"Old Edgar blew a fuse about the 'Bruss decision.' And that's where things stood until that damnable fax appeared." The waiter poured the rest of the wine into T.K.'s glass.

"I still don't understand why we were hired if Bruss had already been sent after Chuck," I said.

He downed the wine in one swallow. "Because Edgar's worried about his cash and is throwing his weight around and changing his mind every five minutes."

I nodded, having known a few Edgars in my time, but I wasn't sure if T.K. was being straight with me. Nobody in that office today seemed overly concerned that a man had been murdered. Maybe old spooks wore heavy armor against unexpected murders, but I didn't.

While we waited for dessert, T.K. asked me to explain what a data warehouse was. "Without the techno-tongue."

"In a nutshell, reams of information are buried in old computer systems. The operational word here is 'buried.' Meaning inaccessible, requiring phalanxes of programmers to dig it up. By the time they do, business needs have changed. The amount of information and the need to manipulate it advances faster than information technology. Smart programs can 'mine' data and extract trends, statistics, good demographics—information companies don't even know they have." I paused and let myself smile. "But data can be dirty."

"I love it when you talk like that."

"Dirty in the sense that it has to be scrubbed, I added primly. "Numeric fields should contain numbers, and you don't want the same customer in the file four times with her name spelled differently. There's a difference between raw data and information. We want clean, accurate information." I had assumed my consultant voice, a little didactic for a casual conversation.

"You really do have a handle on all this stuff, don't you?" T.K. gave me a respectful look.

"It's only technology."

He rolled his eyes.

"I'll be your techno-mentor," I said, "Should I decide to stay."

"Tell me more."

"The most intriguing part of this data warehouse is an ingenious front end that makes data conversion a breeze, maybe cutting development time in half. You save time, you save money." I paused. "What was Chuck's role at Maine Mining? You said he was a marketing genius."

"Old Chuck scrounged up a few million in venture capital from Edgar and his cronies. And Chuck was the player who convinced Software Umbrella to buy Aristotle."

Chuck could talk the birds down from the trees.

For dessert we shared a slab of apple strudel with rum raisin ice cream. T.K. ate a few mouthfuls and pushed the plate toward me. He watched while I polished off the remainder. The boozy ice cream shot with raisins, melting on the warm strudel, tasted far too delicious to leave a single morsel on the plate. I was scooping up the last bite when T.K. said, "Zara, if you keep chowing down like that, there's going to be a lot more of you to love."

I stopped chewing, put my fork down and stared at this insolent man who was supposed to be on his best behavior. One look at my face and he began to back-pedal.

"Er, that is, if and when I am ever afforded..." His voice trailed off.

"We have to talk," I said, feeling my cheeks flush.

The waiter presented the check, and T.K. whipped out an Amex card.

A sharp wind with a memory of spring assailed us as we stepped into the street. T.K. put his arm around me.

We strolled over to Unter den Linden, but that famous boulevard had little traffic and only scattered pedestrians. T.K. pointed to the tall minaret-like television tower that marked Alexanderplatz. Spent linden blossoms, pale yellow and frilly, swirled along our path as we walked alone across vast bare spaces and past the abandoned fifties-style government buildings. The trees' subtle fragrance perfumed the air.

"I never imagined I would cross Marx-Engels-Platz with a lovely lady on my arm. Hell, it was only nine months ago when the old regime celebrated its anniversary. Forty years of oppressing the populace, and four weeks later the Wall comes down and the leaders march into the unemployment line." He hummed a military-sounding march.

"Zara, imagine this vast square populated by May Day celebrations! Forty freakin' years of them. Hundreds of tanks rumbling by the reviewing stand followed by marching battalions. Giving the people bread and circuses."

Now those times were as dead as the crushed blossoms we trod on in this huge emptiness that felt like the last night on earth. The accumulation of this century's ugly history bore down on me as we trekked all the way to Alexanderplatz.

I headed for a bench. T.K. sat next to me and we watched a group of young folks in stonewashed denim jeans trying to decide where to spend the evening.

"When are we supposed to leave for that island?" I asked.

"Soon." Had he heard the doubt in my voice? T.K. lit a cigarette and inhaled the smoke. "Now tell me what's on your mind. Is your divorce final?"

"Very final." I paused to pick my words. "Our split hurt Chloe more than Taylor or me."

"And?"

I took a deep breath. "I tried to resign on Monday." My story came out in a rush of words. "I shouldn't be here, T.K. I have a little girl who needs me. I need to find a job without travel. And now this murder has me freaked out. I don't want to get involved in something risky."

I expected T.K. to react with his typical "oh shit!" and maybe even sympathize or suggest a way out, but he continued to smoke without looking at me.

In a moment I would be weeping. "I really can't talk about this anymore," I said, gulping back my tears.

He remained silent. His head was down, and I couldn't see his face, but I didn't think my sorrowful confession had pleased him.

"What's going on in your life?" I asked when he didn't offer so much as a consoling word.

"Once upon a time there was a pretty woman in Brussels. But since I'm not living there anymore—Zara, did you think I wouldn't ever wise up to your little tricks on that project last summer? You made me look like an ass."

"Sorry," I said, dreading the finger pointing and recriminations. We were both remembering the incident last summer in Berlin. I didn't believe T.K. wanted to re-hash it any more than I did.

He had spoken in an even voice, and his eyes warned: don't pull any more stunts like that. Maybe he did carry a grudge.

"We're colleagues now," I assured him.

"Understood," he said. He threw down his cigarette and stood up. I stood, too. Swamped by waves of jet lag, I wanted to collapse and sleep for days. Alone.

"Another walk?" He suggested. "Coffee in the Nikolai Viertel?"

"I'm beat. T.K., we need to lay down some ground rules."

The faintest irritation passed over his brow. Oh God, I was too tired for another fight.

"I need time to...get reacquainted. It's been almost a year, and—"

"Take as much time as you like." We walked back toward Unter den Linden. T.K. fixed his eyes on the cabstand at a hotel across the street. "How exactly does 'getting reacquainted' translate into a rule?" A puckered brow eclipsed his easy-going expression.

Afraid I wouldn't be able to get so many awkward words out of my mouth, I spoke in a flat, toneless voice without pausing for breath.

"The rule is that we don't unless both of us want to. Another rule is nothing remotely kinky, as defined by your maiden aunt. I didn't come over here for a no-holds-barred orgy. The last rule, well, it's not a rule, but I would like to see a blood donor card or some recent document—of course I will provide same."

He burst out, "Shit! You clinical women can squash a man's romantic impulses quicker than a cold shower." He started across the intersection without even taking my arm.

"These are the nineties, T.K." I was running after him. "Some things have to be said."

We climbed into a cab and nobody spoke all the way back to the hotel. I had sounded like the last of the vestal virgins, but I couldn't think how to make my words less harsh.

I undressed in the bathroom and put on modest white pajamas. T.K. was drinking a cognac from the minibar when I emerged. He didn't even look at me.

I got into bed, clung to my side of the mattress and immediately feigned sleep. T.K. slid in a few minutes later. So much distance separated us you could have plowed a furrow down the middle of the bed and not touched either of us.

~ * ~

Early the next morning while T.K. slept, I jogged past deserted cafés and a street sweeper whistling as he pushed his wide broom along the Ku'damm. A lion roared in the nearby zoo. Blocks later I ran into the Tiergarden, a sprawling park.

The remnants of my jet lag fell away like an old snakeskin, allowing me to think clearly about the misogynist Putnam, the felonious Charles Goodborn, the dead Bruss, and my deteriorating bond with T.K. Logic told me to take the next plane back to the U.S., but I had never been a quitter. If it weren't for the murder, I would relish putting my head down, gritting my teeth and seeing it through.

When I returned to the hotel room, T.K. was propped against the pillow, arms crossed behind his head, looking almost contrite.

"I brought you coffee," I said, putting a Tschibo take-out container on his nightstand.

"I've been such a jerk. How could you stand it?" He removed the lid from the cup and took a sip.

I dropped to the rug and started my push-ups. Five sets of ten. 'Abs tight and breathe through it.' I flopped onto my back and rested a moment before beginning my sit-ups.

T.K. watched me intently. "I would like to apologize and make amends."

"I'm listening," I told him, beginning a set of power crunches.

"We can make a great team." He sipped his coffee. "I'm willing to reform if you'll have me."

"It's not up to me." Pause. "Putnam, Smith and especially," crunch, gasp, "Edgar have to be convinced."

Finished, I stretched out, arms above my head, as far as I could reach.

He said, "We can convince them."

I could see him watching me, trying to decide what was in my head, which was that I was conflicted about staying on the project. "If your associates say *auf Wiedersehen,* I'll be out of here like greased lightning."

After easing into one more long stretch, I stood up and tossed a towel around my sweaty neck. A forage through the mini-bar netted two orange juices. I held one out to T.K.

His eyes hadn't left me. Now he looked like the man I had come here to work with, the man with the wicked gleam in his eye and the crooked carefree smile. I gave him a lot of credit for not propositioning me that very moment.

~ * ~

At eleven o'clock we marched across the square in front of the Europa Center just as we had yesterday. T.K. wore a navy blazer and tan slacks and I had on a navy blazer with a tan skirt, an unplanned Tweedledum and Tweedledee effect that we had only noticed at the last minute.

"Do we look like a team, or do we look like a couple of dip shits?" he had asked, as we gaped at each other.

"A jacket conveys authority. I have to wear a jacket. If we start changing now, we'll be late."

With my jacket distinguished by a red, blue, and gold nautical patterned scarf, we didn't look quite so dorky.

My stomach had more knots than a mariner's handbook and the sight of Putnam made the hair stand up on my arms. I did have a plan to determine if I was still on the payroll.

Like yesterday, Putnam admitted us, and like yesterday, Smith raised his long body out of the chair. I shook hands with as much cordiality as I could summon.

"Putnam began putting glasses on a tray. "No wine for me," I said."

"I'll take a pass, too," T.K. said.

Putnam shrugged and returned with a bottle of Stout and a glass. His shirtsleeves had been rolled up with military precision, exposing freckled wrists and muscular forearms covered with light brown hair. I couldn't help noticing that his scarred and misshapen knuckles bore the history of back alley brawls, while his neat, well-tended nails looked like they had been on the receiving end of manicures and nail buffers.

"I want to clarify a few issues before we start," I said.

Putnam turned, his eyes sharp with suspicion as I stood up.

"We have a contract, executed in good faith by all parties. I expect payment for my services *whether you use them or not*. That's the first issue." My eyes travelled around the room to each of them.

T.K. raised his eyebrows and crossed his ankles.

"Surely Edgar understands about business contracts," I continued. Smith's eyes didn't look so sanguine.

"The second issue has to do with your misconception that I am not a team player." I walked across the room, turned and faced them. "I've been on sales teams, re-engineering teams, and teams brought together to produce computer systems. No one ever intimated I was not a team player."

T.K. examined his fingernails. A flush crept out of Putnam's collar and surged toward his cheeks. Smith folded his hands and looked thoughtful.

The only sound in the room was the faint din of traffic circling the square and a bus shifting gears.

Smith said, "We didn't mean to imply—"

"A SWAT team would have been better than all those other bloody teams together." Putnam cut him off.

He narrowed his eyes. "A mistake could cost your life." He jerked his thumb towards T.K. "Or more likely his."

"You will want time to talk among yourselves as to whether I stay or not."

I opened the door and walked smack into a man on his way in. He grabbed me by the shoulders. He had big hands and white hair and he was very tall.

"Whoa," he said. "No pretty women allowed to leave without introductions." A loud jovial laugh followed.

I rubbed my nose which had been flattened against his chest.

"Blimey, Edgar! What the hell are you doing here?"

"Putnam, I might ask you the same question."

Edgar's smile morphed into a scowl as he looked around the room with tight eyes, noticing the stout glass, the ashtrays and maybe even the lack of purpose. In a booming voice he demanded, "Why isn't the team on that island looking for the goddamn software instead of lollygagging in Berlin? I don't pay for people to sit on their ass."

"We, ah, were getting our ducks in a row," said Smith, who jumped to attention.

Edgar surveyed the room again, and his eyes landed on me. I was still standing by the door dabbing at my nose. He put a big meaty hand out.

"Edgar Standish."

"Zara Gray," I said, shaking with a firm grip. "I'm the technical consultant."

"Ah, good. Very good. Somehow we were expecting a man. Pleasant surprise, I must say. Welcome aboard." He eyed me up and down and didn't neglect any of the female parts. "Please be seated," he said, and when I picked the corner of the sofa, he parked himself next to me, close enough to be off-putting.

Putnam jumped in. "Miss Gray's, ah, suitability hasn't been established yet. We were discussing it."

"I can vouch firsthand for Zara's technical acumen," said T.K.

Putnam looked like he had drunk unsweetened lemonade.

"Then that's settled. What's the plan?" Edgar cast a sharp look around the room, and when no one spoke up, his face reddened. "There has to be a goddamn plan. Let's hear it!"

I was still reeling from the "then that's settled" pronouncement. *Shit.*

Putnam lit an English Oval and moved the ashtray closer. "Drummond and I go in together. He poses as a German, shows me the ropes of doing business in the new climate. Property acquisitions. Investments. All that rot." He inhaled and looked at each of us, as if to challenge an argument.

Edgar looked at the ceiling.

T.K. examined his shoeshine. Smith, pulling at his chin, added, "The advantage is, Goodborn will not likely suspect a German-English team would be coming for him."

"How do you plan to make contact?" Edgar asked.

Putnam shrugged as if to say, easy as pie. "Spread the word around that we've got money to invest. Hope he jumps our way."

"And if he doesn't?" I asked.

Putnam eyed me. T.K. looked at the carpet. Smith stared into his empty cup as if hoping for a genie with clever answers to come wafting out. Putnam got up for another bottle of stout.

Edgar cleared his throat. "What would you suggest?" He turned to me. "If Goodborn doesn't jump?"

Not only did I know some Edgars, I had also met guys like Chuck.

"I think we should appeal to Chuck's basest instincts."

They had all been looking at me, but now they gaped. "But it might be a little dangerous for Mr. Putnam."

While I explained, Putnam had an enigmatic smile. T.K.'s eyes widened and he gave me a dumbfounded look. He recovered, but seemed unenthusiastic, even reluctant; however, he didn't raise any objections. I thought he felt uncomfortable in his newly assigned role.

~ * ~

Waiters scurried by with plates heaped with cutlets and potatoes, and white asparagus stacked like cordwood and garnished with browned butter and bits of *speck.*

T.K. gulped the rest of his beer. His face seemed locked into a perpetual scowl.

My grandma had always warned, *marry the good-natured man, not the handsome one.* At that moment I was happy not to be Mrs. T.K. Drummond.

We were having lunch at an outdoor café in the zoo, which seemed wholly appropriate after the last twenty-four hours. Berlin families had come out in droves and the walks and paths were swarming with strollers and children, lovers holding hands, contented elderly couples, all the things we were not.

Moody and silent, T.K. slumped down into the chair across from me, not speaking. I patted my mouth with the napkin, and took the plunge.

"Look, I'll get on a plane this evening, if that's what you want. It would be my first choice. I can't help it that Edgar liked my plan. I had to say something. I'm paid to think on my feet. Your buddy Putnam obviously has problems dealing with women, and knowing what happened to our predecessor, a hulking body guard with a gun would be a more practical solution than a 'wife.'"

T.K. lit a cigarette, but remained silent.

"You've got to talk to me," I said. "I have to know what's going on."

"Putnam is not enthralled about the idea of sending you and me in after Goodborn."

"What about Edgar?" I asked.

He paused to inhale. "Edgar's a hard-nosed SOB venture capitalist who wants full value for the cash he's invested. Besides that, he's a world-class womanizer, so you're really his cup of tea."

I had figured that out.

He looked at me. "Sometimes Putnam can be an asshole, but he's running the show. Too bad you were so eager to jump into the game with that lame 'plan' involving him. Big mistake. Your plan sucks. I can't believe Edgar bought off on it."

He blew smoke straight up toward the sky.

A sane woman would have given him her most withering look, stood up, and waltzed out of his life forever.

"What's the matter with my plan?" My voice could have quick-frozen lava.

"We don't want Putnam within five hundred miles of us."

"Then why didn't you tell me that last night? I asked you." I stared at him. "Why don't we want Putnam?"

He spoke in a soft rueful voice. "He's a sadist. Enough said. Mea culpa, as usual."

I had involved Putnam because he was pugnacious, and enough of a fighter to protect us. That T.K. didn't want him along was an unpleasant surprise.

"Let's visit the animals," I said.

~ * ~

In the annals of zoo expeditions, this was one of the grimmest ever. Many of the creatures had retreated to shady spots away from the crowds. The animals that were visible looked lethargic; we regarded each other in dispirited commiseration, while T.K. paced up and down in front of the enclosures as if he were the caged one. Then in the primate's area, a big ugly monkey picked up a handful of droppings, seemed to sneer, and without a windup hurled it smack at T.K, who ducked, narrowly missing getting a disgusting mess on his jacket. Everyone around us laughed like crazy, which only made it worse. We left right after that and walked back to the hotel. On the way, T.K. smoked two cigarettes, lighting the second from the butt of the first.

Up in our room, I announced I needed a nap. He nodded irritably, and plopped himself into a chair with a paperback, one of those gory thrillers with people slicing and dicing each other, and some improbable hero saving the world in the last possible instant. Total hogwash.

~ * ~

That evening, Edgar, T.K. and I dawdled over a late dinner off Savigny Platz at Berlin's venerable Lutter & Wegner restaurant. T.K. and I sat next to each other on a banquette with Edgar across from us.

Smith and Putnam, working late, were scrambling to put the last pieces of what was now called "Zara's plan" into place.

Wild horses couldn't have dragged it out of me, but I agreed with T.K. that the plan was lame brained, depending as it did on our unproven acting ability, to say nothing of Charles Goodborn's greed. However, Edgar and even Putnam had warmed to my ideas, and we were leaving for the Baltic Island tomorrow afternoon.

Not for one moment had I ever believed that I would be able to turn tail and go home, Inwardly, I cursed Coppola & Henry. Normally I ran my own show, and I liked managing my own projects. Now Edgar was calling the shots, not T.K. and certainly not me. Putnam was Edgar's lieutenant. Get used to being a player with a bit part, I told myself. *Go along to get along.*

During the meal, Edgar had dominated the conversation, beginning with a cheerful but chilling admission, "Never was much of a student, but I was always very, very good at killing. The army trained me well. Not much call to do that since Korea. Now I'm only good for making money. Very, very good." He had smiled at me. An old man who couldn't stop bragging.

"I hope we don't have you to thank for killing poor Mr. Bruss," I said.

T.K. almost choked on his wine.

Edgar looked at me rather fiercely, and then laughed his loud American laugh.

He stated he was "very, very good" at one other thing, which he couldn't, "ho, ho, ho" discuss in front of a lady.

More hollow boasts.

I watched as Edgar mopped up the last bits of sauce with a piece of bread.

Big-bellied and slightly stooped, Edgar had a long face, and a beaky nose, to compliment the thick turf of coarse white hair. The deep creases etched around his eyes and his leathery face would have identified him as a yachtsman even if Barry Wohlauer hadn't already conveyed that information.

Edgar's eyes, occasionally sweeping over the scalloped neckline of my lavender linen sheath, rested on the pearly Niihau shell beads or more likely on my décolletage. Under the table, his black tasseled loafer grazed my tan pump too often to be accidental. T.K. was right. Edgar was a letch.

"Since you're heading in that direction, tell me a little about all this spying and that Stasi business over there in the East. How will that affect our plans?" he asked, at last broaching a topic other than himself.

T.K. took his package of Dunhill's out of his pocket, and placed it on the tablecloth. He waved his hand in a wide careless motion and said, "Nobody can agree on the exact numbers, but the East Germans had between three and five hundred thousand informers for a population of sixteen million."

Edgar emitted a low whistle.

"Good grief!" I said, "That's one in thirty."

They turned to look at me.

"Good at math. The girl can't help it."

"Right!" said T.K., and continued, "miles and miles—millions of pages of micro-fiche. Gossip. Rumors. Speculation. Lies. Hell, probably even a few facts." He smiled at me. "My 'techno-mentor' here would point out that they compiled a lot of data and not a great deal of information."

Edgar accepted the cigarette T.K. offered, and nodded. His foot found mine again. I plastered my legs as close to the banquette as anatomy allowed.

"The Stasi, that's short for State Security, had files running to thousands of pages on some well-known East German artists." T.K. leaned forward and frowned as he spoke. "The whole system was crazy. Half the people had a good idea not only who the Stasi were, but also of the identity of the informers. Somehow over time most of them managed to adjust to this completely bizarre situation— even to live and let live."

I tried but failed to imagine my co-workers, neighbors and even friends reporting my activities to the security police. The whole system boggled the mind. Edgar sat and smoked, without comment.

T.K. twirled the brandy in his glass, and continued. "When the wall came down, all the files were locked up, but not before some were either copied—or ripped off. Naturally, the Krauts can't agree on how to handle the whole problem. The Stasi tried to melt back into the populace and some are even emerging as part of the new leadership." T.K. turned his head and nodded at me. "Zara and I may be subjected to the usual scrutiny any foreigner provokes, but nothing like in previous years. We can pass inspection."

Edgar added a little cream to his coffee and stirred slowly. "An unbelievable business. And now you will be heading up to the Baltic." He paused, and sipped his coffee. "Never did sail in the Baltic, but it has islands," he paused again, "and I like islands. Some day…" His big voice trailed off. He seemed to be considering something. "Watch out for Goodborn. To my mind, he's a sociopath."

T.K. and I exchanged glances.

"Do you think he could have killed Bruss?" I asked.

"That wouldn't be his style. He'd have someone do the wet stuff for him."

Wet stuff, ick. I shivered.

"How well do you know him?" I asked.

"Sailed with him a few times this spring."

"Tell us about him," I asked.

He sipped his coffee. "Goodborn is competent at what he does— but he's manipulative. Nasty temper, too. Whatever goes wrong is the other guy's fault. If he did poorly in a race, well, some other boat broke the rules, or the wind changed at the wrong time." Edgar looked from me to T.K.

"Goodborn plays the innocent victim. No sense of accountability." He paused. "I heard he once lost a man overboard during a race. Apparently, his crew hadn't practiced the drills before the race. Another boat had to rescue the crewman, and then Goodborn complained when he was penalized. Caused a big flap."

He signaled the waiter to bring the check.

I asked, "Have you ever met Romy, the woman he—"

"Oh yes." He frowned. "Goodborn brought her on one of our sailing trips. Just showed up with her."

He stopped and cleared his throat, but he didn't continue, so I asked, "What was your impression?"

"Not much to tell," he said, exhaling a cloud of smoke. "She brought a first rate potato salad for lunch. She's a good-looking woman. Knows it, too." He licked his lips. "We had barely left the dock, when she took off her shirt and shorts, plopped herself down on the fore deck, unhooked the top of her bikini, and spread eagled herself there half naked in front of God and everybody."

"What did Goodborn do?" T.K. asked.

"He made a worse spectacle. Rubbing sun tan lotion all over her—every damn place, like he owned her. People on boats all around us."

"So what happened?" I asked.

Edgar tapped his ash into the ashtray, and licked his lips again.

"I told them this was New England, not the god-damned south of France, and maybe she should cover up until we got out of the harbor. Pissed him off good. She put on a shirt."

"What did she talk about?"

"The queen bee didn't say three words all afternoon. Kept her nose in a book and sunned herself."

"So besides the business with the sun tan oil, how did they seem to be getting along?" I asked.

"He's crazy about her. She's obviously not one of those church-children-kitchen types. And yet...I wonder how long it will last. Goodborn treated both his wives badly. Never showed a drop of interest in his children." His big foot maneuvered itself all the way to the banquette. I moved my feet in T.K.'s direction.

T.K. broke in. "But as a business man—"

"Bastard is first rate. Smooth. Professional. Very focused. He got three million out of me, and four or five million from my friends." He frowned. "If he won't come back into the fold, and I dare say he won't, grab that CD-ROM. Turn it over to Putnam. Goodborn won't be able to copy it. Not where he is." He paused and glanced from T.K. to me.

"We'll do our damnedest to make sure Maine Mining has clear sailing for the deal with Software Umbrella," T.K. promised. I murmured agreement.

Sailing. Edgar smiled at the mention of his favorite topic. Tomorrow morning, he confided, he was flying to Copenhagen to look at a schooner he might buy.

Now he eyed us again, as if he were trying to assess the dynamics of our couplehood.

He said, "You two make an attractive pair." He continued to glance from T.K. to me. "But too damn serious. You should kick up your heels a bit while you still have an opportunity. Last night before the chancy stuff. I should tell you to get a good night's sleep, but what the hell? You're young. Go out dancing." He looked at me. "Do they still have discos?"

I nodded.

"Find a nice lively disco. Paint the town a bit."

I turned to T.K. who had been eyeing me all evening with his faintly speculative "are you in the mood, yet?" look. I was, but it wouldn't hurt him to wait a bit longer to find out. He nodded approval at Edgar's idea.

"Won't you join us?" I asked Edgar, dreading playing footsie again.

"God, no. Past my bedtime."

We walked him back to his hotel, wished him happy sailing, and caught a cab for a disco T.K. remembered.

~ * ~

Our cabby drove the streets south of the Ku'damm and stopped in front of a gray stone building with a green light illuminating the recessed entry way.

"*Sauvage*," said the driver. "Ring the bell." He chortled. "If they like your looks, they let you in." He laughed again. "I wait."

We got out of the cab and T.K. pushed the buzzer. A large black man dressed in a leopard skin vest and smooth leather trousers answered the door. A half-dozen graduated gold hoops dangled from his left ear. A pulsing beat and the indiscreet laughter of people who have drunk too much came from within the club.

The man looked us over, bowed, and said, '*Willkommen im Sauvage*,' and then repeated the phrase in French and English. T.K. ran back to pay the cabbie.

"I've never had to pass muster so many times in one day," I said, as we walked through a dim corridor painted with larger than life images of lions, tigers, panthers and leopards. Some of the grinning cats were copulating, others ingesting a bloody banquet of wildebeest. The night noises of insects and frogs seemed to come right from urns of bamboo, while a tangle of vines drifted down from a black ceiling. Wicker cages imprisoned parrots, whose glass eyes stared unseeing but malevolent. Snakes with darting tongues coiled around rubber tree trunks.

T.K. wrinkled his nose at the scent of frangipani and put his hand on my waist as we climbed a suspended stairway to a second floor.

Music throbbed even before we entered a big dark cavern of a room lit by torches. We wound our way through lacquer tables and chairs upholstered in faux zebra skin. A bar of chrome and copper ran the length of the room.

As my eyes became accustomed to the dark, I noticed elegant men in black and ultra-thin women in short tight dresses. Looked like an Armani fashion show.

"You dressed up very nicely for Edgar," T.K. said, eyeing my dress as he helped me out of my jacket.

"It wasn't for Edgar."

He said, "I see," and picked up a menu from the table with a pleased little smile. "These Berlin night spots all serve fancy drinks."

"Nothing too ornate for me," I said.

Subdued after our trying day, we sipped "Jungle Rot," equal parts vodka and Bitter Orange. Ten hours of talking, listening, arguing, negotiating, and socializing are activities that energize so-called people persons. Neither T.K. nor I fell into that category.

"Did you believe all that stuff Edgar told us? About being a whiz at killing?" I asked T.K.

"He trotted out that warrior business to impress you."

"Charles Goodborn sounds like a world class jerk."

T.K. said Chuck came from an old but impoverished New England family. A big payout from a previous software venture had allowed him a playboy lifestyle.

"No more Yankee frugality for our lad. He dived into serial monogamy, pricey cars, yachts, a beach house on Martha's Vineyard, and a ski chalet in Stowe—and a yen for cocaine. The good times rolled."

A playboy and a marketing genius, most likely a USBA, or Ultra Slick Bullshit Artist. I stirred my drink. For the life of me, I couldn't figure out why anyone, bullshit artist or not, would take state-of-the-art technology to Eastern Europe. Who would his customers be?

"Want to talk some more shop?" I asked.

"Decidedly not."

Under the table, he tapped his foot. I didn't recognize any of the songs, only the pounding techno beat, aggressive and sensual. I stood up and led T.K. onto the dance floor. I had never seen him so restrained. In that intimate space, we faced each other, barely moving, as if maneuvered by an indolent puppeteer.

Another song started up. First the keyboard, with some heart-stopping chords, then a woman's voice, plaintive and haunted coming into the melody, and then a male voice, suggestive and blunt. Each one sang of a vision: hers of love, his of something more primitive, more—*sauvage.*

I got into the music. T.K. still had a smile flickering around his mouth, and he danced, too. The voices faded out of the song, but the keyboard and drums segued into a frenzied coda, which the dancers appeared to recognize, and as the music grew wilder, red lights played over the room. It felt as if we had joined an orgiastic circle around a bonfire where a pulsing heart and a thrusting pelvis moved to the same drum.

The DJ took a break, and we returned to our table. As I dabbed at the sweat on my temples, T.K. said in a quiet voice, "I trust I'm getting a signal."

I fished a slice of orange out of my drink, and nibbled the pulp. Our eyes met. "Think of me as energetically waving the semaphores."

T.K. kissed my hand and ordered another round of Jungle Rot.

We danced to a slow song, and when he put his arms around me, I melted into him. As the music stopped, he ran his hand down my back all the way to my fanny, and asked, "What the devil are you wearing under this pretty dress?"

"Not much."

"Hmmm. Less is definitely more."

In the taxi, we indulged in a long heady kiss. We dashed through the hotel lobby and kissed again in the elevator; we stood and kissed in the middle of our dark room while T.K. unzipped my dress, which fell down around my ankles. Still clinging to him, I stepped out of the dress and my shoes. His hands felt their way down my back, and over my hips.

"You said, 'not much.'"

"I exaggerated."

"Make us a drink while I catch up."

While I hunted around in the mini-bar, he popped a tape into the boom box. The Righteous Brothers. "Unchained Melody." T.K. still possessed romantic impulses. I poured Bitter Orange into a glass, added a splash of Stoli, and stirred with my finger. T.K. sat on the bed in his shirt and shorts and swore while he struggled with his cufflinks.

"Teamwork, Luv," I said, imitating Putnam's accent and helped him out of his shirt, which I tossed toward a chair. I rested my head on his shoulder. He smelled faintly of talc.

The best feeling in the whole world is bare skin against bare skin. I pulled him close to me, and planted a row of kisses on his neck and across his shoulders.

A gust of wind billowed the curtain. The reflections from the lamps in the street filled the room with shadowy light. T.K. watched our dark reflections in the mirror across the room. I smiled at the man in the mirror.

"Nibble, nibble, little mouse," I said, right into his ear then I bit him on the shoulder, a gentle, tentative bite. "Needs salt."

He turned toward me.

"You are going to pay for that!"

I giggled and clutched him tighter as we sank down onto the bed together.

~ * ~

Next morning Putnam was the wasp that pierced our cocoon.

A Bach Brandenburg Concerto provided a measured counterpoint to the littered still life of open jam pots, egg yolk encrusted plates, and *brötchen* crumbs sticking to smidgens of butter—the remains of our room service breakfast. Dawdling over a second cup of coffee, T.K. smoked and read the *Herald Tribune*, while I browsed through a German phrase book. We held hands, and exchanged smiles. We were going to be all right together on this project.

Someone rapped on the door.

"Must be housekeeping," said T.K. He wore candy-striped boxer shorts, while I was swathed in the hotel's terry robe, modest enough to face the maid. Putnam's rosy face didn't look like the maid.

"Oh! You're really early." By ninety inconsiderate minutes, I was tempted to add. Cool and audacious, Putnam walked right in as T.K. climbed into yesterday's wrinkled trousers.

"Billy Boy, you should have called from the lobby."

"I like to keep my evasion techniques well oiled. Might as well have been invisible. Swooped past the concierge, the front desk, and the bell man."

Evasion techniques my foot! He enjoyed flustering people by catching them in their underwear.

I followed Putnam's censorious gaze. Our room looked like the scene of the great laundry basket explosion. His ice blue eyes swept over my dishabille, the rumpled bed, and the breakfast table.

"Bloody hell," he muttered, and his trim mustache fairly bristled with disapproval. He was looking for a place to deposit his briefcase. I yanked the comforter over the bed and smoothed a spot. Putnam dumped the case on the bed, removed a leather pouch and intoned in a stagy voice,

"Zara Gray and T.K. Drummond, you are now Zara and T.K. Wentz." He gave me a sharp glance. "Your passports, credit cards, driver's licenses, and so forth, please."

"I'll hang on to my passport," I said, wanting no part of forged documents. Putnam should not know how antsy I felt about this whole business.

He flashed an acidic little smile and said, "If you're ever captured by enemy agents, you wouldn't want to be interrogated as to why you're carrying two sets of papers."

"What are you talking about?" I turned to T.K. "He's joking isn't he? About enemy agents?"

Both men burst out laughing.

"Old Bill here is pulling your leg." T.K. paused to look under the bed for his shoes.

No need to be paranoid, I told myself. The wall has been smashed into souvenir pieces, the citizens of East Germany have voted to unite with the West, and the cold war belongs to the history books.

"May I see the new passport?" I asked, feigning interest. I didn't bother to ask its origin. These days Berlin must have entire neighborhoods of unemployed document forgers.

Putnam handed it over along with a big wad of money, a MasterCard, and even some calling cards. I opened the passport. Zara Wentz. An address label was affixed to the inside cover. Lake Shore Drive, Chicago, Illinois. Yesterday's quick photo session had even produced a decent likeness. Everything looked all right, but I felt a hardening resistance to giving him my passport, my blue book, my lifeline.

I took the credit cards and my checkbook out of my handbag, and I dumped everything in a manila envelope and sealed it.

Putnam declined a cup of coffee and tossed T.K. a set of car keys. "I'll be drinking a Pilsener at Zum Nackten Fisch in Sassnitz on Friday evening. The town with the ferry terminal. Plan to make contact around dinnertime. Fellow English speakers and all that rot." He surveyed the room again with a look of distaste, and wished us, a bit ironically, a "safe trip."

~ * ~

The false documents and talk of interrogation by enemy agents gave me a gut-churning feeling of foreboding about Zara's plan, Bruss's murderer, the Stasi agents, and whatever else we might encounter. In spite of Monsieur de Sade on steroids being on the team, T.K. seemed at ease and I didn't confide how frightened I was.

We spent a couple hours at the KaDeWe, Berlin's biggest department store. T.K. fell into his new persona with a short trendy haircut and an even trendier summer wardrobe with lots of Hugo Boss, while I visited the camping and housewares departments.

I ducked away from T.K. for a few minutes to call Colorado and talk to Jody and Chloe. Chloe sounded happy and busy, but Jody told me I should have quit and worried about a job later. "They blackmailed you," she said. "Why don't you get on a plane out of there?"

It was too hard to explain why I couldn't.

What I did do was to call Mark in accounting at Coppola & Henry.

"Hey," he said, "*wie gehts*? Have you found any pretty Frauleins for me?"

"Is this extension recorded?" I asked.

"I'm not important enough."

After I explained a little bit about my situation, Mark gave a low whistle.

"I need a little help here," I said. "You know that expensive P.I. that we used about six months ago? To investigate the client who didn't pay?"

"Frank Girard."

"I'd like for him to get some background on a bad Brit."

"If Girard can't, his contacts can."

"Put it on my expenses. Under miscellaneous."

Mark laughed. "By the time anyone audits them, you'll be gone. Who's the bad Brit?"

"William Putnam. Age is maybe early-forties." I tried to think of what would be specific to Putnam. "Might have been a boxer. Probably was a spook. Maybe a commando background. Sharp dresser. Drinks stout. Hates uppity women."

"This may not be so easy."

"My situation isn't so easy."

~ * ~

Back at the hotel, when I laid the pocket knife, tarp, rope, flashlight, folding shovel, bungee cords, wool camping blanket, roll of toilet paper, Evian water and the duffel bag in which to stash everything on the bed, T.K. laughed and teased me about "going all weird" on him. I assured him these were practical things we might need.

A characteristic rap on the door interrupted our packing.

Putnam strolled in, briefcase in hand. He cast a gimlet eye on the bed and placed the briefcase on the table, snapped open the latches, and extracted my manila envelope, unsealed. "I seem to have come up one passport short."

"I gave you everything."

"I think not."

"Could you have lost it?"

"I think not."

"Zara, sweet," T.K. piped in. "Didn't I see your passport in the wardrobe?"

"You did, but now it's in the mail."

"What?" Asked Putnam. "Where?" His eyes looked like they would pop out of his head.

"I mailed it to myself here at the hotel. I'll tell them to hold it for me until we return," I said. "It will be quite safe."

"Drummond, this insubordination is intolerable."

"No, you are intolerable." I gave him a stony look. "No reasonable assignment would require us to have false identity papers. I want my passport waiting for me when I return."

If I ever did. By now I had the impression Putnam wouldn't let me leave even if I tried to. Wild considerations of attempting to reach the American Embassy crossed my mind.

"Zara, you're being silly," said T.K. We don't want Goodborn or anyone connected with him to know who we really are. It's as simple as that."

Not mollified, I flounced into the bathroom and stayed here until Bill Putnam was gone. I hated him.

Three

In spite of my foreboding, the border crossing from Berlin into East Germany passed uneventfully. The green-uniformed guards gave our travel documents a disinterested inspection, and threw a cursory glance at the contents of the eye-catching blue BMW crammed to the gills with luggage and shopping bags. If we could just make it to the Baltic without incident, I would be a happy woman.

We drove north stuck behind a lumbering, smelly truck with a tarp lashed over the cargo. The old rutted highway required T.K.'s full attention, and I didn't feel like conversation. I slipped the Brandenburg Concerto tape into the player and leaned back to listen.

T.K. turned onto a narrow country road that led us through quaint farm villages with low houses and barns, all strung together by stone-walls. Being in the countryside with Bach made my jitters disappear.

A few minutes later, T.K. took an unpaved road, and I caught a glimpse of willows, sunlight dancing on water, then a shoreline. We pulled into a parking area beside a lake. A rustic restaurant, little more than a pavilion, perched at the water's edge.

T.K. turned off the engine and unbuckled his seat belt. "Hungry?" he asked.

"I'm always hungry."

As we left the car, two couples walked toward a dilapidated Trabbi. The Trabbi or more properly, the Trabant, the East German answer to a Ford, was a plastic box on wheels. Its copious exhaust stank to high heaven, and it broke down with appalling regularity.

The couples covertly stared at the Beemer and us. The metallic color that T.K. called Blitz Blau, lightning blue, screamed, "Look at me!" My denim mini-skirt and white T-shirt, T.K.'s faded Madras sport shirt and Dockers, our hair, our sunglasses, everything about us must have screamed "outlanders." Being noticed was part of 'The Plan.'

Inside, we sipped white wine at a table right by the water. The same song I had heard yesterday in Berlin played in the background. I was surprised to hear English lyrics this far from the beaten track.

The radio played last summer's song.
Your breath touched my cheek like the warm summer wind.
Your lips burnt mine like the mid-summer sun.
Now your love is gone, like last summer's flowers.
I cry warm tears, like last summer's rain.

"Nice," T.K. murmured, and took my hand.

Every summer had an anthem that evoked haunted memories of the past.

We watched a couple in a rowboat drift by. She trailed her hand lazily through the water. T.K.'s eyes, meeting mine again, had that quizzically amorous look of last night, so I wasn't surprised when he asked if I thought "initiating" the new blanket was a good idea.

Even after the wine, Bach, and lunch, I didn't feel *that* relaxed.

"Maybe later." I paid the bill, over-tipped the waitress, and we left, followed by the same curious stares that had greeted us.

We pulled out onto the country road, then T.K. spat out his favorite expletive followed by a whole stream of stronger ones. I thought he was angry about my refusal, but he kept staring into the rear-view mirror.

"What's the matter?" I asked. *Always something.*

He grimaced and made a sharp turn onto another farm road and goosed the accelerator.

"Someone is following us."

I turned around and saw a gray car behind us, not very close. "Why do you think they're following us?"

"Because I noticed that car when we turned off the main road before lunch."

"Who would know where we are? Who would even care?"

He shrugged.

"What are we going to do?" I asked. My heart had begun to pound.

"I don't want whoever it is to know that we've spotted them."

I wished I had thought "roofing nails" during my strafe through the hardware department, but the roofs were of red tile, and being pursued had not been on my radar. I turned around to look; the gray car was still on our tail.

"Could it be the police or someone official? Maybe we should stop and find out who it is."

T.K. said, "Absolutely not!" He hesitated. "There's a little problem."

"Are you going to share?" I hated it when he acted so damn mysterious.

"I've got some goodies for Chuck that we wouldn't want to be caught carrying." He lit a cigarette and popped the dash lighter back into its socket.

Goodies for Chuck? "Do you mean that bottle of Jim Beam?" I asked.

He took a long drag on his cigarette. "No, I mean the Bolivian marching powder and the weed."

"Are you crazy? We cross a border with false passports, you're transporting cocaine and—"

"I didn't tell you because I knew you would get hysterical."

I stopped listening, because I had a quick vision of myself doing twenty to life in a dank East German jail. My skin had turned pasty from no sun and too many boiled potatoes. I wore a dull gray polyester dress with my convict number embroidered on the pocket. My hair, thin and lank, had been hacked off in no particular style. Jodie and Chloe would come every six months to visit. Chloe would cry and scream for me when it was time to leave.

I could make my way back to Berlin by myself, with my guidebook and survival German.

T.K. looked at me. "Sweetie..."

"Don't Sweetie me!"

"Our situation isn't as bad as you think. I have a place to crash around here. A farm. But I'd be an idiot to lead our tail there."

"Ditch the drugs."

"I don't want to if we don't have to." He tossed the cigarette out the window.

Clueless, technical me in a foreign country with a forged identity and a crazy man. Carrying controlled substances. Being followed.

"This Beemer can outmaneuver most cars," I said. "Can you tell what he's driving?"

"I think it's an Opel."

"Piece of cake." Spoken with more bravado than I felt.

"What are you suggesting?" He took his eyes off the road and stared at me.

"The hardest thing will be for you to swallow your male pride and let me drive."

"Sweet Pea, you're going all weird on me again."

"One, I drive a BMW and I know how to handle this car. Two, I once had a boyfriend who was a racecar driver and he taught me some tricks. Like highway patrol U-turns."

"The farmhouse is about twelve kilometers from here."

T.K. turned onto the highway. At the edge of a village he pulled off the road a little beyond a gas station. We jumped out of the car, raised the hood and peered under it. The Opel stopped at the other end of the station. The driver remained in the car. I slid behind the wheel and T.K. slammed the hood and jumped into the passenger seat. I waited until I saw a tandem monster truck that would be impossible to pass. I gunned the motor and pulled out in front of the truck. The Opel waited while the line of cars behind the truck cleared. By then we were already racing along at 140 kilometers per hour, eighty-five mph or so, according to my rough calculations.

In the next village, we pulled behind a brick church with a stark steeple that punched the sky. I eyed the somber gravestones in the churchyard. T.K. lit another cigarette. Then we glimpsed the Opel whizzing by at a good clip, and it looked like the driver was alone. Gender probably male. When he was out of sight, we headed back in the direction we had come from, toward the safety of the farmhouse.

A few minutes later we were stuck at a railway crossing while the freight train from hell trundled by, car after car. Then a gray car approached. Damn. Looked like the Opel, but I couldn't be sure. The freight train cleared the crossing, the gates rose, and in a wild exhibition of acceleration, I shot across the tracks. But the damned Opel was still behind us, two cars back, as persistent as a whiny two-year old. I put some pavement between us, and told T.K., "Hang on!"

I stomped on the brakes, and as we skidded to a stop I cut the wheel sharply, hoping I remembered the intricacies of the turn. The execution lacked finesse. We slued and skidded and left the road, found it again, and headed north, leaving a big cloud of dust, a stunned farmer sitting on his tractor, and the gray Opel still traveling south.

T.K. said, "Holy shit!"

I wiped my sweaty hands on my skirt. T.K. directed me until we caught the highway south again, this time at a slower pace. I put my mind in neutral and concentrated on driving. Thick gray clouds blotted out the sun, and a few minutes later fat raindrops pelted the windshield. The rains came.

A few kilometers down the road, we turned off the highway again.

"We'll just pop into the safe house for an hour to regroup," said T.K., lighting a cigarette. The rain stopped as abruptly as it had begun. In a sleepy village, T.K. pointed me down a pot-holed street.

"In here," he said, "the old place at the end of the lane." I drove a hundred feet and stopped. The safe house didn't look like much. Still, feelings of relief flooded through me, while I relaxed my hands on the wheel and rubbed the kinks out of my neck.

"Might as well put the car out of sight." T.K. jumped out to open a wooden gate and we pulled into a farmyard. Before us stood the most dilapidated half-timbered barn I had ever seen. T.K. struggled to open the wide wooden door. He stopped and stared into the barn. Inside, shafts of afternoon sunlight filtered through missing planks and gaps in the lath where the plaster had crumbled. I saw a half-empty hayloft and, parked in the back of the barn, the rain-spattered gray Opel.

I suppressed a scream.

"Oh shit!" said T.K. "Now everything makes sense."

~ * ~

Through the open car window I saw Bill Putnam bounding round the dung heap. Putnam grinned like a Cheshire cat.

"I say, Drummond that was a nice bit of maneuvering!"

T.K. slumped, and I was surprised how resigned he looked. I had an urge to slap the smug smile off Putnam's face. If following us was his idea of a practical joke, it was in abominable taste.

Putnam walked toward the car and T.K. whispered to me through the window, "Stay cool, and follow my lead. No histrionics." He squared his shoulders to meet Putnam.

I climbed out of the car. The ancient barn mingled smells of hay, cow, and horses. The familiar earthy smell of cow manure gave me strange comfort in this prickly situation. If T.K. and Putnam got into another shouting match or worse, we wouldn't have Smith to run interference. T.K. and I stood together facing Putnam, whose bright smile implied, "Aren't I the clever one?"

T.K. put his hand on my shoulder. Trying to calm me down. Trying to calm us down.

"Zara is an amazing driver," he said in an offhand voice.

Putnam inspected my face like he was searching for "race car driver" genes.

Before he could comment on my Grand Prix abilities, T.K. said, "Billy Boy, just what the hell was that all about?" He scowled at Putnam. "I remember a conversation about teamwork a couple days ago. Since when does one team member harass and endanger the others?"

Putnam's smile looked like a sneer. "Drummond, I merely wanted to find out if you two were being attentive to your—ah, environment or just going for a bit of a ramble in the countryside."

"We stopped for lunch, for Chrissakes! One more smart-assed trick like that, and—"

"My motto has always been 'Trust, but verify.'" Putnam glanced at me, and then looked at T.K.

T.K. rolled his eyes. "Total bullshit."

Putnam watched us intently. His crooked nose was a constant reminder of the fighter itching to mix it up. I would have liked T.K. to knock him flat, but I suspected the Englishman would emerge victorious from any fracas.

"Say hello to Old Mundhenk. I interrupted his early supper."

Putnam seemed intent on defusing the situation.

T.K. nodded. "What an asshole," he said in a voice so low that Putnam, whistling "The Colonel Bogey March" couldn't hear, as he followed us to the farmhouse.

We crossed an unkempt patch of grass, and walked by a neatly tended vegetable garden surrounded by marigolds. I looked around for an outhouse and mouthed 'toilet' to T.K.

The half-timbered farmhouse cried for stucco and TLC. A black and white cat spied us and raced off along the side of the barn. T.K. went ahead of me over a low threshold. Passing muddy boots and a milk can, we walked through a dark hallway. He opened a door to an old-fashioned kitchen. An ancient man with stringy gray hair sat hunched over a sturdy table. In a ragged sweater and carpet slippers, he looked as much in need of attention as the house. T.K. hadn't mentioned tenants or fellow spooks.

As we entered, the man glanced up from the chunk of sausage he was slicing, and gave us a shy grin that showed haphazardly spaced yellow teeth. A sturdy loaf of the type of rye bread the German's call *Roggenbrot* lay next to the sausage, and an uncapped bottle of beer stood at the old man's elbow.

Whatever my idea of a safe house had been, this was the antithesis.

T.K. walked across the kitchen, shook hands, and then hugged the old farmer. He nodded at Bill.

"Show Zara the facilities."

Putnam's thumb jerked toward a dingy hallway. Brushing by him, I hissed, "Teamwork, Billy Boy!" He pretended not to hear me, but I saw pinpoints of anger in his eyes.

When I returned, T.K. and Putnam had joined our host at the table, and a blue cloud of tobacco smoke hung in the air.

Smoking the peace pipe. I would never understand men.

T.K. introduced me to Onkel Mundhenk who spoke no English, so I made a few forays into German of the "nice garden you've got—what's the cat's name" variety. Mundhenk grinned and nodded, but didn't answer.

Putnam's face looked ruddier than ever, while his arctic eyes surveyed the room. "Wherever did you learn to drive like that, Mrs. Wentz?" He asked in his oiliest voice.

While I tried to think of a reply cleverer than "none of your goddamn business," T.K. put his arm around me and mimicked a good old boy country voice. "Oh, Zara has talents that never cease to amaze."

Putnam gave us a sour smile.

"One more stunt like that and we're heading back to Berlin." I said.

"Mrs. Wentz, I think not." Putnam's laconic voice didn't match his steely eyes.

T.K. gave me a warning look.

Old Mundhenk, oblivious to the crosscurrents, creaked to his feet and busied himself rinsing glasses. T.K. jumped up and began drying them, gabbing good-naturedly in such rapid-fire German I couldn't get the gist of the conversation.

Pointedly ignoring Putnam, I looked around, and recognized a kraut cutter like the one from my grandma's kitchen back in Colorado. Herr Mundhenk plucked a bottle of colorless schnapps off a painted shelf. *Korn.*

Still angry, I declined a drink, and while T.K. and Putnam each tossed back a snort, I drummed my fingers on the table, unable to stop thinking of how we might have wrecked the car or been arrested for speeding, and what would have happened if we had been caught with the stash of drugs.

I turned to T.K. "We have a long drive ahead of us."

He jabbed out his cigarette and jumped to his feet. Old Mundhenk tried to give us a sausage.

Putnam muttered an apology—something about "wanting to make up for this little misunderstanding," and insisted on shaking hands. I was afraid he would pulverize my bones, but his handshake was merely firm. Old Mundhenk shook hands, too.

T.K. excused himself for a moment. He returned with the bottle of Jim Beam and handed it to old Mundhenk, who grinned and licked his lips. T.K. hugged the old farmer again, and we retraced our steps through the hallway and back out into the garden.

In the car, I rummaged in the back seat for water, and we passed the bottle back and forth.

"You were great, Zara. Very cool and collected. You didn't raise Billy Boy's blood pressure."

I would have liked to send it into the stroke zone. Instead, I asked, "Who is that old man?"

"My great uncle." He smiled at my stare of disbelief. "Since the wall came down, many of the American nieces and nephews have come to visit. So none of the locals even blink when a big car full of strangers appears. It's the perfect set up."

T.K. reminded me that his mother had been a war bride, hence his excellent German. Herr Mundhenk was her uncle.

I finished the water and tossed the bottle into the back seat of the car. "How did Putnam know about this place?"

"We used Uncle's house a few years ago when we were in a tight situation. Yesterday I mentioned the farm. In case everything went south and we had to have a safe rendezvous point. Just a lucky guess on his part."

"There is an old saying, that if you aren't part of the solution, you're a part of the problem."

"Yeah. I know. We'll give Billy Boy one more chance to redeem himself."

"And if he doesn't?"

T.K. hesitated, and then spoke in an even voice, "Our time over here will be much healthier if you don't piss him off."

Inwardly I cursed T.K. again for not warning me before I had assigned Putnam a role in "the Plan." Now Bill Putnam had become a prickly hair shirt draped over our unwilling shoulders. And what exactly did T.K. mean by "healthier?" Every incident reinforced the knowledge that I should have voiced an emphatic "no" to this operation. If we could just get to the island without more craziness.

~ * ~

We drove past farmland while T.K. flunked quiz after quiz about which fields were rye, wheat, oats, corn, sugar beets and potatoes. I had hooked up with an agricultural illiterate.

In turn, he coached me on some common German words and advised that Germans always called the Baltic the *Ostsee*. "The East Sea?" I asked.

"Jesus, it's the Baltic! *Ostsee* or Baltic."

How many ways can a new language trip you up?

The evening sun found breaks in the cloud cover as we drove north and approached the old Hanseatic port of Stralsund. I read from the guidebook while T.K. drove over a drawbridge, crossed a long causeway called the Rügendamm that put us on the island of Rügen. The Beemer bounced onto an ancient cobblestone road leading down to the water. Across the harbor, the church steeples of Stralsund rose above the treetops.

"I don't see any grain elevators," I said. T.K. pointed across the water to a pair of enormous many-storied red brick monsters along the docks.

"Those are grain elevators?" I had been looking for the white cylindrical silos that jut up from the flat horizon, the cathedrals of the plains that marked every Western Kansas and Eastern Colorado town.

T.K. nodded.

"So one of them is where—"

"Bruss's body was found." T.K. finished my sentence. "We don't ever mention Bruss. That's Putnam's job—to ask Bruss questions."

I turned to him. "I'm afraid of Putnam."

"Just tread lightly around him. And remember he can take care of us if the need arises.

To the music of a Vivaldi Concerto, we crossed the island, driving through leafy tunnels where the trees had been planted close together on both sides of the road. Their arching branches met overhead, creating bowers of sun-dappled shade.

We meandered through villages with thatch-roofed houses where time seemed reluctant to pass. Ducks, geese and chickens roamed in the farmyards, and spotted cows shared pastures with nanny goats.

In this gentle island landscape, we seemed continents away from the massive brick elevators of Stralsund, in a place unfazed by conquering Slavs, untouched by technology, with only a continuum of harvests from soil and sea.

I turned to T.K. "Why would a software pirate like Charles Goodborn withdraw to a place like this?"

Instead of answering, he kissed my fingertips.

We reached the shore of the Baltic at the town of Binz with crumbling old villas of bedraggled decadence lining the streets. The guidebook mentioned a Strand Promenade, and I inhaled warm moist sea air perfumed by *Rosa rugosa*.

The Tee Rose, one of those once Grande Dame hotels, abutted the Promenade. We had agreed to have our first public fight during hotel check-in, the second at dinner, and the third, tomorrow morning.

Americans would be rare birds on this island. A squabbling American couple descending on this seaside spa in their big blue BMW should have no difficulty engaging the locals' attention.

T.K. glanced at me with a guilty face that indicated he was going to say something I wouldn't like.

"I may as well tell you...we'd better act as if our room is "."

"What?" I gaped at him, "Bugged?"

"Just a precaution. All hotel rooms in the East used to be. Who knows what still is? I don't trust anyone."

Between the parking area and the lobby, I expressed my displeasure about the suddenness of this declaration, and his apparent inability to communicate the most basic information in a timely manner. He didn't defend himself, and by the time we had climbed the two tiers of wide stone steps leading to the entrance he had a hangdog put-upon expression, half-scowl, half-pensive, that made me even madder.

~ * ~

The hotel facade put its best foot forward, but the lobby had been stripped of all charm. I was amazed to see old fifties ash blond furniture, a kind of Danish modern meets the Commissar's five-year plan. Stark chairs upholstered in scratchy looking gray fabric sat among the kidney shaped coffee tables. I smelled floor wax, which was odd, because the worn carpets covered drab linoleum flooring.

I stood next to T.K. at the hotel registration desk. He stabbed at the form, writing in an impatient scrawl. Then he started to quibble about the rate of exchange. Ost Marks vs. West Marks. I finally got the gist of what he said. The hotel would take our West Marks, but T.K. wanted a better deal than they offered. I couldn't follow the details of his conversation, which escalated into an argument. The desk clerk waved his hands helplessly while T.K.'s voice grew louder. I tugged at his sleeve.

"We won't be paupers if you will agree to the going rate," I said in English. He glared at me and began haranguing the frazzled clerk again.

Everyone in the lobby had put down books, newspapers and chess pieces to observe our little tableau. A manager was called, and the whole scenario was replayed.

I nudged T.K.'s arm. "You might be a little more sensitive to the local—"

"Will you kindly butt out while I'm trying to negotiate—"

"Could we agree to pay the bill?" I raised my voice a notch. "I don't care how much—"

"You don't care how much they take advantage of us."

"I will pay the damn bill, Mr. Currency Freak, and I would like for you to stop embarrassing—"

"Okay. Shit. Get ripped off." He signed his name and yanked back our passports and stuffed them into his pocket. Negotiations having been successful, the desk clerk and the manager exchanged relieved glances.

I smiled and said, "Thanks, honey."

When T.K. threatened to get into it again about the absence of a bellhop, they found someone to fetch our bags from the car.

The manager led us up a grand but shabbily carpeted stairway to a third floor room overlooking the Baltic Sea.

We could have roller-skated down its length, but in hotel rooms, cleanliness surpasses all other amenities including size. Our room's furnishings, echoing the blond wood in the lobby, were softened by down comforters encased in white linen on the big bed, and scenic prints and paintings of the island. I hastened on to an inspection of the bathroom, an immense white-tiled space with ancient but well-scrubbed fixtures including a monstrous tub.

Through wind-billowed lace curtains, we had a view of green water. I opened the balcony doors and stepped outside to a view of the beach, the long pier, the dunes with their tall grass and hedges of wild roses, and the Strand Promenade. I heard the strains of a barrel organ grinding out "In the Good Old Summertime."

~ * ~

We ate a late dinner in hostile silence at a little café on one of the shopping streets that dead-ended at the Strand Promenade. When the waiter walked by, T.K. snapped his fingers and said, *"Bezahlen, bitte."*

The waiter re-appeared with the bill, and I watched with feigned irritation as T.K. groped in his back pockets, then his jacket pockets, both inside and out.

"You had money this morning." In the voice of a shrew.

"I still do. I must have left my wallet in my other pants." He made a second pass at his pockets.

"You always leave your wallet in your other pants. Or your other jacket. Or in the car."

"Sweetie, I'm sorry."

The waiter, perhaps fearing neither of us had cash, watched T.K.'s gyrations. At the sound of spoken English, heads turned toward us.

"It's not the money, it's the principle," I said.

"I told you I'm sorry. I just—"

"You're hopeless. Utterly hopeless." I hunted in my handbag and pulled out my new Master Card.

"They don't take plastic in this neck of the woods."

My voice rose. "You're kidding." I put my credit card away and produced a big fistful of Ost Marks. "This is so embarrassing. I feel like I'm traveling with a gigolo." I emphasized the word. More heads turned in our direction.

T.K. gave a helpless shrug and tried to take my hand, which I yanked away. "If you forget your cash tomorrow, I'm going back to Chicago. Alone."

"Sweet Pea, I promise."

The waiter, seeing the money, swooped down on our table.

"Is the tip included?" I asked.

T.K. examined the bill and nodded. I counted out what we owed and added ten marks.

"That's too damn much," said T.K. We stood up and I ignored his offered arm. Everyone in the café watched us leave.

Instead of turning right on the Strand Promenade and returning to the Tea Rose, we walked toward the water and onto the endless wooden pier which jutted so far out into the Baltic it looked like we could stroll its wooden planks half-way to Sweden. At ten o'clock the sun was setting, and the darkening eastern sky became by slow degrees a deeper blue, almost sapphire.

A pair of swans bobbed in the waves near the beach, and three boys with fishing poles tried their luck at the end of the pier. A cool wind rustled off the water, and T.K. slipped his jacket over my shoulders.

"The gigolo offers the coat off his back."

Sometimes he was so nice.

"How did we do?" I asked. "Or did we over-do?"

"Perfecto Garcia! The plan is going according to plan."

"And tomorrow?" I clutched his jacket around me as the wind whipped up some waves.

"Another public spat. Let's have it along the Promenade, then you sign up for your beauty treatments and I'll try to find out where Chuck Roast and his lady are hunkered down."

Before this summer, the GDR's exalted honchos had favored the island's better hotels. The more modest lodgings drew trade union types, who apparently stuck together even on vacation. No doubt the former resident Stasi agents had kept their eyes on the *Prominente* and the proles alike.

The town spa, which until last year had catered to the elite's privileged wives, would be a likely place for a rich American woman to indulge herself. Her halting German would mask a keen interest in the local gossip.

T.K. put his arm around me and we trudged back to the hotel. That the room might be bugged was an annoyance, not an impediment. Still, I wondered what the next unpleasant surprise might be.

Four

Late the following evening, we drove along the dark country road toward Putbus, a jewel box early nineteenth century town built by the Count of Putbus. Our objective was a stake out of the cottage, which Chuck and Romy had rented according to the local scuttlebutt. We believed they were not at home.

T.K. had discovered Chuck was sailing back from Rostock in his newly acquired boat, and I had found out Romy had gone to Berlin to visit her sister. T.K. had swapped rental cars with Putnam, and we were driving the inconspicuous gray Opel.

This morning we had staged a noisy argument over my purchase of amber beads at a booth on the Strand Promenade. T.K. had sneered, "Old Commie crapola, probably fake," while I enthused about the reasonable price, and repeated that he could be a little more sensitive to the locals' feelings. As usual, heads turned to watch our squabble.

At the perfumerie, T.K. grumbled, "You'll smell like the inside of a Mexican whorehouse," when I bought 'Crimson Poppies' cologne. The scent was mild and herbal, not cloyingly sweet. I was wearing it tonight.

Earlier in the day, we had "cased the joint." T.K. said I sounded like a fifties gun moll using that old term, which I liked better than his "preliminary surveillance." The "joint" was a white stucco cottage with a steep thatched roof, two chimneys and red-painted shutters sitting by the road some kilometers out of Putbus. No nearby neighbors. A low stockade fence surrounded a garden that stretched from a generous side yard to the back of the house. Sheep grazing in the pasture next door made me think of Colorado. A pond behind the property completed the picture of a delightful place to play house. A shed and an old garage stood behind the fence.

In the daylight, we had made a second pass by the property. In the middle of the garden, greedy finches clustered on a big bird feeder, also with a thatched roof.

"One of these two must have friends in high places to get such a cool cottage," said T.K., rubbing his chin. "Housing like this is at a premium…nothing one would luck into, even with money." He had turned to me. "Ever been on a stakeout.

"Me?"

~ * ~

In the cover of midnight darkness, dressed in black clothing and carrying a newly purchased Thermos filled with coffee, we were preparing to check out any late night comings and goings.

Across from the cottage, we parked in the tractor entrance to a field. T.K. cut the engine and doused the headlights. We had checked for automobiles in the driveway on our daylight visit and had not seen any. Tonight we hadn't passed a single car since we had turned off the beach road.

T.K. retrieved the Thermos from the back seat and I opened a package of butter cookies. Hours ago, we had eaten smoked fish on hard rolls at a little booth that bordered the Strand Promenade.

The moonlight illuminated the white stucco and made the house almost glow in the dark. Our munching the cookies was the only sound. The cottage windows were as dark as the Baltic night.

"Friends in high places," T.K. muttered again as we stared at the property. "Tell me some more about the masseuse who furnished all the primo information. Definitely worth cultivating. I see many spa treatments in your future."

In the dark car, I couldn't read his face. Probably grinning.

I pushed back my Cubs baseball cap and put my sneaker-clad feet up on the dashboard.

"I actually liked the spa, but it's utilitarian by American standards. No thick towels, thicker robes, or new age music. When the woman at the front desk discovered I spoke only rudimentary German, she assigned me to Sabine Schuld, who speaks *ein bischen English.*"

"Is she fluent?" asked T.K.

"Her English is broken but enthusiastic. She studies at night school. We gabbled in a mixture of English and German. She says English is the language everyone is studying."

T.K. passed me a cup of hot coffee. "What else?"

"You wouldn't want to get on her bad side. She's a real Valkyrie. Strong arms. Muscular calves."

He gave a low whistle.

"Her forte is the full-body massage. She almost pummeled me into jelly."

I didn't mention what she had said in her odd English, "So much stress, ja, in ze neck and in ze schulters." This corner of Europe had easily adopted the word "stress" into the vocabulary.

"When I asked if she ever had opportunities to practice her English, she told me she practices during a regular appointment with a woman who had lived in the U.S., another '*schöne Dame.*'"

I sipped my coffee, handed T.K. another cookie and continued my report.

"It was Romy, of course. Chuck's ladylove. Romy gets a massage and a manicure every week. No apparent lack of cash. Frau Schuld even met Chuck once when he came to pick up Romy. She says a lot of people here hate foreigners, but she doesn't."

An owl hooted in a tree across the road.

"Frau Schuld said that her husband had lost his job as a result of the 'changes.' I think it will be easy to find out the local gossip."

"Worth cultivating. Definitely," said T.K. He lit a cigarette. "Nice work."

Did his voice express a smidgeon of surprise?

The cottage remained dark. Only two cars had passed on the road. The problem with a stakeout was you had to pay attention—no napping or crossword puzzles by flashlight. My sunburn from the early afternoon visit to the beach felt prickly, and I envied T.K. his cigarette. I ate another cookie.

While I was at the spa, T.K. had spent the morning going around to all the hotels catering to well-heeled clients inquiring about the best barbershop with the added qualification that someone must speak English. When two hotels mentioned the same shop, he popped in for a shave.

This barber was happy to yak about his American client, enjoying the vicarious good fortune of someone who had found a wonderful cottage to rent, and as if that were not enough, the lucky man was buying a Zeesboot, a classic sailboat, made years ago at a Stralsund boatyard. The barber even knew the harbor where the Zeesboot would be berthed. He had raved about the beauty of the American's companion, a local woman who had returned to the island.

A little more detective work had led T.K. to this cottage.

The headlights of an automobile crawling by the cottage snapped us to attention. We ducked as the driver decreased his speed even more. Finally, the car drove on toward Putbus.

"We're too conspicuous. I better move this crate." Without turning on the lights, T.K. started the engine and drove a few hundred yards up a lane where we had a view of the road passing the cottage.

Minutes later from the direction of Putbus, another car appeared. No speeding tickets for this guy either. He passed our former parking spot at a creep and someone, either driver or passenger, played a flashlight around the area we had just vacated. I grabbed T.K.'s hand, and we watched from our dark cover as the car pulled into the cottage's driveway. We were too far away to determine if this was the same car from a few minutes ago.

Somewhere in the quiet a dog barked. The headlights beamed toward an out-building, and a car door slammed, but no lights appeared in the cottage windows.

Moments later, the driver backed onto the road and traveled again toward the coast.

"What do you think that was all about?" I asked. "It wasn't Chuck or Romy coming home."

"If someone is watching the place for them, it's awfully late to be checking on things," T.K. said. He paused. "I would love to get inside and have a look around for that CD-ROM."

"It could be anywhere. He could have sold it by now."

T.K. had said, "Stakeout," not "breaking and entering." My enthusiasm for B and E hovered around absolute zero.

"Besides, the house is bound to be locked," I said.

"Bound to be," echoed T.K. "You can be the lookout, while I do a tad of exploration."

"What if we get caught?"

Ignoring me, T.K. drove back toward the cottage with the headlights off. He pulled into a field and parked behind a haystack. I heard the owl hoot again, a lonely sound.

Against my better judgment, I crept across the road with T.K. and walked past the fenced garden with the nifty bird feeder. My heart was thumping as we turned into the dark drive. Our footsteps crunched on the gravel.

T.K. used a pocket flashlight to find the latch on the gate. He muttered, "No guts, no glory!" and we entered the back yard. I heard a low sound.

"What was that?"

He said, "Shhhhh."

Shivering in my sweatshirt, I stood right behind T.K. as he fiddled with the door handle. I heard the sound again, but louder this time, like someone gargling.

T.K. shouted, "Shit!" at the same instant I understood that what we heard were growls. We turned and raced toward the gate, and T.K. pushed it open.

A mass of snarling fury lunged at us. T.K. grabbed my arm and we toppled onto the driveway in a bone jarring crash. My scream died as the fall and T.K.'s weight knocked the wind out of me. With his mouth inches from my ear, T.K. was shouting, "*Sitz! Steh!*" at the top of his lungs. The dog neither sat nor stayed, but charged around us in a tight circle as we lay sprawled face down in the driveway, quaking from the animal's menace.

My saliva tasted of blood as I spit pieces of gravel out of my mouth. T.K., still protectively on top of me, felt like a ten-ton weight. He had quit hollering at the dog, which shut up except for intermittent growls.

Movement from T.K. or me, no matter how slight, sent the dog into spasms of snarling. His nails clicked on the gravel as he paced around us, so close I could see the yellowish gleam of his teeth, but as long as we remained docile and motionless, he wasn't going to eat us alive. We would be the little present he was keeping for his master.

T.K. tried to ease his hands out from under me. "Are you okay?" he asked. "I didn't mean to bring us down like a ton of rocks."

"I'm not hurt. Did he bite you?"

"No, but I lost a contact lens." He paused. "Old Fido needs breath mints."

"What are we going to do now?"

He didn't answer for the longest time. Then he said, "Any story we make up is bound to be pathetic, but I'm open to suggestions."

"Can you scoot down? You're squashing me."

With incremental movements, so as not to disturb our guardian, he inched down until his weight was off my back, then he rested his head on my fanny. I made a pillow out of my arms. The cold gravel felt like an icy bed of nails. I started to shiver, and when T.K. moved his arms to hold me, the dog went crazy again, and we had to lie still. Pain turned into numbness, and the dog sat.

"Why didn't he bark at us?" I asked.

"There's an old German saying that a barking dog doesn't bite."

"This one doesn't bark or bite. Yet."

We talked about our options, which was dumb, because our only option was to lie still and wait until someone came to our rescue. I was resigned to being arrested for trespassing. A cot in a jail cell, no matter how lumpy, would be an improvement over the driveway gravel, the waiting-for-an-excuse-to-bite dog and the cold night air. This is where 'go along to get along' had got me. Dreaming of a cot in a jail cell.

"I'll bet he's a wall dog," muttered T.K.

The black beast glowered at us, about a hundred pounds of ill-tempered canine.

"Looks like a Rottweiler to me." The phrase "meaner than a junk yard dog," kept popping into my head.

"A dog from the border patrol. Once the wall was gone, there was no need for all the guard dogs. Big commotion in the German press—these Krauts are worse than the English about their dogs. Lots of hand-wringing about their fate. Just a few of the wall dogs were vicious. I think the rest found homes."

The dog sat and watched us with dark beady eyes, as if he understood every word.

"And we've had the luck to encounter a vicious one who found a home," I said with a shiver.

T.K. turned his head and said, "Yeah," and Fido stopped panting and growled.

"Why would Chuck have a wall dog?" I asked. "To guard the CD-ROM?"

"Something doesn't add up. Chuck and his lady lucked into some very nice housing here, the kind only supremos would have. Now how did he manage that? Somebody pulled major strings for him to rent this spread."

T.K. continued, "he must be doing deals already. But who has such a shitload of information that they need his data warehouse? And who has such a shitload of money to make Chuck Roast an offer?"

Our prospects of finding answers were bleak. We returned to tossing around ideas about a story to legitimize our presence. Pretending to be Jehovah's Witnesses on casual day? I came up with an idea T.K. thought so idiotic that somebody might buy it. We would start with the truth, that we had driven by the house in the afternoon and admired the garden and the pretty bird feeder. I would say that I was so taken with the feeding station that we had actually knocked on the door to ask where to buy one.

"But nobody was home," said T.K.

"We were in Stralsund for dinner," I continued on the same track, "and on the way back I begged you to stop again. We decided to go into the yard to get a closer look. Examine the feeder by flashlight."

"Yeah. You wanted to have a feeder exactly like it for the garden of the summerhouse in Lake Geneva, Wisconsin."

T.K. shifted his weight a little. "Too half-assed. It won't work."

We were silent in the cold night, and our guard dog lay down and stared at us with no particular malice. I may have even slept for a moment. When I stirred the dog eyed us, but didn't growl.

"Nice doggie," I said.

"He only understands German."

The blooms and spiky leaves of iris, the old fashioned kind in colors of pale purple and honey bee gold, stood silhouetted against the sky, as a suggestion of dawn insinuated itself into the east.

"What time is it?"

T.K. braved a growl to peer at his watch. "Three twenty-seven."

I groaned. A rooster crowed.

"Zara, on any other occasion I can't think of anything nicer than using your fanny for a pillow."

I knew he was trying to keep my spirits up, but no amount of self-delusion could paint over the fact that we had blown it, big time, for us and for Putnam. Even if we talked our way out of incarceration, we would always be the couple who had snooped around Chuck's place in the middle of the night. Maybe I would be able to go home early, but I hated to leave in disgrace.

"Where are Chuck's goodies?"

"The coke is in a box of condoms. The hash is—"

I tensed at the sound of a car engine and the dog's ears perked up. The car passed slowly by the house, then accelerated and disappeared, leaving me with a sick feeling in the pit of my stomach. A few minutes later the car was back. The driver stopped on the road and cut the motor.

We lay like corpses fallen on a battlefield. The dog jumped to attention. I heard footsteps on the road. They turned and came crunching up the gravel. The dog gave a low growl and walked a few feet into the darkness. He growled again and the footsteps halted.

"Should we yell for help?" I whispered to T.K.

"Negative."

The footsteps turned and marched back to the street. The dog seemed torn between taking off after this new intruder, and guarding us. He returned, patrolled the area around us once, and sat down, panting, a few feet away.

"Could you see anything?" I whispered to T.K.

"Nada. But that was no friend of Fido."

An engine jumped to life, and we heard the car inching along the road. In my mind, relief jostled with humiliation. God, this was going to be so embarrassing. The police would be summoned. Curious neighbors would come by and stare at the couple lying outside the fence. The dog would be praised, petted, sated with treats. Animal hero first class. Maybe even a medal. We would be manacled and put in the back of a police van.

The dog leaped to his feet again as the auto turned into the drive. No headlights. Something wasn't right. The dog sensed it too. He looked back at us as if to warn "don't anybody move," and walked to the middle of the driveway. He stood waiting with rigid legs.

Piercing headlights pinned us in their glare. The car stopped, the door opened, and a man got out, but I could only see his shadow. Growling now, the dog stood his ground. We heard a click, like someone removing the safety from a weapon. *He's going to shoot us.*

An explosion of noise shattered the night. In front of me, the black dog lifted into the air. He fell in a crumpled heap onto the driveway. The headlights clicked off. Darkness. T.K. raised his head. I looked up, too. A man strode toward us, with brisk steps. Behind him, I saw the blue Beemer against the lightening sky.

"Oh hell, I might have known! Putnam's MO in every detail," T.K. whispered as we scrambled to our feet.

I held onto T.K., weak-kneed.

"Drummond, I promised to make amends." In the early light, Putnam's face wore a pleased smile.

"Billy Boy, that cap pistol of yours sounded like a goddamn howitzer. The neighbors will call the *Polizei* pronto. We've got to get the hell out of here." He nodded toward the dog, lying in a spreading pool of dark blood. "Hide the evidence."

Wracked with shivers, I wanted to find a warm place and surrender to the overwhelming weariness I felt. Instead, I turned to Putnam and pointed at the Beemer. "There's a tarp inside the trunk."

He popped the lid and I grabbed the tarp out of the backpack and unfolded it next to the dog's body. Putnam used the KaDeWe pocketknife to cut the leather collar from the dog's neck. Obviously, he didn't want the dog to be identified. I felt a pang of regret for the animal, which had been doing his job. The two of them lifted the dog by the legs and plopped him onto the tarp. While I rummaged for the bungee cords, they wrapped him like a parcel. Then the whole business, dog and tarp went into the trunk of the Beemer, which Putnam kept calling "the boot." I slammed it shut, and T.K. tossed Putnam the Opel keys. He smirked as he promised to drive back to Sassnitz and "lie doggo."

"What's he talking about?" I asked.

"He's going to lie low—stay out of sight," T.K. spoke in a low voice.

In the distance, a rooster crowed again. Softest gold washed the eastern sky, but our long night wasn't over.

~ * ~

Once we were underway in the Beemer, I stopped trembling. I could even swallow. While we made plans to dispose of the dog's body, we passed the remainder of the tepid coffee between us and mindlessly ate the rest of the butter cookies.

"Why did he have to shoot him? He could have fired a shot into the air. That might have frightened him." I was feeling sorrier than I would have imagined for the hapless dog.

"Bill Putnam doesn't do anything by halves."

After a few minutes, T.K. squinted and swore and admitted he couldn't see well with only one contact lens, so at the *Zirkus* in Putbus, a big roundabout, I got behind the wheel. The town had a dream-like, surreal appearance, as dawn suffused the pockmarked mansions in delicate hues of pink and yellow.

At an intersection where the road was undergoing repair, I stopped the car and T.K. heaved two big cobblestones into the back seat. We didn't talk any more. We didn't listen to music. I put the heater on full blast and drove.

~ * ~

At four-thirty in the morning, we started across the long flat bridge that links Rügen to the mainland. In the West, I could see the dark skyline of Stralsund's church spires. Behind us, a red sun rose out of the *Ostsee,* the Baltic Sea. At the halfway point, with no vehicles in sight, I stopped. We both jumped out of the car. T.K. lifted the trunk lid, loosened the bungee cords and opened the tarp so we could put the cobblestones inside.

Two brown eyes stared up at us. And blinked. The animal let out a pained whimper.

T.K. said, "Holy shit!"

I stood speechless.

"We've got to get rid of him," he said with a scowl.

"Oh no we don't!"

"Zara."

"I did not come here to kill animals."

"He wouldn't have any qualms about going for your throat."

"He didn't touch us. This is your fault. We invaded his yard. I will not be party to drowning an injured dog."

Another whine came from the trunk. I grabbed the backpack and pulled the blanket out of it.

T.K. said, "For Chrissakes he can still bite!"

Ignoring him, I tucked the blanket around the dog. "We have to get him to a vet."

"This could fuck the whole operation."

"You and Bill have done a bang up job of that."

T.K. walked behind the car to the driver's side, and stopped. A bicyclist, coming from Stralsund, pulled even with the car. A young man in jeans and a windbreaker, no helmet. He stopped his cycle and shouted from across the road to ask if we needed help.

"Ask if he knows where we can find a vet."

T.K. muttered something about a good deed that would not go unpunished, but he told the cyclist we had a dog that had been hit by a car. The cyclist shouted "Gebrüder Mertens, Kleintierpraxis in Stralsund," and gave T.K. instructions. He waved and continued pedaling toward the island.

I eased the tarp over the dog, T.K. shut the trunk and we got back into the car and continued into town.

T.K. said, "We leave Fido. And some money. And that's the end of it. If he dies, he dies. No phone calls. No visits under false pretenses. Promise me."

The clinic was a neat one-story stucco building with a sign by the front door that we missed the first time. The practice was attached to the vet's living quarters. Dr. Otto Mertens. There was a fenced yard in back with dog runs. T.K. parked on a side street, and opened the trunk again.

"Easy, boy."

Together, for our cargo was heavy, we hoisted tarp, dog, blanket and all out of the trunk, and lugged it up to the clinic door. The dog whined again, and T.K. repeated, "Easy, boy. Easy, now."

We deposited the patient on the front step. Barking had begun inside the house. I stuck three hundred Marks under the tarp while T.K. took off to get the car.

I leaned on the doorbell, and the chorus of barks and yelps and yaps grew louder. I turned and charged down the sidewalk like the devil was after me. Around the corner, T.K. had the car door open. I jumped in and we did a LeMans start.

We returned to the highway, and I took on the driving duties again until we found an open restaurant where trucks from Poland

and Russia stopped. We shared a breakfast of rolls, ham, cheese and strong tea with milk and sugar. The truckers, with their boots, biceps, and cigarettes dangling from cynical lips, looked like a hard bunch. After our arduous night, T.K. and I, grungy and tired, were a match for them.

Five

At ten o'clock in the morning, with only three hours sleep, I hurried along the Strand Promenade to my spa appointment. The barrel organ man had cranked up "The Skater's Waltz," and I had a memory of my scrawny pre-pubescent self, ponytail flying, gliding backwards on my roller skates, left arm flung out, showing off a little, and leaning into the same music I heard now. I felt a pang of homesickness, for Chloe and Chicago and the familiar patterns of my life.

As she said good morning, Frau Schuld eyed my scraped cheek and bruised chin with dismay. Not a good advertisement for her facial. I made up a quick lie about falling while jogging on the beach. Frau Schuld sniffed and lectured me that women who ran invariably ended up with gaunt faces, flat chests and bad knees. I gave her a thin smile, and went into the locker room.

Today I had scheduled eyebrow and eyelash dyeing and a treatment that in translation sounded like a milk bath with a body brushing massage and packing, whatever that was.

The milk bath had a clean dairy smell and felt very soothing on my sunburn. Frau Schuld must have noticed the no-strap-marks toast acquired at the FKK or nude beach.

The different types of beaches on the island had been perplexing.

That first morning, we had begun workouts with a brisk run along the beach in front of our hotel. As we trotted along, I kept seeing signs stating *Textil Strand*. Then we came to the *Hunde Strand,* or Dog's Beach, and a few hundred yards later another *Textil Strand*.

"Why were the garment workers assigned so many beaches?" I asked, pointing to the sign.

T.K. glanced at the sign and at me, and let out a whoop of laughter.

Over breakfast he had explained that the *Textil Strand* meant the clothing beach, versus the FKK beach, or the nude beach. Dogs were only allowed on the *Hunde Strand*, where we ran with our eyes down.

~ * ~

Before she ministered to me with her brush, Frau Schuld checked my neck and shoulders for signs of tension, and tut-tutted that the benefits from yesterday's massage were so short-lived.

Her probing fingers found what I couldn't hide, that T.K. and I were not here for lazy walks on the promenade and sightseeing excursions. Why, she abruptly asked me, did Americans, who could travel anywhere in the whole world, come here? Telling tales would not be easy, because I liked this big brash woman with fingers like antennae. I sighed, and while she exfoliated my skin with a soft-bristled brush, I fed her a big dose of the misinformation that T.K. always referred to as "our legend."

I had hoped, I confessed, that with his excellent German, my husband might find a vocation in real estate or investments here in the East, now that the border had opened. We had already been in Dresden, Jena, and the Harz Mountains. This Baltic island was our last stop.

She nodded, and made an impatient gesture with the brush. "*Ja. Die Grenze.*" The border. Many people already had that brainstorm. They all arrived driving Mercedes, wearing suits, with bankers and lawyers in tow. Sharks, she called them. *Haifische.*

"Investors, sharks, carpetbaggers, whatever," I said, agreeably, as if confident that T.K. hadn't been included in this grouping.

She asked me to turn over, keeping her eyes discreetly away from my nakedness. She placed a towel across my butt, paused, and her muscular arms swept over my back. I gabbled on, confiding that my husband, T.K., had been lukewarm to the idea, and now professed complete disinterest.

"Teekay," she paused. "That is a new name for me."

"Oh, it's his initials. Stands for Thomas Karl, but everyone calls him T.K."

"Karl is German," she offered.

"Oh yes," I agreed. "A name from his mother. T.K. says it will take years before the East German property titles are squared away."

Everyone knew the state had condemned and confiscated property for years. Absentee landlords had reneged on the taxes. Only the lawyers would make money.

"T.K. wants quick profits, not long-term investments." I gave a loud sigh. "He's so easily bored, so restless."

Sympathetically, she nodded, again as she brushed her way down the back of my thighs, calves and feet. The "packing" turned out to be a full body wrap in big strips of muslin impregnated with soothing herbs, which Frau Schuld promised would pull the toxins right out of me.

With my hair wrapped in a towel and only my face exposed, I lay mummy-like on the table for twenty minutes. My thoughts returned to last night.

The dog had been lucky. T.K. and I had also been fortunate that Putnam had searched for us when we missed the rendezvous. He hadn't had much to go on. 'A pretty thatched cottage halfway between Sellin and Putbus.' He'd spotted the gray Opel behind the haystack, somehow figured it out. I wanted to like him more for rescuing us, but I couldn't.

So far, T.K.'s bad judgment equaled Putnam's. If they had been on one of my projects, I would have sacked them both, but I was the new kid with no authority to dismiss anyone. Go along to get along. I said it to myself ten times a day.

~ * ~

Frau Schuld awakened me for the unwrapping. The dye job came after I was showered and dressed. Lighten the brows a bit and darken the eyelashes. Deep brown, not black. With my lightened hair, with the burgundy streaks I didn't want to look whorish. Frau Schuld laughed and agreed.

While she dabbed glop on my eyebrows, she asked how long we were staying on the island. Ten days or so, I replied. Enough time to wind down. An investment opportunity might still turn up.

"How you and your man meet?" she asked.

I let her pry the story out of me.

Two years ago, a recent widow, I had met him on a cruise.

A cruise! She paused, with her brush in mid-air. How romantic! Where? She wanted to know.

"Oh, nowhere special. The Caribbean," I answered. "Aruba, Curacao, you know."

She probably didn't, but she asked, "And then?"

I exhaled. "Problems." No one ever believed a woman could handle her own affairs. I could feel her nodding vigorously. My lawyers and accountants were so certain that he was a fortune hunter, they had insisted on a mean-spirited pre-nuptial agreement. I had trouble explaining the pre-nuptial business, but she eventually understood.

She had heard of such things. Maybe not a bad idea.

I confided that my husband received a generous allowance, which never lasted from one month to the next. He was so charming, so much fun, but his moods...I sighed again, and asked her if she was married.

Frau Schuld had a husband and a seventeen-year-old daughter, Andrea. Girls were always a worry. And now, her husband's government job had vanished. She had so much anxiety about the future. The loss of direction, of authority, perhaps it was good, but change was so difficult. *So schwer.* Would her daughter be able to continue her education? How would her husband find work? What would happen to rent? To pensions? I nodded in commiseration. She had real worries. It would be a hard row to hoe, as my father had always said, but I couldn't translate that.

A few minutes later, I admired my new brows and lashes in a mirror and smiled at Frau Schuld.

"We're going to the four o'clock tea dance at the *Kurhaus*," I said. "T.K. is a great dancer. Thanks to you, I'll look good."

She pushed a strand of hair away from her eyes, and returned my smile.

"*Auf Wiedersehen*, Frau Wentz."

"*Bis Morgen*, Frau Schuld." Until tomorrow.

I felt so guilty about all the lies that I plunked down a big tip.

After I left, I realized I had been so keen on spinning my tales that I had forgotten to steer the conversation around to Romy. Tomorrow. During my pedicure or perhaps in the intimacy of the tightening treatment for *Hals, Decolleté und Brust*. Throat, cleavage and breast. Then T.K. had read my list of appointments, he leered and raised his eyebrows.

"Zara, they're leaving no part of you untouched."

~ * ~

Sabine Schuld's concerns made the political and social issues real. T.K. read half a dozen newspapers every day, sopping up all the seismic jolts to the collective psyche that the changes rolling across the GDR brought with them. The opening of the border, the great exodus of young people, then the vote for reunification, each event had caused a political convulsion affecting everyone. On the Strand Promenade, at the beach, and in the cafés, the faces expressed hope, despair, exultation, worry, resignation—emotions observed anywhere, but here they possessed a jarring energy, like a row of exclamation points.

On my route back to the hotel, I paused to admire some once white villas with wood-filigree balconies and stylized steel ornamentation. On the sagging porch of a dilapidated house, two T-shirted teenage boys tuned guitars, while a third fiddled with a keyboard. The boys hunched intently over their instruments, ignored by a statuesque young woman who sprawled across the steps, her head thrown back to let her face catch the sun. Everyone wore the ubiquitous stonewashed denim jeans. A tambourine lay on the step next to the girl.

The group began to play when I was well past the house, but I found a bench and stopped to listen as the vocalist sang the English words in a faint German accent, "I can see clearly now the rain is gone." I remembered the old song with the receding clouds and the long-awaited rainbow. Greedy for the future, these young people were unfettered with the worries and pessimism of their parents' generation.

~ * ~

We swooped across the dance floor to the rhythm of the geriatric orchestra's rendition of "Orchids in the Moonlight."

Twice a week the tea dance took place in the ballroom of the handsome turn-of-the-century *Kurhaus*. With gold and white stucco walls and a red-tiled roof, it could have housed a casino in San Remo or Nice. Sunlight reflected off the sea and poured through the tall arched windows overlooking the Promenade. The orchestra occupied the front of the room, and small tables surrounded the parquet dance floor. T.K. and I were the youngest, best-dressed couple and certainly the only Americans.

With two day's growth of beard, designer glasses, and his Berlin haircut, T.K. looked like he had attitude. We moved easily to the music, and I smiled up at him. Sometimes I thought I would wake up in my bed in Chicago's Sandburg Village musing about the unbelievable dream I had just had.

Two men strolled into the ballroom and seated themselves at a table in back where they watched the dancers. They wore sport coats in dull fabrics and no ties. I imagined feet shod in crepe-soled shoes.

They didn't look like gay blades who would stand up and glide across the floor together. Instead, they drank beer and exchanged a few monosyllables while they covertly eyed the crowd.

"Get a load of those two," I whispered.

"Yeah. The dark one looks like an ape with that lowbrow and big jutting jaw. No, he looks even more like a *Gartenzwerg*." T.K. was referring to small statues of red-capped gnomes that populated many German gardens.

"A simian *Gartenzwerg*," I said, glancing back to the impassive duo. "And his friend looks like a satyr. Those eyes. He only needs a flute."

"That's called a pipe, Sweetie, but you're right."

"Chunky Monkey—"

"And Giles Goat Boy," he added. "They keep looking at the pretty lady in the lavender dress."

"The dress Edgar liked."

"It wasn't the dress that old Edgar was ogling."

The mention of Edgar triggered something in memory, but then T.K.'s hand dropped down the small of my back perilously close to my fanny. I watched the faces of the old ladies sitting primly at their tables, pupils widening, eyebrows arching. Some of them smiled "go for it" smiles, while others offered tight frowns of disapproval.

The song ended. "I'm going to powder my nose. Ask a nice Frau to dance."

The orchestra struck up a lively rendition of, "Yes We Have No Bananas", as I left to find the *Damen,*

When I returned, T.K. was escorting a corseted dowager in a tan lace dress back to her table as her women friends beamed at him. I flashed a smile in the direction of Chunky Monkey and his satyr-like companion. They nodded in a curt impersonal way, but I thought they were caught off guard by my friendly gesture.

The orchestra leader made an announcement, which I couldn't follow, and the old folks shuffled out. T.K. explained that disco and rock tunes of various vintages would start in fifteen minutes. A man wheeled in some speakers, and the disk jockey began setting up shop. Chunky Monkey and the goat-eyed man left.

"Maybe we should skip the rock and roll," I said. "I'd like to get back to work."

"We are working."

"I mean on my laptop. Your 'technical resource' hasn't done diddly squat."

"Is that one of those kinky things I am forbidden, or is it something you prefer to do alone?" His face was a perfect deadpan.

"Will you be serious? Today when I came back from the spa, I entered everything that's happened so far into the laptop. With work points and ideas and even biographical sketches I can fill in later about Chuck and Romy." I didn't mention the interesting little journal I kept on the computer.

We had wandered into a large salon. I stood at the window looking out toward the white, filigreed bandstand. T.K. lit a cigarette.

His dance partner came by with two of her friends, and smiled and nodded. T.K. bowed. We left the Kurhaus, and I took his arm as we traversed the broad white steps to the Strand Promenade. He nudged me and said "Eyes left. The gents who 'simply wouldn't dance.'" From a bench on the Promenade, Chunky Monkey and Giles Goat Boy watched the passing parade. The goatish one glanced up, saw us, and spoke to his bench mate, who also turned in our direction. They looked away when they noticed we were looking at them.

Under his breath T.K. said, "Congratulations, Zara, someone has taken your bait."

~ * ~

The nightmare came for the first time that night.

A clearing in the forest, with a frenzied scene around a bonfire. Tongues of flame reached as high as the treetops. Pounding drums. Whirling and howling, half-humans with beaks and snouts, garish plumage and matted hair, dance with wild beasts coaxed from the shadows. A monkey wearing a red cap rides a white lamb into the clearing, jumps off, and joins the dance. A creature with bedraggled red and blue feathers and the fierce eyes of a bird of prey begins to stalk the lamb. A centaur with a shaggy torso and a goatish face joins the birdman, and together they chase the lamb through the writhing mass of bodies.

As I try to reach the terrified lamb, I can only move among the dancers in a mired slow motion. While I watch, the awful pair with their talons and hooves seizes the bleating lamb, and drags it toward the orange flames.

I screamed and woke up.

T.K. brought me a glass of water and held me in his arms until I slept again.

~ * ~

The next morning, still shaken by the nightmare, I lay supine on the treatment table while Frau Schuld's plump fingers delicately applied a firming mask from my neck down to my waist. Even as Putnam, our dog misadventure and the "goodies for Chuck," conspired to frazzle me, the gentle sea and the laying on of Frau Schuld's hands with her scented oils and lotions worked to soothe me.

Eyes closed, I had begun to phrase a question to Frau Schuld, but before I could complete it, she broke in with a barrage of gossip and confidences in her German-English mishmash. I strained to find nouns and verbs among the flood of words. She always referred to Romy as "Frau Motte."

Just a few weeks ago Frau Motte had made a trip to Finland to buy furniture. Then yesterday Frau Motte had returned from Berlin and had come into the spa for her regular appointment. Today, Frau Motte's companion, Mr. Goodborn, was expected to arrive in Lauterbach aboard his sailing yacht.

If I had been having a hair treatment, each strand would have stood on end when Frau Schuld said in a half-whisper that something very disturbing had occurred at the cottage Frau Motte and Herr Goodborn shared, a cottage they rented from her husband's colleague. A watchdog had disappeared, and a pool of dried blood had been found in the driveway.

So much for a zoned out morning at the spa. My eyes shot open and I listened in nervous agitation as Frau Schuld confided her husband himself had fed the animal when the occupants of the cottage were away. The dog, adopted from the border patrol, stayed at the cottage, when it had been rented out.

I asked her to repeat every other sentence, just to make sure I followed what she said.

The dog's disappearance and the pool of blood worried her. She feared such lawlessness would become the norm once the country was reunited. Now they would get the drug problems, the homeless, and the vandalism. She stopped herself.

"Forgive me, Frau Wentz, I do not wish to bore you with our difficulties."

"Oh, no, Frau Schuld," I protested. "I am truly interested."

I remembered sad brown eyes and the pained whine.

"Was the dog a very dear pet?" I asked.

She shook her head. No. The owner felt no sentiment for the animal, but nowadays such expensive training was impossible to replace. That was the true tragedy. An obedient dog secured by a fence, and now gone. *Weg*!

I felt worse for the dog now, with no caring master.

She rattled on. Her husband's colleague had asked the police to conduct an investigation, but the police were so busy. Last year the same police would have jumped to be helpful, but now...

A bead of sweat worked its way from under my arm down along my rib cage. How fortunate that the police were so busy. Kept them out of trouble. Kept us out of trouble. I hoped Sabine didn't notice my heart beating against my bare chest. She set a timer, announced, *"fünfzehn Minuten,"* and left the room.

I willed myself to limpness, closed my eyes again and focused on my tingling skin while the mask dried and the so-called firming action occurred. Still, my brain turned cartwheels inside my head.

No one could tie us to the veterinary clinic in Stralsund and the Rottweiler with the bullet wound. I cringed when I thought about the wad of West marks I had left to pay for the dog's doctoring. How many people on flung around *Westmarks* like they were funny money?

When the alarm rang, Frau Schuld peeled off the mask and sent me to the showers. After the pedicure, while a petal pink enamel dried on my toenails, Frau Schuld stopped by again. A tiny frown creased her wide forehead, and she hesitated for a long moment. I produced an encouraging smile.

She began "Frau Wentz, er, Mrs. Wentz. About the social life on our island there is the following to say." She cleared her throat.

"Yes?"

"We have few...occasions for a pleasant evening."

I nodded and smiled again.

"I tell Frau Motte about my American woman. So sympathetic. Now she likes to make your acquaintance. Your man, also."

"Oh how nice!" I said, inspecting my toenails.

She plunged on. "Herr Goodborn...sometimes a friendly man. Then also moody. Now he has lust to speak English with you and your man."

Our eyes met and hers looked troubled.

"*Ach*!" She exhaled from the effort of picking her way through the minefields of a foreign language. "Frau Motte will telephone to me. I leave message at hotel. When social time is right."

"Of course. Would we go to their cottage?"

"Oh no!" She seemed to find the idea shocking. "Meet at café. That is our custom."

"T.K. and I will be so pleased to make the acquaintance of the other American couple. He always enjoys new people."

"When time is good," she emphasized.

"I'll see you on Monday then. Mud bath and—." The pedicurist returned, and Frau Schuld smiled uncertainly at me and left.

Romy, a.k.a. Frau Motte wanted to meet us. When Chuck Roast was in a good mood. This news wiped out most of the angst I had been feeling. Now I could hardly wait for the second coat of polish to dry, because I wanted to race back to the hotel and tell my "man."

~ * ~

T.K. had been in the lobby all morning, listening to spiels from those looking for investors, but now he was alone, reading a German newspaper and keeping an eye on the World Cup soccer matches on television.

"Buy any snake oil?" I asked, plopping down on the sofa beside him. He put down the newspaper and looked at me.

"How firm?"

"About the same as yesterday."

"You women."

"This woman has received a most interesting invitation." My grin must have conveyed the importance of my news.

He folded the newspaper and placed it on the coffee table.

"May I invite you to reveal the invitation over a pre-luncheon glass of wine?"

We tried not to have any conversations about our assignment in the hotel, because T.K. even thought the lobby, like the bedrooms, might still be bugged from the old days. The restaurants offered more anonymity.

~ * ~

Our favorite sidewalk café was filling with diners, and we grabbed a table for two under a blue and white striped awning, and ordered glasses of crisp Hungarian wine.

"Good. Yes, good," he said quietly, after I had relayed what Frau said. He frowned and didn't even notice the brunette parading down the street in butt-revealing shorts.

"I'd really like to find out why they rate that cottage."

"Maybe Chuck will tell you."

The waiter appeared with my salad, and T.K. waited until we were alone again.

"Do you want to take a look at that harbor in Lauterbach?" I asked. "Where Chuck is docking the Zeesboot? It's near Putbus. I looked in the tourist brochure while my toenails were drying."

T.K. snared a bite of my lettuce and said, "We have an appointment this afternoon. Some gent hopes we'll join a consortium that is planning to erect some windmills. He wants us to show us the prototypes."

After lunch, we took off to inspect the latest investment scheme. Solidifying our legend. T.K. promised we could visit the boat basin on the way back. We left the main highway to Stralsund, drove down a cobblestone country road and turned into a rough lane to get up close to the windmills. A crimson field of wild poppies bent before the assault of the brisk breeze.

Something about the windmill gave me the willies. The polished steel stalks rising out of the farmland looked utterly disengaged from the rural landscape.

The man hoping for our investment money waited in his car. Portly and balding, he gestured at the windmills and spoke a rapid-fire German with a lot of electrical and investment terminology I couldn't make sense of. T.K. squinted and stroked his chin and said we wanted to think about it. The man seemed disappointed.

T.K. said, "Herr Altmann, we'll call you if we want more information."

I reminded T.K. to get a prospectus, a business plan and financial references. "And make sure the windmills aren't in the way of any migratory birds." The man began his story about the economic benefits of wind power in broken English. While he droned on, I stared up at the immense whirling blades, which made the eerie rhythmic sound of a large knife slicing through the air. Whoosh, whoosh, whoosh, like the beating wings of a great prehistoric bird desperately trying to fly out of this desolate place.

~ * ~

Eight streets radiated out of the *Zirkus* in Putbus and we picked the wrong one. A mile outside of town through a tangle of overgrown shrubbery, we sat before Doric columns supporting the roof of a two-story building of dazzling but decayed whiteness. No harbor in sight. T.K. started to turn the car around.

"Wait a minute!" I thumbed through the guidebook. "Here it is... *Badehaus in der Goor*!" We had landed at a stately old bathhouse that, like everything in Putbus, had a shabby Neo-Classical appearance.

We left the parked car to look around. Weeds choked the garden, and the roof tiles, fatigued by history and time, were crumbling into red shards. A granite statue of a woman undressing presided over this scene of abandonment. On a pedestal in front of the weedy overgrowth, she was in the act of pulling a shift over her head. Short legs emerged from thick ankles and grew into thunder thighs, then a generous round belly. Perky breasts were an enigmatic contrast to her ponderous nether regions. Her sculpted arms tugged at the folds of fabric obscuring her head. T.K. stared pointedly at the gray granite breasts and quipped, "Now, that's firm!"

"Crude sexual innuendo will be ignored."

He wrinkled his nose. I would never live down this morning's *Hals, Décolleté und Brust* treatment.

"I can photograph you with the statue," I offered, but I really wanted to leave this place, which in its way felt as deserted and desolate as the field where the windmill blades slashed the air.

T.K. must have felt it too, because he said, "No, let's get out of here."

In the car, I checked the map. We should have veered off to the right instead of going straight.

"This Lauterbach harbor can't be a Baltic Monaco," T.K. said in a pedagogic voice that heralded, "clueing Zara in."

"Until this summer, pleasure boats were scarce and restricted. Not that you could sail anywhere." He gestured toward a water view. "The GDR guarded nautical charts like state secrets. And venturing very far out into these coastal waters would land you in jail. The harbor patrol had radar, fast boats, search lights, and suspicious minds."

"They were afraid someone would make a run to Sweden or Denmark?"

"A lot of people tried. The odds were about even with jumping over the wall."

We drove down a shady cobblestone road which led to a picture book little harbor lined with trees. White clouds stippled the blue sky. The piers and docks, which formed a big "U," looked neglected and rotting. Next to the public pier was a parking lot with the ubiquitous Trabbis.

Two old fishing boats were tied up at a pier on the left side of the harbor. Further down on the right, a small crowd had gathered along a rickety pier, gaping at one of the trimmest ketches I had ever seen.

"That has to be Chuck," I said. "What do we do?" Our clothes would tag us as Americans.

"Let's wander around like the tourists we are."

T.K. pulled in beside a green Trabbi. He slung the leather strap of his Zeus binoculars around his neck. I carried my little Olympus camera. We turned left toward the fishing boats. The planking was old but not rotten. A few sea gulls stood sentinel on the pilings.

Across the water on the Zeesboot, a bare-chested man in faded Nantucket red shorts busied himself wrapping covers around the furled sails. I borrowed the binoculars. The tall, tan man I focused on could have been doing his chores on Martha's Vineyard or in Fort Lauderdale. In scuffed brown Topsiders, Charles Goodborn moved about the boat with an economy of motion that an experienced sailor exhibits from working in cramped quarters. I focused on his face. Forehead, nose, chin all sharply chiseled against the blue Baltic sky. Eyes dark and alert. The sum of his features created a bold striking appearance.

The sun had streaked his light brown hair, and he flashed a dazzling smile of dimples and white teeth at one of the on-lookers. I put down the binoculars. I hadn't imagined that Goodborn would be such a hunk.

Working alongside him, coiling ropes and stowing buckets and cushions was an Asian man, also in faded shorts, but he wore a conical straw fisherman's hat.

I passed the binoculars to T.K. "He has a first mate."

"My guess is Vietnamese," he said, after a long look.

"Is that possible?"

He raised the glasses to his eyes again and took another look. "East Germany imported plenty of North Vietnamese 'guest workers.' Treated some of them like slave labor from what I hear. They'll all be sent back."

"Let's walk over and get a better look."

"Yeah, but not too close."

We sauntered in the direction of Goodborn's boat.

The hull, the two masts, the decks, everything above the waterline was stained a rich mahogany color. From the cabin house with its four portholes, to the graceful curve of the bow, this had been a functional working boat.

According to T.K.'s source, Zeesboots had been used for eeling in shallow coastal waters. Edgar would drool over such a classic vessel.

"We sure as hell don't want to appear too curious about Chuck Roast, and the citizens are starting to gape at the Beemer, so let's drop into that drinking establishment across the street and you can treat me to some local brew." T.K. took my arm. The problem with trying to attract notice is that it's difficult to turn off when you don't want to.

~ * ~

The Aalfischer reeked of the old tavern odors of stale beer and cigarette smoke. We were the sole patrons. The waiter was absorbed in a soccer match on TV.

We took a window table and ordered two Warsteiner while we kept our eyes on the sailboat. Soon the Asian man walked down the pier with a purposeful gait, came into the bar and placed a call from a pay phone by the entrance. He returned to the boat. We stayed put.

Half an hour later, a new Wartburg, the Cadillac of Trabbis, pulled into the parking lot. Chuck and "Hanoi Joe," as T.K. dubbed him, marched toward the parking area with the Vietnamese sailor a few deferential steps behind Chuck. He lugged two big duffel bags, and Chuck toted a third. The driver jumped out of the car, opened the trunk and helped stow the bags. T.K. gave a low whistle.

The driver was Chunky Monkey, the life-sized garden gnome who had watched us at the Kurhaus tea dance. The Vietnamese man climbed into the front seat with Chunky Monkey, while Chuck sat in back in isolated splendor. He lit a cigar as they drove off toward Putbus.

T.K. and I grinned at each other across the table, and clinked our beer glasses in a wordless toast. T.K. lit a cigarette as they drove by us.

"Sweet Pea," he said, "how do you like them apples?"

~ * ~

A few hours later, as we traveled the highway to Sassnitz for our Friday evening hook up with Bill Putnam, clouds rolled in over the water and the sky looked sodden and threatening. T.K. twirled the radio dial and found that pop tune with the sentimental lyrics.

> *Your breath touched my cheek like the warm summer wind.*
> *Your lips burnt mine like the mid-summer sun.*

He hummed the melody after the song had ended.

T.K. looked good this evening, wearing a tan cashmere sweater cut like a sweatshirt and pale linen slacks. His glasses, worn since losing the contact lens in the gravel, had thin delicate frames with amber tinted glass.

I wore jeans, a white T-shirt, and my navy blazer. A generous spritz of *Baltic Breeze* completed my toilette.

We passed the docks where ferries left for Sweden, and continued along the coastal highway into the town, a grimy down-at-the-heels industrial port. The old Baltic buildings cried for paint, plaster and landscaping. It was the kind of backwater seaport I had always imagined tucked into a forgotten piece of Mexican coastline, or some god-forsaken part of Africa. I couldn't understand why Putnam would put up at a bed and breakfast in such a dumpy town.

We found the café at the far end of the main drag, and we parked in the little lot in back. The side street, paved with the usual cobblestones, slanted sharply down toward the harbor. When we got out of the car, I looked back at the water where a few huge ships sat at anchor. T.K. said the Russian navy had a presence here, but would soon be pulling out for good.

Heady whiffs of garlic, wine and fish emanated from the kitchen. I began to salivate.

As T.K. held the door open for me, he whispered, "Remember, we don't know Bill Putnam from Adam."

We crossed the threshold and stepped inside.

The café consisted of three or four little rooms and a bar. Patrons glanced up as we entered. Not Putnam. He sat facing the door at a table in back. A man shared his table. Now what? We could always count on Putnam to complicate everything.

T.K. said, "Hmmmm," and strolled into the back room. I followed. Most conveniently, an empty table waited for us next to Putnam. I let T.K. sit on the banquette right next to him, and I seated myself in a chair beside his drinking partner who gave us a peremptory glance. He must have noticed our foreignness, because I saw his eyes take in T.K.'s haircut, his glasses, then his sweater and finally his wristwatch. He turned his head and gave me a casual but careful scrutiny. No one spoke or made eye contact.

A waiter brought menus and recited the specials; T.K. ordered a bottle of wine. Putnam and his buddy drank beer.

The café had a modest elegance. A small but sprightly rose in a bud vase adorned every table, and prints and watercolors of the island lined the pale yellow walls above the wainscoting.

T.K. and I talked to each other in English, while Putnam and his friend conversed in German. Putnam's German was not fluent, just a little better than mine. His friend spoke with an accent I couldn't identify. They talked about the World Cup soccer matches, which held all males from eight to eighty in thrall this summer.

I studied the man as surreptitiously as he had eyed me. He had a long, rather sad face, tanned, with thoughtful eyes. A deep crease ran from either side of his nose down to his mouth, which was small, but sensual. His brown hair brushed the edge of his collar. Attractive in an offbeat way in his navy turtleneck and jeans.

When the waiter returned, I ordered the halibut, and T.K. hesitated between pork cutlets and herring.

Putnam turned to T.K. and said in his most proper British voice, "I say, the halibut is an excellent choice. The herring is first rate, too."

I said, "Oh God! It's such a relief to hear English spoken."

"*Pojarskiya Koteleti*!" interjected Bill's mysterious friend, nodding at T.K.

T.K. said, "I beg your pardon?"

"Anatoly here is recommending the cutlets," Putnam said. T.K. smiled. Anatoly smiled back, revealing even white teeth.

T.K. stuck out his hand. "T.K. Wentz from Chicago, Illinois." He and Putnam shook hands.

"Bill Putnam from London and this is my friend Captain Anatoly Salenko." I tried not to stare when he explained, "Anatoly lives aboard one of those Russian warships in the harbor."

Anatoly looked about T.K.'s age. Early forties at most. No gray hair. Young to be a captain.

T.K. rested his hand lightly on my arm. "My wife, Zara." I shook hands with Putnam, but when I offered Anatoly my hand, he pressed it to his lips. T.K. looked half-amused, half-irritated at the Russian's gallantry, which I liked.

I couldn't imagine how Putnam had hooked up with a Russian naval officer, but he seemed pleased with himself, as his sharp blue eyes darted around the tables to T.K., Captain Salenko, his dinner plate and then to me.

"Goodness, we're certainly an international bunch," I said. "Mr. Putnam, does Captain Salenko speak English?"

Salenko looked at me with his sad expressive eyes, and said, "much German, little English." He pronounced it "leetle Engleesh."

We continued to chat with our new acquaintances through dinner, mostly in German for Captain Salenko's benefit.

The captain ordered vodka for himself and Putnam, and when we finished our entrees, the waiter delivered two shots in icy glasses to our table. I felt half-sloshed from the wine, but T.K. immediately picked up the glass and said, *"Na Zdroviye!"* At least that's what it sounded like.

Now Salenko watched us carefully and nodded his approval as we both downed the vodka in one gulp. I didn't want him to see me gasp and sweat. T.K. leaned against the banquette and exhaled. He had a faint, almost arrogant smile as he asked Salenko, "Aside from Zum Nackten Fisch here, where does a navy man drink in this godforsaken town—when he has shore leave?"

Putnam jumped in to answer the question. "First rate pub. Down by the waterfront. Anatoly and I got acquainted there over a pint."

He offered a pack of English Ovals, and T.K. and Salenko both accepted a cigarette. Male bonding rite.

Captain Salenko said, *"Der Albatros"* and T.K. raised an eyebrow.

Putnam said, "Name of the pub." T.K. signaled the waiter, and I passed him a wad of bills under the table with which he paid the tab. The captain's eyes didn't miss much, for he honed in on our financial exchange, as well as T.K.'s bare ankles and loafers.

Then T.K. asked for directions to the pub, and nothing would do but for Mr. Putnam and Captain Salenko to escort us down the hill to the waterfront and the seaman's bar.

~ * ~

Der Albatros occupied a one-story brick building facing the harbor. An overhanging roof supported by wooden beams and braces provided a little protection from the sun and rain to those clustered outside around the big hatch-cover tables of bare wood, gray and weathered.

A few colored lights on a low-slung wire were too stark and widely spaced to provide the hoped-for festive air, but by now a fog had barreled in off the Baltic, and only a few men drank in the misty droplets.

Fishing nets were draped over the dark green door in big loops. T.K. started humming, "In the Port of Amsterdam."

Captain Salenko went in first, and Putnam held the door open for T.K. and me. We stepped into a smoky room with a low-beamed ceiling, a wide planked well-scrubbed floor, and whitewashed walls festooned with old nautical mementos. Drinkers occupied the half-dozen wooden tables. A bar ran across the back of the room. No empty stools. The noise of laughter and talk dropped as heads turned to inspect our group. I noticed only two other women. My cashmere blazer seemed so out of place it might as well have been a fur coat.

A frizzy-haired blond waitress swooped by and whispered a few words to the captain, who nodded. She led us through the room, around a corner and into a smaller area dominated by a green tile stove. The waitress plucked the reserved sign off the table and we sat down. The patrons turned back to their conversations.

Putnam said, "A single man can pass a pleasant evening here, right, Anatoly?"

Anatoly nodded.

T.K. ordered a round of beers and when the waitress brought them, Captain Salenko introduced us as his 'new Ami friends.' *American friends*.

She wasn't impressed.

T.K. raised his glass and proposed, "To Glasnost," and we all drank. If anyone had predicted I would ever be sitting in a bar in East Germany with a Russian naval officer, T.K. Drummond and an unpredictable Brit, I would have insisted the crystal ball was cracked.

The Captain discreetly pointed out the nationalities of the sailors at the scattered tables: Russians, Poles, Swedes, Finns and of course, Germans. They all looked alike to me, most of them in dark sweaters and stonewashed jeans. All Nordic and Slavic faces except for the Vietnamese man washing glasses behind the bar. Salenko said a few locals drank here, but we seemed to be the only tourists. A man in an old tweed suit sat by himself and read a thick book. Anatoly nodded, and said *"der Professor,"* under his breath.

When the Captain inquired why we were so far from home, T.K. reeled off his spiel about "researching investment opportunities," Salenko told us the navy would soon be leaving for good. He sighed and looked even sadder. Putnam claimed to be vacationing.

Several times I caught the captain looking at me with his mournful eyes, and I knew I had made a conquest of this interesting man. By the quiver of what antennae can a woman tell? A glance, a gesture, a hesitation? Even tipsy, I knew, for by now I was flying from the strong beer on top of the wine and vodka.

After another beer, T.K. said he had drunk long enough with Mr. Putnam and Captain Salenko, and suggested we do *Brüderschaft,* , or Brotherhood, a bonding ceremony in which everyone drank with locked arms. Afterward, we could call each other by first names.

I told the waitress to make my next beer a Coke, because I kept imagining I saw bubbles rising out of the deep-sea diver's helmet that stood on a shelf behind the bar. In Berlin, Smith had warned us the authorities threw the book at anyone caught drinking and driving, and I could already see us meandering along the coastal highway in an alcoholic stupor and being pulled over and arrested.

While we waited for another round of drinks, the Captain excused himself and headed for the toilets. Before he was halfway across the room, T.K. said, "Billy Boy, what's with Ivan? Don't we have enough complications already?" He lit a cigarette and blew one of his perfect smoke rings.

"Tolya knows the ropes around here." Bill grinned like a Cheshire cat. "And not only the nautical ropes. I've been chatting him up for a reason. The Russkie knows who the resident Stasi were. And he told me Goodborn has cozied up to them. He and his pretty German bird were in here drinking with them last week."

"How did he know it was Goodborn?"

"There's only one other American on this island. And his female companion is said to be absolutely stunning."

I had to give Putnam his due. Not only had he rescued us from the dog, but he had also culled information gold from his new friend.

A few hours later, we left the bar on foot, and sobered up with a long stroll through the dark town. Putnam mentioned the "black beast feeding the fish," and I shivered. T.K. didn't say a word. He had been angry when he found out I left West marks to pay the veterinarian. "For Chrissakes, he'll know it wasn't anybody local. Why didn't you just leave a calling card?"

Now sober, we got in the Beemer and headed back to Binz. As the headlights pierced the mist of the fog-shrouded highway, the rhythmic moans of a foghorn warned sailors away from the coast. In the morning I would enter today's new knowledge into the laptop. Chuck and his Asian crew, Chunky Monkey in a chauffeur's cap, the Zeesboot, Anatoly Salenko, an account of the Albatross— all added to my database of island people and places, a collection that seemed as random as the sea shells, postcards, amber beads and pieces of flint a tourist would carry away as summer memories.

Instead of pretty pieces of driftwood, we were collecting unexploded land mine and trip wires. What I wanted more than anything was to find the CD-ROM and fly back to Chicago.

Six

In those first days on the island, T.K. and I adopted a routine. We continued Zara's plan with public arguments and me paying for everything. We kicked up our heels at the tea dances and listened to the *Kurkonzert* at the bandstand or visited one of the churches for organ recitals. I kept track of everything on the laptop, with the boundaries between work and play always blurred.

Charles Goodborn did not appear in our hotel lobby with hat in hand to beg us to finance a sophisticated data warehouse. Longing for home, I chafed at the passing of days with no contact. T.K. preached patience, but I never had enough to acquire any.

In the evenings, we dined according to our mood, and strolled the long promenade like refugees from a prior century. The twilight lingered as the solstice approached. After we returned to our hotel, T.K. would hassle the kitchen for precious ice, which we carried up to the room. From our stash of Polish vodka, T.K. poured happy-hour-sized drinks and pushed aside the area rugs, while I opened the door to the tiny balcony to let in the sea breeze. We would pop a tape into the boom box and dance, twisting, frugging and two-stepping on the slick gray linoleum clad only in T.K.'s pajamas—I wore the top, he the bottoms.

We had arrived at a spot between serious lovers and friends having a fling, but I worried about succumbing to an emotion-laden disaster that would get bogged down in heavy feelings and worst of all, the perception of a future.

~ * ~

Saturday mid-morning, T.K. tossed down his newspaper, stretched and announced, "Perfect beach weather! Even a workaholic old coot like Edgar wouldn't hold a little 'R. and R.' against us today."

R & R—our permanent lifestyle.

We drove to a smokehouse between Binz and Sellin to pick up some fish and stopped at a grocery for the rest of our lunch supplies. From the beach parking lot we schlepped all our baskets, bags, towels and the beach umbrella along the path through the dunes where the *Rosa rugosa* bushes sprawled.

We hiked away from the sunbathers and volleyball players to a spot where the strand curved inland and the wind felt docile. After setting up, we undressed and rubbed sunscreen on each other. I liked to smooth the lotion on T.K.'s broad tan back. He still sported a baseball cap from The Bass Pro Shop, and I always wore a wide-brimmed straw hat with a red ribbon. I had initiated picnics on the nude beaches and having sex in weird places to keep T.K. interested and even a little off-balance. And no one would ever imagine a couple frequenting the nude beaches were really on a secret mission.

When I peeled off my T-shirt and shorts in the warm sunshine, I also shed my doubts, and the fear that hopped around inside me like a handful of Mexican jumping beans.

After lunch, we waded into the cold surf. T.K. called the temperature "zestful," but sixty-two degrees felt butt chilling to me, so we didn't linger.

Back on the strand, like any married couple, we talked about our kids. I told T.K. about Chloe and my worries about having been an absentee mother. He told me about his thirteen-year-old son who lived with his ex-wife. The conversation always returned to "the operation." T.K. wondered if Anatoly Salenko really was the captain of a Soviet naval vessel. "Ten to one he's a clever KGB *apparatchik* keeping an eye on this part of the world."

With his weary face and mournful glances, Anatoly seemed genuine to me.

Once I thought I spied Putnam's head wearing an old cotton bush hat popping over a dune, but T.K. scolded that I had Putnam on the brain.

"If I thought he was snooping on us, I'd leave tonight," I said, blustering with indignation.

"Billy Boy is too much the uptight Brit to roam around on the FKK Beach. Better worry about that damned dog we rescued."

I stretched out on the towel to get a full dorsal exposure to the sun. T.K. flopped down next to me. We watched the small whitecaps ruffle the surface of the water.

He continued. "Old Fido could have queered everything. So it stays our little secret."

He drew a "peace" sign in the sand with his finger.

"I think you should tell him." I put my hand on his arm. "Otherwise, it will be ten times worse if he finds out."

"And I think you should butt out." T.K.'s brow wrinkled into the frown that always heralded a foul mood. He sat up and rummaged in the heap of clothing for his cigarettes.

"Why are you afraid of Putnam?" I asked. When I first understood T.K. also feared Putnam, that knowledge alarmed me even more than the idea of Bruss's killer. T.K. lit his cigarette and took a long drag without answering.

"I've known him a long time." He exhaled and was silent, apparently lost in thought. "He's all right as long as he doesn't get a bee up his ass about something."

"And if he does?"

"He's the Marquis de Sade on steroids. And meth. And very bad acid."

"Great," I said, while the Mexican jumping beans hopped along my nerves again. "And if the dog morphs into a bee?"

He stared across the water. I couldn't read his face.

"Forget about the dog," he said. "You keep pushing Zara's plan and I'll handle Putnam."

~ * ~

When we returned from the beach, there was a folded note from Frau Schuld in our hotel mailbox. Herr Goodborn and Frau Motte would be pleased to meet us for drinks at a *Kneipe* in Sassnitz about eight o'clock. I already knew *Kneipe* meant bar.

Frau Schuld and her husband would be on hand to make introductions. Once we were in Sassnitz, ask for directions to *Der Albatros*.

T.K. grabbed me and we waltzed around the room.

"I have to hand it to you, Zara. Your plan has been a crazy success."

"And you were right. Patience pays off."

~ * ~

We were prepped for the smoke and noise of a seaman's Saturday night at the Albatross, but to use one of Putnam's Briticisms, the welcoming party gobsmacked us.

T.K. whispered, "Don't show any reaction. We'll play their game, whatever it is."

Next to me, T.K., cigarette in hand, took my elbow as we approached the group at the pushed-together tables in the room with the green tile stove.

Five people, forever frozen in my mind's eye.

I recognized Chuck from the boat. The striking brunette in a sleeveless red V-neck with the soft look of cashmere had to be Romy. Taut and lean.

Next to her sat my new friend Frau Sabine Schuld, with a shy smile. Chunky Monkey and Giles Goatboy sat around the table, too. What were *they* doing here?

I waved at Sabine, with a smile displaying every tooth back to my molars. "Here we are."

They all stood. Sabine, with pauses and hesitations, introduced everyone. Mr. Goodborn, Frau Motte, Herr Schuld and Herr Mueller. Good grief! Chunky Monkey was Herr Schuld, Sabine's "Mann." He was a head shorter than his wife and looked even more simian up close. As he shook my hand, the man with goat eyes, Herr Mueller, smiled with what I imagined was malevolent geniality. I still didn't get his relationship to the others.

An awkward silence ensued, with everyone standing around the table. Charles Goodborn spoke first.

"T.K., Zara, I've had enough of this Herr and Frau horse shit to last a lifetime. My name is Chuck. This is Romy."

The Gorgeous One's pink lips didn't curve in as much as a hint of a smile.

Chuck continued, "The lady next to Romy is Sabine. Her old man is Bodo." Chuck paused and his eyes darted around the table to gauge the effect he was having. T.K. and I smiled politely, while the others looked pained, except for Romy whose expression was still a bland mask. Chuck gestured toward Herr Mueller, and said, "My landlord, Wulf. Wulf Mueller." Giving it an unpleasant emphasis, he pronounced it 'Wolf.' Scratch the Satyr, enter the Wolf. Mueller's predatory eyes were a strange pale brown, which almost matched his dull yellow curls. I didn't like him at all.

Chuck pointed to the empty chairs next to him and we sat down. Another awkward pause. Oh God, we faced an impossible, stilted evening. My eyes roamed over the nautical décor: the sextant, and the seines, life jackets, trophies and ship's bells that adorned the wall. The silence seemed to hold a general malaise. If Chuck had wanted a social occasion with his compatriots, he appeared to have changed his mind. Unlike at the spa, no garrulous stream of words spewed from Sabine's mouth. I didn't like the way T.K. appraised Romy. Chuck didn't either.

Edgar hadn't done her justice. She sat erect with one long tan hand lightly clasping a wine glass while the other hand pushed at her careless mop of dark hair that trailed in tendrilled wisps down in front of her ears and along her neck. She glanced at Chuck, revealing her perfect profile. I noticed that her watchful dark eyes were deeply shadowed in a flattering charcoal shade.

In my chattiest voice, I inquired, "Do we speak English or *Deutsch sprechen*?"

Chuck said, "I thought the whole purpose of this..."he never found the word, "was to network with some Americans."

"Well, then, English it is." I looked to T.K. for help. He gave me a dim smile.

At last Sabine found her voice, and picked her way gingerly through the English. "You must excuse us, Frau Wentz, but we are not feeling like a celebration. Herr Mueller has this week lost his dog."

"Oh, how awful," I said. "I'm terribly sorry."

T.K. turned to Wulf Mueller. "We say a dog is 'man's best friend.'"

Mueller said, "He was a working dog, well-trained and loyal." He pronounced the double-u like a vee.

"Big, black, ugly bastard," said Chuck. "Got loose one day and chased the freakin' sheep next door all over the pasture."

The memory produced a sad smile on Herr Mueller's face.

Our waitress stopped by and T.K. insisted on buying a round. "Wun trink and ve go," announced Mueller.

Chuck smiled for the first time, and his face transformed from petulance to that of an agreeable man.

"We actually found this bar last night," I said. "We met a nice British gentleman and a Russian naval officer."

T.K. nodded toward me. "And Zara said, 'hello, sailor!'"

"The captain was devilishly handsome," I said, mostly to Sabine.

"And speak of the devil!" T.K. looked toward the bar, where Putnam and Anatoly were grabbing the last two stools. They hadn't noticed us.

T.K. gave the group our standard spiel of why we were on the island. Chuck shifted in his chair and looked around the room— bored again. I had a sense that he always had to be the center of attention.

Bodo Schuld wordlessly drank his beer. Squat and muscular, he looked like my idea of an enforcer. Sabine had said her husband had lost a "government job." I would have liked to know what that job was.

Last night Putnam had confided, "The Russkie captain knows who the resident Stasi were. And he told me that Goodborn is already cozying up to them. He and his pretty German bird were in here drinking with them last week."

Romy acted conversationally challenged. "Hello" and not another word. Maybe she was afraid any animation would crack her poreless skin. I wondered if she, not Chuck, was the druggie.

I overheard Chuck complain to T.K. that he couldn't buy nautical charts of the local waters. T.K. said charts had been unobtainable for years, mostly to prevent East Germans from finding their way across the Baltic by boat.

"Now here's a fellow who might be able to help you out," said T.K. I turned my head to see Putnam and Anatoly approaching our table.

How could we explain knowing these two?

Taking stock of the drinkers, Putnam's blue eyes darted from face to face.

"T.K. Wentz, Ha! Ha! Ha! Haven't seen you in a dog's age—or was it only last night!"

He threw his arm around Anatoly's shoulders. "*Pojarskiya Koteleti*!" he bellowed.

"Feesh and cheeps!" shouted the Russian, saluting Bill and then the rest of us with a sweep of his beer glass. They roared with laughter.

T.K. jumped up and introduced the "Glasnost Gang" to our new friends at the table. I couldn't tell if Putnam and the Russian were drunk or only pretending to be. The Germans exchanged glances. T.K. didn't see the warning I tried to send with my eyes.

He squeezed "Tolya" in next to Chuck for a discussion of how to get those precious nautical charts. Anatoly answered T.K. in monosyllables and gazed at me across the table. I mouthed "hello, sailor," but he didn't smile.

Putnam plopped himself down beside Herr Mueller, gave Romy an impudent leer, and announced, "Dog is God spelled backwards."

Mueller and Schuld didn't smile. Next, Putnam extracted a package of English Oval's from his pocket and offered them around the table. Wulf Mueller accepted one, and Bodo Schuld eagerly followed his lead.

Sabine gave Putnam a big toothy smile and said, "God save the queen." She pronounced it 'Gott.' Bill raised his glass and drained it. Bodo muttered a few words under his breath and she blushed. Now another stilted silence descended upon our half of the table, while at the other end, T.K. continued to translate for Anatoly and Chuck.

"Mr. Goodborn has been fortunate to acquire one of the few remaining Zeesboots." I directed my words at Putnam.

"That anything like a dogbody?"

Wulf Mueller's pale eyes narrowed. He understood English.

I gaped at Putnam, who had now mentioned the word "dog" three times.

"Two masted fishing vessel." Putnam paused and thought a moment, then explained, "A bit like a Dutch dogger."

"The Zeesboot is a ketch!" I wanted to gag him.

T.K. and his mates, oblivious to the hole Putnam was digging us into, nattered on in a stream of nautical talk—harbors, tides, shallow waters, Denmark, Sweden, blah-blah.

Nodding toward Wulf, I said, "Bill, you're unwittingly very cruel. Herr Mueller has had the misfortune of losing his dog."

"Oh I say, I hope I'm not in the dog house." His face looked ruddier than usual, and his smile was cherubic.

What was the matter with him? When I became a mother, I reduced my output of profanity but now I turned and hissed, "Will you shut the fuck up?"

"Mrs. Wentz, I don't like women to use that language," he said with an icy stare that brought back T.K.'s warning. *The Marquis de Sade on steroids.*

"Oh, so sorry," I said. I faced Herr Mueller and tried to compose a grammatical German sentence. "Mr. Putnam doesn't mean to be unkind. He didn't know that your dog has disappeared."

Chuck spoke in a loud voice from the head of the table. "Wolf, that ugly Rottweiler of yours was too freakin' mean to die."

Anatoly looked at me and asked in English, "Someone die?"

Mueller answered Anatoly in heavily accented English. "My dog. He is disappeared. There was much blood." He spoke in German again.

"This is what will come with the unification. Anarchy! Drugs! Disrespect!" He pounded his fist on the table. His voice, at first impassive, had become hoarse with emotion. "The capitalist parasites, the western...vermin have arrived!"

T.K. and Anatoly came to attention and Romy's eyes widened. Chuck sat straight and smiled. At other tables, conversations stopped. Mueller stood up so abruptly his chair fell over. Bodo rose, too. Sabine glanced from Bodo to Wulf and seemed unsure whether to sit or stand. Mueller continued his rant.

"It has begun. Foreigners. Pah!"

He stalked away from the table. Bodo grabbed Sabine by the arm, and they followed him out the door while the rest of us stared. A few drinkers made derisive comments, a couple applauded and the noise level returned.

Bill turned to T.K. and said in a cool voice, "Was he ever barking mad! Sorry, Wentz. I should have let sleeping dogs lie."

Chuck said, "Guy's an asshole. Trouble is, he's my landlord."

Romy spoke for the first time. "I 've always been afraid of that dog." Chuck put his arm around her and kissed her temple. She pushed a dark tendril of hair back behind her ear.

Anatoly insisted on ordering a round. We all downed the vodka, which had a mellowing, anesthetic effect.

Chuck returned from the toilet and he was "on," all smiles and white teeth, tipping his chair back and making fun of Bodo, whom he called "Cro-Magnon man," and referring to Frau Schuld as "the Sabine woman nobody bothered to rape."

I didn't understand why Putnam had deliberately provoked Mueller's outburst.

After another round, Putnam yawned and professed he felt "dog tired," and he and Anatoly stood up. I wondered if they were going on the prowl to find ladies of the evening. Sassnitz being a port, there would surely be some. Anatoly, who had stared at me all evening, gave my hand a soulful good-bye kiss.

After they were gone, Romy loosened up and actually smiled. When T.K. politely inquired what brought Chuck to this corner of Europe, he gave us a song and dance about dropping out of the high tech rat race. He wanted to sail his boat and travel around Europe.

"And then?" T.K. asked.

"And then I'll start making money again. Software." Chuck used his big smile to temper his words. "Eastern Europe offers a lot of opportunity. And they have some pretty sophisticated software developers."

Now T.K. looked bored, and I changed the subject. When our little group broke up we arranged to meet again on Monday evening here at the Albatross. Chuck mentioned forming a sailing party to the island of Hiddensee.

After this evening, I didn't think the business of laying our hands on the CD-ROM was going to be so easy. Too many ominous crosscurrents might produce a riptide that would sweep T.K. and me away from our goal. Or worse.

At two a.m., back in Binz with only a few noisy drunks and prowling youths still on the streets. T.K. and I walked arm in arm along the Strand Promenade. A cool breeze blew in off the Baltic, causing me to zip my windbreaker and pull my sweater sleeves down over my hands.

After I vented about Bill's outrageous references to dogs, T.K. reminded me that Bill's part of the plan was to draw suspicion onto himself and away from us.

"If they think Billy Boy is up to no good, they're less likely to suspect thee and me."

"But why did he have to be so blatant? Mueller was really exercised."

"Yeah. Pissed enough to leave after his 'I hate foreigners' tirade. I'll bet Wulf and Bodo are old Stasi goons who would step up and answer 'Yo' to a roll call of former agents." T.K. paused a beat and stared out at the water. "Bodo Schuld and Wulf Mueller. If our Chuck Roast doesn't like those two krauts, then why was he out drinking with them?"

We turned off the Promenade and headed into the dark, quiet town. The breeze rustled the leaves, and the moon played tag with the clouds.

"They give me the creeps." I turned to T.K. "Wulf Mueller is the friend in high places. What reason would Wulf have to make nicey-nice to Chuck and let him rent his house? Especially if Chuck doesn't even like him?"

"Yeah, what does Chuck Roast bring to the party? Besides Romy?"

"A CD with a sophisticated data mining system." I stopped still in the middle of the sidewalk. "Wait a minute!"

T.K. cupped his hand to light a cigarette.

Still thinking aloud, I said, "When we had dinner with Edgar back in Berlin, you talked about the spies and informers and something that the old government did."

I started up the street again.

T.K. fell in step beside me. "The Stasi spied on everyone, and they kept their dirty little secrets in big fat files.

"14 April, 1987." He assumed an officious voice with a German accent. "Bodo S. visited a prostitute at 10:00 p.m. Subject stayed one hour, exited smiling. Told a friend, Wulf M. that it was 'almost like real love.'" T.K. chuckled at his own joke and continued without the accent. "Informers provided so much information their files ran to multi-volumes."

I stopped again. "What kind of files?"

"Micro-fiche, paper, whatever."

"Computerized files?"

"I don't think so. They kept informants' code names in a computer, but not the actual records." He tossed away the half-smoked cigarette.

"What happened to all those files?"

A drunk, staggering and singing crossed the street.

"Most of them were recovered and hauled off to Berlin. Some were shredded or destroyed by the perpetrators. Why?"

"Were any of them stolen?"

"Likely. Stolen or copied. Some of the HVA files disappeared. They were the equivalent of our CIA. External information gathering. Markus Wolf's organization. He didn't trust computers. Rumor has it he had copies in Berlin, Moscow and somewhere in East Europe. It takes an old spymaster to be truly paranoid."

T.K. smiled at some memory and continued. "The Stasi were more like our FBI. Their shtick was internal spying."

He looked at me, still smiling, but with puzzled eyes. "Sweetie, what gives? I can almost hear gears grinding in that clever little head of yours."

We turned back onto the Promenade and headed toward the hotel.

"That night in Berlin you mentioned 'miles and miles of microfiche.' Would that have any value today?" I was talking to myself more than to T.K. "Nobody cares anymore if Herr X planned to fly the coop or if Professor Y harbored non-socialist thoughts."

"You're right. The political stuff is passé. But, Zara, someone might care about who was climbing into bed with whom, and who hasn't come out of the closet yet and who likes to wear his wife's undies."

"Personal information. The kind of gossip that ages well?"

"You got it."

I wondered if we were on to something.

Seven

Sunday morning we motored across the island to Stralsund. In the Market Square, I called my sister, waking her up.

"I was ready to send out a search party."

"You wouldn't believe the Dark Ages telephone system here."

Jody said Chloe was fine and admonished me again to come home.

"Soon." My fondest hope.

I wanted to call my buddy Mark in accounting, but it was too early to wake up anyone but family. I had another task for the P.I. we had retained.

T.K. and I left Stralsund and drove through the green countryside. Red poppies bloomed everywhere, sometimes together in a gigantic bouquet with white and purple wild flowers, and sometimes in a wide red swath bordering a field.

In the artist's colony of Ahrenshoop, we dined on seafood, and bought a print of a thatched-roof cottage overlooking the sea. After lunch we drove to Prerow and worked on our all-over tans at another FKK beach.

T.K. seemed reflective, even a little vulnerable, and as we lay side by side looking out over the water, I broached one of our many taboo topics.

"So, how did you get started in, um, your profession?"

"I lucked into it," he said. "You'd laugh if I told you."

"Try me."

He traced little squiggles in the sand as he spoke.

"I left Southeast Asia in '74, after a stint in Nam, and then Thailand. After that I bummed around Europe for a year. Visiting friends, living on the cheap. Met a guy in Paris. In a bar. He found out where I'd been, and what I'd been up to, and said he had a friend.

He smiled at the memory. "The friend was an American. Middle-aged, nondescript, nobody you'd remember. I never did find out who he worked for. He said I was just the man they needed. He handed me $25,000, and an old briefcase full of photos of aircraft and tanks—Russian stuff—and said to go find out 'how many planes and tanks the Syrians have that match those photos.'"

"So did you?"

"Not right away. I called up a girlfriend in Hamburg, and told her I needed help spending some money. She flew in, and we moved into the George V and did some serious partying. Eating. Drinking. She went shopping. A drunken evening at the Crazy Horse Saloon."

"My God, did you spend all the money?"

He grinned and smoothed over the squiggles in the sand.

"Barely dented it. But I did some thinking and decided if the Syrians ever looked into that briefcase I would be dog meat."

"So what did you do?"

"I gave the briefcase to the young lady, and she carried it to Hamburg and stashed it in the back of her wardrobe. I got on a plane for Damascus."

"And?"

He smiled again. "Got a cab at the airport. Told the driver to take me to the desert. He drove out to the edge of town and said, 'This is the desert.' No goddamn planes or tanks anywhere.

"I spent two weeks in the hotel bar. Establishing my legend, as a burnt out veteran drinking himself to death. Thousands of those back then. Saigon had just fallen. I ran into a girl from Iowa, a belly-dancing student and we lived it up a bit."

"Well, did you ever, like, spy?"

"On weekends, I'd rent a car and she and I would take a drive out of town. Once we drove all the way across the desert. Mostly we stuck close to ruins and tourist sights, way the hell away from the Golan Heights."

He squinted at the water.

"The military presence was hard to miss. I scouted with my friend at a safe distance, with a tourist guidebook and a fifth of Scotch."

He paused and lit a cigarette. "I kept count of the Russian planes and tanks I saw. But mostly I sat in the bar with the would-be belly dancer. Over a bottle, I could pick up more news in one day than on all my scouting expeditions."

"Did she ever dance for you?"

He smiled and exhaled a cloud of smoke.

"What about your embezzled employer?"

"A couple weeks later, I hopped a plane to Hamburg, picked up the briefcase, and scurried back to Paris."

"So what did you tell them?"

"I was nervous as hell, but I dished out a spoonful of facts, a big bowl of rumors, and a whole platter of lies and half-truths."

This adventure sounded totally typical of T.K.'s antics.

He turned to me and traced his finger along my arm. "I haven't thought about this for years. The man was convinced I'd given him first-rate information, and thanked me for my efforts. Said if I ever needed a reference...and I still had twelve thousand dollars."

"Did you call up more women and carouse the rest away?"

"I studied economics and political science in London. Crossed paths with Billy Boy for the first time."

"Tell me about Putnam."

T.K. frowned. "Very smart. A true soldier of fortune. Did some boxing in his younger days. Billy Boy has a bit of a literary bent. And he likes rough sex."

A real Renaissance man.

"Can we trust him?" I looked T.K. square in the eye.

He didn't answer for the longest time.

"I sure as hell hope so."

~ * ~

'Red sky at night, sailor's delight.' Awash in hues from palest pink to a deep crimson, the sunset looked like a beating heart exploding, smearing bloody streaks and purple blobs and great clumps of red across the sky behind Stralsund.

A large black freighter with a Polish flag sat at anchor in the harbor, and tinkling music drifting from the open door of a nearby tavern had tempted us to stop in for a few beers.

Afterward, at my insistence, we walked along the waterfront near the huge grain elevators that stood side by side in red brick solidarity, each with a ship in full sail emblazoned on the facade facing the harbor.

Closed for only a year, the elevators already had a derelict appearance, with broken windows, paint-chipped doors and weeds sprouting out of the gutters. No more golden wheat would shoot down the conveyer into the holds of ships bound for foreign ports.

We crossed a railroad track and a wide empty parking lot to get close to the brick behemoths.

"Why here?" I asked. "Why kill somebody here?"

No Trespassing and Entry Forbidden signs were posted around all the doors.

"I don't know. Deserted. Isolated yet easy to find."

"Who would Bruss have been meeting? Or do you think it a random attack?"

T.K. ran his hand through his hair. "Dunno."

We were getting close to the biggest building. Dark and solid, it loomed like a fortress. No light shone from the scattered windows, and now that the dusk had deepened, I noticed streetlights were an absent amenity.

I stared up at the few dark windows scattered across the acres of brick. "Do you think maybe Chuck?" My voice dropped to a whisper.

T.K. thought for a moment. "The doors are bolted. The ground floor windows have bars. How would Chuck manage to get inside? If he's our man, then he had insider help."

We were standing in front of one of the heavy wooden doors. I climbed up on a concrete pad and peeked in the tiny window. Pitch black.

"Do you have your pocket flashlight?"

"Never mind. Let's hustle back to the car before we run into a watchman."

"My sandal rubbed a blister on my heel. Swing by and pick me up over there." I pointed to the second brick building next door.

"You sure?"

I nodded.

He shrugged and took off toward the parking area. I walked along the street until I came to the second building. No crime scene tape. I wondered why not. Maybe the murder had happened somewhere else. Maybe the fax had been wrong. The arched wooden doors were bolted shut. From another small window, I peered into inky darkness. I walked a few more steps and found yet another door. No bolts across this one. A tentative pressure from my fingers and the door creaked open a few inches. I jumped and backed away.

The car pulled up and I turned around. "That was quick. There's an unlocked—."

The car wasn't the Beemer, and the driver wore a black ski mask.

Two other masked men jumped out and rushed me. I screamed and started to run, but one of them grabbed me, pinning my arms to my sides and pulling me toward the half-ajar door. When I screamed again, one of them clamped a gloved hand across my mouth. The second man forced my head back and put his face so close to mine that I got the full force of his bad breath and stale body odor.

He snarled an incomprehensible phrase. The one word I understood was *gefährlich*. Dangerous. Then he leaned his face even closer to mine, until I saw only his dark pupils through the narrow slits of the mask. In accented English, he rasped, "Dangerous to spy, Frau." When he tried to drag me toward the open door, I bit his gloved hand and kicked at him.

The piercing blare of a car horn made them freeze. Then I was shoved roughly and sprawled backwards, falling shoulder first into something hard. My ankle twisted under me. My attackers jumped into their car and took off, tires squealing, turned the corner by the elevator and were gone.

Caught in the headlights from another car. Racing toward me. Screeching to a stop.

I got on my hands and knees and lurched to my feet on legs that didn't want to stay upright. My shoulder felt like it was undergoing acupuncture with red-hot skewers. With numb relief I watched T.K. come running. In the headlights glare, he looked as scared as I felt.

"Are you all right?"

He put his arm around me and I wailed from the pain in my shoulder. He dropped his arm, said, "Oh, shit, I'm sorry," and steered me around to the passenger's side. He opened the door and half-lifted me in.

As soon as the car began to move, I started sobbing. T.K. drove into the downtown and parked in the middle of the square across from the old *Rathaus* right under a street lamp. He kept repeating, "Sweetie, it's going to be all right," but I couldn't stop. He turned on the overhead light and looked at my shoulder, barely touching it with his fingertips. My T-shirt looked like a rag, ripped and filthy.

"Can you move your arm?"

I nodded and stuck out my elbow. The sharp pain of the motion caused me to wince. T.K. handed me his handkerchief, and I blew my nose, and sat for a moment gathering my wits.

"I'm okay now."

"I'd better take you to the emergency room."

"No way."

"We could concoct a story. You wouldn't have to—."

"Absolutely not."

"What, then?" He looked so stricken I felt like the dumb shit I had been. Hanging around that place alone in the dark.

I hiccupped, then I started to laugh, with a few last straggling sobs interspersed with more hiccups.

"What?"

"You could leave me on the front step at the Kleintierpraxis with a big wad of West Marks."

His mouth opened a little, like he was going to protest, but instead he took the handkerchief, and dabbed at my eyes.

"Sweet Pea," he said, "you break the mold."

~ * ~

With my shoulder still throbbing, I fell into a half-slumber while we were crossing the Rügendamm, that long bridge connecting the mainland to the island, and didn't fully wake up until we were almost back to Binz. T.K., holding his cigarette next to the cracked window, drove with his right hand. He stared straight ahead except when he gave me a quick glance.

"This...what we're doing isn't all wild nights at the Crazy Horse Saloon and sitting in bars with belly dancers, is it?" I asked.

"No, that tale had a happy outcome."

"Are you going to tell Putnam what happened?"

"Have to."

"Will he be angry we were poking around the grain elevators?"

"At first. Then I think he'll be...interested." T.K. rubbed his chin "Maybe he can persuade the esteemed Captain Salenko to have the ship's doctor take a look at your shoulder."

"I'll be all right. Don't you like Anatoly?"

"Not nearly as much as Anatoly likes you."

"I can't help it."

"I know. Can you tell me what happened back there?"

The whole encounter had been so scary I only remembered black masks, the hand over my mouth, how scared I was and my futile struggle.

T.K. didn't think we were followed during our meandering day, and he didn't have any ideas about who those goons might have been.

More to the point, did they know who *we* were? Had our cover been blown, or had we blundered by at the wrong time? More questions to add to the long list in my log. 'Spying is dangerous, Frau'. Was this only a warning to butt out? To me, the eyes and voices had conveyed real menace.

Whenever I recalled my assailants, the fear rushed over me in waves. Up the inside of my arms and down into my legs, then coiling into a queasy knot in my belly. The old grain elevators must be more than a meeting place, or a spot to dump a body. Something even more sinister.

~ * ~

Everybody was on my case.

On Monday morning, Frau Schuld's scowl, when she noticed my purple and blue shoulder, indicated she didn't believe I had fallen twice in one week.

"I'm kind of a klutz," I admitted as she slathered me with mud. The mud wasn't the gritty kind, but warm and smooth like melted chocolate, only odorless.

She let out an exasperated gasp and dipped her wooden trowel back into the churn.

"It's really not what you think," I told her.

"No matter what I think," she muttered, and gave a loud indignant sniff.

"My husband would never hurt me," I said, looking up at the ceiling.

She heaped on more mud and plastered the front of each leg. Then she placed a big sheet of plastic over me from neck to toes, and commanded, "Turn." As an afterthought, she added, "*bitte*." Please.

It took a while because I had to avoid putting any weight on my shoulder as I awkwardly flipped over onto my stomach. She watched me with a pained frown.

Uncharacteristically, she didn't seem to want to talk today, but that didn't mean I had to clam up as well.

"We enjoyed meeting Mr. Goodborn and Frau Motte," I said. She didn't respond, but smacked a big glob of mud across my back.

"I'm sorry that Mr. Putnam was so rude to your friend. I think he was drunk—of course drunkenness is no excuse. It's so novel for us to meet a Russian. T.K. was pleased to be able to translate for the captain and Mr. Goodborn. It's good when he can feel useful."

She said, "Ja."

"We're meeting them again tonight. Monday nights can be so dreary."

"Ja. Us, also. Frau Motte invite."

"Oh, good!" I enthused. "Will Herr Mueller come, too?"

"I do not know." She slapped another big trowel full of goo onto my butt and then smeared it down the back of each leg. Another sheet of plastic went over the mud, and now I was turned again—she helped this time, and then left me encased in the purifying brown mud, with only the ticking of the timer for company. My chocolate-like coating felt silky, and I could have relaxed completely if I wasn't wondering why we couldn't meet our new American friends without these German chaperones.

~ * ~

Over lunch in Sassnitz at the Köpi Eck, Putnam gave me his standard dressing down.

"The *Schweinerei* in Stralsund was the result of more bloody stupidity than I imagined even you, Mrs. Wentz, were capable of."

I didn't argue, because in his perfect hindsight view, it had been risky to go poking around the grain elevators.

His blue eyes narrowed. "However, my American beaters flushed some interesting quail out of the bushes."

He turned back to his meal. "Tolya and the ship's doctor will meet us in an hour on the beach below the chalk cliffs."

I turned to T.K. to protest, but he continued cutting his potato. "Sweetie, you're much too crucial a player to go on the disabled list."

"What kind of a cock and bull story did you tell Anatoly?" I asked, glowering at Putnam.

"Rather more or less the truth. Tolya thinks he might even know who attacked you. And why."

Putnam obviously enjoyed watching me sit there with my mouth agape, with my forkful of fish poised between plate and lips.

An hour later, T.K., Putnam and I walked along the narrow beach toward the base of the cliffs. A hundred feet away I recognized Anatoly strolling toward us. A muscular bald man with a fringe of salt and pepper hair walked beside him, carrying a little black bag.

"I don't like this one bit," I said.

"For Christ sake, he's a doctor and your shoulder looks like hell!" T.K. took my arm like he thought I would bolt.

"I'm not getting undressed."

"Zara, Anatoly is doing us a big favor so let the doctor look at your shoulder and I'll give you a dime and a root beer sucker if you don't cry."

If Putnam hadn't been present, I would have given a succinct but crude retort.

Putnam and Anatoly made a big pretense of recognizing each other from a distance. First waves, then smiles, and as our two groups met, hand shaking and introductions. Anatoly's shorts revealed the sturdy legs of a soccer player. He wore thick leather sandals and a T-shirt from the Moscow Olympics. The doctor, who was very tan, wore baggy cotton slacks and a sport shirt. He didn't speak, but his affable smile signaled that he took the situation in stride, as if he examined foreign women on the beach every day. We walked away from the water and stood on the sand at the base of the cliffs. A few people were scattered along the long strand, but none of them within earshot.

Anatoly's deep eyes looked sadder than ever. When I unbuttoned my blouse and began to slip my arm out of the sleeve, T.K. said, "a gentleman would take a hike," and Anatoly and Bill left the group and walked further up the beach.

The doctor touched my shoulder, upper arm, and neck. On command, I raised my arm and moved it this way and that while the doctor prodded my shoulder until I gasped with pain.

T.K. translated the diagnosis, which was "Only a bad bruise." I slipped my arm back into my blouse. "No pushups for a few days," he continued. "And no sexual athletics."

"He didn't say that! You are so full of—."

I smiled at the doctor and thanked him. He bowed. Bill and Anatoly re-joined the party. Bill stared up at the sheer wall of chalk and declaimed:

> *"...these steep and lofty cliffs,*
> *That on a wild secluded scene impress*
> *Thoughts of more deep seclusion; and connect*
> *The landscape with the quiet of the sky."*

T.K. said, "Now Billy Boy is going all weird on us."

Putnam darted a smile at me. "Wordsworth, Mrs. Wentz."

The doctor, clutching his black bag, headed up the beach. Anatoly stayed with our group. Together we walked along the base where the cliffs were the steepest. Way up on top, we could see the tourists on the observation point. A trio in front of us started the climb up a steep path to the top. Anatoly offered a flask of vodka around and everybody tossed back a slug.

Bill asked him to repeat that "interesting story you told me this morning."

I understood most of Anatoly's German, and later T.K. filled in the rest.

"Perhaps ten or twelve weeks ago, a political officer assigned to ship, was called back to Moscow. Very sudden, but we did not mourn departure. He was arrogant bastard. Crew hated him. After he left I determined to maintain...relaxed discipline and finish time here enjoying life. When we return to home port, I don't get brass band with welcoming delegation." His lips compressed. "No money for wages. Probably not enough for government to feed us."

He picked up a stone, turned it over with his fingers, and skipped it across the water.

"No money. No future. Cabbage soup, not cutlets." He skipped another stone in the sea. "My men have not sold uniforms. We remain good Soviet sailors, not flea market entrepreneurs."

I thought he was disgusted by the selling frenzy in Berlin by the Brandenburg Gate where the Soviet army did a thriving business peddling hats, belts, medals, even entire dress uniforms from tables set up in the open air.

"Of course I have been ordered to dispose of much equipment: trucks, small boats, naval supplies. Everything at a good price. For West marks or dollars. I give you list."

When we didn't respond, Anatoly shrugged and continued.

"A few weeks after officer left, one of crew swore to me that he had seen him walking on docks in Stralsund. Then we hear many rumors. I neither believed nor disbelieved until Bill told me what happened last night. If thugs threatened you in Stralsund, then rumors real."

"And the rumors were?" asked T.K.

Anatoly stared across the deep green water, a jade color hinting of restlessness under the calm surface.

"When Berlin Wall came down, the HVA, that's East German Secret Service, were desperate to get documents away from West. Too many to shred or burn quickly. Faster to load trucks. Department XXII was entrusted with task. Papers sent to Moscow for safekeeping. Copies of records already in Moscow." He paused. "But in these times where can anything be truly safe?"

No one had an answer.

"A freighter was coming from Riga for purpose of collecting files. But I am told—and this is still rumor— freighter never arrived. So records may be stored in old storage buildings by wharves, waiting for transport, guarded by Department XXII. You were lucky they did not kill you."

Before I could ask if they might have killed Bruss, T.K. glanced at me and shook his head. His bantering smile and careless posture disappeared during Anatoly's story. With his hands clasped behind him, he bent forward a little as he walked. Frowning, he didn't have the air of a paid-for husband squiring an insecure woman about. He looked grim.

Over here it was impossible to know what was permissible. Anatoly and Putnam seemed to be confidantes, but I hoped Putnam hadn't told the Russian why T.K. and I were on the island. On the other hand, why would we visit the ship's doctor when we could have walked into any clinic? Placing so much trust in Anatoly seemed crazy to me. He might be tempted to sell a few of our secrets along with his trucks and supplies.

All the Cold War rules lay in the rubble heap with the crumbled Berlin Wall and the failed socialist dream. New opportunities, along with unknown risks and dangers poured through the open borders. New rules would inevitably follow, but this summer, there were none.

Anatoly said he had to return to his ship. We drove Putnam back to his boarding house in Sassnitz. He promised to stay away from our little group this evening, "in order that Mr. and Mrs. Wentz can do a spot of bonding with their fellow Americans."

As he left us, he paused and asked, "Interesting turn of events, wouldn't you say, Drummond?"

T.K., who hadn't said a word since we left Anatoly, scowled and didn't answer.

T.K. said nothing on the way back to Binz. I had begun to pick up some bad vibes. He parked behind the hotel.

"I want a drink." He set a hurried pace along the Strand Promenade to the main drag. Down the street, I heard the barrel organ playing the "Beautiful Blue Danube". We turned into our favorite café with the red and white awnings. I ordered a lemonade and T.K. asked for brandy.

"I don't know how our livers can survive all this booze," I said, making conversation.

His face wore a grim frown.

"I didn't realize you were so sensitive to remarks about drinking." What was eating him? I wanted to talk about Anatoly's story and what it meant.

Still frowning, he said, "I am sensitive to the fact that you have no business in anything that remotely involves Department XXII, the HVA and the KGB. They are players in a deadly game where amateurs always lose."

"You spy people have more acronyms than us geeks." I tried to make light of what he had said, but if he wanted to frighten me, he was doing a damn good job.

"When I first heard about Chuck's wondrous software, I thought it sounded like something the Soviet Institute of Cryptography, Telecommunications and Computer Science would have a hard-on for."

"Computer geeks would never get their tongues around a mouthful like that." I still wanted to bring a little levity into this scary conversation.

T.K. didn't even look at me. "It's a joint project of Russian defense and the KGB."

Those dreadful initials again. "Are you saying I should leave?"

The waitress brought the drinks. T.K. didn't warm the brandy between his palms, but downed it neat in one gulp. "Any arguments from you," he said, "will be futile."

I didn't plan to argue. I would tell old Dungeons and Dragons we had blundered into various East Bloc espionage systems, and leave it at that. Who would argue? Still, I couldn't believe T.K. would actually pack me off after the time and energy we had invested. After all, the Iron Curtain was coming down and the show was over for the bad guys. He must think they were going to take a couple of curtain calls.

Our eyes met. T.K.'s were cold, like an unfriendly stranger's.

"This evening you'll make excuses for leaving. A sick aunt in London. An emergency meeting with your financial advisers. Think of something. And make it believable."

When T.K. and I returned to the hotel, I said I needed to buy some toiletries, but what I really wanted to do was make a phone call.

"Why buy East German stuff when you can get whatever you want in Berlin tomorrow?"

"To help the local economy."

He shrugged and stepped out on the balcony for a cigarette.

Downtown, I went to the post office and placed a call to Mark in accounting. The six-hour time difference made calls back to the states impossible before mid-afternoon. While waiting for my call to go through, I wondered if it was a good idea, but my sales and technical experience has taught me, usually the hard way, not to leave any loose ends.

"It's Mata Hari," I said, when Mark picked up.

"Are you all right?"

No mindless banter. What was going on?

"Did that PI find anything worth reporting about the nasty Brit?"

"He found someone, but it has to be the wrong guy. He's going to dig a little deeper. That man couldn't possibly be your colleague."

"Why do you say that?"

"What is his role in your assignment?" He had not answered my question.

"I think he's running the show." I picked my words carefully. "I also think the guy who hired me is afraid of him. They seem to have been collaborators for a long time. It's all very murky."

Mark's silence worried me more than anything.

Out on the street, everyone was coming back from the beach with bags, damp towels, and tired, whiny children. I wanted to see Chloe so badly that I felt close to tears.

"Something has come up and I'm leaving tomorrow."

"That's the best news yet. Is there anyone you trust absolutely?"

"T.K."

"But you said he's friends with this Putnam."

"I'm not sure."

"Stay on everyone's good side. Kiss ass and all that."

Not reassuring. I told him I would be back in the office in a couple days. "I'll be the one with her tail between her legs."

On the way back to The Tea Rose, I wondered if I should confront T.K. with the PI's information. Since the PI might have zeroed in on the wrong man, I decided not to rock the boat. Whatever was so bad it couldn't be told wouldn't matter in twenty hours.

I got out my suitcases and started to organize my packing. T.K. still stood on the balcony where he watched my activities with his face frozen into that harsh frown. Did he think I actually wanted to stay?

At last he came into the room.

"It's still afternoon and we've hours before dinner. Let's take a walk up to the hunting lodge," I suggested.

"Nothing you say will make any difference."

"You don't seem to realize that I am not unwilling to leave. I never wanted this assignment to begin with, but there are a few things we need to clarify before I go."

My reasonable voice must have convinced him he would get no arguments. We changed into walking shoes and took off through the town to catch the road that led up to the old Schloss.

We walked the first kilometer in silence. T.K.'s gait had relaxed and he was not so ramrod straight. I didn't speak until we left the main road and turned onto the broad uphill trail.

"My view of the situation is this," I began. "I still have a contract, and the payment for my services will be made whether I stay or go. I do not plan to take a haircut."

T.K. stared down at the ground with that tedious face.

"If I say something that's not true, please interrupt."

Silence.

"Anatoly's story apparently gave you a case of acronym angst, and you're worried about my safety with respect to the HIV and the KGB."

"It's the HVA for crissakes."

"Sorry. Edgar sent us in as a team. I will be very nervous about leaving you here if they are unaware of your unilateral decision to send me home."

"Edgar and Bill won't have to live with the consequences." The toe of his shoe sent a stone skittering up the hill ahead of us.

"Let's review the facts. Bruss is dead, and his body was in that old granary. I was attacked and warned—and I believe now that it was only a warning—in the same place. If the HVA is storing their old records there, I can see why they are a little edgy, but on the other hand, why would they stash Bruss's body so close to their treasure? Have you wondered about that? When a deep harbor is right outside the door?"

"Maybe they didn't have time to get rid of it."

"Exactly. We don't know any details about the murder. If I were going to be around longer, I would suggest we visit the local newspaper office and read the back issues of the paper from the weeks after the crime. Then at least we wouldn't be operating in ignorance."

A tour bus barreled down the hill. I continued, "the other thing is, Chuck and his friends are on the island, not in Stralsund, and it's possible there's no connection at all between them and these guys you're so panicked about. You told me the Stasi were internal security and the HVA was the external agency. They are probably just as communicative and cozy with each other as our FBI and CIA."

"We don't know anything about that."

"But we can surmise that no sane agent is eager to provoke the investigation dead Americans would cause."

T.K. didn't respond. My bruised shoulder had begun to ache. The road up the hill wasn't steep but the grade was constant. The hikers and tour busses were on their way down this late in the afternoon.

"I don't want to get off on the rabbit trails, but do you want to hear my 'Chuck theory?'"

"I'm listening." He cupped his hand to light a cigarette. We plopped down on a picnic table bench at the trailside snack bar.

"We keep hearing about all these missing files: the HVA files, the Stasi files. I can't help but wonder if Chuck hasn't sold someone a bill of goods."

I left him with that thought while I bought a bottle of currant juice. I turned back to watch him. He sat slumped at the end of the bench, one leg crossed over the other, brow puckered while he smoked and stared off into the green beeches.

When I returned, he looked up and said, "Go on."

"Let's go back to the idea of the data warehouse. I mentioned before that data has to be scrubbed to go into the warehouse, even if it's already on computerized files. Does 'A' stand for accident or adultery? You had better know. And you had better be consistent.

"Can you imagine trying to input typed or handwritten reports? Someone's surveillance notes with no special structure. It wouldn't be like a purchase order form or a requisition. How could you possibly codify this kind of information on, say, a spreadsheet? It would be the classical case of garbage in, garbage out."

T.K. shrugged again.

"I'm not saying it couldn't be done. It's a huge effort in time and manpower, but if Chuck found someone with a bunch of files and an 'idea'...well, he might tell them he could make it happen."

"Take the money and run?"

"Or sail."

T.K. ground his cigarette out in the dirt. I stood up and tossed my juice bottle into the trash.

"It's the only thing that makes sense. He must be pulling a scam."

We climbed the rest of the way up the hill in silence. The Schloss Granitz, a large sand colored building with a crenellated tower at each corner presided solidly over the scene, with a great four-story tower rising out of its center. The narrow arched windows commanded a view of the Baltic and the countryside. To me, the term "hunting lodge" conveys a rustic affair with a few antlers hanging over a big stone fireplace and a canoe tied to a dock out front. This so-called lodge looked like a palace. We sat on a bench in the gravel yard in front of the broad steps to the entrance.

"If we could have gotten close enough to Chuck, we might have been able to figure it out."

"But you're leaving tomorrow, so I'll have to figure it out alone."

"You really are paranoid."

"I've run into the Department XXII hoodlums before. Zara, these guys are pros. Nasty ones. With contacts in every terrorist group on the globe. Don't make this any harder for me than it is."

I knew I was no match for the rough and tumble guys that rubbed elbows with Carlos the Jackal, and God knows I wanted to go home, but it bothered me to leave everything hanging.

~ * ~

Monday evening we drove the familiar road that followed the coast to Sassnitz. T.K. said I would be a passenger on the 1:30 train to Berlin tomorrow. In the morning, he would arrange for Smith to meet me at Bahnhof Nord and return the contents of the manila envelope. I could pick up my passport at the Kempi and board a plane to the States.

He reached into his shirt pocket for a cigarette. Since Anatoly told us about the missing files and the organizations with numbers and letters in their names, T.K. had seldom been without a cigarette.

As usual, he parked a distance away from the pub.

Walking down the hill, I said, "You should really discuss my leaving with Putnam."

"He never wanted you here in the first place."

"He may have changed his mind."

"Then he'll have to change it back."

"He'll take his anger out on you."

In the long twilight, drinkers had congregated around the hatch cover tables in front of the tavern. T.K. adopted his trademark careless posture as he took my arm. I forced myself to smile up at him. Inside, our friends waited at the table in the little room with the green tile stove.

Chuck sat at the head of the table, Romy on his left. Next to super-slim Romy, Sabine's shoulders and breasts looked massive. At the opposite end of the table, Wulf Mueller with his gold chia curls faced Chuck. No-neck Bodo, with his back to us, occupied the chair on his left. Two empty places waiting for T.K. and me. Chuck made a welcoming gesture. Bodo turned his head. Everyone's eyes on us, expectant, not friendly but—appraising. T.K.'s denim shirt noticed and admired by all.

I sat down by Chuck, who flashed his dimpled smile and a planted an enthusiastic kiss on each cheek. T.K. shook hands with Bodo, Wulf and Sabine, and then said something to Romy, which made her blush and Sabine smirk. He slouched down next to me, nabbed the blond waitress as she sped by, and ordered schnapps and beers for the table.

I had decided not to drink, so when everyone toasted "Prost," with raised glasses and tossed back the colorless schnapps, I put my glass back on the table.

"Hey, what's this?" asked Chuck, nodding at the brimming glass.

"Not in the mood to celebrate," I said, unzipping my tunic and struggling to extract the arm with the sore shoulder.

T.K. had everyone's attention with some long involved East German joke.

Chuck reached around and helped me. "I think I'm in love," he whispered.

I was wearing a thin white silk T-shirt.

"Not in the mood for love," I said, putting my hand on his arm. His mouth dropped open and he tore his gaze away from my transparent shirt and looked right into my eyes.

"Jesus, I sure as hell am."

"I probably have to leave tomorrow." I made a sad face and feigned devastation.

"Shit, no."

"Yes. I forgot to give power of attorney to one of my investment people, and now there's a problem. I said, 'it's only money,' but T.K. thinks I should go back." I paused. "So I guess I have to."

Chuck's smile vanished and the sparkle faded from his eyes. "But you can't leave! I wanted the four of us to sail over to Hiddensee. I had everything planned."

"T.K. is going to stay on and try to find some investments. He can still go sailing with you."

"No offense, but T.K.'s company is not what I was looking forward to."

T.K. finished his joke, and Wulf laughed with everyone else. I swapped drinks with Chuck, who downed my schnapps and started on the beer. T.K. ordered another round. Wulf began apologizing to T.K. for Saturday night's outburst, something about all the strain of unification and his fears of the unknown future.

Romy kept her eyes on Chuck and me while she and Sabine exchanged housewife chit-chat, but when I overheard them talking about what to do with left over pork roast, I spoke up. "Pork fried rice."

Chuck burst into the conversation. "I would kill for decent Chinese food!"

"We saw an Asian restaurant in Stralsund," said T.K.

"Yeah, the one with skinned rats hanging by their tails in the freezer and wonton stuffed with dog food. Somebody saw the cans in the trash," said Chuck.

"You always exaggerate," said Romy frowning.

"Not much." Chuck spoke to T.K. "Don't make my pretty friend leave."

"Oh, business before pleasure," T.K. said very coolly.

"If I were staying, I'd make you the world's best roast pork fried rice," I promised Chuck.

T.K. glowered. Maybe I was laying it on a bit thick.

"You are leaving us, Frau Wentz?" asked Wulf.

"Alas, yes, tomorrow." I stood up and went to the ladies room.

T.K. ambushed me when I came out of the toilet. "What the hell do you think you're pulling?"

Before I could come up with an answer, he ordered, "Drink up and say your farewells because we're out of here in five minutes."

~ * ~

On our private little balcony overlooking the Baltic, T.K. said, "I'm reasonably sure I can get to Chuck alone. He seems pretty uncomplicated."

"I wouldn't count on that. He doesn't like you."

"As soon as I have the CD, I'll come and get you and we can deliver it to Edgar together. Everyone knows you were a big part of this."

I wondered if he was trying to soften me up for a final fling in the bed with the moonlight streaming in through the balcony door, but I felt too antsy to dredge up any passion, and now more than ever I wanted to avoid an emotion-laden night together with glib promises of future meetings. I spent so much time packing up the laptop, winding cables and rearranging everything that T.K. became irritated all over again and feigned sleep by the time I climbed into bed.

What crossed my mind was that T.K. might be packing me off for some ulterior reason I didn't know, maybe to concentrate his attentions on the beautiful Frau Romy Motte or even something more ominous. I couldn't very well share my suspicions.

~ * ~

The next morning, I stood again on our balcony. My packed suitcases and the laptop waited by the desk. T.K., always fearful about phoning from our turf, had driven to the Sellin Post Office to call Jesse Smith in Berlin and arrange for my pickup.

I looked at my watch. Eleven-thirty. What was keeping him? Maybe a parking problem or a long wait for the phone.

I tried to read the novel I had saved for the train. *Westsee Piraten.* West Sea Pirates, a young adult book in German, the swashbuckling story of fourteenth century buccaneers who preyed on Hanseatic cities and shipping. I would keep plugging away at improving my German, no matter what.

I felt time pass, watched seconds become minutes, minutes multiply. It was impossible to concentrate.

Twelve o'clock. Why was T.K. so late? We wouldn't have time for lunch, and the train didn't have a dining car. Twelve-thirty came and went. By now I was worried. I went down to the lobby where I could watch for him. One o'clock. I marched up and down the lobby fighting feelings of panic. One-thirty.

I heard the train whistle. *Shit.*

A man came up the hotel steps. Navy blazer hanging on wide, slightly stooped shoulders. Not T.K. Something familiar about the white hair. He opened the door and stepped into the room. The big belly. The beaky nose. The shrewd eyes.

"Edgar!" It wasn't until he stopped and stared at me that I realized I had spoken his name.

"Zara Wentz, what a very pleasant surprise!"

I couldn't stop staring at him, while my mind churned over this odd predicament.

"I would like to invite you and, ah, 'Mr. Wentz' to lunch. Have you eaten?"

"Not yet." My mind spun in circles. Edgar was on the island.

He paused in the middle of the social niceties and asked, "Is anything wrong. You look...distressed."

"I'm so surprised to see you. I...we didn't know you were coming. Wouldn't it be awkward if you were seen here?"

"Oh, I was a mite concerned—hell, I was worried about your, ah, situation. Flew to Berlin last night from Copenhagen. Rented a car. Decided nothing beats a firsthand look. Where's 'hubby?'"

"He's not here just now."

"On the prowl for the CD? With you know who?" His eyes seemed wary.

"He's got a lead on something." I didn't elaborate.

Edgar arched his unruly white eyebrows, seemingly puzzled by my vagueness.

"I'll tell you over lunch. Let me run upstairs and grab my handbag."

Back in the room, I dabbed at my face and wrists with a damp towel as I tried to compose myself. It didn't seem like a world class idea to tell Edgar T.K. had disappeared, that I was supposed to be on a train back to Berlin, and Bill Putnam was unaware of this change in plans. Why was Edgar running around in public? It would be a disaster if he ran into Chuck. I went downstairs to face the music.

He spurned my choice of a quiet indoor restaurant where we wouldn't be seen, insisting instead on lunch at a sidewalk café. I gave him an edited status report, omitting Putnam's tailing us, the business with the dog, my attack at the Stralsund docks, even Anatoly. Edgar wasn't a glasnost kind of guy. I reported solid social contacts with Romy and Chuck and the promise of a sailing party. Edgar nodded. I felt his foot moving around under the table. *Not again.*

Ignoring the game of footsy, I shared my theory that Chuck was trying to pull a swindle by making pie-in-the-sky promises to some techno-naïfs, promises his software couldn't deliver. Edgar drank more wine and nodded again and his foot found mine. I gave his shin a little kick and said, "Oops, sorry."

When he asked for the third time where T.K. was, I had no choice but to begin a contrived explanation. When I was running out of words, and Edgar's knee was pressing against mine, I spied Chuck and Romy walking along the sidewalk toward us, only half a block away.

"You've got to disappear! Chuck is coming. Hide in the men's room."

For a large man, Edgar moved fast, and by the time Romy and Chuck had reached the café, he was safely out of view.

"Zara, love." Chuck's greeting was puzzled. No dimples today. I wasn't even sure he was pleasantly surprised. Romy's watchful eyes and half-open mouth didn't move when she spotted me. I wondered what it would take to get a reaction out of her.

"T.K. changed his mind at the last minute. I'm not leaving, at least not today."

I could see Chuck pumping himself up. First he squared his shoulders, next his eyes lit up, and then came the engaging, confident smile, followed by a flash of white teeth and lastly, the dimples. From zero to sixty in ten seconds.

"Hey, Rügen's first roast pork fried rice party! Tomorrow night, okay? And if the weather holds, we can all sail over to Hiddensee this weekend. The four of us—without chaperones! That sound good, sweetheart?"

Romy nodded with an absolute lack of enthusiasm.

"Where's T.K.?" asked Chuck.

"He's out with someone who's looking for an investor," I lied.

His eyes took in the two plates and two glasses at my table. "Another potential investment opportunity. Herr Something-or-other. In the john." I gestured toward the back of the restaurant.

"You two are really serious about dropping some cash over here, aren't you?"

"That's the idea." Even though an umbrella shaded the table, I was starting to sweat.

From the depths of the restaurant, "*Aufmachen!*" Open up! Someone was desperate to get into the toilet Edgar was monopolizing. Any moment, I would get palpitations.

"See you this evening?" Chuck always had a special intimate smile for me. "We can plan the party."

"I guess."

More commotion back by the bathrooms.

"Where will I ever find soy sauce and sesame oil?" I asked.

Chuck said, "There's a little Vietnamese grocery in Stralsund. For the guest workers. I'll bring Ho Dung. He can translate. Tomorrow morning."

"Who?" No one I remembered.

"Vietnamese guy. He crews for me," Chuck said.

"See you tonight." If T.K. returned. If I could get rid of Edgar. If the anxious man didn't break down the door to the toilet and expose this farce.

Romy said, "Ciao," and they left me sweating in the shade.

Edgar crept back to the table. "Listen, you better eat and get out of here," I said, none too diplomatically. "If Chuck had seen you sitting with me, it would have queered the whole operation. Do you want to take a status report home on a diskette?"

"No, Mrs. Wentz. Your summary was quite adequate. I'll be out of your hair directly."

He ate a few more bites, finished his wine and said good-bye.

Back at the hotel, I checked the parking lot but the blue Beemer and T.K. were still missing. At the desk in the lobby I got a bus schedule for Sassnitz. No matter how I dreaded it, I would have to tell Bill that Edgar had come and T.K. had gone and Chuck expected me to cook roast pork fried rice tomorrow evening.

Eight

Putnam wasn't in his room at the boarding house, an old three-story villa long past its glory days. The white paint had peeled off the elaborately carved wood filigree, and the sinuous steel ornamentation was dented, broken and bent. I took off my blazer and folded it, and then I sat down on the wooden steps and waited glumly, my chin cupped in my hand. The sky was a pale gray mother-of-pearl wash, and the air had a sultry feel, as if a thunderstorm lurked beyond the horizon.

I sat in the warm air and my bones shook. Something had happened to T.K. Something bad. He had been hell bent on protecting me. Had he run into the goons who had attacked me in Stralsund? Somebody from a past life? The KGB-HVA-Department-something-or-other uglies? What kept running through my head was something Putnam had said back in Berlin. At one of those dreadful meetings in the Europa Center office. "A mistake could cost your life...or more likely, his." It had been a big mistake to visit the old grain elevators. My mistake.

T.K. had actually been nice to me. I wished I hadn't been so cold on our last night. In the twenty minutes I sat and waited for Putnam,

I got myself into such a funk that I could not sit still for one more instant. There was no one I could ask for help, not Sabine, not Chuck, absolutely not the police, not even Anatoly, supposing I could figure out how to reach him. I decided to find the post office and call Mark at Coppola & Henry.

His assistant told me he would be back in twenty minutes. I trudged up the hill to Putnam's place again, and moped some more on the front porch. Next door I could hear someone strumming a guitar, the same sad chord, over and over. The somnolent afternoon, the salty air and the sad notes made me want to sit and cry. Instead, I clenched my jaw and walked back to the post office.

When Mark answered the phone, I told him what had happened including the chronicle of this God-awful day.

"Get the hell out of there, Zara! It doesn't sound right."

"How can I leave when I don't know what's happened to T.K.?"

"Just leave now."

"I'm going to make one more attempt to find him."

"You're crazy."

"Listen, in the unlikely case I do stay here, there are a few people involved in this business who are behaving very strangely."

I stopped to think how to word my request. This didn't seem like the right time for subtlety.

"The venture capitalist's showing up today could have blown our cover and the entire project. Can you ask that P.I. to dig into his background?"

He gave an unenthusiastic grunt that must have meant yes.

"Once before, I asked you about Bill Putnam. I'm still waiting for an answer."

"The P.I. says he's nobody you want to know. Will you get out of there before you run out of options?"

"As soon as I can leave in good conscience. I'll call you." I hung up before he could scare me any more than he already had.

Tourists returned from the beach or wandered out for a cup of coffee and a slab of strudel at the nearby café while I waited once more on the porch of Putnam's lodgings. In the distance, I heard thunder reverberating across the water.

I wrote to Putnam:

TKD has disappeared down the rabbit hole while he was trying to hustle the Clueless Technical Type back from whence she came. This happened at a very bad time, as relations with the lad from the New World and his lady were becoming very congenial. The CTT has decided to go back to Chicago. The beautiful blue sedan has also fallen down the rabbit hole. Should you have a pressing need to communicate, the Chicago number is...

I saw Putnam's gray Opel pull into a parking space down the block. He got out of the car and bounced up the hill with a strong springy gait. Legs like tree trunks. He wore shorts and an old cotton bush hat and carried a canvas tote bag. The hat looked like the one I'd seen at the FKK beach. I just knew Putnam had spied on us. He was so slimy. Hiding my revulsion, I stuck the note into my handbag, grabbed my jacket, and ran to meet him.

He halted in the middle of the sidewalk, and eyed me with distaste. His expression said a plague of locusts would be more welcome than the sight of me scurrying toward him.

"Mrs. Wentz! Now why am I gripped by a foreboding of bad news?"

"T.K. disappeared this morning. I'm afraid something has happened to him."

A few fat raindrops pelted us, then the sky opened, and as the Baltic equivalent of the monsoon hit, we made a dash for the Opel.

Putnam tossed his soggy hat in the back seat and used his beach towel to wipe the water off his face, and I blotted mine with a handkerchief. The car windows had already steamed over.

"Let's not be rash, Mrs. Wentz," he advised.

"You are perfectly free to call me Zara, luv," I said rather coldly. He stared at me with his glacial eyes.

I told him everything that had happened since yesterday when Anatoly told us about the rumors involving the grain elevators. Putnam seemed more shocked by Edgar's unannounced visit than by T.K.'s having gone AWOL.

"Damned stupid, that. Supposing you'd been sitting there having tea in the lobby with Goodborn when bloody Edgar strolled in." He cast his usual icy glance at me. "I told Drummond all along this scheme would never work, and now there's going to be hell to pay."

"What should we do?"

"We'll motor back to Binz. Everyone leaves a trail, Mrs. Wentz. Even your...ah, husband." His eyes burned with a blue flame. "We all leave a bit of spoor. The hunter knows where to look."

"I have to call my office."

"Right-o."

Putnam's unnatural calm, controlled and almost radiant, scared the hell out of me. He hummed a little as he drove me to the post office. I dashed through the rain, and ducked inside. They recognized me by now, but I didn't care.

I told Mark I couldn't leave yet.

"Zara, I didn't want to tell you this, but the P.I. made an effort to find out what he could about this Motte woman. He called in some favors. Conferred with some FBI contacts." Mark sounded distraught, almost breathless.

"And?"

Mark's news was rather chilling, if you put it into the context of Anatoly's story, the incidents at the grain elevator and T.K.'s disappearance. Now I was even more frantic to find him.

~ * ~

Putnam drove me back to Binz. He didn't utter one word, yet his erect driving posture, with his pink and white scarred hands placed at precisely ten o'clock and two o'clock on the steering wheel and his humming the Colonel Bogey March, gave me the impression he was wired. I looked out the window at the rain.

No note or any other sign of T.K. at the hotel. In our room, my suitcases were sitting neatly on the floor, right by the desk where

I had left them. Still humming, Putnam took off for Sellin to check whether anyone remembered seeing T.K. at the post office. I lay down on the bed to think, and immediately fell asleep.

I heard the sound of a key rattling in the big brass lock, and woke up with a start, expecting to see T.K. step into the room. Silence. Nobody. I must have been dreaming.

I went down to the front desk and threw my uncertain German and myself on the mercy of the manager. My husband, I explained, had left this morning to run a quick errand and hadn't returned. Would he mind checking with the police to find out if there had been any accidents? Or the hospital, perhaps? He picked up the receiver and dialed. I caught the German word for "accident." He looked at me and shook his head. The conversation continued. An American, he said. Mr. T.K. Wentz. He glanced at me again, as his eyebrows sprang halfway up to his hairline. "*Ach*, so. Yes. Immediately. *Ja. Ja.*" He palmed the receiver. Your husband is in Stralsund. At police headquarters. The Binz police will take you there. Please bring your passports. They will pick you up in a few minutes.

I stared at him while he repeated everything very slowly, as if I was an imbecile, then I turned and ran upstairs. I grabbed our passports, and changed into a clean T-shirt, ran a comb through my hair, and put on my navy blazer. In the mirror, my reflection looked normal with no trace of the woman whose world was cracking open.

Back downstairs, I tried to explain to the manager that our friend Mr. Putnam was looking for T.K., and that he should tell him where I had gone.

A twenty-something green-uniformed cop with unruly blond hair came into the lobby, and the manager introduced me to Klages of the *Volkspolizei*. The People's Police. I didn't catch his title. Maybe it was 'Comrade.' We exchanged a firm handshake, and I followed him out the back door.

He inquired rather officiously if I knew how to drive. I asked him if he was making a little joke, but his earnest blue eyes denied any attempt at humor. He pulled a set of car keys out of his pocket, the keys to the Beemer. We tripped and stumbled over the language barrier, until I realized he wanted me to drive him to Stralsund while his colleagues followed in a squad car. I nodded agreement. We walked a few blocks and there sat the BMW, parked on a side street. His fellow cops must have been circling the block, because a police car arrived moments later. He gave me the keys. I unlocked the Beemer and sat in the driver's seat, feeling both numb and edgy while they had a cop powwow through the window of the police car.

Then Officer or Detective or Comrade Klages climbed into the passenger seat, and fastened his seat belt. He put his head back and sniffed slightly, then gave a faint sigh, as if reveling in the discreet smell of the leather upholstery. I adjusted the seat and the mirrors, and powered down the windows.

"*Wunderschön,*" he said, more to himself than me, "*Wie Gott in Frankreich!*'" Like God in France. I took off down the street toward the main road. The other two cops fell in behind us in their Wartburg.

"My husband," I began.

"A small matter."

"Please tell me."

"They will tell you in Stralsund."

"Can't you—?"

"No. Sorry."

I went over the same ground again with the same results, except the second no sounded firmer than the first. He wasn't paying attention to anything except the damned car. His eyes swept back and forth over the dash, not missing a single dial or knob, and he exclaimed, "Super!" when I popped the Beatles into the tape deck. He pronounced is 'zooper.'

We traversed the long Deutsche Allee Strassen to "Strawberry Fields Forever" and "Penny Lane." He laughed when we zoomed around a tractor and left his colleagues lagging. He gestured at the speedometer, and I thought he was indicating for me to slow down.

"No, No. Faster. Now, how fast?"

We were doing one hundred and forty kilometers.

Now he pointed up the street. "Straight road ahead."

He grinned as I gunned the engine. The car purred and leaped down the road, but I felt like a croquet ball had lodged in the pit of my stomach. Under a compulsion to make polite conversation, I told him how much I liked this idyllic island. I gestured toward neat fields, the chickens, ducks and geese waddling and pecking in the grass around the old farmhouses, and the pastures dotted with brown and white cows.

Fiddling with the power windows, inching his up and down, and glancing in the side mirror for a glimpse of his colleagues, he only nodded.

I turned up the volume on the tape deck, and then I put the car through its paces, accelerating through the curves, hurtling down the straightaway. The rains had long passed, and the countryside was drenched in a haze of golden afternoon sunshine.

Soon we were traveling over the Rügendamm, the long bridge that carried us off the island and into Stralsund. Officer Klages directed me right and left and up and down one-way streets until we pulled up at the blue lights in front of an old brick building which housed the police department. The car had been my safe womb, and out of it, the bravura I felt while driving immediately deflated. I even started to feel a little queasy as he held open the heavy wooden door and I entered the police station. I wiped my sweaty palms on the back pockets of my jeans and went in to face whatever music awaited, certain it would not be "Strawberry Fields Forever."

~ * ~

Desks, chairs, typewriters, more green uniforms. Teutonic orderliness. No weird characters hanging around. Different, but not that different, from an American police station. Klages walked up to a counter and spoke with a middle-aged woman in uniform. His voice was too low for me to catch what he said, but she asked me for the passports.

"Why do you have my husband here?" In my best German.

I didn't understand her answer. "Excuse me?"

She didn't try to explain. "*Die Pässe, Bitte.*" The passports, please. With a prayer they didn't scream forgery, I handed over the two little navy blue books. She disappeared through a door in the back of the room. I turned to Klages and repeated I didn't understand why my husband was in the Stralsund jail. We were tourists on vacation. We had broken no laws. What business did the police have with us?

He said it was about the dog.

I must have looked astonished. The dog, he repeated. A giddy feeling suffused me, and I wondered if I would faint, right there on the floor between the old wooden desks on the drab tan linoleum. I asked for water. A few minutes later Officer Klages came back with a bottle of apple juice. He said "*auf Wiedersehen*," and thanked me for the ride.

"You can't leave me here," I wanted to say, but of course he could, and in fact, after a handshake, he did.

I sat there for thirty-seven minutes, while my mind wandered in a maze of futile speculations, and awful possibilities. No one spoke to me, although sometimes I received quick curious glances. *Don't make waves*, I told myself, when I really wanted to swear and demand to see T.K. It was almost seven o'clock, and I had promised to meet Chuck and Romy at nine in Sassnitz. Our whole operation was unraveling into a shambles.

The passport woman came back into the room, followed by a man in a sport coat, then T.K., with rumpled clothes and a sheepish grin, and yet another cop. I stood up. T.K. saw me and winked. He walked with his usual assurance, almost arrogance. I ran up to the counter.

"Frau Wentz." The man in the sport coat spoke to me.

T.K. said, "My wife speaks only a little simple German."

He answered in a brusque voice, "And I will ask her only some simple little questions."

He held a blue passport in his hand, and he beckoned me with it. I looked back at T.K., who gave me what I interpreted as an encouraging smile. The man ushered me through the door and turned into a small room with a metal table and three wooden chairs. Drab gray walls. The interrogation room. We shook hands, and I was quaking in my loafers. He bowed a little stiffly and said,

"Kriminal Kommissar Mann." A uniformed cop carrying a notebook came in and sat down. The giddy feeling returned.

"The dog you and your husband left at the Kleintierpraxis..." He hesitated, and I nodded to let him know I understood.

"Where did you find this dog?"

"On a country road. Before the bridge. I'm not sure exactly where. It was dark, and we had driven over some cobblestones."

He frowned. "That could be anywhere, Mrs. Wentz."

"I'm so sorry. I can't tell you more."

"Where were you going in the middle of the night?" He got up and walked around the room, but his eyes never left my face. Brown eyes, brown hair, brown jacket, brown shoes. T.K. and I hadn't prepared a reason for our late night wanderings.

"Out driving. It was *jet lag,* I guess." I used the English phrase, hoping he would understand it. He nodded slightly. "Where we live, in Chicago, we would have just finished dinner." He nodded again. "Here in Rügen it was the middle of the night."

He stopped pacing and frowned. I attempted a hopeful smile. Silence.

The cop stopped scribbling. The brusque one cleared his throat, as if preparing for more questions. I resisted the urge to wipe my damp palms on my jeans again.

He said, "Okay." in a tired voice, and the scribe jumped up and opened the door. Able to breathe again, I got to my feet and he escorted me back into the big room with the metal desks. He handed my passport to the woman.

T.K., in the middle of signing something, glanced up. I couldn't read the expression on his face. Bemused, even calm, inured to these awful scrapes.

"How is the dog?" I asked my interrogator.

"Healing." Only that word.

The woman did not return our passports. The plain-clothes cop said something to T.K. An apology or a warning? I couldn't tell.

"May I please have my passport?" I asked in my best German.

"No." Something about continuing to investigate the shooting. A few days at most.

T.K. gave me his, "don't rock the boat" look. He took a package of Marlboro's and offered them around. Like magic a little crowd assembled around the cigarettes.

"Ach, nehmen Sie ruhig mehr als eine."

Take more than one. Was he crazy? They were keeping our passports and he was giving them cigarettes? I wanted to throw a fit, but what would that accomplish?

"Zara, run out to the car and get the extra smokes out of the glove box."

I gave him an incredulous look, but did as requested. When I returned, a little breathless and still beside myself at the loss of my passport, no matter how fake and how temporary, T.K. was holding both documents, and from the sound of it, telling an East German joke. *To the East German police.* I froze until he finished to great guffaws of laughter. I handed him the Marlboros, which he tossed to the man who had interviewed me.

We seemed to be free to go. I pushed open the heavy wooden door, surprised to find that it was still daylight.

On the sidewalk, T.K. and I spoke at the same time. I said, "Oh my God, I've been so worried!"

"I was afraid you would be gone!"

I hugged him. "I couldn't leave until I knew you were all right."

He put his face in my hair and held me so tightly I could barely breathe. We stood together for a long time, and then he took my hand. "Let's get the hell out of here."

In the car he said, "They picked me up on account of that damned dog." He pointed at the ceiling light, signaling we should have an "assume someone is listening" conversation.

I nodded.

T.K. continued. "I was driving back to the hotel, and these cops stopped me. 'You will have to come with us to Stralsund. A procedural matter. To clarify a situation,' and a lot more crapola." He stopped to light a cigarette. "So I was more or less arrested." He sounded almost euphoric. "My God, you'd think someone had shot Honecker, not a damned dog."

He said he wanted to grab a bite to eat, but he really wanted a drink. We stopped at a little place on a street before the main road to the bridge. Over beer and more cigarettes, I got the unadulterated story.

"The charge was suspicion of animal abuse."

"How did we get found out?"

"Remember the man on the bike who recommended the Kleintierpraxis in Stralsund?"

"Yes."

"He called the vet a few days later asking if a couple had brought in a dog hit by a car in the early morning hours. Wanted to know how the dog was doing."

Amazingly, T.K. wasn't angry with me.

"The vet told him someone had left a dog and a fortune in West marks on his front stoop. But the dog had been shot, not hit by a car. The vet had already called the police to report a gunshot wound. Then the cyclist provided a description of our car."

"So some cop recognized the Beemer from the 'wanted' list?"

"Yeah. Private citizens aren't supposed to have guns. Any shooting has to be investigated. And thanks to my little techno-mentor and her big wad of West marks, they knew whoever left the dog wasn't a local." He gulped the beer and wiped his mouth.

"This doesn't make sense. They thought you shot the dog and then took it to the vet?"

"Sweetie, they were making sure." He gave me an impudent grin, and gestured to the waiter for another beer.

"So what did you did tell them?"

"T.K. never tells a lie when a half-truth will do. I told them we saw the dog lying in the road. Being good Samaritans, we stopped to investigate. He was still alive. We put him in the trunk and were headed for Stralsund to get help. Stopped to check on our cargo. Saw the bicyclist, got the vet's address. Dropped the dog off. Naturally we knew he was bleeding, but we'd no idea he'd been shot. Not our dog, didn't want to be responsible, on vacation and so on, left money, took off."

"They believed you?"

"Only because I told the same story five or six times without changing it."

"Where did you say we found him?"

"On the road to Stralsund." He gestured toward the highway. "They still have no clue whose dog he is. And we want to keep it that way. They asked where his goddamn collar was. Said all dogs have to wear a collar." He paused. "What did they ask you?"

"Where we found him and what we were doing driving around in the middle of the night."

"What'd you say?" He looked at me intently, squinting through the smoke of his third cigarette.

I told him, and then I asked. "Did you give the same reason for the late night rambling?"

He finished off this glass of beer. "Sweetie, I said you were an insomniac."

"Close enough."

I arranged the cardboard coasters, the *Bierdeckel* into a neat pile on the table.

"Does this mean we've blown it? Now that we've drawn the notice of the police? Sabine told me Wulf Mueller tried to get the cops to investigate his dog's disappearance. But they weren't interested."

"That would have been either the local Putbus cops or in Bergen, the county seat. Stralsund is in a different district."

"But they could talk to each other."

"They can and they will. Sometime, someone will have a conversation."

I could hear the thinly veiled insinuations already. "Mrs. Wentz, if you knew the dog belonged to Herr Mueller, why didn't you tell him where the animal was?"

T.K. said, "So we've got to put this business to bed before they do. Find out a way to put the screws to Chuck Roast." T.K. put his hand on mine and squeezed it.

"I did some thinking. You were right. We'd both be pushing up daisies if anyone was seriously worried."

Then I told him about Edgar's surprise visit, his almost running into Chuck and Romy, and my trek to Sassnitz to find Bill Putnam.

~ * ~

Putnam was stomping up and down in front of the hotel like an enraged bull. The look he gave me made the memory of the Stralsund police station seem downright homey. He hadn't talked to the manager, because he always prided himself on his ability to sneak past any front desk. Today it had backfired.

We all climbed the stairs up to our room, but T.K. pulled me aside and whispered, "I'll deal with Billy Boy." Aloud he said, "Sweetie, could you run down and see if you can wheedle some ice cubes while I brief Bill?"

Apparently T.K. didn't want me around when he told Putnam about his arrest, and especially about our saving the dog. I went downstairs and sat in the lobby for a few minutes, and then I stopped by the front desk where we had to explain daily that Americans could not survive without at least one bucket of ice. With his usual warning that cold drinks would cause stomach cancer, the manager gave me a little milk can full of ice. As I came up the stairs, I heard raised male voices behind the door to our room. I stopped to listen. Putnam was speaking.

"This whole bloody business is her doing, and she's leading you around by the nose. You should have thrown the bloody dog into the harbor like we planned."

They had both forgotten about the possibility of the room being bugged. I edged closer to the door, as Putnam continued to rage.

"I've been running my own investigation. Maybe you know while she poses as your wife, she's married to a man who comes from money. So why is she here?"

I couldn't believe Putnam had had me investigated. What a jerk. He hadn't found out about the divorce yet.

"I've watched her. Brazenly parading along the beach in nothing but that bloody red hat. Anatoly is under her spell. Bloody Goodborn will be next, but I'll wager he won't hand over his CD-ROM in exchange for a little snogging."

I stood by the door, as his words rained like blows.

T.K. murmured something, and Putnam interrupted.

"Drummond, tell me one thing. Is the fucking you got worth the fucking you'll get?"

My heart raced, and I took half a step back.

"Billy Boy, stay the hell away from our beach and butt out of what doesn't concern you. But for the record…"

I didn't catch the rest. Completely rattled, I crept back downstairs and tried to calm myself. A few minutes later, I trudged back again, this time bouncing the ice around noisily in the milk can and whistling disjoined snatches of, "The Colonel Bogie March."

When I entered the room, Putnam's cheeks were flaming red, and his eyes looked right through me. T.K. had a quirky smile that looked more bitter than cheerful.

Putnam stalked out of the room.

"That was lovely," I said. "Now we know who's really not a team player."

"He's angry because sneaking past the front desk was counterproductive." T.K. pulled off his shirt. "Get dressed. We'll be late for the Albatross."

He went into the bathroom.

Putnam hated me even more than I despised him, and his lobbying against me would be relentless, but I had some aces up my sleeve. I held the technical suit as well as the sexual one, trumps I wouldn't hesitate to play. In addition, now I knew something else. The reason T.K. was a failed spy had dawned on me. He had a soft heart.

Nine

Ho Dung was late. Chuck and I waited for him outside the hole in the wall Asian grocery store in a rundown neighborhood a block off the Frankendamm. Drab pockmarked stucco buildings housed a gaggle of funky stores and shops. Next door to the grocery, a tattoo parlor offered sailors indelible memories of this Baltic port.

Chuck paced up and down the sidewalk, looked at his watch and swore, then looked up at the noonday sun in the diffuse blue sky.

Bored with his profanities, I walked a few doors along the street to a tiny antique-cum-junk store and bought a cut-glass vase with a chipped rim to hold the luscious wild poppies that bloomed everywhere.

"God, that's ugly," said Chuck when I showed him my purchase.

"It's Bohemian glass. After the hotel kitchen cleans it up, it will sparkle."

"It'll still be ugly."

Not as ugly as your disposition. Earlier this morning, at the produce market, several women had turned to eye the smiling long-legged man in khaki shorts and salmon colored polo shirt. Cracking jokes in a combination of German and English, we had filled a string bag with scallions, peas, onions, lettuce, button mushrooms, oranges and strawberries.

Now he scowled and fidgeted, annoyed by having to wait, by the vase, by me. The absent Ho Dung was scheduled to navigate us through the grocery store. Besides rice, I needed soy sauce, sesame oil, bean sprouts and rice wine vinegar.

~ * ~

Last night at the Albatros, our group had planned the party. Anatoly and Putnam had been invited. Anatoly was bringing the ship's doctor; Wolf Mueller would have a schoolteacher in tow, and I had taken Sabine's wistful hint and included her daughter Andrea along with her and Bodo. Twelve for dinner.

After T.K. and I had left the bar and were walking up the hill, he said, "Chuck is courting you."

I noodled over that remark all the way to the car. Side by side, we leaned against the Beemer. "What will it buy him?" I had asked.

"Information. Find out if our 'marriage' is stable, if you like to blab when I'm not around, if you're available to interesting suggestions."

I could see his pleased smile in the glow of the street lamp.

"So what do we do?"

"Talk a little, flirt a little—humor him."

~ * ~

Which was what I did now, sitting next to Chuck on the curb in front of the grocery.

"So how did you meet Ho Dung? If he's a guest worker, what work does he do?"

"He's Mueller's gofer. Sort of like an indentured servant. Sometimes he repairs computer equipment."

An interesting fact that I should tell T.K.

"He helped you bring the boat down from Rostock?" I asked.

"Yeah, I sailed here with a goddamned boat person."

"How did you communicate?"

Chuck scowled at the memory. "I pointed and yelled and he scurried around the boat like a goddamn rat. After two days he knew the English for everything. Now, can we talk about something else?" He paused, and then grinned. "What do the Vietnamese do with their dogs?"

"I don't know."

"They wok them!" He guffawed at his outrageous pun while I rolled my eyes.

He looked at his watch again and sputtered, "Jesus!"

Last night T.K. told Chuck and me at least 60,000 North Vietnamese, mostly skilled workers, were living in East Germany. Practically slave laborers, they were paid a pittance and worked in five-year stints. When the wall came down, many of them had tried to escape to the West. Those remaining would be sent home soon.

I stretched my legs out in front of me. I wore my denim mini-skirt, sandals and a soft pink cotton T-shirt.

"Nice tan," offered Chuck. Not bothering to hide his interest, as his eyes traveled up and down my legs.

"We go to the beach." I leaned back on my hands. "So, how did you and Romy meet?"

"The usual way. Introduced by friends." He didn't contribute any details.

"She's so quiet," I said.

"Yeah, Romy's a lover not a talker."

"She's very pretty."

"Old T.K. thinks so, too."

"He looks, but he doesn't touch."

"How do you know?"

I turned to Chuck and smiled, a "just between us" smile.

He said, "You hold the purse strings, don't you? God, I couldn't stand that."

A bicycle came round the corner and sped down the street toward us. A lean Asian man jumped off, and propped the bike against the building. Breathless, he apologized for being late, while Chuck stood up, and apparently relishing every moment of his righteous anger, chewed out the man in a bizarre combination of gutter English and pidgin German. Seemingly used to the tirades, Ho Dung stood and stared stoically at the sidewalk.

"Could we please get the groceries?" I asked, interrupting the harangue. "I've got to get back and cook the rice." Chuck scowled and pulled open the door to the grocery store.

"Probably try to sell us water buffalo testicles."

I offered Ho Dung my hand and spoke in German. "Zara Wentz. It's very nice of you to help us out." He answered in an idiomatic German that put mine to shame. I handed over my translated ingredient list that he scanned, nodding.

The interior of the shop was dark and even out on the sidewalk we had received whiffs of pungent and medicinal smells.

The tiny store was jammed floor to ceiling with dried everything— octopus, mushrooms, whole ducks, and piles of things I couldn't even guess at. Boxes competed for space with dark jars and baskets and burlap bags. While Ho chatted with the proprietor, Chuck muttered, 'eye of newt and toe of frog.'

We waited, with Chuck drumming his knuckles on the counter, while the proprietor found each item. In a few minutes we had everything. Ho Dung, who had been pressed into service this evening to slice, chop and serve, promised he would meet up with us at Chuck and Romy's place in a few hours.

Chuck and I got into the Beemer and I drove down the Frankendamm, turned and started across the long bridge toward the thatched roof cottage on the road between Putbus and Sellin. Echoing Edgar's phrase, Chuck told me again, in his smooth, glib voice, how very good he was at making money, and what a bundle he was going to make in a few months.

"Not as much as your late husband piled up, but enough to buy the cottage, refit the boat, and buy Romy a crown Sable."

"Oh, fur!" I wailed. "One doesn't wear fur anymore."

He didn't hear me. "I've got some gilt edged software. And so many buyers, that it's...it's kind of a candy store problem."

I smiled at him, and didn't ask a single question.

~ * ~

Romy's cottage kitchen was high on charm and low on convenience. I liked the cat-patterned lace curtains lining the window overlooking the garden, the copper molds above the worktable, and the red tiled floor. The appliances looked like miniatures lined up against one wall of that boxy space: a two-burner stove and the refrigerator barely big enough for a dorm room. Forget about a dishwasher, microwave or Cuisinart. Forget about cupboards.

I had two pots of water boiling for the rice, and now I needed a burner to scramble the eggs. Julia Child and Betty Crocker between them would have been challenged to put a meal together.

Romy had co-opted T.K. for a shopping trip. Alone with Chuck, I put him to work sharpening knives. If he reminded me one more time that he absolutely hated celery and "don't sneak any in, because I can detect two parts per million," I would whack him over the head with the closest blunt object. The rolling pin, however clichéd, would do nicely.

~ * ~

Yesterday after T.K. and I left the Albatross, we met up with Putnam in a dark bar in Binz. The boys had seized on the advantages that access to the cottage would bring in a social situation. Putnam even complimented me on my cleverness in arranging a party. I accepted the kudos.

Over a few Pilseners, T.K. and Bill debated whether to use this opportunity to search for Chuck's stolen CD. They implied their activities were men's work, and if I promised to be vigilant, I would be allowed to act as lookout.

Sometime during the drinking, I had been jarred into the realization that Zara's plan was toast. T.K. and I had pinned our hopes on the birds of a feather theory, assuming Chuck would sense the kindred spirit of a con man in T.K. and strike up a palsy-walsy friendship. But Chuck didn't like T.K. Why bother with him when Mrs. Wentz had the checkbook?

~ * ~

In the cottage kitchen, Chuck offered to make us salami and cheese sandwiches. I watched while he sliced a tomato and a pickle, and opened a bottle of wine.

"We can sit in the garden," he said. "It's the best thing about this place." He put our lunch on a tray and headed out the door. Looking over his shoulder, he winked at me. "No, the garden's the second best thing. The first is my new cook."

Talk a little, flirt a little—humor him.

~ * ~

Back in our hotel room before the party, I asked T.K., "Who were the West Sea Pirates? They were raiding the coast here in the 14th century, and the town is plastered with posters for a festival. It's also the name of that rock group."

T.K. interrupted the buttoning of his shirt and paused to reflect. "This island is still swarming with West Sea Pirates. All the carpetbaggers from the West, trying to make a buck off the reunification, with Chuck the biggest buccaneer of them all." He gestured toward the balcony and the water. "The Russkies, of course, living off this land since the war. Include the Stasi, feeding off fear and secrets." He went back to his shirt buttons. "Even you and I, Zara, we're all West Sea Pirates."

T.K. finished dressing and began to roll a few joints, which he stashed in a leather cigarette case. The goodies for Chuck.

"In case we need to escalate our friendship with Goodborn," he said glancing up at me. He noticed I wasn't displaying any enthusiasm.

"An adventurous girl like you must have done a few drugs."

"Quite a few," I said, "but that was a long time ago, and I never pushed them on anyone."

"Nevertheless..." His voice trailed off.

From day one, I hadn't liked the "goodies" idea, but I hadn't won that argument.

I began pawing through the wardrobe for something to wear, selecting black silk slacks, black sandals with a little heel, and a white linen shirt. Later, when I emerged from the bathroom with makeup and good hair, T.K. looked up and said, "Very, very nice! No wonder you had old Bill speculating you were a sex spy!"

I winced at the memory.

"With Putnam's rants and your arrest, I forgot to tell you what I found out about Romy yesterday."

T.K. raised his eyebrows. Well-versed in recent German history, he knew the sex spy background. During the years when the Cold War sizzled, East German spymasters had advised, "Go West, young man," and sent out agents whose mission was to seduce secretaries and administrative assistants with jobs in sensitive government bureaus in West Germany. After pillow talk, and even marriage, some women had been sweet-talked into spying for these Romeos. When they tried to branch out to the United States, the East Germans discovered American women were too independent to want to marry these smarmy Don Juans, but the resourceful spymasters had also recruited a handful of attractive German women to reel in the American men.

"The PI discovered the FBI investigated Romy," I said. "Twice." I paused to put on some big hoop earrings. "Except for the fact that she's a woman, she'd fit the profile of an East German Romeo spy perfectly. Young. Single. Good looking. Opportunistic. She went from a modeling job in Düsseldorf to Los Angeles, then on to an administrative assistant position in a high-tech firm. She worked in three different firms. Two in Silicon Valley and then in Portland, at Maine Mining. One of the outfits made cryptology software. Every career move gave her access to better information-stealing opportunities."

"They never pinned anything on her?" He rubbed his chin.

"The PI said they followed her and tapped her phone. Found out zilch. She always had a boyfriend where she worked, but never a live-in. Weekend sex only. If she was getting information from the boyfriend, she was discreet and professional."

T.K. grinned. "My kind of woman."

"She lived on her salary. Went back to Germany for a vacation every year. While she was at Maine Mining, she went on vacations with Chuck."

"Anything else?" T.K. lit a cigarette and tossed the match into the ashtray. "The PI thought we should know her profile tripped the FBI alarms."

I grabbed my handbag and stood by the door, waiting for T.K.

He frowned while he smoked. "If she was spying, it would be dangerous for her to come back here. Her name might be in one of the files that never made it to Stralsund…or to the shredder."

He opened the door and we stepped into the hall.

"The locals wouldn't care if she spied on foreigners," I said. "But the West Germans might have passed the names of the old agents to their allies. It would have been even more dangerous for her to stay abroad."

We chewed on the subject of Frau Romy Motte all the way back to the cottage.

~ * ~

That evening Chuck was in a foul mood when we arrived, stalking around slamming doors, hassling Ho Dung and storming through the kitchen.

"Will you lighten up?" I was trying to slide my short cakes into the oven. From the way he stopped and glared at me, I had the impression no one ever crossed him.

"Everyone gets party jitters."

"Does T.K. get party jitters?" he asked in a sneering tone.

"T.K.'s a party animal. He's jittery when he can't party."

Chuck perched on a kitchen stool and watched critically as I sectioned an orange.

"Is the cook up for a glass of wine?" he asked in a civil voice.

"Is she ever!"

When he handed me the wineglass, he stared at my linen shirt. "I liked the see-through number a lot better."

"My husband thought it was immodest."

Chuck took a sip of whatever he was drinking. It could have been ice water, vodka or any of the colorless varieties of schnapps. My vote went to vodka.

"So the guy isn't really so careless of his wife?"

"He isn't careless at all."

He shrugged and wandered off.

My plans didn't include having to fend off Chuck this evening. Full of jitters myself, I roamed about with my Olympus capturing the final moments before the guests arrived.

Ho Dung posed wearing a wide grin, a chef's hat and a white apron, stirring rice in a big iron skillet. The camera caught T.K., sleeves rolled up to his elbows tossing the salad in a big white enameled dishpan.

Chuck changed into tan linen slacks and a soft polo shirt the color of ripe strawberries. I snapped his photo as he pulled the cork out of a wine bottle.

Romy, glamorous in a pink silk shirt and a long, sinuous, sarong-styled print skirt greeted the guests, who arrived en masse.

Anatoly, Bill and the ship's doctor drove from Sassnitz. Putnam's eyes glowed like cobalt beads as he purred, "Good evening, Mrs. Wentz. Haven't seen you in a dog's age."

My nerves would snap if he went into his dog routine. Only a week had passed since The Night of the Dog.

The ship's doctor's name was Vladimir, and T.K. whispered, "beware of Vlad the Impaler."

Sabine and Bodo arrived with their daughter Andrea. She was the girl with the strong, supple figure who had been on the porch stairs with the "It's gonna be a bright, bright sunshiny day" musicians. The band's concert posters were plastered all over Binz.

Andrea had her father's dark hair and eyes, without his brooding, feral features. Chuck wandered over and whispered in her ear. Whatever he said made her smile. Edgar was right. Chuck attracted women like ants to a picnic.

Wulf Mueller appeared last with the teacher. A brunette with a sharp nose, thin lips and eyebrows like swallows, she wore a halter that exposed the top of her ample white breasts. In a strong voice she said the inevitable "Hallo."

Chuck, shook her hand, let his glance linger on her chest, and said, aside, "I think I'm in love."

He insisted on first names—none of that "Herr and Frau horse shit" at his party. The teacher's name was Uta, and not only did she have the breast advantage but also the linguistic advantage, for she spoke excellent Russian and passable English.

The cottage was furnished in a mixture of casual wicker and more formal year-round pieces. Pale blue runners covered the parquet in the living room, where the Germans stood uneasily. Sabine and Uta cast unsocialistic glances of envy at the yellow and white upholstery of Romy's new Finnish furniture.

As the filmy curtains lifted on the evening breeze, the guests, primed by alcohol, strayed from their tight little cliques and gradually began to mix. Wulf's friend Uta, looking serious and intellectual in spite of her décolletage and frizzy hair, held T.K.'s and Anatoly's attention while she lamented about the lost chance to create "our long held dream of a democratic socialist state." From time to time she glanced at Wulf, who stood in a huddle with Bodo and Sabine at the other end of the room.

With his golden goat eyes beaming a satyr-like smile, Wulf constantly turned his head to observe everyone, paying particular attention to Putnam and Vlad who were chatting up Romy. Chuck kept glancing at those three while he made his rounds with the wine bottle. He poured Andrea an extra-large portion, and gave her a dazzling smile, setting off a danger ahead alarm in my brain.

Conversations remained muted, and the guests acted extravagantly polite, as if everyone waited for something to happen. We hadn't yet drunk enough to ramp up the noise level, and I began to wonder if we were going to eat the roast pork or wake it.

At eight o'clock, Romy lit the hurricane lanterns on the long table in the garden. The guests charged out of the house in a body, like an edgy, combustible herd primed to stampede.

~ * ~

As we ate the roast pork fried rice, Bodo got a big laugh from the group when he wondered when the always-present-at-every-German-meal steaming bowl of boiled potatoes would be served.

Looking down the long table, I couldn't believe that only a week ago, these people had been strangers. *They're still unknown quantities.*

Both Uta and Andrea looked animated as they listened to T.K., who wore an easy smile while he delivered one of his endless supplies of East German jokes. Chuck gazed at Andrea until her father noticed and never took his eyes off Chuck. Anatoly left the table and returned with two bottles of chilled vodka. Romy brought out little glasses, and the toasts began.

I excused myself to return to the kitchen and show Ho Dung how to assemble the strawberry shortcakes.

In the garden, each toast turned up the noise level. I checked to make sure everyone was at the table, and then I scooted down the hall toward the back of the house and opened the door to the master bedroom. I slipped in and stood for a moment, looking around. Instead of a closet, German bedrooms have ungainly crate-like wooden wardrobes. The bedroom held two of these monsters. Feather beds. Clothes tossed all over, even on the floor. Romy's dressing table a jumble of cosmetics and brushes. A laptop, undoubtedly Chuck's sat on an old-fashioned treadle sewing machine cabinet. Would I ever love to get a look at Chuck's computer files. I listened by the door to make sure no one was coming before I did a furtive perusal of the drawer in each nightstand. Nothing very interesting, like a CD-ROM. I knew the CD bore Maine Mining's logo and the word 'Aristotle.' It was the third copy of five.

Muted voices, coming closer, outside the window. A man and a woman. I ducked down below the windowsill. Staccato bursts of German. I caught words, but nothing that made sense. Ready to duck again, I peeked over the windowsill. Romy and Wulf stood not two feet away. She had her back to me, and I couldn't see her face. He spoke in quiet, menacing voice, *"Sei vorsichtig! Das kann schief gehen!"*

Sei vorsichtig. "Be careful."

I couldn't translate the other phrase. Wulf grabbed her arm above the elbow and she angrily wrenched it away.

Still ducking, I scuttled across the room, opened the door and charged smack into T.K. I gasped and nearly screamed. He inhaled sharply. It was a tossup who was more surprised.

"Holy damn!" he said. "What are you doing? Hustle your buns back to the garden. Your dessert is being served."

"What does '*Das kann schief gehen*' mean?"

"Who said that?"

"I'll tell you later. Tell me what it means."

"Literally, 'it can go crooked.' Idiomatically, it can blow up in your face...it can shit the bed...it can—."

"I got the idea."

~ * ~

Carrying the last strawberry-piled plates, I walked into the garden. Romy and Wulf appeared from different directions and took their places at the table. They looked nonchalant, except Romy's cheeks were mottled, as if she had applied rose blusher with a bad case of the shakes.

Flushed from the vodka, Uta stood with her glass raised. She offered her toast in three languages; first in German, which caused Sabine to wipe away a tear, then in Russian, while Anatoly and Vlad nodded their heads. She brushed her frizzy bangs out of her eyes, and started again in English.

"Until this year such a night as tonight, and such a gathering as this, could not take place." She looked around. "With Germans, Americans, Russians, British, even Vietnamese, coming together in friendship." Everyone looked solemn. Chuck, smoking a big cigar, leaned back in his chair. Carrying back the used dessert plates, Ho Dung paused respectfully on the grass.

She continued, "Some of us had a dream of creating a truly democratic socialist state, a state which would combine many of the freedoms from the West with the respect and nurturance of working people and their needs that we always maintained here in the East."

Putnam glanced at T.K., who stared off into the distance beyond the garden. Impassive, Bodo and Wulf sat clasping their glasses.

"We are regretful our long held dream will not become reality."

Chuck began to fidget. Ho Dung disappeared into the kitchen. Andrea yawned.

"A friendly international occasion such as this with people of different ideologies, gives us the hope that the future will also be replete with friendship and good will for all."

Under his breath, Chuck muttered, "Merry Christmas to all and to all a good night."

Uta raised her glass. "To the future."

I took a sip, slipped my glass under the table and poured the vodka onto the lawn. Other toasts followed, to the host, to the hostess, to the chef, even to me. Andrea was knocking back the booze with the adults.

Chuck plopped down on the bench next to me and threw his arm around me like we were old friends.

"How did you like the toasts?" I asked.

"Too much Commie claptrap."

T.K. came up to the table and asked very casually, as if he didn't much care, "Goodborn, are you trying to put the make on my wife?"

"I would, but she refuses to get drunk," Chuck said, dropping his arm. "She's all yours." He stood up and lumbered into the house.

"Who did you overhear?" T.K. asked, sitting down next to me.

"Wulf and Romy." I told him how I happened to be in a position to eavesdrop. He said, "Buttercup, you never cease to amaze." He paused, and added, "But let Billy Boy and T.K. handle the operational areas."

We parted after deciding I should flirt with Chuck while Putnam kept Romy occupied, so T.K. could have another go at the bedroom.

Before I could look for Chuck, Anatoly found me. "How is arm?" He asked, in very halting English, brushing my shoulder with his fingers.

"Arm is much better."

"We walk, Okay?" He opened the garden gate to the driveway, where the dog had jumped us.

Anatoly took my hand and we strolled down the driveway toward the road. The roseate clouds hovered above the horizon, and overhead, the pale blue bled into a darker Prussian blue. Anatoly plucked a few daisies.

"You marry wrong man." He turned his sad, handsome face to me, and his mournful eyes met mine.

"I don't think so." I tried to keep my voice light.

"Why him?" he demanded, waving his hand in the direction of the cottage. "Why him?" he asked again when I didn't respond.

"I bought him," I said, somewhat coldly. He nodded, as if my explanation had already occurred to him. Then he switched to German, and when I grasped what he said, my cheeks must have rivaled the sunset for color. "You need a lover." He paused, and said matter-of-factly, "I am artist on mattress."

I didn't know whether to be appalled or amused, and I stared at him.

He frowned slightly and he threw his shoulders back like he was ready to salute. "You need real man," he said. "Not gigolo."

"We'll talk about it later," I said, and turned to the short path leading to the front door of the cottage. He followed, unperturbed, and held out his handful of daisies. "You are very exciting, Zara, very exciting."

In the living room, they had rolled up the rugs, and Putnam and Vladimir were doing an energetic Cossack dance to Russian music pounding out of the boom box. Squatting with their arms crossed in front of their chests, they thrust their feet out in front in a movement requiring thighs of iron. Sabine flushed when Bodo jumped in to try. Strong, but awkward, he grunted and sweated and eventually got the hang of it. Everyone stood around the dancers, applauding. Wulf Mueller emitted a bleating laugh that matched his goat-like features.

When the music stopped, Putnam sat down on the love seat and T.K. joined him. They talked quietly, heads together, while Putnam caught his breath. The signal. I found Chuck in the kitchen and asked him to scare up a drink for me. His eyes had a glassy, truculent look, but he opened a bottle of Mosel and poured a glass. I led him away from the sink where Ho Dung was finishing the dish washing, and to the cozy corner table with the upholstered bench.

"So, Chuck," I said, sitting close to him. "Tell me how you plan to make all this money you keep talking about."

Instead of an answer, Chuck thrust both hands under my shirt.

"God, I've wanted to do this all week," he murmured, moving his fingers across my breasts. I grabbed his wrists and forced his hands away from me.

"Keep your paws to yourself!"

There was no fine print in my contract requiring me to submit to anyone's groping, but I wanted Chuck to stick around until T.K. and Putnam had finished snooping.

Chuck's eyes had a stony look, and for a moment I thought he would storm off.

"So prim and proper, Mrs. Wentz. I'd like to see you sloshed some time."

"Oh I'm not as big a stick-in-the-mud as everyone thinks."

He stood up and went round the corner into the kitchen, shouting, "Ice cubes! *Mach schnell!*" Ho Dung answered softly and I heard the refrigerator door open. Chuck returned with a bottle of vodka and a glass. A moment later, Ho Dung placed a bowl of miniature ice cubes and a plate with slices of lemon on the table and left.

As he set about making his drink, Chuck asked, "Know anything about computers?"

"I love my word processor and my electronic address book," I gushed, slipping back into my Mrs. Wentz persona.

"Ever hear of a data warehouse?" He jiggled the ice around in his glass and took a big swig of vodka.

"That's something for big businesses, not a lady with a laptop."

"I've got one to sell. And I've found a couple of customers. Right here." He drank again.

"That's wonderful," I said. "Starting your own business? There's so much opportunity here, long term."

"I think short term. In and out."

"You and T.K. think alike." I didn't want to appear too curious or knowledgeable.

Chuck continued in a voice of absolute confidence. "With my software, they can leapfrog three or four generations. Practically from punch cards to client-server in one big jump."

"I'm not very technical, but I'd love to hear you explain how it works."

I could barely contain my excitement. Chuck was ready to spill the beans.

"This weekend," he said. "On the boat there's nothing to do but talk. At least nothing you would want to do." His eyes had that mean stare again.

"Sorry." I put my hand on his and took a sip of wine, wondering if I could mend fences without awkward sexual overtones.

"Will you go skinny dipping off the boat?" he asked, leaning back against the bench.

"Oh, I might. Now, tell me more about the new business of yours. Do you have customers lined up?"

"Yeah. Wulf has an interested 'friend.' He's trying to raise cash. I wonder if the 'friend' isn't Wulf himself. He was some big Commie honcho until last fall. Lost his job. Likewise old Bodo. Those two are thick as thieves."

"Whatever would Wulf do with a data warehouse?" I asked. Chuck's elbow dug into my ribs about the same time I noticed Wulf standing not six feet away from us, eyeing Chuck and me at the table, a picture of coziness. I hoped he hadn't overheard us.

I motioned for Wulf to join us. "We were just talking about you," I said. "This is such a terrific house. How can you bear not living here? That wonderful garden."

He flashed his caprine smile, raised his glass in a silent toast, and seated himself on a chair across from us. Did he give Chuck a cold and cautioning stare?

Chuck rattled the ice in his drink again and didn't seem so ebullient. Wulf had not responded to my question. Just then Sabine came into the kitchen, interrupting the awkward silence. She said that she had to be at the spa early in the morning, and thanked us for the evening.

Probably wanting to see Andrea before she left, Chuck leaped up and followed Sabine. As the always-scrupulous-in-the-performance-of-her social-duties Mrs. Wentz, I made my apologies to Wulf and went into the living room to say goodbye to the Schulds.

The tape serenaded an empty room. On the lawn, still tossing back the vodka, Anatoly and Vlad sprawled in the garden chairs. Why wasn't Putnam talking to Romy, dancing with Romy, drinking with Romy? This didn't look like plan A.

Ho Dung left on his bicycle, and the Schuld family drove off after Chuck had a quick whispered conference with Andrea.

When I asked Anatoly and Vlad where everyone was, Anatoly answered, "You are here is enough."

I stayed to chat for a moment, still wondering where the others were. T.K. presumably, was snooping.

In the woods behind the garden shed, a woman shrieked with laughter. We heard the sound of running feet, then splashing water, and a male voice roared *"Koteleti Pojarski!"* Another splash and more feminine laughter.

Anatoly and Vlad left through the garden gate and down the dark path toward the noise. I followed, picking my way through the murky shadows. When I came into the clearing, the moonlight revealed two heads bobbing in the silvery water. Uta and Putnam! Putnam, not distracting Romy, but cavorting in the pond.

I did a double take as I realized Anatoly and Vlad were stripping off their clothes. Before their white butts and thrashing legs disappeared into the water, T.K. popped up by my side.

"Putnam is in the pond. Have you seen Romy?"

He was already out of his shoes and shirt, saying, "Come on, there's nothing like a bare naked party to cement international friendships."

"Are you mad?"

Someday I would write a job description for this assignment, one that would include getting naked on every possible occasion.

"I'll explain later." Off came the khakis.

"Did you find out anything?" I slipped out of my clothes. T.K. and I looked ghostly pale, like celadon statues, posing in the moonlight.

"Nada."

I hung the white linen shirt and my slacks on a bush. "Well, did you snoop or plant a bug?"

"Zara, for Chrissakes, hurry up! It's not every day we have a chance to skinny dip with the KGB."

"What?"

But T.K. was already running toward the pond. Not knowing what else to do, I followed him into the water. Go along to get along had created bizarre experiences. This would be another one.

Gasping from the cold, we splashed around. Soon the temperature felt fine. Chuck and Wulf appeared, and Chuck shed his clothes and waded in among us. He had a nice body.

Wulf skulked along the path, insisting he was "standing guard."

At last Romy appeared and walked down to the water's edge. The guys all wheedled her to come in, but she put her hands on her hips and said we were *verrückt*.

Chuck bellowed, "Sweetheart, pretty please with plum butter," and T.K. yelled, "it would be the perfect end to a perfect party," but Romy couldn't be coaxed. The Russians shouted something unintelligible. Putnam's bizarre battle cry, "*Koteleti Pojarski*!" sounded again.

While they were all distracted by Romy, I made a break for the shore. T.K., that rat, roared, "another moon is rising in the south," and the men hooted and applauded as I yanked my big linen shirt off the bush and tried to pull it over my drippy wet back and arms. I grabbed my underwear, shoes and slacks and ran shivering toward the cottage, right past Wulf, who again raised his glass in a priggish little salute.

While the swimmers staggered out of the water, dried off, and dressed, I made a pot of tea, and laced it with rum. Now more subdued, we huddled around the big white table in the living room, warming our hands on the hot cups. The cold dip, for all its hilarity, had a sobering effect on everyone, and the others left after midnight.

In the living room, Chuck dimmed the lights, and put on a tape, while Romy poured refills from a second pot of tea. T.K. and I sat on the love seat. I rested my head on his shoulder while he rubbed the cold out of my feet and ankles. He was unusually quiet.

Chuck stared at Romy. "You were a real party pooper."

"I didn't feel like getting naked with that crowd."

He made a disbelieving face.

"It's a girl thing," I said, backing her up.

T.K. pulled the leather case out of his pocket.

"What ya got there, T.K.? More cigars?"

T.K. said, "Such a great party shouldn't end without smoking some first rate weed."

Chuck said, "Amen, brother."

Romy's face was impassive. Chuck looked from her to me and said, "Will little Miss Party Poop and Little Miss Prim and Proper take a few hits?"

"I might," I said.

After a long pause, Romy answered, "A few."

The joint made us mellow, and we sipped tea and listened to the pulsing song from the Berlin disco with the lyrics about a special night of lust and love.

Romy sat on Chuck's lap and T.K. and I curled up together. He seemed subdued. I told them about Bill and Uta racing naked into the pond from the garden shed. Chuck said there was an old chaise longue in the shed. Romy guessed Uta, as a frequent guest when Wulf was living here would have known about the chaise.

In a dreamy voice Chuck said, "Uta really has nice big bazongas."

"And nice big feet to match," I added.

Chuck and I got pretty silly, until T.K. looked at the clock and said, "The sun also rises."

It was two a.m.

When we got up to leave, Chuck said, "Nine o'clock Friday morning, Lauterbach harbor. You girls can get together tomorrow and plan the food. Wentz, if you have any more of that great weed..."

"Gotcha."

~ * ~

On the way back to the hotel, T.K. drove slowly, with his arm around me, sometimes taking his hand off the wheel to rub his chin. If he didn't want to talk about his search for the CD-ROM, I had another topic even more interesting.

"Why did you say we were skinny dipping with the KGB? Anatoly bad-mouthed the KGB. Don't you remember?"

"Sixth sense," said T.K. "Those two have too much freedom to socialize."

"Anatoly hates the KGB," I repeated.

"We'll see." T.K. leaned over and kissed my hair.

At least nothing had derailed the evening and scrambled our plans. Home free.

When we got out of the car at the hotel T.K. said, "Zara, sweetie, I fucked up big time."

"What happened?" I asked, turning to face him, uncertain whether I even wanted to know.

We stood in the parking lot behind the hotel. My one desire was to shed my clothes, crawl into the big bathtub, rinse off the moss, the sand, and the pond scum, and fall into bed.

T.K. didn't answer as we trudged around the hotel to the Strand Promenade. The night was so still that I could hear the water sloshing against the pier. T.K. let out a sigh that sounded more like a groan, and took my arm. We started to walk toward the quiet center of town, and I asked again, "What happened?"

He turned right at the intersection and we walked past the bandstand and the big placards where the town posted the water temperature, and began the trek down the long wooden pier. Our hollow footsteps and the little waves lapping at the shore were the only sounds. There was a whispery smell of ocean. T.K. lit a cigarette, and tossed the match over the railing.

"I told Bill to distract Romy, because I was going to search the bedroom. You were to keep company with Chuck. I thought I had clear sailing."

T.K. stopped in the middle of the pier and faced me.

"The lady of the house caught me red handed. Going through one of her wardrobe shelves."

"Oh God, what did you do?"

He started walking again. Out at sea, the lights of a lone freighter tracked slowly across the water.

"I made it worse."

"What could be any worse? What did you say?" I felt like jumping off the pier in utter frustration.

"She was all whipped up. Looking at me like I'd climbed out of the sewer. So I tried to make love to her."

"You did what?"

"It was all I could think of. I said I was looking around while I waited for her."

"Oh, T.K., really." I felt completely deflated.

"I laid it on with a trowel. Said she was the most beautiful woman I'd ever met. Confessed I was crazy about her." He gave a rueful shrug. "Christ, she got even angrier. Totally bullshit. Obviously didn't believe a word of it. Said I was a 'disgusting parasite,' and a 'rotten excuse for a man.'"

"Well, at least she bought into your character," I said feebly, but I was actually feeling stabs of jealously, even as he confessed to being turned down. Tonight when he had danced with her, he had turned on his magnetic mix of boyish charm and suavity.

"What?" T.K. asked, looking at me.

"Nothing. I'm cold."

"Oh God, I knew telling you would only make it worse."

"Don't be silly. Please explain how this awful scene played out."

"She threatened to tell Goodborn. She said she wanted to 'put an end to this ugly charade.' I had to find out what she meant by that. 'What charade?' I asked. She clammed up." He hesitated, staring out at the water. "I threw her words back at her. What she told Wulf. '*Ja, das kann schief gehen.*' I said. 'It can go crooked.' I've never seen the color fade out of anyone's face so fast. Then we heard all the shouting at the pond. I said, 'sorry to have been such a royal pain in the butt,' and I left."

"Why didn't Putnam distract Romy as planned? Is he trying to sabotage us?"

T.K. shrugged. "Very uncharacteristic of him to bungle like that."

Nobody spoke for a few moments.

"As for being caught snooping," I said, returning to a hateful subject, "We can discuss damage control—do a worst case, best case analysis. But not tonight. I'm too tired."

We were at the end of the pier, surrounded by restless black water. The faint breeze blew through my shirt, making me shiver. Somewhere across the water lay Sweden. Along the dark horizon, a thin gold thread became visible. T.K. put his arm around me. "I only want one girl and that's you, Sweet Pea."

Yeah, right.

Ten

The morning sun beamed out of a blue sky spotted with plump white clouds. A light breeze ruffled the trees and played through the halyards of the scattered yachts in the little basin, as t*he Painted Cow* left the Lauterbach dock and motored out of the harbor.

I stood on the bow, and as the breeze freshened, I jammed the Chicago Cubs baseball cap down on my head and smiled back at T.K., who lounged in the cockpit looking cool in a soft denim shirt and tan shorts. Chuck had the tiller, and Romy was below in the cabin stowing provisions. From the dock, Putnam gave us a crisp farewell salute.

We "girls" had not gotten together to plan the food. The day after the party Romy had left a message that she would take care of everything.

Our worst-case scenario, Chuck rescinding his invitation, had not occurred, which meant we were either in best case, or most likely case. Best case was that Romy had kept her mouth shut. Most likely case was that she blabbed to Chuck about T.K.'s snooping and his proposition, but Chuck, according to his own agenda, would sever diplomatic relations later or not at all.

Now, with all the klutziness of hopeless landlubbers, T.K., Romy and I hoisted the mainsail while Chuck, having morphed into Captain Bligh, alternately swore and yelled directions at us. Then T.K. held the tiller while Chuck continued to mutter about our inadequacies while he raised the foresail, as if to say, "look, you idiots, it's this simple."

Moments later, he cut the engine, and the only sounds were the creak of the boat and the wind filling the dark maroon canvas.

My ex and I had cruised out of Chicago's Burnham Harbor aboard a friend's yacht, but content to work in the galley, I hadn't mastered sails and winches. T.K. professed "a total lack of knowledge of all things nautical except for the cocktail flag." And on the Zeesboot, Romy seemed as clueless as the rest of us in managing the baroque suite of strangely placed sails and the gaff rigging.

In the cockpit, T.K. and Chuck lit cigars, and although it was only ten in the morning, Chuck hollered down through the companionway. "Bloody Marys, right away, chop! chop!" Romy murmured it was a "little early for that," and Chuck frowned and stuck out his lower lip, so T.K. tried to smooth things over, the sun had to be over the yardarm somewhere, and offered to mix the drinks.

Romy snapped, "I'll do it!" and I could see her below in the cabin, making an angry face as she pulled a big can of tomato juice from the depths of the built-in ice chest. The galley had primitive cooking facilities: a two-burner gimbaled alcohol stove, and an old copper sink with a pump. A charcoal heater would furnish warmth, if needed.

Chuck said the boat had been remodeled into a cruising yacht after its days as an eeler had passed, but one glance at the bunks and the primitive head made me pity the hardy eel fisherman, if this was the renovated Zeesboot.

Romy brought up two drinks; one festooned with a stalk of celery. "You, too?" she asked, coolly. I said, "Oh, why not? After all, we're on vacation."

"Do I have my first mate trained or not?" Chuck asked. T.K. smiled and nodded.

Romy disappeared back into the cabin and again I heard the vicious chip, chip, chip of the ice pick. She remained an enigma to me, for although she always chatted easily with Sabine and Uta, in the time I had known her, we had exchanged only a few words. I felt her mistrust, and held back from pushing unwanted intimacy. When she came up on deck, she handed me a drink, then stood close to Chuck, rubbing his neck and shoulders with her long fingers.

While I sipped my drink, I studied one of the charts that Anatoly had given Chuck. Hiddensee, a thin island shaped like an underfed sea horse with his tail dragging, lies directly off the west coast of Rügen, just north of mainland Germany. We could have cruised out into the Baltic and all around Rügen, approaching Hiddensee from the north, but a Zeesboot was designed for coastal waters, so we were keeping to the shallow bay or Bodden, and sailing around the southwest tip of the island and through a narrow passage that would take us into the Stralsund Harbor, and on up to the island. Protected from the open sea and never far from land.

The wind picked up as we sailed across the Bodden.

"For lunch, we'll drop anchor inside a little cove." Chuck pointed to the chart. "Right there. Glewitzer Ort. Kubitzer Bodden..." He pointed to a bay north of Stralsund. "God, these names can sprain your tongue."

Except for a few fishermen and an excursion boat, we had the bay to ourselves. Chuck mentioned yachts from West Germany, Sweden and Denmark were beginning to visit the island's harbors now that the "politics were friendlier." He reckoned we would reach Stralsund and the Rügendamm around four or five in the afternoon, and if we didn't have to wait around "for those goddamn lazy clowns to raise the drawbridge," we would make Hiddensee about nine, just in time for a swim and a late dinner.

The morning passed pleasantly, with the brisk breeze moving us along, the green coast and the fields of Rügen in the distance, and captain and crew hammered on Bloody Marys.

Anatoly had provided enough charts of the Baltic waters to supply an armada. As we rounded a spit of land, Chuck sent me into the cabin to look for one of them. "In the cupboard above the bunk," he said.

That's where I was searching when I stumbled on the CD-ROM. With Aristotle written across the building blocks on the label, it was stashed inside two zip-lock bags. My fingers began to tremble, because I recognized it right away, and at the same moment my heart started pounding, Chuck yelled, "Never mind! Never mind!" sounding kind of panicky and I just knew he had remembered what was hidden away under the charts. I grabbed the one marked Greifswalder Bodden and carried it topside. When I re-joined the group in the cockpit, Chuck gave me a suspicious stare, so I took off my sunglasses, looked him right in the eye, and gave him a big dumb smile.

"When can I take the helm?"

Chuck said, "As soon as we round that point."

T.K. slouched against the cushions, gazing across the water as he rubbed sunscreen over his nose. My heart was still a jackhammer against my breastbone, and I couldn't wait to tell him my astonishing news.

A few minutes later, we rounded the point amid a stream of contradictory instructions about the sails and the winches and a barrage of swearing, then Captain Bligh was all sweet reason again, and I took over the tiller and managed to keep us on course even though my thoughts were totally focused on the CD. Romy went below to fix lunch, while Chuck clambered to the bow to adjust a sail.

"I found it, I found his CD-ROM," I whispered to T.K.

"No shit?" He stared at me.

I told him where it was hidden.

"Zara, you are positively amazing. Are you sure?"

I told him I had seen the production label on the CD.

"I didn't have time to check the serial number."

Just then Chuck returned to the cockpit, and we had to change the subject. I wanted to get another look at what lay inside that plastic bag.

Savory smells wafted up from the galley. Captain Bligh took the helm again, and we tacked and headed up into a long, narrow inlet.

On the shore, we could see farmhouses, outbuildings, and spotted calves tethered to trees in an orchard. We brought the sails down with a whoosh and a clatter and another round of profanity from our captain. Of course, I screwed up, because I couldn't concentrate on anything except my new knowledge. T.K. looked blasé, but I wanted to jump up and down and yell "Eureka!"

Thinking maybe I could find another moment to myself in the galley, I helped Romy carry lunch up to the deck, but she was always right on my heels coming down the companionway.

We ate potato salad with long skinny frankfurters and thick sauerkraut tasting of bacon. Finding the CD-ROM had made me so jumpy I found myself taking a second helping of everything. Total pig out. Smacking his lips, Chuck admitted, "This Kraut food is all right."

Half an hour later, when we were underway again, Romy and I went below to clean up. I waited, dishtowel in hand, while she stood at the tarnished sink, lean tan legs bracing her body against the heeling of the boat, and methodically washed each blue plastic plate. The tendrils of dark hair trailing along her neck and ears curled slightly in the moist sea air. She wore a long-sleeved red sweater with a rolled collar, casually elegant against her white shorts.

Had I ever seen her smile except at Chuck? I felt torn between pity for a young woman whose life T.K. and I might casually wreck, and our suspicion that she was a hardened spy who was playing by her own secret rules. She had mentioned her family fled to West Germany the year before the Wall was built when she was just a little girl, but we had no way of verifying her history. If she were one of the sex spies, she would have an excellent legend. T.K. suspected her and Wulf Mueller of conspiring against Chuck. We still didn't know what her relationship to Mueller was.

Anatoly told Putnam Wulf and Bodo had been Stasi, but we hadn't verified that. We hadn't verified anything. Vlad and Anatoly could be KGB officers assigned to the Russian ship, having a terrific laugh playing doctor and captain to our gullibility. If Putnam's motto was "trust, but verify," why had he taken all these people at face value?

T.K. stuck his head down into the cabin and said, "You ladies are awfully quiet. Not plotting against us men, I hope." For an answer, I stuck my tongue out at him.

Around two-thirty the wind died, and we took down the sails and put-putted through the passage that ran between the mainland and the island. Chuck downed bottle after bottle of beer, insisting, "Help me out, Pete. I hate to drink alone."

I had no opportunity to sneak another peek at the CD.

As predicted, we reached the drawbridge a few minutes after five. Heavy traffic crossing the Rügendamm caused a delay in its opening, and half a dozen boats waited for passage. Beside himself with impatience, Chuck narrowly missed ramming another sailboat. In an endless litany of blame, he cursed the drawbridge, the other captain, the Germans, and even the foreign buoys.

Quite sensibly, Romy climbed into a bunk and read a book, and I followed her lead, but Chuck's ranting was impossible to block out. When at last the drawbridge clanked and groaned and lifted to let the assembled flotilla pass through to the harbor, I went on deck to watch. Altefähr, the old town where T.K. and I stopped our first day on the island was on our starboard side. On a distant hill, I could see the lonely windmills with their blades turning slowly in the quiet afternoon air.

Presiding over a backdrop of trees and ancient church spires, the abandoned brick granaries of Stralsund were to port. Several freighters were tied up at the docks. A gigantic boat we had noticed on that first afternoon still floated stolidly in mid-harbor.

"What the hell is that big white tub?" Chuck asked.

"The *Fritz Hecker*," said T.K. "Offered cruises for the masses... for the Bodos and Sabines of the Democratic Republic. Except the workers didn't build a very reliable vessel. In fact, it should have been christened *Fritz Wrecker*." He paused. "Now it's confined to the harbor. A barracks ship."

"How the hell do you always know the stupidest damn details?" Chuck turned and stared at T.K., who never hesitated to share his knowledge of all things East German. More knowledge than a frivolous man ought to have. Chuck obviously thought so, too.

"Oh, my barber likes to gossip," T.K. said easily.

"My barber likes to cut hair and bore me to goddamn death with World Cup soccer chitchat. Like maybe I give a shit."

Chuck steered us toward the city side and flung his arm out in the direction of the largest storehouse.

"Big ugly suckers, aren't they? Some poor guy turned up dead in one a few weeks ago. A German, but he'd been in the States. Knew him slightly. We'd worked at the same company a while back." He hesitated, and spoke again in a matter-of-fact voice. "But you knew that, didn't you?"

I froze. Chuck had brought up the subject of Bruss, even insinuated we knew him? I looked from Chuck to T.K., whose brows contracted in puzzlement.

Chuck, hand on the tiller, smiled at our consternation. In the cabin, Romy still had her nose in a book. T.K. inclined his head toward me, a suggestion of a nod. Why did he want me to carry the ball? I could hardly breathe, but the voice of my alter ego, dim Mrs. Wentz gushed into the silence.

"Chuck, why didn't you tell us that you had lived in Chicago?"

Chuck's turn to be baffled. "I didn't."

"But you said we knew your colleague."

"Not in friggin' Chicago!" he barked. His furious eyes locked in on mine. T.K., staring across the harbor at the big granaries, smiled slightly.

"Well, how then?" I persisted. "How do we know him—what's your friend's name?"

"Your buddy Putnam," Chuck began, but I interrupted before he could continue.

"Oh, Bill Putnam. You mean Bill knows this man?"

Chuck's face reddened. At any moment he would lose his cool and start swearing at me, at T.K., at the world.

"Jesus, will you shut—your 'friend' Putnam has been all over town asking nosy questions about this guy."

T.K. chimed in. "Goodborn, what are you getting at? We only met Putnam the night before we met you."

"I don't know if Putnam knows your colleague, but he certainly knows Uta." I said, with a smug smile.

"Most likely in the biblical sense." T.K. stretched, grinned at Chuck, and took a swig of beer.

"Just forget the whole thing," he said, glowering. His bomb had fizzled into comical misunderstanding and sexual innuendo.

"Where did you say this man died?" I asked.

Chuck pointed toward the waterfront. "Over there in those goddamn bricks."

Romy joined us, and I turned to her and said, "Chuck was going to tell us about his dead friend."

Her lips parted slightly and she pushed a strand of hair behind her ear. She turned to Chuck. "What are you saying?"

"No one on this boat has an IQ over sixty!" he exploded, his eyes ferocious and even predatory. "You're all as dense as those freaking brick monsters. Nobody is dead! I never lived in Chicago. Bill Putnam is an English tourist and I am the King of Prussia!" He gave the tiller a savage twist, and the boat made a big sweeping arc and turned away from Stralsund. No one spoke as we headed back to the middle of the harbor.

T.K. disappeared into the cabin and came back up the companionway holding a bottle of beer, which he handed to Chuck.

"Sorry, Goodborn," he said. "It takes my wife to get everything totally twisted around."

Chuck said, "Yeah," and chugged the beer down in hasty gulps. Stifling a belch, he flipped the bottle overboard.

Romy, dark eyes wary, lips still parted, looked from Chuck to T.K. and then at me. "Who would they blame if there were no women?" she asked.

"Damned if I know," said T.K.

She turned her back and threaded her way to the bow where she sat for a long time, looking straight ahead, hunched up with her arms wrapped around her knees.

Chuck kept eyeing me, so I stayed away from the CD's hiding place. I wondered if he had bought our innocent routine.

As if to support Chuck's mood, ominous gray clouds appeared in the southwest, and soon the winds burst on us, first in puffs, then strong gusts. Romy returned from the bow and took the tiller, while T.K., Chuck and I scurried about yanking on lines, cranking winches, and raising the heavy canvas sails that luffed like crazy as Romy headed too close to the wind.

Heeling sharply, *Painted Cow* sluiced through the waves up the Kubitzer Bodden toward Hiddensee, and Chuck's mood became more frenzied as the hull picked up speed. He whooped at the wind and hoorayed as the instruments showed us edging up to six knots. The rain squall, driven by fierce drafts of wind, made the boat heel at an anxiety-producing tilt, and then we heard crashes in the galley as dishes and pots rattled around.

Oblivious to our discomfort Chuck seemed invigorated by the downpour. He only carried foul weather gear for two and we all looked like drowned rats with soppy clothes and wet hair plastered to our heads by the time he dragged the yellow slickers out of the locker. He and T.K. put them on, and I found a moth-eaten navy wool sweater, which provided enough warmth to keep my teeth from chattering. I would have been happy to drop anchor in a secluded cove and attempt to haul a few eels out of the Bodden, but Chuck's face showed wanton glee as he confronted the wind, the rain and his crew's wimpiness. Romy went below in the cabin and worked on getting the charcoal-stove going. Would I ever find another opportunity to check the CD?

At last we sailed into the lee of Hiddensee, where the boat was protected from the gusts. The rain settled into steady light drizzle.

"No skinny dipping tonight, Goodborn," said T.K.

Chuck grinned as he flicked his soggy cigar downwind into the water. "Now, Wentz, we'll allow the ladies to make that decision."

Romy, coming up from below with three mugs of steaming tea, winced at Chuck's words.

Oh God, it was going to be a long night.

~ * ~

It was still daylight when we came into the small harbor at the northern end of the island of Hiddensee. A cluster of houses with red tile roofs and stately trees sprouting out of the flat coast indicated a settlement.

No one appeared to admire the Zeesboot while we tied up to the small pier. Our only neighbor, anchored in the small basin on the opposite side of the pier, was a trim cruiser that looked spanking new. I borrowed Chuck's binoculars. The boat was the *Little Mermaid*, flying a red flag with a white cross.

"Danish," said T.K.

Half an hour later, toweled off and in dry clothing, we climbed onto the dock and went in search of the only restaurant, which was inside a small hotel, one of the red roofed buildings facing the water.

I had formed a tentative plan for getting the CD to safety, and craned my neck looking for a post office.

"Tomorrow, I'd like to buy postcards. For friends back in Chicago."

T.K. gave me a curious look, but I only smiled at him. With every minute that passed, I grew fonder of my idea, which followed Einstein's advice: "make everything as simple as possible, but not simpler."

We walked across the restaurant's veranda, where puddles had collected on the seats of the chairs and the tabletops, and water still dripped from the trees onto us and the gray flagstones.

T.K. sang a few bars of "McArthur Park."

"I always thought that was one of the saddest songs ever," said Chuck, in a wistful voice.

Inside the inn, we could hear animated talk and boisterous laughter. We climbed a half flight of stairs, entered a large dining room and found ourselves in the midst of a noisy gathering. The room, lit by masses of candles on the tables, was festooned with hay and garlands of herbs woven into rustic wagon wheels. Milk cans held big bouquets of purple and blue larkspurs.

The innkeeper escorted us to a secluded table in a small area adjoining the dining room.

"What's going on?" asked Chuck.

"Tomorrow is midsummer," replied the innkeeper. "The village will celebrate with a bonfire on the hill near the lighthouse." He smiled at us. "You would be most welcome. The young couples will dance around the fire. The older boys will light torches and run through the fields to scare away the witches. It's how we celebrate the solstice." He smiled again. "Would you like to join us?"

Chuck declined, saying we would be sailing back to Rügen. "What a bunch of superstitious crap!" he muttered after the host left the table. "We might as well be in the goddamn dark ages."

We walked back to the dock through a fine misty fog, and behind us, the lights of the inn faded into diffuse golden halos. The trim little Danish boat was gone, and *Painted Cow* had the waterfront to herself. We climbed aboard and sat in the cozy cabin. T.K. retrieved our bottle of brandy from a duffel bag, Chuck lit a sconce on the cabin wall, and Romy added charcoal to the stove. All the fresh air had put us in a tired stupor, and we sprawled around the table on the damp cushions, sipping brandy.

Through the open port holes I heard the water lapping against the hull and the creak of the boat straining against the mooring lines. The cabin felt warm and close, with our shadows large in the dim light. Chuck stretched his feet out as much as the cramped space allowed, and suggested we each confess something that would surprise everyone else at the table.

"Doesn't have to be dirty," he said. He looked at me and grinned. "Can be. Romy can start."

Romy's face flushed. She said, "Oh, let's not..." Her voice trailed off.

"Tell what you do at those goddamned hen parties. You and Sabine and Yvonne and—what's her name, with the dog? Irene."

"But I've only been twice," she protested.

"Tell them what you told me."

"We...we just give each other pedicures." Even in the murky light I could see that she was blushing to the roots of her hair.

"Sounds rather harmless," I said, trying to think of something I could admit to, nothing too weird or personal.

"Tell them what Irene's ugly dog does," he demanded. Chuck had turned into a manipulative jerk again, badgering Romy who looked as if she might burst into tears.

"Tell them!"

She spoke so quickly that I could barely hear her.

"He eats all the dead skin and nail clippings from the pedicures."

"Isn't that the grossest thing you ever heard of?" Chuck asked. T.K. laughed and lit a cigarette.

"Now, Zara." Chuck was looking at me. "What does Miss American Pie do with her girlfriends when T.K.'s not around?"

"He's always around." T.K. cocked an eyebrow.

"Well, supposing he wasn't. Confession time!"

"When I was working," I began, "my girlfriends and I—there were five or six of us—would get together and we'd rent 'Dirty Dancing.'"

"Yeah?" said Chuck. Now T.K. looked interested.

"We'd make popcorn, stock up on sodas and wine and plop down in someone's living room and crank up the VCR."

"And then?"

"Afterward, we'd dance with each other. Like they danced in the movie."

"T.K., I think these women are all closet lezzies. What do you think?"

T.K. smiled and blew a perfect smoke ring.

"It's a coming of age movie," I said. "Getting laid the first time is a big deal. We're sort of celebrating it."

Romy said, "They don't understand."

"Then we send out for pizza," I continued, "and watch the movie again." I stopped, realizing that 'getting laid' wasn't exactly the phrase genteel Mrs. Wentz would use, but no one had noticed. Chuck lit a cigar and looked first at Romy and then at me.

"She's right. I will never understand you women." The cloud of smoke drifted toward the open porthole.

T.K. broke the silence. "You're next Goodborn."

I waited for Chuck to tell some whopping big lie. Instead he said, "This is God-awful boring."

No one spoke. Chuck was a manipulative jerk and I was about ready to tell him so when he said,

"If I had access to some capital, I could make us all rich." He winked at me and mouthed, "richer." Chuck settled himself against the cushions and puffed on his cigar.

"What's the deal?" asked T.K., rising from the table and rummaging in his duffel bag, bringing out his cigarette case which he opened to reveal four neatly rolled joints. He took out the plumpest one, lit it, inhaled deeply, held the smoke in his lungs, and passed it across the table to Chuck. Romy reached into the cupboard by the table and got out a scented candle, which T.K. lit with his cigarette lighter. Anyone out for a stroll would smell the mingled scents of cigars, cigarettes, charcoal, and vanilla wafting out of the portholes. Hopefully, the pungent odor of grass would get lost in the potpourri.

The flickering light of the candle played on the polished wood of the cabin, and the air became even more turbid and claustrophobic as we passed the joint around. I had to keep nudging myself to pay attention as Chuck began detailing how we could make big bucks peddling his data warehouse software to "those slimy ex-Stasi and some creeps from the—I think they're the stooges of the KGB."

We sat around the table, faces inscrutable in those dim shadows, as if airbrushed to reveal only the histories and legends we strove so hard to present.

"Fella I knew back in Portland couldn't pay me back a wad of money from a business deal," said Chuck. "I was already itchy to cut out of the country, so I didn't want his house or his Aspen condo." He took a hit, reflected a moment, and continued. "Finally he offered to slip me the computer system his company had just developed. Brand new technology. I said, 'What am I supposed to do with this?' 'Sell it!' he said. 'Who to?' I asked. 'You're the boy wonder marketing genius,' he said. You'll find a customer.'"

"Oh, is this the data warehouse you were telling me about at the party?" I asked. Romy frowned. Under the table, Chuck's foot nudged mine. A signal to shut up?

"Guess I did," he said slowly.

"The one Wulf wants? And the KGB wants it too?"

Romy's eyebrows knit together another quarter inch. Chuck had been telling tales out of school.

T.K. chimed in, "Goodborn, you'll have to forgive my wife. When anyone mentions money, she stops being a ditz and starts asking questions like a bean-counting banker."

"If I have a flair for investments it's because I always dig into the facts and figures," I said.

"And I like that kind of shrewdness in a woman," said Chuck. He sipped his brandy and found the thread of his story again. "You know Wulf Mueller's our landlord." He nodded at Romy. "One of her connections. Got to talking one day. I happened to mention I had a computer system to sell. Explained what a data warehouse was. I didn't expect Wulf to understand. Naturally I was speaking English, probably got a little too technical, but he perked right up. Said he had some Vietnamese guy fixing old computers. Can you believe it? That gook Ho Dung turned out to be a geek!

"A few days later Mueller showed up again. Inspected the garden. Fed the dog. Wondered whether to paint the shed. Beat around the bush for fifteen minutes. Later came up with a 'friend' who just might be interested in my data warehouse software. Someone who had 'a million kilometers of tape.' I could tell from his questions that somebody knowledgeable had been coaching him. He wanted to know if they could 'mine' the data—what kind of ad hoc queries would the database support? That kind of thing."

"Please don't get too technical or you'll lose us," I said.

"Right," said Chuck. "We wouldn't want to lose our little banker here, would we?"

I giggled.

"Old Wulf eventually got to the point," explained Chuck. "His 'friend' had copies of thirty years' worth of Stasi files. Reports from thousands of informers. Not just from around here locally, but half of East Germany. Turned out the people responsible for transporting the files used to photocopy the juicy stuff before they turned the paperwork over to headquarters in East Berlin. That's where everything was stored."

T.K. gave a lazy nod. "What did our friends do with the copies?" he asked, casually, as if he were just making conversation.

"The gang of couriers tried to get a little blackmail business going on the side, but since nobody had any money, it wasn't too profitable. And it was damned hard for them to get access to the Stone Age copy machines."

"But they kept on copying?" asked T.K.

"Yeah. Typical Kraut efficiency, with everything neat and orderly. Except the files were still on paper. After a while, they couldn't store all that bulk without someone noticing, so they started copying everything electronically. Low-tech punch cards, then tape. They invested the blackmail money to hire a few Bulgarians and Hungarians to do a little programming. Then the Vietnamese showed up and they worked even cheaper."

"And then the wall came down." T.K. looked bored, with his eyes half-closed, leading Chuck along.

"Yeah, the wall came down and all the files were put under Western lock and key. Of course nobody knew that most of them had been copied. But Wulf and his pals saw the value of what they had."

"And they knew it would be even more valuable in a sophisticated electronic format," I said.

"The astute Mrs. Wentz," mocked Chuck. Romy appraised me from across the table, gimlet-eyed. T.K.'s foot gave mine a sharp nudge.

Better watch out. Don't overstep the boundaries.

Chuck indicated that T.K. should light another joint, and the cabin grew even smokier. Romy got out a nail buffer and an emery board and started in on her nails. She pretended not to pay attention, but I knew from the intense look on her face, that she was digesting every word.

"Electronic format," coached T.K., trying to get Chuck back on track.

"Yeah. They're pretty shrewd," answered Chuck. "Just think about it. Once the country gets on its feet and people have some money, the old Stasi gang will be ready." He squinted at an imaginary screen as he pretended to type at a keyboard. He gave us a sidelong glance. "Show me all the men in Stralsund who cheated on their wives." Another knowing look and more pantomimed keying. "Now show me all the men who cheated with their wife's best friend."

"Gotcha," said T.K., smiling a little. He was cleaning his glasses, polishing each lens with his handkerchief, taking a lot of time.

"But they can't use your system on old-fashioned computers, can they?" I asked. "And what about the KGB? What do they want with your data warehouse?"

Chuck held up his hand. "Banker lady only gets one question at a time.

"Computer question?" I asked.

"Yeah, they need the latest hardware, and it doesn't come cheap."

"Banker lady requesting permission for another question."

"Shoot."

"How can a bunch of unemployed Stasi afford the latest hardware?"

"That's where banker lady comes in. They need venture capital."

"You must be joking," I said. Out of the miasma of dope and booze I found the perfectly indignant voice of Mrs. Wentz. "T.K. and I would never invest in such a sleazy, disgusting business."

T.K. said, "Sweetheart, we might just want to think about it."

"There's nothing to think about. Blackmail and extortion are completely reprehensible."

T.K. looked at Chuck and shrugged. "Is the KGB a more simpatico group of guys?"

Chuck doused the half-smoked joint in his brandy glass, and blew out the candle. He regarded me with a sarcastic stare across the narrow table.

"Goody-two-shoes doesn't know shit about this. These people have been spying on each other for forty years. With them it's a disease. They can't stop. They don't want to stop. At least we can trust Mueller. He's practically family.

"The KGB—actually it's some bunch from the other side of the hall in East Berlin who are in bed with the KGB. They moved their files before the West took over. Now they want their information in nice neat rows and columns before they ship it off to KGB headquarters in Moscow for safekeeping. Those guys play rough. They were in charge of terrorism and all that shit. Now, who would you rather do business with?"

"Neither blackmailers nor roughnecks." I said firmly.

"Has to be somebody," Chuck said in a triumphant voice. He beamed like a poker player laying a royal flush down on the table. "Because there's this funny business with Wulf's dog." With my heart in my gullet, I gaped at Chuck.

"What about Wulf's dog?" My question was drowned out as T.K. pounded his fist on the table, making the glasses, the ashtray and me jump.

"Dammit, Zara, I told you hauling that—that ugly mutt off the road would bring us nothing but hassles. You and your pathetic little heart bleeding for everything on four goddamn legs."

He was admitting our entanglement, and for an instant, I wasn't sure whether he was putting on an act or not. Chuck and Romy watched while he continued to rail at me.

"I said that must be Wulf's dog. I told you we should tell him where the dog was. Whatever gets into you..."

I crossed my arms and produced a stubborn scowl. "Wulf doesn't deserve the dog." I looked at Romy. "I'm sorry if he's your friend, but I really don't like to see animals mistreated."

Her stony-faced response was to get up from the table and put the glasses in the sink. Then she turned and began making up the bunk next to the table.

I couldn't imagine why T.K. had admitted our link to Wulf's dog. Chuck certainly didn't seem any happier with our "confession" than he had when we bamboozled him about Bruss and the grain elevator. He sat there with a sulky, narrow-eyed look.

I took the glass with the old cigar and the dirty ashtray out of the sink and held them at arm's length while I asked T.K. to dump them into the harbor.

Chuck said, "You two aren't a whole lot of fun tonight and I want to go to bed." Nobody answered him. "There are two sleeping bags and two bunks."

"T.K. and I always sleep together."

"Gonna be like sardines," said Chuck, leering a little.

T.K. shrugged. "That's cool."

"Bunch of freakin' love birds. Romy can take the other bunk. I'll sack out on the deck."

He took a plaid-lined green sleeping bag from a locker and climbed out of the cabin. T.K. went after him, carrying the glass and ashtray, and I heard them talking and Chuck laughed at something T.K. said. Romy went into the head and I took a quick peek to make sure the CD was still under the charts, before I made up our bunk.

Romy joined Chuck while T.K. and I slipped into sleeping attire: An old Henley shirt and pink leggings for me, sweat pants and a long-sleeved T-shirt for him. We brushed our teeth over the tarnished copper sink.

Then T.K. and I went on deck to give Romy a little privacy. Chuck had laid out his sleeping bag in front of the big wooden box where the eels had been kept in seawater. Now a storage space, it offered protection from the evening breezes. Chuck had the best quarters, under the stars in the fresh night air away from the stale smell of weed in the cabin.

Chuck sat on the eel box with his legs dangling down, and I could feel him appraising us. He spoke in a low voice.

"Mr. and Mrs. T.K. Wentz, or whoever the hell you are. As wriggling and slippery as the eels that used to be hauled up in the nets." He patted the box. "But even the slipperiest eel ended up in the smoker with a stake through its head."

Chuck's words made me shiver, and T.K. touched my arm.

"Get some sleep, Goodborn," he said. "The grass made you paranoid."

Romy was in the bunk with her back turned when we re-entered the cabin.

T.K. and I curled up together under the coarse wool blanket, and the gentle motion of the boat put me to sleep immediately.

~ * ~

T.K.'s warm hands under my shirt awakened me. Faint moonlight filtered into the companionway, but the cabin lay in darkness. His hands moved again.

"Not now," I whispered.

He whispered back, "Sweet Pea, pretty please."

"They'll wake up."

"Not if we're quiet."

"How can we be that quiet?"

"It will be a lovely challenge." He met my protest with a kiss. A few minutes later my leggings and his sweat pants were at the bottom of the bunk, and we were meeting the challenge pretty well, actually.

From the channel I heard the noise of a diesel engine, which grew louder. We froze. The pulsating throb of the engine seemed to be coming right at us, but sound on water is deceptive.

T.K. whispered, "Oh Shit! Take a look, would you?"

"Are you crazy? Why me?"

"You're on top."

Neither Romy nor Chuck stirred. I disentangled myself, slipped out of the bunk and peered out the porthole. Not able to see the boat, I yanked my shirt down over my butt and stood in the companionway, peering out at the water. I guessed this was the little Danish boat slowly returning to her anchorage on the other end of the harbor. Her flag had been taken in for the night. A moment later, the skipper cut the engine, and a deep silence enveloped us again.

Romy sighed and turned over. On deck, I could hear Chuck's rhythmic snores.

I returned to the bunk. "Just the *Little Mermaid.* Now, where were we?"

He pulled me close and we continued our stealthy activities under the coarse blanket.

~ * ~

T.K. had fallen into a sated slumber. Feeling drowsy, almost drugged, I debated whether to leave the warm bunk for a visit to the head, when I heard a splash, like a fish makes when it leaps out of the water. The boat tilted to port, and didn't right itself, then I heard another sound of movement in water. The boat rocked back to an even keel. I nudged T.K. with my elbow.

There was stillness, as if someone waited and listened. Then faint sounds came from the bow. A furtive tread? I nudged T.K. again. "Jesus, wake up! Somebody's on the boat!" I lurched out of bed and groped at the bottom of the bunk for our pants.

"What?" He was sitting up.

"Somebody just climbed onto the boat," I whispered again, tossing sweat pants in his direction. I grabbed my leggings. T.K. climbed into his pants. A shape passed the porthole, as T.K. flew up the stairs of the companionway.

I heard T.K. yell, "hey!" and running feet flew past the portholes, then a splash, more running and a smaller splash and T.K.'s expletives.

I made a heroic effort to pull the leggings on.

Chuck hollered "Wentz, what the fuck?"

A few feet away from me, Romy's sharp voice, asking if everything was okay, when obviously everything was not. She jumped off her bunk and ran up the steps. I got the leggings on, no mean trick in the dark, and followed Romy out of the cabin. On the horizon, a pale purple band signaled the first light of dawn.

Chuck was shining a flashlight in the water off the port side. The light raked the surface, revealing—only water. I caught the end of T.K.'s breathless words.

"...some guy creeping up on you when I came out of the cabin. He—he saw me and ran toward the bow and took a dive before I could get to him. I threw a winch handle at him, but I'm pretty sure I missed."

Chuck continued to criss-cross the water with the flashlight beam. "Probably some damn thief. Can't even get a night's sleep in a middle-of-nowhere place like this."

He turned the flashlight on the bow, and we all gaped at a line of wet footprints, then a puddle of water and two black flippers glistening beside a coiled line. The sight gave me goose bumps. Romy gasped and looked at Chuck, who picked up one of the flippers and put it down again.

Then T.K. and Chuck climbed onto the pier and looked around. There was no moon, and the shadowy trees cloaked the village except for a few patches on the white houses.

Romy turned to me and said, "I think we should leave." She was clutching her arms to herself as if she was freezing.

Chuck and T.K. climbed back on board, and T.K. suggested Chuck might want to share the bunk with Romy. "It's not as crowded as you think," he said, as we all traipsed back down into the cabin, and Romy lit a lantern. She turned to Chuck with an enigmatic look on her face and repeated, "We should leave now."

"Aw, God, no." he grumbled. "It's the middle of the night."

"Did you get a good look?" I asked T.K.

"Yeah. He or she was wearing a wet suit.

In the dim light, his eyes were rimmed in red, and his shoulders slumped. My brash, silent lover of an hour ago looked defeated. I didn't share my thought that an ordinary thief wouldn't wear a wet suit and flippers. Just then we heard the blub-blub-blub of a boat engine, and everyone scrambled back on deck. Chuck's flashlight didn't carry that far, but I knew it was the Danish boat that had interrupted our late night lovemaking.

T.K. whistled and lowered his voice almost to a whisper. "Shiver me timbers."

"I don't get it," said Chuck. "Why would someone from Denmark come snooping around my boat in the middle of the night? If that's who it was."

Romy and I exchanged glances. "I want to leave," she repeated, but Chuck only scowled.

My thought was maybe someone else knew Chuck had the CD on the boat, but it would be crazy to try to steal something with four people on board.

Romy doused the lantern and we climbed into our bunks. I dreamed that Chloe was crying and I couldn't get her to stop.

~ * ~

In the village of Kloster, a rooster crowed. I rolled over and peered at my watch. 7:45. Next to me, T.K. stirred. Chuck and Romy, entwined in the bunk across from us, were dead to the world.

"Let's go for a run," I said, whispering. "So we can talk."

T.K. stretched and yawned.

I scribbled a note and stuck it under the ashtray by the sink. "8:00 a.m. Went for a run. Be back in an hour."

Minutes later we were jogging along an unpaved road lined with sprawling beach roses. Cows grazed at the edge of a salt marsh, and the long clean beach stretched to our right.

We loped at a steady pace. I was primed for an A to Z postmortem of last night: from why T.K. had admitted to our involvement with Wulf's dog to the possible motives of the frogman who had left his black flippers on the deck.

We turned off the road where there was a narrow path giving access to the empty beach.

"About last night," I began, when T.K. said, "We've got to grab the CD and sky out of here. Off this island. Back to Berlin."

I turned and searched his face. "Is there something you would like to share?"

He stopped and rummaged in the little backpack that held towels and water. "Someone came on board to kill Chuck last night."

More stupid "spy" stuff. I just knew it.

"What makes you think that? And why would anyone even want to kill Chuck?"

T.K. glanced at the sea and then back at me. He spoke in a flat voice. "Our visitor was sneaking up on Goodborn...with a knife."

T.K. paced up and down on the sand, then stopped and searched the backpack again. He didn't face me, but stared out at the water.

"What I am going to say will scare the shit out of you, but for your safety, I have to tell you."

Scare me? I had been scared since I found out about Bruss's death. Now, my adrenaline surged like a tsunami. I could probably run all the way back to Berlin.

A bird called shrilly and dived into the surf. T.K. turned away from the water and met my eyes.

"What?" I asked.

"Putnam," he said. "Heavy legs, big butt, and the way he moves. That was Billy Boy in the wet suit. He's trying to kill Chuck."

Crazy, unpredictable Putnam. A loose cannon, yes, but an assassin? And why Chuck?

In the pasture across the road, calves bleated.

"I'm pretty sure, but not one hundred percent." T.K. picked up a stone, examined it and tossed it back to the sand.

I heard myself speak reasonably, like I was inquiring about a business problem. "You saw a man in a black wet suit in the dark for a few seconds, and now you think that was Putnam? You're making an awfully big assumption."

"I recognized Putnam's commando knife," he said in a toneless voice.

"What commando knife?"

"His Fairbairn-Sykes fighting knife. For killing in close combat. Big ugly toad stabber. He's had it for years."

"Oh, my God!" Putnam had brought a gun along. He could have an arsenal from garrotes to grenade launchers with him.

T.K. turned and walked up the beach toward the access path. Feeling a little spacey, I followed a few paces behind him until we reached the road. He stopped and waited for me to catch up.

"What's your plan to get the CD off the boat?" T.K. asked. "We sure as hell can't risk getting caught with it."

"I'm mailing it. Just as I did my passport. There was a map of the village at the inn. The post office isn't far from the harbor. There's a little cardboard box in one of the boat lockers, and every boat has twine."

We walked back toward the village now, passed by an occasional cyclist.

"I'll slip the CD out of the plastic container and into my handbag. Stroll into the ladies room at the inn, pop the CD into the box, wrap it up, and mail it to myself at my Chicago office. Last night I mentioned I was going to buy some postcards."

T.K. agreed it was simple and practically foolproof. The German postal system was sacrosanct, West or East.

"Then we'll sail back to Lauterbach with them," he said, planning aloud. He pulled a broken-in-half cigarette out of his pocket and looked for matches in the backpack. No luck.

"As soon as we can, we'll check out of the hotel and drive to Berlin. Probably late tonight." He rubbed his hand through his hair. "Save your questions for later. The important thing is to grab the CD and get away. Today we have to stay in character. Gullible Mrs. Wentz should reconsider the loan to the ex-Stasi. Promise Chuck something to keep him happy."

We walked back on the meandering beach road and into the shady village of Kloster. T.K. had his hands clasped behind his back. I couldn't stop thinking about what T.K. said.

"Who is Bill Putnam, and why is he working against us?" My voice was level, with no evidence of the panic I kept trying to tamp down.

He stopped and draped his arm over my shoulder. "Sweet Pea, I promise I'll tell you everything, but now I have to think. Please?"

I pulled away from him. No point discussing how Chuck knew about the dog now, when we were getting ready to make a run for it. We had gone out of our way to attract attention. And somehow Chuck found out. Chuck knew an awful lot that he shouldn't. About us. About Bruss. About the dog. I didn't like it at all.

We strode along under the big trees that lined the path through the village, and while T.K. was thinking, my mind circled around why Putnam would want to get rid of Chuck. And how to warn Chuck without blowing our cover. Somehow, we would have to alert Chuck.

It was almost nine o'clock when the path turned and we found ourselves walking by the inn where we had dined last night. I hoped

Romy had been awake long enough to make a pot of coffee. A little breeze had come up, promising a good sail.

The waterfront came into view. As we approached the pier, I stopped and stared.

"Oh no!"

T.K. said, "Holy shit!"

Our duffel bags sat forlornly on the dock's gray planks. The gauzy curtain of morning mist had risen above the harbor, and far out, in the expanse between fog and water, the maroon sails of *Painted Cow* were outlined against the sky.

Eleven

We exchanged incredulous looks.

"Damn it to hell!" T.K. shook his head.

Watching those dark sails cross the Bodden, took the wind out of ours. In mid-channel, *Painted Cow* tacked and headed north toward Wittow.

T.K. talked to himself. "Was it us or was it the frogman? Had to be Chuck's decision. But she wanted to leave last night. Something we said or something we did."

While he continued his monologue, my thoughts orbited our bizarre situation. We had reached the FUD factor: Fear, Uncertainly and Doubt.

"Now why did those two leave us high and dry?" T.K. repeated. "Why?"

He turned to me. "You didn't by any chance filch that damned CD before we left the boat this morning, did you?"

I met his gaze. "You know, I considered it, but I was afraid one of them would wake up while I was groping under the charts. And the other thing was they might have checked for it while we were gone."

I looked up at him. "Let's jump on the first ferry to Stralsund. We can catch a train to Binz."

"No, we check into the inn." He grabbed the duffel bags and started walking down the pier.

"The inn? What for?" I ran to catch up with him.

"I'm thinking about a cup of coffee, a shave, a bath, and a place to make a phone call."

When I didn't respond, he continued, "Listen, no matter how weird it feels, we have to carry on as Mr. and Mrs. Wentz would."

The Wentzes, either angry or amused, would regroup at the inn. Over breakfast, we could decide on a plan.

When we reached the street that led to the inn, T.K. plopped our duffel bags down on the gravel. Without a word, he unzipped his bag and began groping around in it.

"Oh God, do you think they snooped in our bags?"

T.K. fished around and extracted his brown leather Dopp kit. He unzipped it and peered inside.

"Is anything missing?"

Without answering, he zipped the case. Then he retrieved my shoulder bag, and started searching again.

"They went through our luggage and the goodies and our passports are gone."

"Oh, T.K."

"The joints were in my cigarette case. The coke, ah, we hadn't quite reached that degree of intimacy yet, where we could bring out the coke. I thought maybe today."

"Where had you stashed the coke?"

"I moved it a few days ago. It was in that little sewing kit you carry around."

"Are you crazy? Oh, really! If we're caught, then I take the fall? You bastard!"

He lit a cigarette and stood looking half-defiant, half-contrite.

"It's gone, damn it, so you can quit your rant. Captain Goodborn has probably done a line or two, unless, of course, steely Frau Motte has forbidden him. Now I am going someplace where I can brush my fucking teeth."

He picked up our bags and began trudging toward the inn. I couldn't believe he had set me up with the coke. Not for the first time, I wondered how far I could trust T.K. My real passport was in Berlin and my faux password sailed off on *Painted Cow*. I didn't see how the situation could get much worse.

~ * ~

I left our room at the inn to make my telephone call while T.K. sat up to his armpits in water, soaking in the big white porcelain tub with claw feet in our *Doppel Zimmer mit Bad*.

The post office had one room. I waltzed into the now familiar routine of forties phone technology. At the counter I said, *"Ferngespräch."* Long distance. The clerk, a middle-aged woman with a no-nonsense expression, eyed me as I gave her Mark's number in Chicago. My call would wake him up at an ungodly early hour on Saturday morning. I hoped he had spent the night at home and not at his girlfriend's apartment.

The clerk dialed, actually dialed, from a phone behind the counter, no push buttons here, and pointed across the room to the public telephone booth. I knew the drill from Sassnitz, but it still seemed like an incongruous way to make a phone call.

Mark picked up the phone on the third ring.

"Oh God, Zara, Do you know what time it is?" He yawned into the phone.

I apologized for waking him, and using big-time circumlocutions, because T.K. was convinced that the telephones might still be tapped, I gave Mark the gist of the last twenty-four hours.

My private opinion was by now we had reached FUBAR, "fucked up beyond all recognition," but I didn't offer this to Mark.

He cleared his throat. "The venture capitalist's second installment for your services, the one for thirty percent of the total hasn't been deposited in the escrow account," he said. "D & D were totally bullshit when I told them. They said you might as well cut our losses and come home."

The good news and the bad news: come home, but without the CD.

"The other thing is your contract may not be worth the paper it's written on. Edgar Standish has a reputation in New England. He's been indicted for illegal financial dealings. Not once, but twice. Indicted, but never convicted. The rumor mill has it he's made some risky investments. That he may even be broke."

Bloody Edgar! I felt like someone's head had butted me in the stomach. The woman behind the counter was eyeing me between weighing parcels and selling stamps. Maybe it was bad etiquette to tie up the phone.

"What else?" I asked, trying to keep the despair out of my voice. "Any more background on William Putnam?"

"We're going to owe the PI a bundle. He found out his Putnam always lands in trouble spots. Southeast Asia, Northern Ireland, the Falklands. He used to be employed by his government, but he was 'selected out.' The PI thinks his current occupation could best be described as a mercenary."

"That sounds about right." I sighed. "Don't suppose you have any good news?"

"I don't suppose that I do. Why don't you move into friendlier territory?" He yawned again.

"We are planning to do that. Tonight."

Two men stared at me, waiting for me to get off the phone.

I said goodbye and traipsed back to the little counter and paid for my call.

I couldn't believe it. The fantastic fee Coppola & Henry were expecting was up in flames along with our chance of getting our hands on Chuck's CD.

Outside, I passed a vendor displaying some locally made linen clothing. Remembering that I was still Mrs. Wentz, whom I thoroughly disliked by now, I bought a longish skirt, eyeballing the fit, and a knitted linen top to wear with it. Then I hustled back down the shady walk to the inn.

~ * ~

I saw T.K., long legs crossed at his ankles, sitting outside on the patio. On the table sat two cups and two individual pots of coffee. What, I wondered, besides expletives, would T.K. have to say about Edgar's stiffing us? He glanced up, saw me coming and smiled the lazy smile that hadn't deserted him in spite of this horror show.

Feeling angrier by the minute, at Edgar, at myself for being such a fool and not listening to the inner voice that had cautioned against this asinine escapade, and at T.K., who, after all, had gotten us into this mess and had fobbed the drugs off on me, I just wanted to throttle somebody.

I strolled up to the table, tossed my parcel onto an empty chair and sat down. I looked T.K. square in the eye.

"What did your associate have to say?" he asked.

Something about my mood made him attentive. He cocked his head and held my eyes with his, taking in my anger.

My voice dripped acid. "I didn't think twice about exposing my bare butt to the Baltic Sea breezes. I've tolerated Putnam's badgering and Chuck's groping. I endured a mugging by goons and a close encounter with a guard dog. But these escapades and indignities have paled in comparison." I stopped to inhale.

T.K. shifted in his chair and asked, "In comparison to what?"

"We were stiffed by Edgar. There's no second payment in the escrow account."

T.K. gaped at me with incredulous eyes. "Mr. Moneybag's didn't make the deposit?"

"That's right. You better call your bank on Monday."

"You're shittin me!" His shoulders slumped.

"Unfortunately, no," I said, and the anger that had been pumping me up was now fizzling into dejection. I poured myself a cup of coffee. The cup jiggled on the saucer because my hand was shaking so.

T.K. rubbed his fingers over his chin. "Then we don't have to worry about Chuck and his CD anymore." His eyes narrowed. "From day one, this has been one big rat fuck. We're not exactly over here saving the world for democracy," he continued. "No pay, no work."

He looked at me across the table. "We do exactly as we had planned. Only minus the CD. Back to Berlin tonight." He looked at me. "You're pale. Are you all right?"

"I'm in shock." I didn't want him to know how lousy I was feeling, so I changed the subject. "Listen, what about Putnam? Isn't Edgar paying him, too?"

"Good question," said T.K. "Not a word to Billy Boy about that check. I'm going to ask him to give us a lift from the ferry back to our hotel."

"Are you crazy? He tried to kill Chuck. Anyway, he's probably still on that Danish boat. How would Putnam have access to a boat like that?"

"Resources we aren't supposed to know about." He stood up and took a few coins out of his pocket. "Be a good wife and order up some breakfast. A four-minute egg and some currant juice for me. A basket of rolls. Orange marmalade if they have any. I'll run to the post office and ring up the frogman."

"I don't want him to pick us up. He wanted to kill Chuck. As in murder. How do we know he won't kill us? We'll take the train."

I didn't want to see Putnam. Not today. Not ever.

T.K. said, "Okay, if he's not there, I'll try to leave a misleading message. Then he knows we attempted to make contact."

"This is suicidal, T.K."

Ignoring my protests, he stood up. "Stiffed by Edgar. Why am I not surprised?" He stopped and his mouth curled in disgust. "It always sounded too good to be true."

I ordered breakfast, and then I sat slumped in my chair with waves of anxiety and despair washing over me. Edgar and Putnam had ripped a canyon through the project.

Not only would we not be paid, we wouldn't get the CD-ROM, and we might be on the hit list of the Marquis de Sade on steroids. I dug my notebook out of my handbag and began jotting things down in a kind of shorthand code.

I tried to understand the big picture, starting with the actual chain of command. Edgar gave orders to Smith and Putnam who passed them on to T.K. and me. Were the Maine Mining people even involved? It was their company going down the drain. What had Wohlauer said? "Mr. Standish is making all those arrangements."

Like who to kill?

If Edgar was corrupt and Putnam was a killer, where did that leave T.K. and Zara Wentz? "Sucking hind teat," is the phrase they used on the farm.

My imagination was in free fall, and meanwhile the feeling of fear that had been skittering about in the last two weeks was hopping like drops of water on a red-hot skillet.

I wrote in a tight little script, trying to make sense of all this madness.

T.K. wanted to get back to Berlin. God knows, so did I, but we owed Chuck a warning about Putnam. Something indirect, but enough to make him cautious, although Chuck and caution didn't inhabit the same planet.

T.K. walked up the path toward the inn, looking relaxed in his faded navy sweatshirt and old jeans. His face and neck were sunburned over his solid tan, giving him a rugged outdoorsy look.

I should have done a background check on T.K. A bit late now. I scribbled more notes, and looked up from my writing again.

T.K.'s walk was easy, more like a saunter. That could mean Putnam hadn't been available. I took a deep breath. One needle of good news in a haystack of trouble.

~ * ~

Men and animals should be left alone while they eat, and I waited until T.K. had smeared the final smidgen of marmalade on the last bite of roll before confronting him.

"How would you describe Putnam's profession?" I asked, keeping my voice pleasant and conversational.

T.K. finished chewing and didn't meet my gaze but looked across the patio toward the waterfront. "Can't you guess?"

"Words like terminator and assassin come to mind. Occupations that don't seem relevant to retrieving a CD-ROM from a white-collar thief."

T.K. lit a cigarette and blew one of his perfect smoke rings.

"You said you met him studying economics in London," I said, persisting.

"And political science. Turned out to be a perfect cover. Business people can go anywhere. Trade delegations, export fairs, embassy staffs, that sort of thing. After London, our paths crossed a few times in Eastern Europe. We were friendly enough, and we had an assignment or two that required..." he paused, searching for the right word..."cooperation." That's how he knew where old Uncle Mundhenk lived."

"We're working for Edgar, not for Maine Mining?"

"Edgar told the people in Portland that he knew the right crew to go after Chuck." He stubbed out his cigarette on the flagstones. "Maine Mining people—they're software developers. What the hell would they know?"

It seemed crass to keep harping about our payment, but I didn't care. "Tell me about the money."

"Edgar was offering a cool million for the CD-ROM. Plus expenses. Obviously that was just a fraction of its worth. But Smith and Putnam didn't know data warehousing software from Shinola. Putnam knew I'd had something to do with a software project in Germany." T.K. scowled at the memory. We both always tried not to think of my shenanigans of last summer.

"They offered me a pile of cash. I didn't know any more about the technology than Smith and Putnam, but I did know a lady who gets off on bits and bytes, and eats this stuff for breakfast. I figured she could be my tech backup, so I made a more-than-generous offer to Coppola & Henry for your expertise."

He reached across the table and took my hand. "It seemed like a perfect solution. Christ, I thought it would be easy cash."

The waiter brought the coffee and T.K. ordered a *Frühschoppen*.

The waiter returned with a bottle and poured clear liquor into two tiny glasses. I scowled at T.K. Hitting the sauce this early in the day wasn't a good sign.

"Cuts grease and aids digestion," he offered by way of an excuse.

The alcohol would hack away at the little packets of fear. Maybe T.K. felt them too.

"Hair of the dog," he said. "So to speak."

"So to speak."

We clinked glasses and downed the firewater.

"You didn't realize Edgar was a bad actor?" I asked when I could breathe again.

"The only hint was he hired Billy Boy."

"And the details of the financial arrangements are—"

"My God, you're starting to sound like Mrs. Wentz."

I gave him a look.

He shrugged and continued. "Naturally old Edgar was too canny to hand over a million bucks at once. The deal was, we would be paid twenty per cent cash up front, thirty per cent into the escrow account when we located Chuck, and the other fifty when the CD was recovered." He paused. "Once you came on board, Edgar had instructions on how to divide the payments."

"Why would Putnam try to kill Chuck before we had the CD? He couldn't know that I had found the hiding place. And how did he even know where we were?"

T.K. winced, and lit another cigarette.

"He couldn't know, could he?" I repeated. No matter how far down I pushed the fear, it bubbled up again.

I recognized his guilty, belligerent expression from earlier confessions of misdeeds.

"Jesus, T.K., how did he know?"

"I called Putnam from the inn last night. When I went to the john. I told him you found the CD."

I stared at him.

"Edgar's orders. Putnam's orders. They wanted to know the minute we located it."

"So Putnam knew the CD was on the boat. He knew the four of us were on board. We're always talking about playing the tape out. Let's play this one out. Was he going to kill all of us? Or was he going to kill one or two of us and make it look like the others did it?"

T.K. looked just as tired and defeated as he had last night. "I don't know," he said. "Zara, I absolutely do not know."

~ * ~

At noon we caught the little ferry that shuttled passengers between Hiddensee and Stralsund. Our fellow travelers were a young couple in stonewashed denim and two old ladies togged out in their best finery. The wind had died, and the smooth greenish gray surface of the water looked like polished metal.

T.K. reported the young couple spoke Polish. He drank a beer and she peered into a hand mirror at her eyebrows and teeth while the ferry put-putted sedately through the Bodden.

Next to me, T.K. collapsed on the hard seat and fell into a sweaty slumber. Sunlight glinted on his sunglasses until he shifted restlessly and shielded his eyes with his arm. I sat beside him in a kind of sun-dazed stupor.

The light reflecting off the glassy metallic water created a sensation of sailing through a blinding world of surfaces. Images reflected one another, creating gross distortions, and impenetrable meanings. We inhabited a perilous world of mirrors, a glittering fractured world where everything was assumed, and nothing was known.

~ * ~

I awoke parched by thirst and with a crick in my neck. The ferry was entering Stralsund's harbor. Chirping and pointing, the old ladies noticed the mammoth white whale of a boat floating in the harbor. As we got closer to the ship, I could see the rusty watermarks and dull paint of the failed socialist dream.

T.K. woke up, with the strap of the duffel bag imprinted on his face. He yawned, stretched and sat up. I began to gather our belongings together.

"Oh, hell!" he squinted at the waterfront. "Don't look now, but our ride home is waiting!"

I saw the dreaded figure of Putnam pacing up and down the pier, almost strutting. Red countenance, strong, stout legs. As he made a crisp about-face, I saw he did have a big butt, probably hard as granite. He looked fanatically neat as always with his shirt tucked into his creased khaki shorts and his gleaming white socks. Loafers polished to a gloss. As the ferry edged closer to the pier, my heart dived into my stomach. Bill Putnam was the last person I wanted to see.

"How did he get here? I thought you left a misleading message."

I no longer trusted T.K. to be up front about his relationship with Putnam.

"Either he figured out we would be on the ferry or he has helpers keeping an eye on us."

"What kind of helpers? What are you saying?" It was bad enough to know about Bill and his knife without the idea of a whole band of faceless threats who "kept an eye" on us.

"Okay, I was kidding about the helpers; he just made a lucky guess. There, he's spotted us. Give him the Zara Wentz blast of charm."

My blast seemed more like a sputter, but I smiled and T.K. and I both waved. Putnam stopped pacing and approached the wooden pier as the little ferry docked. A deckhand tossed the line to a waiting sailor, and there was the usual noise and commotion while the boat tied up. As we marched down the gangway, I suspected walking the plank would be a better option than promenading smack into the clutches of Bill Putnam.

T.K. called out, "Billy Boy! You must have a goddamned crystal ball!" Putnam's sunburned nose seemed more out of kilter than ever. He barely glanced at me as he stepped right up and took my duffel bag.

"Mr. Wentz and his digerati diva. Flotsam from the isle of Hiddensee!" His blue eyes shone with malice. "Bungled it rather badly, didn't we?"

T.K. must have spilled the beans that Chuck had abandoned us. Putnam always scared the hell out of me. He began walking along the waterfront toward the parking area near where the goons had attacked me at the grain elevator. I glanced up at the impenetrable bricks, and even in the afternoon sun of mid-summer they had a cold, foreboding look while the rest of the port dozed in the torpor of the afternoon heat.

"Couldn't you wait until we're in the car before you launched into finger pointing and recriminations?" asked T.K.

Putnam looked back over his shoulder. "Drummond, we will review the performance of you and your wife," he glanced at me with his usual distaste, "later. Uta is with us today."

A short distance away, I saw a woman standing next to a gray Opel. She smiled and waved. Shorts, tank top, big clunky sandals and frizzy hairdo. I looked closer. An unshaven armpit and breasts bobbing as she waved her arm back and forth. T.K. offered an appreciative smile.

"Hallo, Zara and T.K.!" she called. She pronounced T.K.'s name the German way, sounding like Tay Kah.

I raised my hand in recognition. "Hallo, Uta!"

Putnam dumped our duffel bags in the "boot" as he always called it, and we piled into the gray Opel. Uta and I sat in the back seat.

T.K. put his neck against the headrest and said, "We had a lousy time and we got no sleep. Just point this baby toward Binz and wake me when the hotel is in sight." He closed his eyes.

Turning to Uta, I said, "I've never met anyone so incredibly rude as Chuck and Romy. They sailed off and left us stranded. Without a word. Can you imagine? T.K. and I went for a run and when we got back, *Painted Cow* was gone."

"Wore out our welcome, did we?" Putnam's hands with their white-scarred knuckles gripped the steering wheel as he stared straight ahead.

Uta was an unwitting shield from Putnam's anger. She turned to me as if about to share a confidence. "We have so many plans for the four of us today and this evening, too. You will forget this bad experience."

"Oh, sorry, no plans," I said with a little groan. "T.K. and I are much too exhausted for plans."

"You will be our guests at the tea dance," Uta said, as if she hadn't noticed my lack of enthusiasm. "Some special live music. Then Bill will treat for dinner." She gave Putnam a little tap on the shoulder, which he ignored. Her voice faded into a tentative recitation of the hoped for events of the evening.

"After dinner we all go to the *Kreidefelsen*, you know, the Chalk Cliffs, for the festival of the summer solstice. Today is mid-summer."

Putnam added, "Mustn't miss the festival. Already, three ferryboats of Swedes in Sassnitz. Drunk already, like as not."

I said, "I don't think—" and Putnam broke in.

"If sitting on Goodborn's boat swilling beer was too tiring, Mrs. Wentz, you can have a bit of a lie down after the dance. But we wouldn't want to spend our whole vacation in bed now, would we?" In the mirror, I could see his icy eyes and off-kilter nose, which reddened, as he no doubt considered our deficiencies.

"I'll go along with whatever T.K. decides," I said primly. This business with Putnam and Uta would foil our plan to go back to Berlin tonight.

We were crossing the Rügendamm. Today no sailboats circled in the windless heat. In the car, conversation had died. I didn't want Uta to think we were avoiding her. She sat slumped next to me looking disconsolate as she curled a strand of hair around her finger. T.K.'s remark about Bill liking rough sex came back to me. I hoped he was being nice to Uta. I didn't see any bruises.

"I bought a new outfit in Hiddensee. Local linen. Do you want to see it?" I pulled the skirt and top out of the bag.

Uta said, "That's very pretty. You could wear it to the dance." She paused, crossed her legs and gave a little laugh. "I like linen, but I would never buy it. I hate to iron." She grasped the same strand of hair again, and rolled it around her finger.

Uta acted nervous and unsure of herself. I wondered what Putnam had told her.

~ * ~

In spite of the tension, I had fallen asleep in the car. We were driving through the outskirts of Binz.

"In Bergen?" T.K.'s voice was brimming with exasperation and his profile looked downright flinty as he turned to look at Putnam. Putnam began an involved explanation about the car, which didn't make any sense until I realized they were talking about the Beemer. Something about a repair shop in Bergen and the part not being available in Stralsund. Putnam muttered darkly about the Socialist work ethic while Uta stared at the back of his head with defensive angry eyes and T.K. looked more incredulous by the moment as he listened to Putnam's explanation.

"The mechanic dribbled on about how they would have to order the distributor cap from Berlin, but they would make every effort, and blah, bloody blah, and I said my friend expects his car on Monday—"

"Holy Shit! I expected it tonight!"

"Sorry, Drummond. You'll have to make do with us chauffeuring you."

"Oh, we can just rent another car," I said.

Three faces turned and stared at me. Putnam looked back at the road and his voice had a falsely jovial pitch. "Not this year on this island. It may be the 'Year of Miracles,' but not that sort."

I suspected Putnam had seen to it that we wouldn't have a car for days, as if he had read our minds not only about which ferry we would take, but that we were planning to sneak back to Berlin.

~ * ~

While T.K. changed clothes, I stood on our balcony and watched a freighter disappear over the eastern horizon. Green and glossy, the Baltic still looked smooth as enamel. Shrill voices of children playing tag on the beach punctuated the afternoon air, while an endless stream of strollers patrolled the long pier.

Exuding whiffs of Armani, T.K. joined me, resting a possessive hand on my fanny. Eyeballing the linen skirt for size had been a bad idea. T.K. had already quipped, "great glutes" and "terrific butt." Instead of another remark about the tight skirt, he moved his hand to my shoulders and neck. I gasped.

"You're one big knot."

"I just want to leave this place."

"Without a car?" He seemed dubious.

"We can take the train."

"Is that what you want?"

I looked at him. "Anything with wheels or propellers."

He dropped his arm and gripped the railing with his hands, focusing his eyes on the green water. "Such a half-assed cobbled-together scheme, and for a while I started believing everything would be all right. In spite of Bruss being dead, Bill Putnam, the Stasi and the damn dog. Yesterday when you told me you had found the CD, I thought we were actually going to pull it off."

"But we didn't."

We watched the pair of swans bobbing together near the pier. Contemplating the water had an almost hypnotic effect.

T.K. rested his hand on my arm. "We'll get through the dance and dinner, and then we're out of here. Hitchhike if we have to."

~ * ~

Arriving at the old Kurhaus, we walked through long corridors with frayed Oriental carpets and drab paint. The gilt had peeled off the big mirrors, and the chipped plaster ornamentation cried out for a phalanx of handworkers. We climbed stairs with ragged runners and stopped to admire the seascape afforded through the tall windows.

T.K. smiled at me as we performed the boxy steps of the rumba. A few yards away, the gold fringe on the red scarf Uta had slung low over her hips fluttered as she and Putnam executed their own version of the Latin beat.

As he danced, Putnam made a series of strange noises deep in his throat, little grunts, accompanied by hums and faint snorts and clicks.

Sabine and Bodo entered and grabbed a table in back. Sabine arched her eyebrows and opened her mouth in an "O," apparently surprised to see us. The music ended, and we joined them for a drink, but the encounter was stiff. Bodo didn't speak to anyone, Uta retied her scarf with nervous fingers, and Putnam's sharp eyes scanned the room. T.K. seemed the only one at ease as he explained to Sabine we had left *Painted Cow* in Hiddensee, and that Chuck and Romy had sailed north, probably to the Cap Arkona lighthouse.

When I asked if Andrea was playing with The West Sea Pirates, Bodo glowered and Sabine nodded toward the big speakers. Disco and rock and roll would soon shake more plaster off the walls. She told us that the band would play a few numbers to promote their evening appearance at the Midsummer Festival.

Moments later, a dark-haired man with scraggly hair and black boots plopped himself down by the microphone. The disk jockey.

An hour later, in the now packed room, we had boogied up a sweat and a thirst. I had to dance with Putnam twice. While I forced a bland smile, he gyrated in some Zen-like state of concentration with his eyes centered on a fixed point and the series of strange sounds emanating from his throat again. T.K. had been coming on to Uta, grinning at her flashing gold fringe and bobbing breasts in his careless familiar way. Now he was dancing with her again, and Putnam had gone to the men's room.

Perched on a chair at our table, I had just drained my second glass of black currant juice, when Captain Anatoly Salenko appeared. He looked more morose than ever, and not at all nautical in a black turtleneck and slacks and a sharply tailored loden-green jacket. Without a word, he made a suggestion of a bow, took my hand and led me onto the crowded dance floor.

I hadn't seen him since the night of the party when we had walked in the garden and he boasted he was an "artist on the mattress."

"You were so beautiful in the moonlight," he said in his excellent German. He must be referring to the skinny-dipping—that's what a male would remember. I made a stab at translating "all cats are gray in the dark." He smiled in his soulful way and didn't answer.

The West Sea Pirates came into the room with Andrea Schuld looking great in a red suede mini-skirt and a crazy-quilt patchwork vest. I said, "hallo," and then, "break a leg!" which none of them understood.

Anatoly put his arm around my waist. He watched Bodo and Sabine as he talked about the crew wanting to leave the ship to celebrate Midsummer, and how hard it was to maintain discipline in these strange times. His eye had a tiny tic, and he seemed bursting with nervous energy.

The disk jockey introduced the West Sea Pirates, and the vocalist began crooning, "I can see clearly now the rain is gone."

We had edged into the throng jamming the dance floor. I saw T.K.'s head bobbing above the dancers, the quintessential American: tall and handsome in his rangy way, with cool glasses and a generous sunburned nose.

Anatoly pulled me close to him, much closer than called for, and put his hands on my fanny, firmly clasping each cheek. I gave an astonished gasp.

"I like sexy dress." He spoke English.

When I tried to pull away a bit, he just gripped me tighter, and began to speak into my ear in his strange Russian to English sentences.

"Now please to listen. Very serious, you understand."

Still shocked, I nodded faintly.

"Cover is blown, like you say."

I whispered, "Cover is blown?"

He brushed my cheek with his lips and whispered into my ear again. Anyone watching would think we were making out.

"Everybody know T.K. not real man, I mean not husband. Everybody know about CD-ROM."

My heart had started to pound. "Who is everybody?" I whispered.

"Everybody. Me. Stasi. Americans."

One of his hands left my butt and settled firmly on my breast.

"Jesus, Anatoly!"

"Very exciting, Zara. Anatoly is like Napoleon. Do two things at once. Make love and give warning. You must listen. Very dangerous here. Go back to west with T.K. Go now! You understand?"

I nodded and made another attempt to extricate my various body parts from his hands, but he didn't loosen his grip. I hope no one had noticed our little tableau.

"Cover is blown. You understand? Many enemies."

"Yes." I felt somewhat faint as the significance of his message became clear.

"I have not means to assist. You understand? Please say yes again."

"Yes."

"Much danger. Not to trust anyone. Bill. The financier. Even Anatoly."

"I understand." I knew he was delivering an ominous warning. But I understood nothing. Anxiety, perplexity, and even disbelief whirled together through my head, creating a vortex of doubt and fear. Why was he saying not to trust him? And who was the financier? Was he talking about Edgar? My God, how would Anatoly know about Edgar?

"I feel heart beating through breast. Ah, Zara—-"

The song ended and everyone applauded.

"Here comes T.K.!"

Anatoly dropped his hands and was offering a cavalier's kiss to mine when T.K. popped up next to us.

"Tolya! I hope you're taking good care of my wife."

"I take good care of all wives." His eye twitched and he smiled his sad regretful smile.

Twelve

T.K. and I stood on the balcony, out of earshot of the supposed listening devices.

"Putnam said another five minutes Anatoly would have had you on your back right on the dance floor."

Putnam had watched Anatoly and me and blabbed to T.K., but Putnam didn't know Anatoly had whispered warnings in my ear, not sweet nothings.

"He saw what he wanted to see." I rehashed the scene, including the bits about Putnam and the "financier."

A faint whiff of smoke from the bratwurst grill down the street reached my nose. We hadn't eaten lunch, and I was so hungry I felt a little nauseous. Or was it fear gnawing at me again. I couldn't tell.

T.K. asked me to repeat every word, every nuance, and while I talked, he smoked and looked across the water with narrowed eyes, concentrating on our worsening predicament.

"The gist was that everyone," I paused for emphasis, "Everyone knows who we are and why we're here, and not a man jack of them can be trusted. He even said not to trust him. Why would he say that?"

When T.K. turned to look at me, his eyes looked so weary I wanted to weep.

"Captain Salenko is certainly not the ship's captain. I'm sure he's the ship's KGB officer. You've made an interesting conquest." T.K. gestured across the water toward Sassnitz. "Salenko definitely stated he couldn't save us? Not even you?"

I nodded. The memory of that afternoon on the beach when Anatoly brought Vlad to examine my shoulder came back to me. The plastic box the ship's doctor had carried but not opened had looked like a fishing tackle box.

"You always wondered." I turned to T.K. "Anatoly seemed to be able to get away from the ship whenever he wanted to. Never in uniform. Always at liberty. Going to parties." I stopped, recalling something else. "And he practically admitted to us that the KGB was stashing documents in the old grain elevator."

"He may have believed we already knew. And he would have wanted to seal our friendship." T.K. lit another cigarette.

"How would he know about Edgar?" That had been the most shocking news. "Do you think that's who he meant by the financier?"

"Who else could it be?" Our eyes met.

"Let's get out of here tonight," I said, almost in a whisper. "After the Midsummer party. Lose Putnam and Uta. Grab a train to Berlin. Or pay a cab to take us. Don't even bother to check out of the hotel. Just take our cash and go."

"That would work." He put his finger to his lips and we went back into the room. Yesterday morning before we boarded *The Painted Cow*, I had stuffed my laptop, most of our cash, and all but one of our credit cards into T.K.'s big suitcase and locked it. T.K. had heaved the whole business on top of the wardrobe.

Now I pointed to it. While I got the key out of my boat bag, T.K. lifted the suitcase down and put it on the bed. His brow wrinkled, and his mouth had a quirky twist as it always did when he was puzzled. He didn't wait for the key, but pressed the latches with his thumbs. They snapped open.

Surprised, I started to say, "I know I locked it," but before I could get the words out, T.K. lifted the lid.

The suitcase was empty.

We stood side-by-side and peered into the gaping gray canvas interior where the laptop had been. T.K. put his hand in the zippered pouch where our cash and credit cards should be. Empty.

"Oh my God, T.K.!"

He put his finger to his lips, and led me back out onto the balcony.

"What are we going to do?" I whispered.

"Zara, how much cash do you have?"

We had paid for dinner last night, and bought rounds of drinks at the tea dance.

"Maybe a hundred marks. Plus a little mad money. Chuck left my new Master Card alone."

"We're not at the Grand Hotel in Berlin. This is still the Deutsche Demokratische Republik."

He pulled his wallet out of his back pocket. "Thirty marks." He counted the pile of change on the nightstand.

"Fourteen more. Maybe a hundred and fifty total."

"Do we have enough to take a train?" I tried to tamp down my panicky feeling.

"For two?" He shook his head. "Dunno. Doubtful. We can find out."

"A bus?"

"Too risky. There's nowhere to hide on a bus. A boat or train is better. And we sure as hell don't want to stick around long enough to have someone wire money."

I thought of calling Dungeons & Dragons to charter a plane to pick us up, but if the island had an airport it was hidden away from tourist eyes. Stralsund was thirty miles away, too far for a hurried hike out with so little darkness to hide us.

"We'll steal bicycles or hitch a ride," I said with more bravura than I felt. "We can show up without papers and tell the authorities our passports were stolen."

T.K. had been looking at the crowd on the Strand Promenade.

"There are two guys down there who could be watching the hotel." He continued in a conversational voice. "I thought somebody fell in behind us when we left for the tea dance. The other one probably followed us back. One of those 'many enemies' of ours must have called in reinforcements." He paused, and I tried to keep breathing.

A dark wind had blown in, chilling even a cold warrior like T.K. I imagined the awful finality of doors banging shut and gates slamming, leaving no exit.

T.K. put his arm around me and spoke softly. "We will get out of here. In the meantime, we won't give Billy Boy any reason to suspect we're onto him." He gave my arm a little squeeze. "We'll act as meek and docile as bunnies."

~ * ~

Midsummer's Eve had become a Midsummer's Nightmare.

We ate Koteleti Pojarski at the Köpi Eck, with Putnam appraising us with a malevolent gleam in his cold eyes and Uta offering schoolmarmish lectures about the history of the summer solstice in the Baltic countries. If I hadn't been so intent on thinking of how to leave the island, her myths and folklore might have been interesting, but my nerves felt like a cat's cradle of fine wires. Her voice droned on, but her words were lost to me.

We hadn't mentioned the theft to Putnam. If he were the perpetrator, he would think we hadn't yet discovered his robbery. Hoarding our precious cash, we hadn't offered to pay for wine or beer at the Albatross, nor did we offer to share the fare for the cab that drove us half way up the big hill north of Sassnitz to the Chalk Cliffs.

Private cars were not permitted on the hilltop, and when the cab was stuck in the throngs of people trekking up the road through the tall beech trees, we got out and joined the revelers. I still carried a midsummer bouquet Uta had given me: St. John's Wort with its petite yellow flowers, wormwood with silvery gray leaves and purple larkspur.

Many of the celebrants had obviously been drinking all afternoon. "It's going to be a bloody Bacchanal," Putnam muttered.

T.K. smiled and said, "A thousand Swedes came out of the weeds."

Uta with her flushed face and overly bright eyes looked a little tipsy, while Putnam's vigilant eyes never strayed from T.K. and me.

Looking at the smooth gray bark of the tall beeches, I stifled an urge to run, to take off through the forest of charcoal colored trunks, straight as telephone poles, and run to freedom. T.K. must have understood how I felt, because he kept a grip on my hand.

The big hill we climbed was flat on top, and revelers swarmed around the makeshift booths selling beer. A field kitchen had been set up, and Putnam gestured at the huge iron cookers and said, "*Gulaschkanonen*." T.K. and Uta laughed. "Goulash cannons," T.K. translated. He seemed carefree and natural, another happy partier.

In the center of the clearing, bundles of fagots had been stacked around an immense triangular pile of birch logs. I glanced at my watch and could just read the dial. Almost ten-thirty, but darkness was falling fast, and the sun had now settled behind the island and the sapphire sky would soon be dark.

The chalk cliffs, offering a long vertical plunge into the sea, were a few hundred feet away, and two cops blocked the narrow path through the forest that led to the lookout points and to the steep trail down to the beach.

A red rocket fired from the clearing lit up the dark sky above us, and the crowd became still. We heard a far off sound of bells, dissonant and arrhythmic, then atonal horns, low muffled drums, high reedy flutes and pipes. Louder and closer came the primitive sounds, eerie but compelling.

In a procession of bells and drums, holding flaming torches aloft, two creatures in masks depicting a rooster and a dog entered the clearing, followed by several musicians, also masked. A duck rang the bells, while a cow with her horned head bedecked with flowers rattled a tambourine. A piping brown goat danced suggestively, thrusting his pelvis at a white sheep that pounded a drum. After them came a slinky black cat blowing a horn trotting next to an eel banging on a milk can. Bringing up the rear was a red-eyed demonic looking donkey that beat upon a large hollow drum.

The noise, hallucinatory in its intensity, filled the mountaintop. The motley band, wearing skins, feathers and rags below their masks, dipped and swirled in a clamorous dance as more rockets spiraled into the dark sky. The audience sent up a hoarse cheer.

"This music will scare away the witches and evil spirits," muttered Uta.

The tumult of sounds grew more intense, and the crowd parted for three men rolling an immense flaming wheel, which they directed toward the tower of birch logs. I couldn't see over the people in front of me for a moment, then I caught a glimpse of a boy lighting the fagots. The spectators gave a wondrous "ahhhh," as the bonfire was lit. Moments later red flames blazed and surged up into the night and while the birch logs burned, the musicians whirled in their dervish dance.

"The fire purifies," chanted Uta. "The fire is magic."

The mesmerizing masks and the pagan rite reminded me of my lamb nightmare. I moved closer to T.K., who still held my hand.

We had to retreat, as smaller fires were laid around the bonfire. A pungent smoke drifted into our faces.

"Burning herbs keep away the spirits that do mischief to the cattle," intoned Uta. Her face with its sharp nose and eyebrows like swallows in flight looked rapturous in the firelight.

Too bad the burning herbs didn't keep Putnam at bay.

I looked across the clearing and nudged T.K. Romy, with a garland of flowers in her dark hair stood with Chuck and Wulf Mueller. Chuck's glassy-eyed stare focused on the cat's jutting breasts. He looked either drunk or stoned. Not a good time to inquire about our passports.

The buxom cat reminded me of Andrea Schuld. I watched as Sabine and Bodo joined Chuck's little group. T.K. eyed them, too. So did Putnam. Uta, the high priestess of midsummer, had wandered off.

"Everyone knows," Anatoly had said. "Many enemies."

The crowd seemed restless now, always in motion, waiting for the fires to burn low enough for the couples to jump.

"Can I bring you a beer?" asked T.K., turning to me.

"No. Please don't leave," I whispered.

Putnam heard T.K.'s offer and insisted, "Two more for Uta and me."

T.K. hesitated, winked at me, and motioned toward the beer tents. I tried to follow, but Putnam grabbed my arm.

"Enjoying the little festival are we, luv?" His voice had an insolent sneer.

I turned to face him, the man I now thought of as my jailer. Our eyes met, and in that instant I hated him.

"I am so bloody tired I could damn well fall asleep standing up," I said, paying particular emphasis to the word "bloody."

His eyes bulged slightly, and I wondered if his scarred knuckles would knock me into the middle of next week, but he dropped my arm, turned about face, and walked in the direction T.K. had gone.

If I could only find T.K. before Putnam came back, we could merge with the crowd and run away into this crazy night. Why was T.K. buying beer when we had to hoard our little bit of cash? I was fixated on the idea of escape. We could use the darkness to hike down the long hill. Maybe hitch on one of the descending shuttle busses. With Putnam hovering, we hadn't had a chance to look at a ferry schedule or price tickets. If we had watchers, they would have to contend with the confusion, the smoke and the crowds.

Alone, I cruised by the beer tents, hoping to find T.K. without bumping into Putnam, but I didn't see either of them. I glanced over at the group that had formed around Romy and Chuck. Sabine was talking while Bodo glowered. Chuck looked around in his supercilious way. Was he looking for the sexy horn-blowing cat?

I wondered where Chuck had moored *Painted Cow*. The northern trip around Rügen was much shorter than the route the four of us had sailed. He might have cruised into Sassnitz harbor.

Romy said something to Chuck and his answer was a scowl. She looked like a pagan goddess with her dark flower-laced hair and her smoldering watchful eyes.

Ho Dung and a few young Asian men stood in the dark shadows away from the fire, watching the festivities. When I glanced their way again, Wulf Mueller had approached them. His stiff posture, furious eyes and rapid speech told me he must be haranguing them about something. Ho Dung and his friends looked pained, and they faded into the darkness as Wulf turned and stalked away.

A huge crowd surged around the fires, with whole groups chained together hand in hand, swaying and chanting while the drummers beat out a savage rhythm. Cowed by the Babel of foreign voices, I moved in the shadow of the tall flames, with the acrid smell of burning herbs in my nose, and the disorienting music in my ears.

Where was T.K.? What would I do if he didn't come back? I would have to find my way down the hill alone, and try to stow away on the Swedish ferry.

Why wait?

One person would be less conspicuous than two. After all, I was supposed to be back in Berlin by now, with my own passport, on a flight back to Chicago. Where had "go along to get along" gotten me? Into this mess. If I could find the path down the cliff, I could hitch a ride from Sassnitz to Stralsund. Get back to Berlin somehow. There might even be enough money for one third-class train ticket.

I edged through the crowd to the wooded area where the path led to the cliffs and the observation point. A policeman stood in the way.

With a painted-on smile and a slight stagger, I stood in front of him.

"Toiletten?" I asked with a giggle, indicating the path.

He shook his head and pointed in the other direction.

I feigned another laugh. *"Zu lange Schlange. Zu viel Bier."* Too long a line, too much beer.

He grinned.

"Ich mach' schnell." I'll be quick. I gave him my best smile.

He shrugged, and I darted around him and ran down the path to the cliff.

A moonless night. Now it was dark as pitch, but the white chalk of the cliffs and even the path should be visible. My pulse out-paced the now distant drumming. I could still smell the herby smoke, but the noise and chaos were behind me. It would be stupid to wander around and get lost. I could barely make out the path.

Right away I abandoned all ideas of climbing down to the beach in this cave-like darkness. T.K. and I had seen reproductions of the famous Caspar David Friedrich painting of the chalk cliffs, with the vertical plunge down to the blue green sea. I remembered the rocks on the beach and the pieces of driftwood. There was no soft sand to break one's fall.

The night air, cool and damp, made me shiver, and I zipped up my hooded sweatshirt. The road offered a safer escape. Still, I walked forward a few more yards, using dead reckoning in the darkness. In the direction of Sassnitz to the south, a roseate glow in the sky. East toward the Baltic, ebony black.

Straight ahead of me, in the direction of the cliffs, I heard raised male voices and froze. I crept a little closer, primed to leap into the bushes to avoid exposure.

Arguing in German. I couldn't make out the words. I heard rustling and thrashing. As I edged closer, a man's panicked voice yelled, "*Nein, nein!*" No. No. There was a hoarse protest and heavy grunting. Then a long terrible scream than echoed into the dark night. I stood rooted to the spot.

Footsteps pounding my way. I could see nothing, but I lunged off the path and ducked into some shrubbery, scratching my hands on the twigs. The person passed close by. Heavy breathing, almost gasps. Then silence, there was only the noise of the drums in the distance, shouts from the mob of people, and the pungent smoke.

With my heart racing, I scuttled back along the path, with the flames lighting the way. I hadn't realized I had traveled such a distance toward the cliffs. The German cop wasn't at his post, and I merged into the anonymity of the crowd.

The smaller fires had now burned low enough for the young couples holding hands to leap over them. Exuberant boys showing off jumped, too.

"The flax will grow as high as the highest jumper," Uta had prophesied.

"There's my girl!" A familiar low voice spoke behind me. I turned and noticed T.K.'s goofy smile. He wasn't carrying any beer.

"Where the hell—?"

"Shhhhh. Tell you later. Where are our 'friends'?"

"Oh my God! I was looking for the path that goes to the beach and I overheard two men fighting. I'm sure one of them pushed the other one over the cliff."

T.K. frowned, and I realized it could have been him. After all, I had seen nothing. Before he could speak, Uta, holding a beer bottle popped up next to us.

"Hallo again!" Her nosegay was gone and she looked rumpled, with bits of dry grass in her hair "You and T.K. must jump through the fire," she said, smiling at him.

"Oh, I don't think—."

"Come on, Sweet Pea! We'll make a magnificent leap!"

After what I had just heard, how could he think I would jump through the fire? The horrendous scream still sounding in my head, the leaping flames, masks and thrashing drums were too nightmarish to lure me close to the fires.

"No, you two should have a go at it," I said rather nastily.

"I jump with Bill—-after the cattle ceremony."

The Romy-Chuck group hadn't appeared again, but it was difficult to recognize anyone in the smoke and the darkness and the crush of bodies.

"Let's get out of here," T.K. whispered.

Just then Putnam walked out of the darkness like a skulking ghoul. Mr. 'always-perfectly-groomed' looked so tousled that T.K. said, "Billy Boy, have you been out in the bushes wrestling maidens?"

Had T.K. lost his mind? Uta giggled while Putnam glowered, and the moment was interrupted by the sound of cattle lowing. We watched a herder, wearing heavy boots and looking none too sober, pull two brown and white cows, unhappy campers despite their garlands of flowers and herbs, toward the smoky clearing. One of the smaller fires had been raked and sprinkled until only ashes remained, and the man led the balky cows through the cinders, as the onlookers emitted a raucous cheer.

Then Uta pulled Putnam toward the "jumper's fire." As they vaulted over the flames, Uta's breasts jiggled and bounced, gaining the noisy approval of some gawking beer-guzzlers, but Putnam's eyes never left us. Still holding Uta's hand, he hauled her around to where we stood watching.

"The obligatory cow-dragging and fire-jumping are behind us," he said sourly. "Now we need a beer."

The firelight cast a shadow on Putnam's face, forging his crooked nose, hard eyes and cruel lips into a more horrific mask than any of the creature band.

He and T.K. left for the beer tent. Back in high priestess mode, Uta babbled something about love magic and all the girls who would find their future husbands this evening. She announced that a dip in the water would be especially healing and lucky tonight.

"I've had enough celebrating for one midsummer," I said, feigning a yawn. "If you two want to stay, T.K. and I will catch a bus back to town."

"No, you won't!" Putnam's voice barked. T.K. stood right behind him. They both held beer bottles.

Before I could react, we heard the nasal 'ta ti ta ta' of sirens. A convoy of police cars came blaring up to the top of the hill and stopped, with blue lights flashing. The crowd became subdued as a swarm of cops descended on the festivities.

People were asking, "*Was ist los*?" Slowly the news passed from one group to the next. A horrible accident. A man had fallen down the chalk cliffs. All the way to the pebbled beach. Killed, of course.

Uta had said midsummer was a day of victory of sun and light over darkness and death. Not for the poor soul tossed over the cliffs.

~ * ~

The police herded everyone into four long lines, and processed the entire crowd, taking down names and addresses. I had steeled myself for awkward explanations about the whereabouts of our passports, but the young cop from Binz who had drooled over the Beemer recognized me, and didn't ask for identification.

Tourists like us who were staying on the island were asked to inform the police before they left. If the chance to leave presented itself, I would be out of here like greased lightning.

A pall had fallen on the hilltop. The bonfire had burned down to smoldering logs. The animal band wandered away. The donkey, mask off, ears a droop, left with his drum under his arm, walking side by side with the dog and the duck whose bells sounded an irregular plaintive chime as she strode along.

The Swedes became sober and orderly. The locals spoke to each other in low murmurs. At last, the first group of chastened celebrants was allowed to board the shuttle buses for the short trip back to Sassnitz. Putnam, never more than a few feet away, tried to herd us toward a bus, but one of the cops knew Uta, and he took her aside and whispered something in her ear.

She screamed, *"Nein! Nein!* Wulf!"* Then she hunched down on a tree trunk away from the embers, and wailed.

Had someone thrown Wulf Mueller over the chalk cliffs? Wulf Mueller, ex-Stasi field officer, dog owner, former colleague of Bodo and landlord of Chuck was dead? Wulf Mueller with his unspecified relationship to Romy, dead?

Wild horses could not drag out of me what I had heard but not seen by the edge of the cliff. *You know nothing.* I said it to myself over and over.

I walked over to Uta, patted her shoulder, while she covered her face with her hands and bawled in loud breathy sobs.

Someone told T.K. that campers on the beach, who found his broken body, had heard Wulf scream as he plunged over the white precipice. That scream would haunt my nightmares forever. Shocked by his death, I tried to summon feelings of sadness, but I had never liked him. I remembered his goatish face surrounded by tight ringlets, his pale golden eyes, his braying laughter, and his hatred of foreigners. Still, he hadn't deserved his horrible fate.

Wulf would have enemies from his past, many with motives for wanting him gone. What bothered me was everyone had disappeared for a while, right before his death. T.K. Putnam. Uta. The group around Chuck and Romy. Everyone.

Someone had brazenly seized an opportunity. Where had T.K. been? What if he were involved?

All of us hovered a few feet away from the weeping Uta, and even Putnam seemed undecided as to what we should do.

She shook her head back and forth and choked out incoherent words. Then she cried, "Wulf! Wulf! Wulf!" She kept blubbering the word *Vergeltung*. I noticed blades of grass were stuck to her big square knees.

T.K. watched Uta with an odd expression on his face, half worry, and half puzzlement. When I asked what *Vergeltung* meant, he paused before answering.

"Retribution."

Retribution for what, I wondered.

Sabine, her face full of woe, ran up to Uta and bent down to her and they hugged each other and set off a chorus of fresh sobs and wailing. Bodo stood stiffly off to one side, looking angry and a little uncertain. Had he pushed his old boss off the hill into oblivion? He would have sufficient strength, as would Putnam.

Now Romy, with the garland of limp flowers still adorning her dark hair walked up to the two crying women. She didn't join in the hugs and weeping, but stood by them, hands at her sides, clenching and unclenching her fists. Romy had argued with Wulf at the party. I didn't think her lean arms could send Wulf spiraling off the cliff. Still...

Sabine noticed Romy standing by and put her arm around her, trying to pull her into the mourning sisterhood, but Romy sat by herself on the rustic log chair next to Uta and stared into the darkness. Her dark eyes looked stunned, as if she couldn't believe what everyone now knew.

Wulf Mueller was dead.

Chuck had disappeared. Did Chuck hate Wulf enough to kill him? I wouldn't put anything past Chuck.

I walked over to the women. Romy looked up, and I wasn't sure she even recognized me. "Will you take Uta home?" I asked. "She'll want to be with close friends or her family at a time like this."

Romy nodded. She seemed totally out of it.

"We'll be going then." I hesitated.

Romy nodded again. Sabine and Uta burst into fresh tears. I gave Uta my package of tissues and returned to T.K. and Putnam.

Putnam said, "The time has come for the Wentzes performance review, and what a bloody sorry performance it's been!"

"Billy Boy," T.K. said, and then paused. "We can listen to your rant over breakfast tomorrow. Now I want to go back to the hotel and make love to my wife." He sounded so sincere that I turned and stared at him.

Death brought out strange reactions. Putnam considered T.K.'s amorous suggestion for about three seconds.

"Not bloody yet, you won't," he said in a cold, steely voice. "I want to discuss the balls up the Wentzes made of their sailing trip. Edgar will be aerated when I tell him that instead of the CD-ROM you two got the bloody boot."

"Billy Boy," T.K. said, and stopped and opened his mouth in an exaggerated yawn. "Can't this tiresome old rant wait until tomorrow?"

Putnam, his eyes angry slits, offered no response, but continued to escort us into the parking area where a trio of shuttle buses waited with engines idling.

T.K. said, "On the other hand, I would love to hear you explain how you single-handedly managed to toss the primo ex-Stasi over the side of the cliff. The self-same ex-Stasi who wanted to buy Chuck's data warehouse."

Putnam still didn't speak, but his eyes were murderous.

Oh, God! What is T.K. doing? Now we're really in for it.

We boarded the bus. Putnam tried to grab the seat directly behind T.K. and me, but a large woman planted herself there, taking up two places, and Putnam had to sit in the row behind her. Moments later, standees reeking of beer and smoke crowded the aisles. The driver closed the door, and pointed the bus down the hill.

"Why did you accuse Putnam of killing Wulf?" I said in a whisper. "He was already angry. Now he's totally bullshit."

He draped his arm over my shoulders, speaking softly so no one could overhear.

"Sometimes I make an educated guess."

I didn't understand T.K. at all. Why enrage Putnam, putting us even more at risk? While the bus rumbled down the hill, my thoughts twisted like the road. I leaned against T.K. as the driver, who apparently thought he was maneuvering a Porsche through the Grand Prix, careened through a curve. As close as we were, I still felt lonely and desperate. We didn't have the CD-ROM. Two men were dead. Putnam was insane, and now T.K. was acting like a lunatic.

"Where were you?" I asked in the whiny tone I hated. "We might have had a chance to escape."

T.K. didn't answer right away. Then he answered in a glib voice, "Oh, I was information gathering."

"Did you talk to somebody? Were you anywhere near the cliffs?"

Another pause.

"No. I was in the woods. I, ah, was with Uta."

"With Uta? What kind of information does she have besides Midsummer blather?"

He didn't answer. Uta had had relationships with both Wulf and Putnam. She might have information. But why would she share it with T.K.?

I turned and looked square at him. "What were you doing with her?"

His hand waved in a vague gesture, brushing against a man standing in the aisle.

I glanced around to make sure Putnam was still far enough not to overhear. "What did she tell you?"

"She may have saved our butts. She said the old Stasi gang was watching the exits from the island: cars crossing the Rügendamm, the ferries, the train, even bicycles."

"Why don't they want us to leave? Do they think we have the CD-ROM? Or are they in cahoots with Putnam?"

"She didn't know the reason, but we're going to be the patsies. Maybe we've seen something. Maybe we know too much." He paused and frowned. "She warned me...that Billy Boy was—-feeling his oats, itching for combat, so to speak."

"Then how dumb was it to accuse him of killing Wulf?"

"Just let me handle Putnam," he said with a scowl.

Astonished that Uta had betrayed so many confidences, I asked, "So, what did Uta want in return for this information?"

"She, um, she wanted..." His voice trailed off and he didn't meet my eyes.

"She wanted what?"

"Shhhhh. You know..."

"No, I don't know. What did she want?"

T.K. still avoided eye contact. From the window of the bus I could see Sassnitz below. In the harbor, lights shone aboard the Russian ship.

"She wanted, er, she asked me to...do her." He tried to cross his long legs, but the seats were too close together.

"Do her? What does that mean?" I must be a few mouse clicks behind.

"Do her. You know."

"No, I do not know." I had a perverse pleasure in seeing him squirm.

"Jesus, Zara, don't be so dense."

"You had sex with her? Oh really, T.K.!"

"Shhhhh. For Christ's sake. Keep your voice down." He fidgeted and tried to cross his legs again. "It wasn't exactly sex."

"Either it was sex or it wasn't."

"Technically, it wasn't," he muttered.

Anger was overtaking my feelings of jealousy.

"Did she say how you stacked up against Wulf and—?"

"Will you shut up?" His hands were clenched and he stared straight ahead.

T.K. and I had been very tight with each other. I had believed that he cared for me, and yet he couldn't be faithful for two weeks, two goddamned lousy weeks.

In the back of the bus, a chorus of voices began singing in Swedish. The tune had the monotonous rhythm of a summer camp song with forty verses. I wanted to scream at the singers to shut up, and I wanted to cry and to pummel T.K. at the same time. Most of all, I didn't want to let him see how devastated I was.

"Sweetie I had to find out what she knew."

"Don't sweetie me!" Pressing myself against the wall of the bus, I moved as far away from him as I could.

He grabbed my wrist and pulled me back.

"The Sunday school picnic is kaput." His voice, right into my ear, was hoarse with tension. "We are in deep kimchee, and I will do anything necessary to get us off this goddamned island alive."

"And how is screwing Uta helping this endeavor?"

"Will you get it out of your thick head that I screwed her? And even if I had, this is not the time for any squeamishness." Then he lowered his voice even more, and spoke so softly I couldn't hear him. Something or other about "Billy Boy," then "I am going to try to..." but I couldn't make out the rest.

"I didn't understand a word you said."

Just then the bus arrived in the center of Sassnitz and the driver stopped at the intersection that led down to the Albatross.

"I'll tell you later."

When the lights came on, I turned to look behind us. Putnam had left his seat and stood squeezed up right next to our row. When he put his hand on T.K.'s shoulder, the sight of his scarred knuckles gave me such a feeling of dread that I could barely stand.

He just said, "Right-o! Here we are."

Nobody spoke as we walked toward the parking lot behind the Köpi Eck where Putnam had parked the gray Opel. The air smelled briny and fetid, like a salt marsh. Putnam told T.K. to drive and made me sit in the back seat with him. He kept referring to me as the digerati diva, and I realized in the last two weeks he had never spoken my name.

T.K. looked at Putnam in the rear view mirror and asked, "Where do you plan to give us our dressing down?" but Putnam didn't answer.

"Billy Boy, now would be as good a time as any."

Putnam still didn't respond and instead began to hum "The Colonel Bogey March" in a disjointed monotone, adding the hums and clicks—those strange sounds he had made at the tea dance this afternoon.

I didn't like this at all. T.K. glanced back at Putnam, lit a cigarette and rolled the driver's window all the way down.

Putnam stopped humming and stated, "Order. Counter-order. Disorder." An ominous pause followed each word.

At the intersection where we would normally turn into town, Putnam told T.K. to keep driving and directed him to take the road to Putbus.

"Zara is tired," said T.K. "I'll just drop her off at the hotel. You and I can have a little stag party tonight."

"Not in a million years. The digerati diva stays with the group. Who knows? Maybe our boyo Goodborn has sailed his pretty yacht back to Lauterbach Harbor. Maybe the CD-ROM is still aboard all snug and nice. Maybe she can retrieve it. Never too late to redeem ourselves, is it now?"

He spoke with a false heartiness that set my teeth on edge.

T.K. echoed, "Never too late for redemption," and lit another cigarette. Putnam directed T.K. through Putbus and along a dark rocky road, ordering "left here" and "next right."

I sat next to him in the back seat and quailed.

The cacophonous beat of the menagerie band with its pounding drums and tuneless horns still pulsated in my head. Maybe T.K. heard it, too, because he turned on the radio.

> *Your breath touched my cheek like the warm summer wind.*
> *Your lips burnt mine like the mid-summer's sun.*

"Turn off that bloody drivel!" Putnam barked.

T.K. doused the music.

The road narrowed to one lane and a stark white-columned building loomed out of the darkness. T.K. slowed down to a crawl and said, "Billy Boy, you missed the Lauterbach road. We're at the old bathhouse. Interesting statue of a girl undressing you might want to inspect. One of the island's unheralded sights."

Putnam rolled his window down and peered into the night. "Right-o! Drummond, turn in here and stop."

T.K. pulled into the deserted parking area. Putnam spoke in a level voice.

"Now turn off the motor and give me the keys." He gestured at me. "The digerati diva will remain inside. If she decamps, the whipping boy will pay dearly."

T.K. looked at Putnam, started to say something, and stopped. My heart raced and I felt nauseated. T.K. turned to look at me. Our eyes met. He squinted and nodded slightly, but I didn't understand what he was trying to tell me.

Putnam ordered T.K., "Get out!"

T.K. opened the driver's door, then hesitated. He turned and said to Putnam, "I thought you had graduated from the sadist's twelve step program."

Putnam said, "Drummond, you know no one ever changes."

After one last drag, T.K. tossed the cigarette out the window. He was looking at Putnam in the rear view mirror.

"The keys, Drummond."

T.K. just sat there. I froze when Putnam put his hand on my face and ran his index finger roughly down my cheek, and over my chin. I gave a little shriek as his hand pressed against my neck.

T.K. tossed the keys at Putnam, who caught them in his right hand. Putnam's left hand still touched my neck, making me crazy with fear.

T.K. opened the car door, then he took off his glasses and handed them to me, but he looked at Putnam. "Leave her alone."

Putnam took his hand away and opened the door on his side.

I just didn't understand what was happening. "What's going on? Where are you guys going?"

T.K.'s answer was full of careless bravado. "Oh, Billy Boy is going to administer his brand of tough love."

"Can't we be civilized?" I asked as they got out of the car. "Bill, please, can't we talk? Let's talk it over. Okay?"

The car doors slammed shut.

"No! Wait! Please!"

They disappeared into the blackness, Putnam behind T.K. Then I could only see the white pillars rising out of the greenery, and in the foreground, the gray statue of the woman pulling her dress over her head. Some insects were buzzing in the thick silent night. Then I heard the smacking sound of a fist battering flesh followed by a muffled groan.

I had to save T.K. before Putnam beat him to a pulp, but my pulse hammered so loudly in my ears that I couldn't think. Trying to staunch my panic, I groped around under the Opel's back seat. Maybe I could find Putnam's revolver or commando knife. Nothing.

I opened the trunk with the inside latch.

"Calm down," I whispered, as I climbed out of the car into the darkness. In the distance by the bathhouse, I heard voices. T.K.'s sounded furious, and Putnam answered with the sweet reason of madness.

I moved around the car on trembling legs and slipped into the front seat to continue my search. Nothing there either, but I did find a flashlight in the glove box. I got out of the car and again heard the sickening sound of fist pounding flesh.

Putnam swore, endlessly repeating the word, "bloody."

"Calm down," I whispered to myself again. "Jesus, just calm down." Creeping around the car, I lifted the trunk lid and aimed the beam of the flashlight inside. Putnam had stashed everything in the Opel. I noted the backpack with emergency supplies, our picnic gear, and Putnam's beach bag. Under the backpack, I found the two gray paving stones we had picked up to sink the dog's body.

Two hands were required to grab hold of one of the heavy pavers. I clasped the stone close to my body and pulled the folding shovel out of the backpack with my left hand. Trying to decide what would be the best weapon, I vacillated between stone and shovel.

Carry them both.

I forced myself to move with deliberation as I unfolded the shovel with my awkward left hand. The sound of another blow made the paralyzing fear return. I stood still, listening, but now the only noise was the insects calling and the blood rushing around in my head.

My mouth felt like dry cotton, and I couldn't swallow. Using the shadows of the tall bushes lining the parking lot as cover, I crept toward the disrobing statue, shovel in one hand, paving stone clutched in the other. My feet crunched on the gravel, but the insect chorus in the bushes covered the sound. Moisture made the air heavy, and although the night was cool, I had started to sweat. With each step the paver felt heavier.

Behind the tall evergreens, Putnam croaked, "I don't enjoy this, Drummond, I really don't."

T.K. answered, "Fuck you."

"Drummond, listen to reason. Goodborn's expendable. The Stasi are out of it. She's expendable."

T.K. grunted and said something I couldn't hear.

"She can meet with an accident. Like Mueller did."

T.K. said, "No way," in a hoarse wheezing voice.

"It can still be old Drummie and old Bill dealing with the Russkies." Another pause to inhale. "Like in our glory days, except now we're independent businessmen." Putnam kept a reasonable tone. "You always used to adapt to these situations."

T.K. didn't answer.

A path led around the statue toward the bathhouse. I continued to creep through the darkness, then stopped. The starlight reflected off the white temple-like building, and I could see both men in stark relief, just a few feet away. Putnam's broad back was turned to me and now T.K. moved out of the darkness. His bloodied face hammered home the reality of Putnam's beating. I gripped the paving stone like a shotputt and placed my feet shoulder width apart for balance. I still held the shovel in my left hand.

Quicker than I could have imagined, Putnam put up his fists, took a step forward and launched a pulverizing blow at T.K., who turned to deflect the punch. It landed on his shoulder, sending him reeling.

Putnam stepped back again. Now I summoned all my strength and heaved the stone. Hearing me grunt, Putnam turned just as my missile arrived. It caught him in the stomach and he made an "oooof" sound and lurched backward, but didn't fall. In some invincible Zen-like state, I moved toward him, grasping the shovel with both hands. Putnam was bent over clutching his stomach, and T.K. was on his hands and knees scrabbling around in the gravel.

I raised the shovel over my head like an ax and brought it down, but Putnam edged out of the way, and the shovel smashed into the ground and flew out of my tingling hands.

Putnam clambered to his feet and said, "Bloody hell!"

My feet were nailed to the ground.

T.K. yelled, "For Christ sake, run for it!"

Putnam grabbed my arm with a hand slick with blood, and held on with a terrible tenacity. When I struggled and kicked at him, his grip only tightened. His free hand clamped on to my other flailing arm, as I screamed and struggled. I couldn't believe how powerful he was. I knew he would kill me.

Then I glimpsed T.K. behind Putnam, staggering but hanging on to the paving stone. Putnam was so focused on me he never knew what hit him. The stone only grazed his head, but he released his grip as he collapsed onto the gravel, as solid and quiet as the granite that had bashed him.

T.K. stood and stared down at Putnam. I should have felt relief, but now I was even more frightened

"My God, is he dead?"

"I doubt it." T.K. used his shirttail to wipe the blood from his face.

Kneeling next to Putnam, I felt his neck. "Faint pulse," I said, looking up at T.K. for guidance.

"Let's get out of here. He's likely to wake up in a few minutes." He spit in the dirt and dabbed again at his bloody nose.

I fumbled through Putnam's pockets looking for his car keys, and when I found them, my hand trembled so much that they clinked together like little chimes. I took the money out of his wallet, dropped some bills and groped for them on the gravel.

"Take his wallet along. We'll ditch it later." T.K.'s voice was hoarse and still breathless.

I wobbled to my feet and leaned on the shovel. T.K. was weaving round as if punch drunk; he had picked up the paving stone again and refused to put it down. I steered him back to the car by his elbow, but I felt so dizzy and numb I wasn't sure who propped up whom.

"How badly are you hurt?" I asked, looking at the blood-soaked front of his shirt.

"Broken nose. Plenty of bruises."

"Should we find a doctor?"

"I'll survive. We have to get off this island."

I helped him get into the car. Then I handed him Putnam's beach towel from the trunk. He picked up his glasses from the dashboard where I had left them. If I could just get the car started, everything would be all right, because driving always calmed me.

My shaking leg slipped off the clutch as the car lurched out of the parking lot, and I turned onto the road before I remembered to flick on the headlights.

In the east, the horizon had a fine gold line that heralded the arrival of dawn.

"We're going to be okay," I said to T.K., trying to convince myself as well. "Everything is going to go right from here on out."

Thirteen

The smoky dawn couldn't penetrate the torpid mist hanging over Sassnitz. T.K. and I slouched in the gray Opel outside Putnam's lodgings, making sure the house wasn't being watched and checking for wakeful neighbors, pedestrians, barking dogs, anyone who might notice two people entering a place where they didn't belong. Nothing moved, not even the white cat that watched us from the porch across the street.

T.K. had it in his head that Chuck had given our passports to Putnam. Maybe Uta had told him. We wanted to steal them back from Putnam's room because we'd have a better chance to escape if we had travel documents.

An hour ago, after we had left Putnam unconscious at the *Badehaus in der Goor*, I had made a middle-of-the-night stop at our hotel. While T.K., whose denim shirt looked like Jackson Pollock had gone at it with a tube of crimson, waited in the car, I had rung the bell and awakened the night manager. I pretended to be a little tipsy, and favored the gentleman with a toothsome, louche smile. What clinched his cooperation was a fifty-mark bribe. Putnam's fifty marks. The manager gave me a bucket of ice and a ferry schedule. It was amazing how the simple need to survive focused one's priorities. In a mad scramble through our room, I crammed warm clothes and first aid supplies into T.K.'s duffel bag along with snacks and booze.

We changed clothes in the car, the same dark outfits we had worn to watch Chuck and Romy's cottage on The Night of the Dog.

"I vote to keep the Opel and drive back to Berlin," I said. "Tonight. I want to get off the island now. T.K., I will swim across the harbor if I have to."

"It would be suicidal to stay with Putnam's car when he might be dead." T.K. had wrapped the ice in a towel that he pressed against his nose. "Or worse yet, alive and on his way to file a stolen vehicle report."

Putnam might be dead. We would be held responsible. I knew we had left clues and evidence everywhere. Too late. Too late for everything, even for tears.

T.K. shifted the ice to his left eye. "We're safer on the Swedish ferry. Wulf's murder will have thrown the old Stasi watchers into confusion. I'm certain no one has been following us. No more discussion. We're going to make a run for Sweden."

Anywhere in the western world away from this island was all right with me.

"Did you remember our stash of vodka?" he asked.

"Yes, and the nuts and chocolate bars."

"I want some vodka."

Surveying his bruised face, I said, "T.K., we've got to keep our wits about us. And we'd better move. Get in and get out."

"Just give me the damn bottle."

I retrieved the bottle from the duffle bag and T.K. took a hefty swig and passed it back to me. I took a gulp, too. It burned all the way down.

With the money from Putnam's wallet, we had enough cash to buy tickets for the ferry to Trelleborg in Sweden. After liberating our passports, we were going to hustle down to the harbor and lie low until a few minutes before the first ferry departed. T.K. didn't know how much the rules had relaxed. In the old days an ordinary citizen wouldn't have been able to buy a ticket to another country without reams of permission slips and red tape. Of course, we weren't ordinary citizens, and in this "time of the turn," anyone might be able to buy a ticket, but we didn't think it would be as carefree as catching the Lake Michigan Ferry to Mackinac Island.

T.K. shivered, as he had been doing since we left the old bathhouse. I handed him a sweater. "Are you sure you want to do this?"

The idea of sneaking into Putnam's lodgings was scary. Putnam seemed like the sort who might set a booby-trap, or plan an unpleasant surprise for the unwary intruder.

"We have to get those phony-baloney passports back. They're better than nothing." T.K. dabbed at his nose. "Before Billy Boy or his ghost shows up." He hesitated. "Not a soul in sight. Only that white cat."

"We'll ditch the Opel here."

"Yeah. And leave the car keys in Putnam's room. With his wallet." He rubbed his chin. "Wipe it off with the towel and don't touch it again. Use your tissues. Where's that shovel? Stuff it in the duffel bag." He wiped the steering wheel with his old shirt. "Now, give me the keys."

I didn't let on how frightened I felt.

We left the car and crossed the street. I schlepped the duffel bag over my shoulder and carried the flashlight. The street was quiet, too quiet, almost like it waited. *Get a grip on yourself.*

We climbed the porch stairs of the boarding house and T.K. unlocked the front door. We slipped into a dark space. I flicked on the flashlight. A hallway. T.K. motioned me to follow him. We passed several doors and T.K. stopped at room number five. I fixed the flashlight on the lock, while he inserted the key. Trying not to make any unnecessary noise, he turned the handle slowly. The lock clicked. My heart raced as the door opened. With a shaky hand, I let the weak light play around the room.

A bed with rumpled covers. Someone snoring. I gasped as the light illuminated two big bare feet. White legs. Purple shorts with giant yellow polka dots. A massive belly, a strong chest. We must have taken in the whole scene instantly, but it seemed to last an eternity. The flash light beam traveled further up the body. When it reached the man's face, he snorted and opened his eyes. He froze.

One of those defining moments that stays with you for a lifetime. We froze.

The beaky nose, the white hair. My God, it was Edgar!

He squinted into the narrow beam of the flashlight, then in a quick movement he reached toward the nightstand. The shaft of light followed his outstretched arm. I saw a bottle, eyeglasses and a handgun. Edgar reached for the gun. I threw the keys and Putnam's wallet on the floor as we backed out of the room. T.K. shut the door.

I expected a barrage of bullets as we bolted down the hall and out onto the front porch.

T.K. gasped orders as we ran.

"Into the next yard! Stay by the houses! Keep going!" He was already panting. "Don't get too close to the walk!" We raced across the lawn, and tore through a flowerbed. Right on through the adjoining neighbor's yard.

T.K. wheezed more instructions as he ran. "At the corner, stay out of the street light. Left toward the harbor."

We charged on down the block. Somewhere behind us, a dog barked.

Then T.K. rasped, "For God's sake, don't outrun me. Stay together."

After our hundred-yard dash, we stopped so he could catch his breath. He seemed ready to collapse. I had visions of Edgar, his big belly flopping over the waistband of those shorts, hurtling down the street after us, firing his gun.

The dog had shut up and the neighborhood remained quiet in the smoky gray light. Somewhere out on the water a foghorn began sounding its mournful warning. I slung the duffel bag back over my shoulder and whispered to T.K., "Are you O.K.?"

He nodded. "Damned sore and dead tired. Let's keep going. We'll take an indirect way down to the harbor."

"Won't Edgar come after us?" I asked.

"He never saw us. He knows someone opened the door and shone a light in his eyes."

"Won't he wonder where Putnam is?"

"That he will. Now let's put some distance between us and bad Edgar."

I kept looking over my shoulder as we wended our way street by street down to the harbor. The old houses appeared derelict and deserted. The cobblestones gleamed, all slick and shiny with moisture. T.K. and I both shivered in the damp air. He seemed lost in his own thoughts as he dabbed at his still-bleeding nose.

"Thanks for saving my butt."

"You saved mine at the grain elevators," I reminded him.

We walked on in silence.

Edgar. What was Edgar doing in Putnam's bed? He had appeared once before without a plausible explanation. I noodled over what Putnam had said to T.K. between punches there at the Badehaus. Something about the Stasi being "out of it," and "old Drummie and old Bill dealing with the Russkies." The Stasi would indeed be out of it if Putnam pitched their leader over the chalk cliffs.

Had old Ed and old Bill decided to deal directly with Anatoly? They might be selling him Chuck's software, cutting Chuck and Romy out of the equation, cutting T.K. and Zara out. Cutting Wulf Mueller out. Way out. Still, I didn't think they had Chuck's CD-ROM. Not yet. I wondered what T.K. knew that he hadn't shared. I wondered if I would ever hug Chloe again. I tried to push these bleak thoughts out of my mind.

How we would board the ferry without passports? Maybe the local officials wouldn't care if foreigners leaving the country had papers on not. But what would the Swedes say? T.K. was keeping his own counsel, never a good sign. My bruised shoulder throbbed from the weight of the duffle.

Yachts with midsummer celebrants had overloaded the dock space, forcing some of the boats to anchor in the basin. At the waterfront, a bunch of dilapidated rowboats were tied up to the pier.

"What now?" I asked. We had been running on adrenaline all night, and an overwhelming weariness was creeping into my bones. Too tired to think or run, I wanted to collapse. T.K. must feel crummy. He already had two black eyes and I wondered if he had a concussion.

"We could find a dry place to sit down," he said, glancing around. "We sure as hell don't want to arrive at the ferry terminal at four-thirty in the morning."

"How about if we climbed into one of those rowboats? If we can find one that isn't leaky." I peered into the hull of one that looked promising. An inch of water.

"We could sit on the dock," T.K. said, "and wash those nuts down with some vodka." The sound of a car driving slowly along one of the nearby streets interrupted T.K.'s proposal. We stood motionless until the sound faded into the distance.

"Let's walk a little further," he said, pointing to the end of the wharf, "and we can prop ourselves up against those pilings. I definitely need propping up."

The fog had rolled in and settled a few feet above the harbor, causing the masts of the sailboats to disappear into the cloudy soup. Calling in shrill voices, two gulls swooped over the water in the gray light.

We approached the pilings, but someone else had gotten the idea first. He jumped up as we approached.

"Hi, what are you doing here?" I blurted, forgetting he spoke only a smidgen of English.

Ho Dung stared at us with alarm, then recognition and relief. He hesitated and looked around, his eyes wide with fear. "The police are searching for me," he said in German. Someone told them I pushed Herr Mueller off the cliff."

The surprises kept rolling in like the fog.

"Wulf looked angry when he was talking to you on the hilltop," I said, switching to German.

Ho Dung nodded. "He told us that we must go. That we had not right to be at festival." He frowned at the memory. "Herr Mueller said Asians have not understanding of Nordic symbols." He paused. "My friends and I were disappointed, but we did not kill him."

"They're afraid of foreigners here, because they've isolated themselves so long," said T.K.

Ho Dung stared at T.K.'s battered face with the dried blood still caked around his nostrils, and two shiners.

"We had our own bad luck tonight," I said. "We want to get off the island."

Ho Dung pointed toward the basin where the fog hovered above the boats. "*Painted Cow* is anchored there. I thought Mr. Goodborn's boat would be good hiding place, but now afraid—if he find me there."

I looked at Ho Dung. "Is anyone on board? Did you see a light in the cabin? Chuck was at the festival, but he disappeared."

"No lights."

I turned to T.K. and said in English. "We could borrow a rowboat to get to Chuck's boat. Catch a few hours sleep."

Sleep. It beckoned like an addictive drug.

T.K. touched his nose and winced. "I don't see any oars."

"At the Albatross!"

They both stared at me.

"I'll be right back," I said. The prospect of sleep gave me a shot of energy. I put down the duffel bag and took off.

When I returned with oars, T.K. and Ho Dung were sitting hunkered down in a disreputable looking rowboat, with bare wood showing through the chipped paint. T.K. had our duffel bag across his lap, and he and Ho Dung were smoking cigarettes and speaking softly in a language I didn't know. Vietnamese? T.K. spoke with a lot of pauses and hesitations. They must be determining facts that would establish their relative positions back in that time. Ho Dung seemed to me in his early thirties. He would have been a boy during the war.

I handed him the oars, one of which had a broken blade. Then I delivered the bad news. "Half the cops on the island have congregated at the ferry terminal."

T.K. muttered, "Cripes!" Ho Dung gave me a hand while I climbed into the boat and sat down. We seemed dangerously low in the water, and I hoped the boat wouldn't swamp.

T.K. said, "*Di di Mau!*"

"What?" I asked.

"*Di di Mau!*" T.K. repeated. "That's Vietnamese for 'let's get out of here.'" T.K. made one of his broad sweeping gestures, stopped and grimaced, still in pain. He continued speaking Vietnamese to Ho Dung, who began rowing with steady workman-like strokes, propelling us forward. We skimmed past a dozen or so boats anchored in the basin, including some old rust buckets.

Then dead ahead through the fog I saw a familiar trim boat. It was the *Little Mermaid*, anchored a bit away from the others. I put my hand on T.K.'s arm and pointed. We scrutinized the shipshape little Danish boat. The flag had been taken in. T.K. motioned to Ho Dung to give the boat a wide berth, as I scanned the cockpit for signs of life. Nothing stirred. Then in the distance, through the fog I spied the pristine hull of *Painted Cow*.

An eerie noise floated over the water. At first I thought it was a boat straining against the anchor line, but then it sounded more like sea birds calling to each other. Ho Dung continued to row. I listened, and the nearer we came, the more enigmatic the noise. Then all three of us must have had a simultaneous understanding that we were hearing the moans and cries of a woman in a sexual frenzy. The commotion came from Chuck's boat.

Ho Dung lifted the oars out of the water. T.K. and I exchanged looks.

"Is that what I think it is?"

T.K. said, "Chuck and Romy." He grinned. "Particularly Romy."

"Let's wait here until they're finished," I said, for now we were only a few yards from the boat.

"No. The elements of surprise and embarrassment will work in our favor," T.K. whispered.

Looking as uncomfortable as I felt, Ho Dung fidgeted with the broken oar, running his hand over the uneven paddle. T.K. motioned to him to keep rowing.

As we closed in on *Painted Cow*, I noticed little ripples around the hull. They were literally rocking the boat.

"This is awful! T.K., please, let's go back."

T.K. shook his head.

Yesterday in the hour before dawn, the Danish boat had interrupted our furtive coupling. These lovers would be unluckier still.

In complete silence, we glided up to the stern. A trim rowboat was tethered to the Zeesboot.

We heard a male voice panting, "Oh, baby, oh, baby, oh, baby!"

Ho Dung stood up, grabbed a stanchion, and then the lifeline. Ever solicitous of the Zeesboot, he climbed on board and threw down a fender to put between our rowboat and the hull.

The occupants wouldn't have noticed if the Loch Ness Monster had snorted and swum alongside.

I pulled myself onto the boat and T.K. handed up the duffel bag. The groans and gasps continued unabated. This was going to be so embarrassing. When I looked for a place to drop the duffel bag, I noticed the black hood, and a mask with cat ears and whiskers, then cat's paws and even a long black tail littering the cockpit. Chuck was with the sexy creature in the cat costume. Good Lord, if it was Andrea, this was going to be even worse than I imagined.

T.K., with only one good arm, had heaved himself onto the boat while Ho Dung tied up the rowboat. Then Ho Dung crept up to the bow and sat down, facing the water. T.K. disappeared down the companionway while I cowered in the cockpit. I heard him say in the cheeriest of voices, "You lovebirds better hurry it up, because the passengers are ready to sail."

Complete silence.

Then Chuck went ballistic, screaming and swearing and threatening mayhem. Amid the noise and profanity I heard a feminine voice trying to interject some reason into the scene.

T.K. came out of the cabin. "They're getting dressed," he said in a low voice, adding, "It's Andrea. The sexy cat girl. Old Bodo would be lathered if he found out Chuck was skizzling his daughter."

"She's only seventeen."

He shrugged. "Pay attention and don't say a word. I'm going to get us out of here."

We waited a few minutes until Chuck came up the companionway in bare feet and faded red shorts. He gave us the hairy eyeball while he buttoned a blue flannel shirt, and almost lost it again when he spotted Ho Dung sitting on the bow. "What the fuck is he doing here?"

"He's your crew." T.K. said quietly.

"The hell you say." Chuck's jaw jutted out with a stubborn thrust and his eyes were raw with rage. He looked at T.K. "Who beat the shit out of you? I'd like to shake his hand."

"The same man who was going to kill you last night," T.K. said in a matter-of-fact voice. He had Chuck's attention now. "If Zara hadn't been awake, we might all be dead."

"Okay, Wentz, who's this mystery man?"

Andrea came out of the cabin, wearing the black shirt and pants of the cat suit. Neither blushing nor the least bit abashed, she said, "hallo," plopped herself down next to me, opened a can of Fanta, and took a big swig. *Sang froid* to the max.

Chuck perked up. "Sweetheart!"

T.K. said, "Someone will row the young lady back to shore."

Chuck put his arm around Andrea's waist. "Andy's my crew today."

T.K. scowled. "Out of the question, Goodborn. Why would you put her at risk? Bodo will come after all of us."

"She stays," insisted Chuck, thrusting out his jaw even further.

"She goes," said T.K., and his voice had that dangerous edge that always made me quiver.

Andrea nodded agreement, and began gathering up the bits and pieces of the cat costume, and found a plastic bag to stash them in.

Obviously, this wasn't her first visit, for she seemed to know her way around the boat.

"I'll row Andrea back to the dock now," I volunteered.

Chuck automatically said, "Ho Dung can take her."

"No, he can't." I said, "The police are looking for him." After I explained why, Chuck grinned, and called out to Ho Dung, "So you played ultimate Frisbee with the head Stasi?"

A long pause while Ho Dung mulled over Chuck's phrase. *"Nein! Herr Goodborn."*

I climbed down into the rowboat that rocked until I sat down. T.K. helped Andrea in, who sat holding her drink and the plastic bag.

Chuck made a kissy face. "I'll catch up with you later, sweetheart," he said in a saccharine voice.

We pushed off from *Painted Cow*, and as I maneuvered the oars, it became painfully obvious that Zara Gray would never qualify for the Head of the Charles regatta.

"Oh, this is so stupid!" Andrea blurted out as I struggled to keep us on course. She gave me a scornful look. Even with tousled hair and smudged eye makeup, she was pretty.

"What do you suggest?" I asked, panting slightly.

"Give me the oars, and I'll take you back to the boat. I can row myself to the pier. It will be better if no one sees you."

The young lady had a head on her shoulders. She drained the juice, tossed the can overboard, and took over the oars, rowing with a practiced motion. She deposited me back at the boat in a fraction of the time it had taken me to row the same distance. A quick *"auf Wiedersehen,"* and she disappeared into the mist.

"Andrea wanted to go back alone," I explained once I was back aboard *Painted Cow*.

Ho Dung still sat on the bow. T.K. had taken off his shoes and plopped himself down next to Chuck in the cockpit, sharing the nuts and chocolate.

Chuck must have been told the identity of his would-be assassin, because he was venting in typical Chuck fashion.

"Putnam's your goddamned friend, right? I never trusted him or that oily Russian. You can't trust anyone in this God-awful backwater of a place!"

T.K. didn't react, but took another handful of hazelnuts and offered the bag to Chuck, who helped himself. Chuck sat with a stony face, daring anyone to cross him.

"I know you must feel betrayed," T.K. began. "Particularly since Putnam seems to be in league with one of your old backers, an Edgar Standish."

Chuck slumped down in the cockpit. "You're shittin' me!"

"Edgar and Putnam are, to put it mildly, pissed off at all of us." T.K. paused for emphasis, then continued, "but Mueller's murder has created a, shall we say, a window of opportunity for getting out of here." He paused. "You know Edgar. We know Putnam. We have to put our heads together, look at the possibilities and try to form a plan."

"I'll have to think about it," said Chuck, scowling again. He was staring at T.K., perhaps wondering about the great tectonic shift, about T.K. talking of plans and cooperation.

"We're all their quarry now, and we need to get out of here. What do you think of sailing out of Sassnitz while the fog is giving us some cover? We could lay over in an out of the way cove, and when the fog lifts, you and Ho Dung can sail us all across the Baltic." He paused. "The Danish island of Møn is a popular destination for refugees."

Chuck stared into the fog.

"Ho Dung will ask for political asylum," explained T.K.

"Hypothetically, what's in it for me?" asked Chuck.

"Hypothetically, your life."

Chuck digested that bit of information, shrugged, and relaxed his shoulders. "Suppose I turn you two over to Putnam and Edgar?" he asked. "They might be willing to deal." He looked from me to T.K. and beamed at us, apparently relishing his idea.

In spite of Chuck's threat, T.K.'s voice remained even.

"Putnam's deal would be to hold your feet to the flames until you revealed where you've stashed that CD-ROM."

T.K. abruptly stopped talking as a new sound, a boat with a rumbling engine entered the mooring area. We sat still, listening, except for Ho Dung, who left the bow and slipped down the companionway into the cabin, quiet as a cat. Chuck glanced at T.K. then peered into the fog. The engine seemed to be coming right at us, like a torpedo zeroing in through the filmy blanket of white. A big boat, maybe forty feet long, a cutter, loomed out of the mist and into view, only a few yards away. I saw the GDR flag. A spotlight played over *Painted Cow*. My God, were they going to board us?

T.K. waved. I made a half-hearted little gesture. A moment later, Chuck smiled his five hundred watt smile and raised his hand in a quasi-salute. The cutter's crew scrutinized us with blank faces, then one of the sailors returned our greeting. The cutter passed back into the white curtain of fog. I could breathe again.

T.K. continued as if nothing had happened. "A few weeks ago we had dinner with Edgar in Berlin." He lit a cigarette and offered one to Chuck.

"You had dinner with asshole Edgar?" Chuck accepted the cigarette but didn't light it. He seemed to be trying hard not to show any surprise.

T.K. said, "Let's cut the crap about playing pretend. We know who you really are and what you did and we were sent here to find you. That's all ancient history and we have scrapped our mission, so to speak. Okay?"

Chuck nodded, but his eyes looked wary. His confidence had disappeared when the cutter came by.

"Old Edgar told us the army had trained him to kill and that he was 'very, very good' at it," T.K. said, looking hard at Chuck. "Do you know anything about that?" T.K. asked. "Was Edgar telling the truth?"

A police siren wailed somewhere down by the docks.

"Edgar always lies." Bitterness replaced his old cocksure tone. The siren's wail became fainter. Chuck sat up straight and returned the bag of hazelnuts. "You're right. Let's get the hell out of here.

High tail right across the freakin' Baltic." His blue eyes challenged T.K. "Nobody could find us in this fog!"

T.K. didn't move.

"Only a fool," he said, emphasizing the 'fool,' "would try to cross the shipping lanes in this pea soup. I don't see any radar reflector on your mast. It's safer to wait until the fog lifts."

"Bunch of goddamned wimps," muttered Chuck. He repeated in a falsetto voice, "It's safer to wait it out until the fog lifts."

Imperturbable, T.K. sat and smoked.

"All right! Damn it! Have it your way!" Chuck climbed out of the cockpit. "I'll find us a place to hide out and when this shit lifts, we'll run for it."

He stopped and turned to T.K. "The way you sneaked onto the boat this morning—that was a rotten dirty trick!"

"Yeah," agreed T.K. "We arrived at a bad time. Sorry about that, Goodborn."

Chuck stared at him, trying to judge if the apology was real, decided it was and barked, "Let's get going."

T.K. ordered, *"Di di Mau!"* and Ho Dung scrambled out of the cabin. Moments later, he pulled up the anchor. Chuck turned on the engine and slowly maneuvered the boat out of the basin and smack into the most viscous fog bank I'd ever seen.

~ * ~

Feet up, brain on autopilot, I sat in the cockpit, sipping coffee from a white plastic mug festooned with nautical blue anchors, and keeping Chuck company as he navigated toward a marker buoy somewhere in the waters northeast of Sassnitz. T.K. and Ho Dung slept in the bunks.

While Chuck went below for a coffee refill, I held the tiller and tried to keep the compass steady on forty-five degrees. The visibility hovered at about ten feet as the gauze curtain of fog enveloped *Painted Cow*. Every few minutes I put the mug aside and blew into an old brass foghorn, producing a bleating signal of our presence.

Chuck returned with a cigar in addition to his coffee. He plopped down beside me, and took over the tiller. "So, Zara, who are you and T.K. really? Is your name even Zara?" he asked.

I didn't trust Chuck any further than I could throw him, and he had reasons to feel the same about me, but I was just plain tired, tired of running and lying and posing as the oh-so-correct Mrs. Wentz. I called up some morsels of candor and told Chuck a little bit about Zara the systems integrator consultant and T.K., the man who "found people and fixed situations."

Chuck, staring into the fog and puffing on his cigar, showed no surprise at my admissions.

"Gonna be a hell of a job to fix this situation," he said, stretching his legs. The damp air had curled his hair.

"The idea of fixing the situation has tanked," I said, "since the people who hired us appear to be trying to kill all of us."

We noodled over that thought for a moment then I perked up. "On the other hand, your data warehousing software is safe under the charts on its CD-ROM!" I turned and smiled at him.

"You bitch!" he said, returning my smile. With his impish grin and curls he looked like a naughty cherub, and his voice held so much admiration that my hackles didn't rise.

"How the hell did you find it?" he asked, still grinning.

"By accident."

He shook his head.

"Now it's your turn to share," I said. "Who's going to buy this technological toy? And is that," I pointed down into the cabin, "your only copy?"

"In a week I'm supposed to go to Berlin and have some Russian geek burn in another copy. Pick up some of the hardware—the main server and a couple of PCs. Arrange for some technical people to come on board." He took a sip of coffee. "Banker lady still want to be the project angel?"

"Oh, Banker Lady was a myth." I paused. "What about the buyers? Who will become the owner of *Aristotle*?" I didn't say 'illegal owner.'

"The KGB gets one copy. Wulf and his old cronies were to have the other. In return for negotiating the deal with the Russkies."

"But Wulf is dead."

"And the doo-doo is piling up too goddamn deep." With a disgusted wave of his arm, he tossed the cigar into the sea.

"Can Bodo take over?" Old Bodo had always seemed the perfect lackey, loyal but with the IQ of an eggplant.

"He's the muscle," said Chuck, "but maybe he can finish the deal." He handed me the foghorn and I sent another lonely bleat into the mist. I turned to give Chuck a stern look.

"Wouldn't it be prudent to keep your hands off Bodo's daughter?"

He scowled. "Andy's very mature for her age."

"That's a copout," I said, "and Bodo will kill you."

"Shut the fuck up. I know what I'm doing."

We sat in sulky silence. Then Chuck ventured, "That was some pretty good shit in your sewing case. Things definitely go better. Any more of that around?"

"No, that's all we had."

"Not even a joint left?"

"Nothing." I stifled an enormous yawn.

~ * ~

By some navigational miracle, Chuck found the buoy in the fog and changed our course to north-northwest. He studied the charts again, and decided we could dip into Vitt, an old fishing village just south of Kap Arkona. We would be poised for a run across the Baltic, straight from the lighthouse at the northern tip of the "Kap" to the island of Møn, lying just off the Danish coast. Thirty-seven nautical miles to safety.

Safety. I tried not to let myself yearn for it too much, but Chloe's tear-stained face was always in my mind's eye.

We motored along in silence with the Baltic a greenish slate, flat and oily-looking. I took the tiller again while Chuck went below. He returned with a bottle of rum and dumped a big slug into my coffee without even asking permission, and then he doctored his mug with a bigger jolt.

"So you and T.K. aren't really married?" he asked, fishing around for more salacious little details I knew he liked to savor. "You have a 'real' husband?"

"Does it matter?" I asked.

He answered with a leer.

When I didn't respond he said, "I always like to get a take on the person I'm dealing with."

"This woman is technologically savvy. This woman works for a company who expects to be paid. And this woman wouldn't run off and leave her so-called friends stranded on Hiddensee."

"Oh that!" he shrugged.

"Yes, that!" I said, glaring at him.

"Not my idea. Romy was awake when you guys left. She was rummaging through your stuff when I woke up. I said that sporty little boat was an American boat, and maybe you and T.K. were collaborating with the guys in the flippers. She said she found T.K. snooping in our bedroom the night of the party. She said you two were going to steal the CD-ROM and take off." He paused. "I didn't know what to believe. Got a bad case of the hoo-hahs and decided to get the hell out of there."

"That boat with the Danish flag is American?"

"Wellcraft Scarab. Lean and fast. Mercury engine with a lot of horses."

"Edgar mentioned he was going to Denmark," I said. "To look for a sailboat, but I'm wondering if he hasn't chartered the *Little Mermaid*."

"Edgar!" Chuck spat the name like an oath.

"Your once upon a time bankroller!" I reminded him.

"Greedy S.O.B."

"Well, he's in Sassnitz now, with a gun, and boxer shorts loud enough to give you a headache. In cahoots with Bill Putnam."

Chuck shrugged and said, "Yeah, I still can't believe it. Two lousy birds of a feather. That really sucks." He frowned. "A few months ago Edgar was...my partner in this deal. If he hired you two, it was just to get to me."

Edgar's partner? My mouth dropped open, but I didn't say anything, because just then, yawning and stretching, Ho Dung came out of the cabin and joined us.

Chuck let him take over the tiller and we continued our course north-northwest into the filmy curtain of fog that showed no signs of lifting.

I went below, made a pot of strong tea and scrounged up a breakfast of stale bread, scrambled eggs, sliced tomatoes and Friday's leftover potato salad. Not my finest effort, but filling.

We ate on deck and let T.K. sleep. Chuck got out another chart and calculated we were just a few miles south of the cape. While I was gathering up the dirty plates and cups, I heard the sound of an engine nearby. In the fog, sound travels over water like an unfaithful lover's words, confusing and untrustworthy. Hesitantly, I picked up the foghorn but didn't put it to my lips. Ho Dung put his hand on my arm. Chuck, suddenly alert, squinted into the fog. We waited, each of us trying to get a sense how far away the phantom boat was, in which direction it was moving, even measuring the size of the boat from the noise of the engines. An inboard motor with the familiar purr. Chuck cut the engine on *Painted Cow*, and we sat listening. Low male voices, a whiff of cigarette smoke, and that engine noise, passing us somewhere in the fog, then doubling back, passing again, much closer, then fading in the distance.

Three times. My nerves felt scraped and raw.

The ghost boat was criss-crossing the waters of Tromper Wiek. Probing. Searching.

We waited, dead in the water, until the engine was inaudible, then Chuck started up the outboard again, and we headed west into the shallow coastal waters.

Nobody spoke, and I carried the dishes below, dumped them in the tarnished copper sink and sat down on T.K.'s bunk. I touched his shoulder, then remembered, and placed my hand on his arm.

"Wake up!" I whispered. "I think somebody's looking for us."

T.K. opened his bloodshot eyes and gazed at me with a puzzled frown, as if he didn't remember where he was or who I was. After I repeated my words, he closed his eyes again. His temple felt hot and clammy.

In the head, or toilet to us landlubbers, I pumped cold water into the tiny sink, wet a clean cloth, wrung it out and returned to T.K.'s bunk. He opened his eyes again and I wiped his face.

"Zara." His voice sounded uncertain. He stared up through the open hatch. "I had your dream."

He sounded dazed and disoriented. Did he have a concussion? In all the dicey situations we had come through, wisely or not, I had relied on T.K. one hundred percent.

"You are scaring me to death. Are you all right?" I used the cloth to dab the last of the dried blood from around his nostrils.

"The dance around the fire." His voice full of puzzlement, he repeated, "I had your dream."

Oh God, he was totally out of it! I put the cloth across his forehead, left the bunk again and poured a cup of tea for him. He eased himself into a sitting position and still holding the cloth to his head, downed the tea in a series of slurps and gulps. I took the cup, walked two steps back to the alcohol stove and poured a refill, and then I sat down on the bunk beside him. I had to make him understand the seriousness of this new predicament.

"In the fog, we heard a boat, cruising back and forth like in a pattern. Maybe searching for something. As I talked, I watched his face. No reaction. "The engine sounded like the *Little Mermaid*'s." I watched him for a reaction.

"Just because you're paranoid doesn't mean they aren't out to get you." He had a crooked smile and he closed his eyes again. "You think it was Putnam?" He looked up and took another gulp of tea. The dreamer had disappeared. T.K. was back. His weary eyes met mine.

I nodded.

"It figures." He drained the second cup. "If Putnam somehow got back to his room, and Edgar told him what had happened, they would have decided to track us down. They would have noticed that Putnam's car was parked across the street, and then—."

"They would have realized that *Painted Cow* was no longer at anchor."

"So," he said, rubbing his chin, "they sure as hell wouldn't want to lose Chuck, who, after all, has laid the golden egg."

"Or has stolen it."

"Right." T.K. stood up stiffly by degrees, like an old man, and touched his shoulder. He dumped his cup into the sink. I found his glasses on the table and handed them to him. He looked at his image in the little mirror by the companionway and winced.

Back on deck the gauzy shroud still hunkered over the water, in fact it seemed even thicker, and from the cockpit we could barely see the bow. Ho Dung had the tiller and Chuck, in a yellow foul-weather jacket, frowned as he measured a distance on a chart with a pair of dividers.

"Lost at sea?" quipped T.K. "No LORAN? How about a good old fashioned Radio Direction Finder?"

Chuck's frown deepened. "These Ossie Krauts haven't done jack shit to make navigating these waters easy." He looked up at T.K. "I have to do it with a compass, charts and a depth finder." He jerked his thumb over his shoulder. "And him. Ho Dung's worth half a dozen electronic gadgets."

"What did you make of that boat?" T.K. asked quietly. "Zara said they seemed to be searching for something...

"Maybe we over-reacted." Chuck squinted into the fog. "And maybe we didn't. But we're hugging the coast all the way up to Vitt."

"How can we do that? Without running into the coast?"

Chuck pointed to the chart. "See this area here?"

T.K. nodded.

"Depth is always around twenty meters. We take a reading every minute or so. Try to keep the course at that depth. Take us right to the Kap Arkona Light."

"We have enough fuel to get across?" asked T.K., eyeing the outboard.

"I'd like to take on more in Vitt. If we ever find the damned place."

For two hours, I stood in the companionway and fed Chuck and Ho Dung the numbers from the depth finder, while T.K. dozed on some cushions. We always had our ears pricked for the sound of an engine, but there was only the lap of the water against the hull and the soulful cries of some sea birds. Everything I touched felt damp: my own lank hair, my sweater, the ropes, the chart and even the teacup.

At last, Ho Dung estimated we must be close to Vitt, and turned toward the shore. Or what we assumed was the shore. The numbers on the depth finder indicated that the keel was very close to the sea bottom. In a moment we would surely run aground, which would the last straw. I would wade to shore and walk back to Berlin.

Then through the nebula of fog, I inhaled loamy whiffs of land, with the heavy odor of salt marsh.

"Land!" I said, leaving my post and coming back on deck.

Ho Dung sniffed the air and agreed with me. Then the fog lifted a little, and through the vaporous curtain we saw the ghostly outline of trees and even a thatched cottage. Then came another cottage, and in a clearing, a white octagonal chapel. Only the put-put of our motor disturbed the perfect stillness as we entered the tiny harbor of Vitt. An errant rooster crowed, as if to announce our arrival.

On shore the fog was not so thick, and we could see the dock and even a beat up gas pump sitting at the end of the pier. T.K. woke up when we pulled up to the dock. He spoke his fluent German to a grizzled old man with a brimmed cap who emerged from the mist to find out what we wanted. Chuck filled the fuel cans, paid, and we took off right away. T.K. said he didn't want the locals to get a look at us or at *Painted Cow*. When the old man asked where we were going, T.K. said, "Sassnitz."

If anybody came around asking questions, that might throw them off our trail.

We motored out and headed north.

"Where are we hanging out until the fog lifts?" I asked Chuck.

"We aren't. We're rounding the Kap now, and then we're making a run for Klintholm harbor on Møn."

"In this fog?" I asked. I looked around but neither T.K. nor Ho Dung offered any arguments. Ho Dung didn't meet my eyes.

"Are you crazy? Sailing right through the shipping lanes with no visibility? T.K., stop him!"

T.K. sat down next to me. "Zara, if Edgar and Putnam are looking for us, this boat is not the place to be. Edgar's got a powerful engine. We've got no wind, and a crappy little outboard. We can't outrun or out-maneuver the *Little Mermaid.*"

He was right. We had a Hobson's choice. On Chuck's boat, we were like big, plump mallards; afloat and waiting to become duck à l'orange. But it would be suicidal to sail through the shipping lanes in this white murk.

"I suppose freighters have good radar?" I asked, hopefully.

"They can see a friggin' flock of geese." Chuck said, grinning at me.

"How long will it take to cross the shipping channel?"

Ho Dung grabbed the chart and pointed to a long string of buoys that marked the narrow passage, hardly wider than the Rügendamm. "Every boat pass through here."

"Zara, Sweetie, the odds of colliding with a freighter are really very slight. We'll be cautious."

He hadn't mentioned the tugs and barges that might also be in the shipping lanes. It was three against one. I didn't like it, but I told myself that the afternoon sun would burn off the fog and visibility would be ten clear miles. I told myself that T.K. was the picture of health and sound judgment. I told myself many hopeful lies that I wanted to believe, but a dull feeling of doom settled into me like an anchor into soft sand.

Painted Cow, which I now saw as a ship sailed by fools, rounded the marker buoy at Kap Arkona and Ho Dung set a course due west.

Although I had no appetite, I made the condemned crew a hearty lunch. The larder contained a can of long hot dogs like Romy had served and a tin of sauerkraut. In a mutinous mood, banging pots and pans, I dumped the kraut on top of the frankfurters, and lit the alcohol stove. I found an onion and an apple and began grating them into the sauerkraut. While I worked I brooded on the testosterone-driven decision T.K. and Chuck had made, with the usual bullshit justifications. We passed a bell buoy, clanging in the mist, and someone on deck created a desolate counterpoint with a half-hearted squawk on the foghorn.

If I was honest with myself, I had to admit part of my anxiety was based on guilt about agreeing to this one ludicrous last trip, based as it was on greed and sex. I gasped as I grated my knuckle, and a drop of blood spattered into the sauerkraut.

A little extra protein.

On deck, we were finishing lunch, when we heard a powerful engine coming through the fog. Ho Dung cut the outboard and we sat and listened, anxious, with everyone frozen in place, Chuck poised for an instant with his fork in mid-air, and Ho Dung with bits of sauerkraut sticking out of his mouth. The other boat seemed to be maneuvering around us in a series of ever tightening circles, until I calculated they must be only yards away. We waited. A British voice boomed out of the fog "Ahoy there!"

My worst fears now true. Putnam.

T.K. shouted something gruff and unintelligible in German.

The voice roared again, "Ahoy, *Painted Cow*!"

T.K. replied in the same strange German accent. All I could catch was "Anna Katerina."

A low male voice sputtered, "Dammit to hell!" American English. That would be Edgar.

They circled us again and took off.

"What did you say to them?" I asked T.K.

"The first time I said 'that noisy boat is scaring the herring away.'"

"And the second time?"

"I said my boat was the *Anna Katerina* and they were infringing on my fishing grounds.

"Did they buy it?"

"I don't know. They left."

"Scaring the herring. I like that." Chuck looked at me and gestured at the remains of our lunch. "Get rid of this mess," he ordered, and went into the cabin.

Kitchen patrol was not how I envisioned spending what might be the last afternoon of my life. I hurled the plates, one at a time, into the Baltic, dumped all the utensils into the water, then heaved the empty cook pot after them. A stub of frankfurter and strands of sauerkraut floated alongside the boat. T.K. and Ho Dung both stared at me as if I had lost my mind.

"He said to get rid of it." All my rage and frustration had been exorcised in those rebellious gestures.

Ho Dung, at the tiller, gave me a gleeful grin, almost conspiratorial. T.K. said "Holy shit!" and burst into laughter.

Just then Chuck came out of the cabin carrying an automatic.

It hadn't occurred to me that I might have committed a capital offence.

T.K. said, "Christ, Goodborn, what the hell are you doing with that .22?"

"Those pirates get close to this boat again, I'm gonna let them have it."

"A better idea would be if we had a plan," I suggested, hoping Chuck had forgotten all about the dishes. He stashed the .22 in the storage compartment amid the sheets and the fenders.

"Zara's right," agreed T.K. "We need to figure out what to do if they return. Until now, we've been just been putting the wheels on the cart as it goes along."

"Okay. Dammit!" Chuck motioned at T.K. and me to go into the cabin.

"No," I said. Ho Dung has a say-so, too. Everyone on this crew has got to have a voice. We're in this together."

"Oh my God," Chuck groaned and rolled his eyes. "We're being stalked by pirates and Ms. Politically Correct climbs on her soapbox."

"What we need to do," I said, ignoring him, "is to figure out what Putnam and Edgar have in mind. Will they try to board us? Do they think Chuck and Romy are on board alone?"

"And a fisherman who speaks Platt Deutsch." added T.K., referring to his recent conversation with Putnam.

I continued to think aloud. "Are they coming after the CD-ROM? They may have decided to cut all the middlemen out and just deal with the KGB."

Chuck curled his lips and muttered, "Bastards!"

"Someone could have seen us rowing out to the boat and tipped them off," T.K. said.

"Today only, buy two, get four." Chuck snorted. "They'll be bug-eyed to find all of us."

T.K. turned back to Ho Dung and they spoke in Vietnamese, with Ho Dung gesturing nervously, his voice high-pitched with agitation.

Then T.K. said, "Ho Dung doesn't think anyone saw us rowing out to the boat."

"What else did he say?" asked Chuck. The conversation had sounded too emotional for T.K.'s simple answer.

"Chuck mentioned pirates. Someone in Ho Dung's family had a bad experience on the South China Sea, and he's afraid."

"Did he tell you what happened?" I asked.

"In graphic detail. Torture, rape, mutilation, and murder with the bodies thrown into the sea."

Chuck said, "This sure as hell isn't Southeast Asia."

Under my damp sweater, the hair on my arms rose. I tried to push the information about Edgar's being "very, very good at killing" and the fate of the unfortunate Bruss out of my mind. All that and my first-hand knowledge of Putnam's sadism threatened to ratchet fear up to a heart-pounding terror.

T.K. didn't smoke because the smell carried across the water, so he chewed on one toothpick after another.

We turned the situation this way and that, and took an inventory of possible weapons, and then we settled on a plan that was so off-the-wall that it just might work.

Everything would depend on Ho Dung. He insisted he felt up to it, but I had my doubts.

I laid the life jackets on the port bunk in case the situation really deteriorated, and then I stretched out on the empty bunk for a nap, but I lay awake for a long time, and my short sleep was fitful and restless.

In a groggy stupor, I woke up and climbed back onto the deck. The fog hadn't lifted, and the little outboard propelled us onward across the glassy water, accompanied only by the marine chorus of jangling bell buoys, occasional "groaner" buoys and the melancholy sound of a foghorn calling off in the distance.

Then we heard the familiar sound of the powerful Mercury engine racing our way.

"Dammit!" Chuck peered into the fog and thrust his jaw out.

T.K., at the tiller, said "Ah, hell!"

Ho Dung didn't say a word, but scurried back to the stern and took the tiller from T.K.

There would never be a good time for the *Little Mermaid* to reappear, but this hour was critical with our course northwest now toward Møn, and *Painted Cow* ready to enter the shipping lanes.

Impossible to estimate direction and distance in the fog, but the powerboat seemed to be coming at us smack out of the east, racing kamikaze-like toward our starboard bow. Chuck darted to the locker and got out the .22. Fighting off panic, I grabbed the boat hook. T.K. took the fish boning knife out of another locker, then like mice watching for the snake to strike, all of us stared in the direction of the engine noise.

The fog, now a faint luminous curtain, had a wispy ethereal look, and with no warning, we moved into an unclouded space, a transparent hole the size of a football field.

"Yikes! They'll see us!" I gasped.

Weak sunlight flickered down into the water. T.K., Chuck and I nearly trampled each other attempting to go below into the cabin before the enemy boat came into view.

When I put on my life jacket, Chuck sneered, and then of course T.K. refused to wear one.

"If they sink the boat out from under us, you are going to be one sorry drowned rat," I warned.

He whispered, "Sweet Pea!"

I wanted to pound his stubborn hide, but instead I knelt beside him on the bunk. We stationed ourselves, heads almost touching, at one porthole on the starboard side, and Chuck glommed onto the other one. I shivered when I thought of our plan, brazen yet risky, with its absolute reliance on Ho Dung.

The *Little Mermaid* entered the fog-free hole and made straight for our vessel. As she got closer I could make out Edgar, at the controls, wearing a yachting cap, and Putnam, ramrod straight as always, standing next to him. Putnam had a strip of white cloth tied around his head, a bandage whose ends blew rakishly in the breeze. Like a wounded tiger, he would be more dangerous than ever.

A moment later the *Little Mermaid* circled around us and pulled up a few feet away from our starboard side. The boat rocked wildly back and forth in the wake, making me nauseous in the close confines of the cabin. Edgar set his big engine to idle, and turned his head toward the man at our tiller.

T.K. whispered, "Now we'll find out what those dirtbags are after."

We couldn't see Ho Dung from the cabin, because the eel box was in the way. Putnam was only a few feet from us, but he wasn't looking at the narrow portholes, he was staring at Ho Dung. From my view, I could observe Putnam's narrowing icy eyes and the ruddy color flooding his face. He must have expected to find Chuck at the tiller. Edgar stared at Ho Dung without emotion. Ho Dung, stoic and silent, kept *Painted Cow* on course for Møn.

"By God, Ho Dung, I believe you've done a runner. What in bloody hell are you doing with Goodborn's boat?"

Putnam's voice bristled with indignation. Ho Dung didn't respond. Then Putnam phrased his question in German, somewhat more politely.

Ho Dung responded in kind. I couldn't catch every word, but it sounded like he said something about sailing to Denmark for political asylum.

His voice aghast with indignation, Putnam turned to Edgar. "He's made off with Goodborn's bloody boat."

Edgar said something I couldn't hear.

Putnam yelled, "Is anyone else aboard?"

I couldn't hear Ho Dung's quiet voice, but I knew he would claim to be alone.

So far, in spite of his pirate fears, he was doing a first rate job. I hoped he hadn't noticed the knife in the sheath around Putnam's waist.

"Asking permission to come aboard. There's...there's some computer related items that belong to this gentleman," Putnam indicated Edgar, who nodded curtly, "and we need to, ah, retrieve them now." Putnam's voice had become polite, even ingratiating.

Ho Dung yelled, "Very sorry. No one can come aboard without Captain Goodborn giving permission."

"Don't feed me a load of codswallop! You've stolen this pigging boat, and the authorities will lock you up and throw away the bloody key."

Ho Dung's voice quavered, but I caught his words, "permission to sail boat."

"Like hell, he does," barked Edgar. "He's feeding us a crock of crap. Tell him if he won't give you the CD, you'll slice him up like sushi. Say you're coming aboard to get the CD. Show him your goddam knife."

Chuck muttered, "Asshole Edgar!"

Putnam took his knife out of his leather scabbard and stared in Ho Dung's direction with a look that made the back of my neck constrict. If Ho Dung was anywhere near as scared as I was, he had probably jumped overboard.

"Yup, it's Billy Boy's good old Fairbairn-Sykes fighting knife," said T.K. "Okay boys and girls, time to get the weapons ready." He looked at me and I gave a weak nod.

Chuck took the .22 out of his jacket, and T.K. reached for it. Chuck hesitated, and T.K. said, "I've had some experience in this kind of situation." Chuck looked like he might argue, and T.K. hissed,

"Jesus, he'll be right on top of us." Chuck handed over the pistol and grabbed the boat hook and the boning knife. I held my sturdy folding shovel, gripping it tightly to keep my hands steady, while my heart threatened to pound its way out of my chest.

Weapons in hand, we crept back to the portholes to see what Putnam would do.

Chuck said, "Pete, why don't you plug the bastards right now?"

T.K. shook his head.

While we watched, Putnam, still poised with the knife, looked aft, and stared into the fog, and said something to Edgar, who looked in the same direction. They seemed irresolute, and put their heads together for another conference. Putnam returned the knife to its scabbard. I heard the faint growl of a diesel. Edgar had backed away from us, and he and Putnam looked in the direction of the diesel sound again, then they took off at a full throttle.

The enemy had withdrawn.

"Now why," T.K. asked, "did those two act like the Russians are in Jersey?"

Our boat started to make an erratic turn, when Ho Dung came running toward the cabin house. "Come, Captain Goodborn! Come!" he shouted. "I cannot be seen," and he practically dived into the cabin. Chuck threw down his weapons and raced up to grab the tiller.

Except for Ho Dung, we all returned topside. A big gray boat had entered the hole in the fog. Was this going to be a case of "out of the frying pan into the fire?"

"Hmm," said T.K., in a low voice, "a *Grenzboot*."

A border patrol boat. I had noticed the GDR flag, and the blue hats of the crew. The boat was at least seventy feet long. This summer they wouldn't be stopping escapees from crossing the Baltic to freedom, but I felt uneasy. The boat bristled with radar and searchlights and the man with the megaphone, obviously about to hail us, didn't look like a people person.

"*Achtung!*" he shouted.

Chuck managed to look bored.

A long harangue came out of the megaphone.

"What's he saying?" I asked T.K.

"We're in the shipping lanes in the fog and it's very dangerous. To ourselves and to other boats. We're weekend idiots." He paused. "We should set a course for southwest. There's a big harbor in Warnemünde." He grinned. "They say that they are busy sailors. Don't expect them to come and bail us out of trouble again." T.K. listened to more of the harangue. "We must get out of the shipping lanes. Now."

T.K. shouted that we would head southwest right away.

Chuck glowered, although he probably hadn't understood ten words.

The sailor with the megaphone gave us a haughty look and the big gray boat turned and plowed back into the fog. The entire crew must have been on deck to witness our dressing down.

Then, as quickly as it had appeared, the hole in the fog vanished and we were in the soup again.

"Friggin commies. This fog is going to lift any time now." Chuck yelled in the direction of the cabin. "Ho Dung, get your yellow butt back out here!"

Ho Dung, looking nervously in the direction that the Grenzboot had gone, appeared on deck again. Chuck pointed at the tiller, "Three hundred thirty degrees for Klintholm," he ordered. "We'll be there in a few hours."

Ho Dung put us back on course and we almost rammed into the first buoy that marked the entrance to the shipping lanes.

~ * ~

We soldiered on in our blind world, Ho Dung at the tiller, Chuck barking orders, and T.K. and I harkening to the slightest sounds disturbing the gray silence of the fog. Over the lapping of the water and the blub-blub-blub of our motor, I listened for the return of Edgar's big Mercury engine, and for the foghorns and bells that signaled of an approaching freighter. Chuck had explained we would know of a nearby ship in plenty of time.

"They've got to follow the International Rules of the Road," he said. "A vessel in the fog has to sound its horn once every minute.

These Baltic ships will have alarm bells to warn off nearby boats. So, no problemo."

"What about us?" I had asked. "We aren't warning anyone of our presence. We don't even have a radar reflector."

"We have a special situation."

Edgar and Putnam, our special situation. They didn't know Ho Dung wasn't alone aboard *Painted Cow*. They would be brazenly confident that they could handle one scared sailor, and when they confronted all four of us? How many times would our luck hold out before we were boarded, murdered and thrown to the fishes?

Chuck heard the engine first and held up his hand, as if for silence. We were all tuned into the sound of the *Little Mermaid* coming across the water.

"Screw 'em! I'm not cutting the engine, and we're not going to cower in the cabin like a bunch of goddamned sheep!" He didn't look at us for confirmation. "We keep going. Nobody, not even big Ed and bloody Bill would be stupid enough to try to board us while we're underway. Not in this soup and not in the shipping lanes."

He clambered around the cabin housing onto the fore deck, peering into the fog.

"If things start to get dicey," T.K. whispered, "go below and put on your life jacket."

"I feel so trapped down there," I said. "I'd rather be on deck." Nevertheless, I scooted into the cabin and slipped into my life vest, and came topside again. Now, in the distance we heard the foghorns and the chorus of jangling bells of vessels transversing the shipping lanes. Fear crawled over me like ants. I told myself I would do whatever I must to survive.

One of the blaring horns seemed to be getting closer. "Sounds like a water buffalo in heat," said Chuck. T.K. nodded. Chuck laughed at my pained expression. "Zara, they're not even close."

He ordered Ho Dung to change course toward the northeast, perhaps hoping the duo aboard the *Little Mermaid* would mistake our boat for a Copenhagen-bound yacht.

Unfazed, our stalkers continued to hone in on us. That ominous circling had started again, coming nearer with each pass.

"Ahoy Ho Dung aboard *Painted Cow*!" Putnam's voice bellowed into the fog above the Mercury engine. "We're ready to make a deal." The fog sat so thick they couldn't get close enough to see us without being in danger of ramming us.

"*Falscher Dampfer*!" shouted T.K. "*Hier ist das Aalboot Ostsee Prinzessin.*"

Wrong vessel! This is the eel boat *Ostsee Princess*.

"Bloody hell!" exclaimed Putnam. "That's Drummond's voice."

I looked at T.K. who had turned pale except for the skin around his discolored eyes. He leaned against the eel box, put his hand to his brow and whispered, "Shit! It worked before."

I grabbed his arm. "Sit down. You look like you're going to pass out." He slumped down on the deck beside the eel box.

The *Little Mermaid* emerged from the fog, only yards away. Putnam stood forward at the bow rail with his knife unsheathed, his terrible eyes focused on Ho Dung at the helm. Then he noticed the rest of us, and his eyes seized on me with a look of pure hatred.

"Mrs. Wentz!"

He glanced at the water and back at me. "A nice cold bath will be in order. And without the life vest."

"You killed Wulf didn't you?" My voice was little more than a squeak.

"He was nothing. You're nothing."

As I went jelly-kneed with fright, Chuck rushed out of the cabin with the .22. He took aim at Edgar and fired. An enormous bang jolted our fog-shrouded world. I heard the bullet zing off The *Little Mermaid*, which made a wide sweeping turn as Edgar, not noticeably impaired, maneuvered to put a little distance between the two boats. At the sight of Chuck's automatic, Putnam had literally hit the deck. Chuck fired again, shooting blindly into the fog.

"Goodborn, your stupidity will get us all killed." T.K. spoke in a hoarse, angry voice as he pulled me down behind the eel box. Someone aboard The *Little Mermaid* returned fire. Chuck ducked back into the cabin, as a shot ricocheted off the capstan. I heard Chuck firing out of the forward hatch, and imagined Ho Dung cowering in the cockpit. Two more shots came from Edgar's boat. Chuck must have scored a near miss on The *Little Mermaid,* because I heard the Mercury engine rev up and take off toward the southwest. I peered over the eel box and caught a glimpse of Putnam through the mist, gripping the bow rail like grim death. As The *Little Mermaid* zoomed by our boat, Edgar fired one last shot and disappeared again into the fog.

"It was your phony accent they recognized." Chuck looked down at T.K. who was still propped against the eel box, pale and quiet.

"What's the matter with him?" he asked me.

"I think he has a concussion."

"Screw everybody! I'm getting the fuck out of here," he said, going aft to take the tiller from Ho Dung. He turned the outboard on full power, and we took off in a zigzag pattern.

I hunkered down by the eel box with T.K. Ho Dung scrambled up to the bow to stand watch. The *Little Mermaid* circled back on our tail. She was coming up right behind us.

Even before Ho Dung yelled, I felt a great, resonating presence approaching our starboard side. I jumped to my feet, all senses alert, straining my eyes in the direction of the eerie reverberating hum.

Something dark coming through the fog, something huge. Blotting out the sea and even the sky, a black behemoth bore down on us. I screamed, but a blast from the oncoming ship's horn obliterated every sound except the clanging of bells, right on top of us. In a pause between the warning noises, I heard Ho Dung shouting again, and Chuck yelling, "Whooeee! Come on, baby, Move! Dammit! Move!"

Relentless in its advance, the enormous prow edged closer, promising annihilation.

Acrid whiffs of diesel fuel spewed into the air, with the monster so close, moving forward to crush us. T.K. stood up and wrapped his arms around me. Ho Dung yelling, Chuck's banshee shouts, our imminent destruction only seconds away. I saw Cyrillic lettering in faded white paint, and towering above us, a deadly looking anchor protruding from a rusty hole.

Then an instant of wild uncertain hope.

Yes. No. Yes. No.

Yes.

Our boat heaved and lurched crazily in the bow wave, Chuck yelled, and the water was calmer again. Dumb with shock and relief, we watched the giant ship glide by. A big band of red paint showed above the waterline.

"She's friggin' empty," yelled Chuck, from the cockpit.

Now I saw t*he Little Mermaid* again, careening around the freighter's stern at high speed, coming after us once more. The radar aboard their boat would have warned them from the freighter's path. I faced the bitter realization we had survived one death only to face another.

They hit the freighter's immense wake at high speed, and as if in slow motion, the *Little Mermaid* lifted straight into the air. As she flipped over, I saw human form hurtling into the water like a toy action figure. Then we heard a noise—as if a giant egg cracked open. The boat splintered into pieces. While we watched, The *Little Mermaid* disappeared into the Baltic.

Then Chuck was yelling again as the freighter's powerful wake smacked into *Painted Cow.* I could feel the battle between the suction from the big ship and our tiny vessel. In a surge of seawater, T.K. and I tumbled against the eel box. We were going to capsize, with water sloshing everywhere, swamping us, with our boat floundering like a bathtub toy.

I crawled to the handrail and hung on. Chuck screamed something about getting more weight to starboard. Still clutching the handrail, I tried to get to my feet. Heedless of Chuck's yelling, a half-drowned Ho Dung still clung to the bowsprit. The water washed over the deck and down the scuppers as Chuck fought to get control of the boat.

"We did it! Whooee, baby, yes!"

The freighter, serenely unaware of the chaos in her wake, headed west.

T.K. soaking wet, leaned against the eel box, glasses askew, and produced a damp, disoriented smile.

Moments later, we rounded the black buoy that signaled the far side of the channel. *Painted Cow* had survived her passage across the shipping lanes.

Dazed and dripping, I looked around. Where The *Little Mermaid* had been there was only water. That we were alive seemed a miracle. I could see across the water with other ships in the distance. The fog had lifted.

Fourteen

Still without wind, we motored north toward Møn, weary, wet, and relieved. In the sunny cockpit, sprawling on the sodden cushions, we shared a bottle of rum and a post-mortem. T.K. and Ho Dung smoked cigarettes, and Chuck sucked on a big fat cigar.

"Were we wicked lucky or not?" asked Chuck with a chortle. "Old Edgar got it right. He was 'very, very good at killing.' He got himself killed along with your buddy Putnam."

"Could they have survived the boat breaking up?" I asked.

The rest of the crew felt certain Putnam and Edgar were dead, but I extracted a promise that if we got within range of another boat, we would hail it and ask the skipper to radio for help.

"How could Edgar have screwed up so...so royally?" I asked, not really expecting an answer, "and steered his boat right into the freighter's wake? They could have waited until the wake was gone and still caught us. They didn't have to be such hotdogs."

T.K. lit another cigarette and closed his eyes.

Ho Dung thought the midsummer spirits made Putnam and Edgar feel immortal. "Powerful spirit drummed to life. Festival madness."

My conjecture was in the heat of the chase, Edgar, his reflexes and faculties showing their age and with a crazed Putnam egging him on, had simply misjudged the turbulence.

"You're all wrong!" Chuck grinned and flipped the empty rum bottle into the water. "Edgar's a sailor, not a power boater. A sailboat's keel stabilizes it...so you roll with the goddamn waves. Edgar's used to a boat with a keel, not a friggin' stinkpot with a flat bottom."

T.K., still silent, didn't offer his usual quips, and I wondered if he mourned for "Billy Boy," and their adventures and the good times before everything turned sour.

What I felt went beyond tiredness to a bone-weary exhaustion, but I didn't trust Chuck, and with T.K. alternating between coherence and confusion, I had to stay awake.

Chuck asked Ho Dung to take the tiller while he went below to look for another liter of rum.

Always a bad idea to self-medicate, but I needed the rum's anesthetic to mute the emotions of surviving this endless day that began eons ago with fire and drums on the hilltop.

Chuck emerged from the cabin with a fresh bottle.

"How much farther to Klintholm?" I asked, sounding like the pesky kid who keeps demanding to know, "are we there, yet?"

"Three to four hours."

I must have made a long face, because Chuck said, "closer to three."

T.K. pointed to a spot of the horizon. "You'll see chalk cliffs, just like on Rügen."

"Take it easy," I said, but Chuck ignored my protest as he poured me a hefty portion. As usual, T.K. held out his glass for a refill. Only Ho Dung declined.

"Go below and get some sleep," Chuck ordered his first mate. "You don't want to be babbling about some damned festival spirits when the Danes question you." He looked at me. "I'm hungry as hell. Can you find something for us to eat?"

I went below to look for the chocolate bars and nuts. While I was out of sight, I dredged up enough energy to take care of a little task involving the CD-ROM. After that, off came my yucky wet bra and on went a dry sweatshirt. I found Chuck's automatic in the pocket of his foul weather jacket and hid it in the galley under the plastic dishpan. Ho Dung came into the cabin and collapsed onto the bunk.

Too tired to make a pot of coffee, I drank this morning's tepid dregs while I trimmed a bit of mold off a piece of Emmental. I chopped up the chocolate bars and dumped them with the hazelnuts into a bowl. Little squares of Swiss cheese went into another bowl.

When I came up on deck with the snacks, Chuck said,

"I've been filling Wentz in on how I happened to land on that damned Commie island with all those Krauts." He grinned, showing deep dimples, and reached for a handful of nuts. "Pete says no need for secrets now that we'll all be parting company in a few hours."

I took a sip of rum.

"I asked Chuck how he and Romy met," explained T.K.

"Romy is Wulf's niece," began Chuck. "She wanted to get out of East Germany, travel and see what life was like in the West. She didn't want to change politics, just get off Rügen for a while. Old Wulf suggested she might do a bit of spying, not really spying, but you know, meet some guy, liquor him up, get nice and cozy with him and...encourage him to talk, then report what he blabbed. Piece of cake with her looks. So she learned English and went through a regular training program."

I glanced at T.K. whose lethargy had vanished as he smiled expectantly at Chuck.

"She was one of Markus Wolf's sex spies?" I asked.

Chuck's jaw dropped. "How did you know about that?"

"How dumb do you think we are? I asked someone to do a little research. He said she was investigated by the FBI."

"No shit?"

He popped a piece of cheese into his mouth, chewed for a moment, and continued. "She landed at my company and we hit it off right away. One thing led to another—I had some bad luck with the IRS and a vicious ex-wife, a few other problems..."

His voice trailed off and I nodded with as much sympathy as I could muster.

"Romy thought I could sell the data warehouse software in East Europe and make a bundle. She arranged for us to go on a 'vacation.' We met Wulf in Mallorca, and he promised to get us a good offer. Then I did something so goddamned stupid that—." He stopped, shook his head and attacked the rum again.

"Chuck, we all make mistakes," I said. T.K. nodded.

"Yeah, but I invited Edgar in. I knew he had negotiated a few not-so-honest deals, and I was nervous about bargaining with those Commie bastards on my own. Big Ed wasn't afraid of anybody."

"And that changed everything," T.K. said.

"He muscled himself right into the project, and then he wanted a bigger cut." Remembering Edgar's offenses, Chuck's eyes narrowed. "We had more meetings. Romy worked with Wulf and his cronies to set them up. Those guys were cagey. Always met in a different city. Berlin once, then Hamburg. Finally we came up with the right laundry list for their 'clients.' And all the time Edgar butted in wanting more."

"Greedy, greedy Edgar," intoned T.K.

"Then I had some bad luck." Chuck paused and reached for the rum again. "The Berlin Wall came down."

"Poor baby," I muttered under my breath, but he didn't hear me and prattled on.

"That threatened to kill the pretty deal Wulf was cutting for all of us."

"With the Russians?" I asked.

"Yeah, I told you. They were the clients who were so hot to buy the software. Wulf's cut would be an extra copy of the CD-ROM. He could do whatever he wanted with that. He and Bodo with their old Stasi gang were going to blackmail the whole friggin' country, once they got their data warehouse filled with all the dirt."

"Instead they got their asses kicked big time," said T.K. "Lost their power and their government financing."

"Yeah. Bummer. Then I had to get out of Maine. I was broke and some guys I owed a little money were looking for me. Edgar said he had put our down payment 'in escrow.' Grand Cayman bank account. What a bullshit artist! So Romy and I took off with the software CD." He adjusted our course and stared across the water with a faraway dreamy look in his eyes.

"Of course Romy knew where to go?" I asked.

He answered slowly. "Yeah. We flew to Berlin and then came to Rügen. She knew one thing that Edgar didn't, and that was how to find Wulf."

Chuck stopped his narrative to light another cigar. Hoping for a spark of energy, I ate the last piece of chocolate. T.K. and I had pieced everything together except Edgar's endless perfidy.

"Back in Portland," Chuck continued, "Edgar had to play dumb. My partners went into a massive panic after I left and they sent a guy named Bruss over here. Still don't know how he found us. Anyhow, the last thing Edgar wanted was for anyone from Maine Mining to locate us. Edgar showed up, arranged to meet Bruss and killed him. Dumped his body in that ugly brick monstrosity."

Edgar had killed Bruss. And I always suspected Putnam. A few days ago, Chuck's candid revelations would have been electrifying, but the rum and most of all my fatigue made it hard to ask bright questions.

"That must have been a wake-up call for you," I said.

Chuck nodded. "I didn't find out right away." He looked at T.K. accusingly. "Big Ed hired your pal Putnam. And from what I hear, Putnam brought you in," he scowled at T.K., "along with 'Miss Prim and Proper.' To find us. But I always smelled a rat." His eyes shifted to me and his smile raced from zero to sixty. It was hard to tell the difference between Chuck flirting and Chuck enjoying his own cleverness.

The sun disappeared behind an immense cumulous cloud and the afternoon air felt chilly again. Conversation died. I touched T.K.'s hand and he didn't respond. Asleep. Sleep! Heaven would be a clean bed in a safe place and twelve hours of deep, dreamless uninterrupted slumber.

Chuck stared at the cloud and then at me.

"There's an old sailor's legend that if a beautiful woman bares her breasts to the elements, the sun will shine and the wind will blow." His knowing leer turned into a smirk as he watched my face.

"Too bad Romy's not on board," I said.

"You know who I mean, Zara."

"Stuff it!" I spoke louder than I meant to and T.K. opened his eyes.

"Little Miss Prim and Proper is a real drag," Chuck complained, looking at T.K.

"I'm not taking off my clothes!" I sputtered.

"Oh, she won't even undress for me unless she's in the mood," T.K. said easily.

Pleased that I had risen to his bait, Chuck sat with a self-satisfied grin.

"Say Goodborn, do you know those thugs who mugged Zara at the grain elevator in Stralsund?" T.K. asked. "Did you ever hear about that?"

"No. Hey, you two weren't poking around there, were you? That's where those Stasi bastards had their files locked up."

"We just walked around the outside a bit," I said.

"Lucky they didn't kill you."

"Anatoly told us that was the HVA group, not the Stasi," said T.K.

"Anatoly wanted to scare the shit out of you." Chuck continued to look knowing and smug.

"What I don't understand is why Edgar didn't pop up here and try to relieve you of that software himself," I said, intent on gathering one more fact.

"Edgar doesn't speak German, and a little island in the Baltic is a helluva long way from his turf. Advantage, Goodborn!"

"And you had that ferocious guard dog and old Bodo hanging around," I added.

"It was a hell of a lot safer," agreed Chuck, "for Edgar to have you dumb pigeons find me, and then he and Putnam came in for the kill." He grinned again. "But we outfoxed them. Poor bastards."

"Did you know about Edgar?" I whispered in T.K.'s ear.

"Of course not."

Did he sound a little glib? I wondered how much T.K. had known up front. My bitter thought was, more than he would ever tell. Before I could fall into a big gloom over the shifting sands that constituted the connection between T.K. and me, I saw a boat speeding our way.

We all perked up. "Let's hail them if they get close enough," I said.

The boat, stunning in its sleek lines, slowed as it approached.

"Oh yeah!" said Chuck. "Big sexy Italian number. Technomarine. I've seen them in Mallorca and the Caribbean. Suckers can cruise at thirty knots."

As the boat came nearer, I waved, and the skipper decelerated his craft down to our turtle speed and pulled alongside *Painted Cow*. '*Godiva*' was stenciled across the transom in dark blue letters.

Four men had crowded into the cockpit. Dumbfounded, I recognized three of them. Bodo Schuld, neither waving nor smiling, in a tight dark jacket, stood next to a solemn man wearing a skipper's cap. Beside them, looking not one whit friendlier were Anatoly Salenko and Vlad the Impaler.

This didn't look like a social call.

Vlad shouted down into *Godiva*'s cabin and two muscular men carrying sub-machine guns across their chests appeared.

T.K. whispered, "Shit! They've got Kalashnikovs." He walked back to the stern and spoke to Chuck. I only caught the words, "for Chrissakes don't piss them off."

Chuck reduced our speed to about as fast as a duck could paddle.

Anatoly and Vlad neither spoke nor smiled, but scrutinized *Painted Cow*'s occupants. They made no eye contact, but moved with purpose as they prepared to board us.

In a robotic state beyond fright, I felt as if a vast space had opened between me and the other players, an isolated area where I existed with deadened feelings.

Rubbing his eyes, Ho Dung came topside, discerned the situation and fastened a couple of fenders along the port side between *Godiva* and us. His expression proclaimed, "I will never see Denmark."

I recalled Vlad playing doctor with the fishing tackle box on the beach Sassnitz, Anatoly, Bodo and Vlad dancing like Cossacks. We Americans must have seemed such gullible dupes. And Bodo? What was he doing here after Wulf was killed? Obviously in bed with the Russians.

"We come aboard, okay?" Vlad asked now in rather decent English. His fringe of salt and pepper hair puffed up in the moisture-laden air. He and Anatoly both wore dark blue windbreakers.

Chuck said, "Sure. I'll hoist the cocktail flag."

Without the party flag, we'd been pounding down the drinks for over an hour. I gave myself a quick half-hearted lecture to sober up, but my anesthetized state felt almost safe.

Vlad and Anatoly jumped onto the deck. Vlad, a heavy man with a muscular build, caused the boat to rock, and I had a stomach-churning flashback of our encounter with the freighter's wake. The apes with the Kalashnikovs stayed on *Godiva* where they had a clear view of our boat. Bodo still stood impassively in the cockpit of *Godiva*, while crew and visitors on *Painted Cow* were crammed into a tight little grouping amidships. Chuck stayed at the tiller. Anatoly, with his sad eyes, thin lips and the deep creases etched from nose to mouth, looked more morose than ever.

"How many passenger?" demanded Vlad, whose one-time affability had disappeared.

"Four," said T.K., with a hand gesture that paused shortly on each of us.

"Where are Standish and Putnam?" Vlad peered down into the cabin.

We all spoke at once.

T.K. stated matter-of-factly, "At the bottom of the Baltic," while Chuck said, "They hit the freighter's wake and their boat flipped and sank," and Ho Dung uttered, "Unlucky bad fortune, those two."

Anatoly exchanged an unhappy look with Vlad, who said, "We spoke by radio at twelve hundred hours." He paused, and asked in a sharp voice, "Where is CD-ROM?"

None of us responded. Vlad gestured to Ho Dung to relieve Chuck at the tiller. Chuck joined the group standing in front of the eel box. Anatoly pushed Chuck to his knees, pulled a handgun out of his windbreaker and placed it against Chuck's temple.

Vlad demanded again, "Did Putnam and Standish have CD-ROM?"

"No, dammit, I have it!" Chuck's face had turned red, but he didn't seem particularly afraid. I clutched T.K.'s arm.

Anatoly put the gun away.

"Now we talk business," said Vlad, almost jovially.

Anatoly shouted something to the muscle on the Russian boat, and one of the gorillas disappeared into the cabin. He reappeared carrying some papers and a laptop in a black leather case. Criminy, it looked like my laptop! He handed everything down to Anatoly. It *was* my laptop!

"Present for you," said Anatoly handing me the case.

"How—?"

"Not to ask question." Anatoly made eye contact, but his eyes were inscrutable.

Don't trust Anatoly. I took the laptop, wondering if he had found the demo CD of Aristotle I had stashed in one of the laptop case's many compartments.

Moments later, we were all squeezed around the little table in the cabin, Vlad and Anatoly across from Chuck, T.K. and me. Everything in the cabin felt clammy from when the wake sloshed water everywhere. Anatoly produced documents, apparently the agreement that Chuck and Edgar had entered into through Wulf's negotiations.

"Here is English copy," said Anatoly, handing a few pages to Chuck. "We start on page two, right after the section about down payment."

Chuck winced. Reading over it, he pursed his lips and scowled. No way, no way in hell," he continually muttered. "No matter what

Edgar promised, I'm not jumping through any friggin' hoops for these guys."

"Is problem?" asked Vlad.

Nobody heard Chuck's answer, because T.K. slumped down onto the table in a dead faint. I put my hand on his forehead, which felt as moist as everything else in the cabin. His face was a ghastly pale mask except for his two black eyes and bruised nose.

"I don't suppose you really are a doctor." I said, nodding at Vlad.

"Once I was." He pronounced the words as 'vunce I vas.'

"Can you look at him?" I got up from the table so he could tend to T.K.

"What has happened to him?" he asked, taking T.K.'s pulse. He pulled T.K.'s eyelid back and looked at his pupil.

I told him about the beating.

Vlad's diagnosis: "I think he has concussion and is also drunk."

The two Russians hauled T.K. up on deck, and I found a dry blanket in one of the boat lockers and put it over him. The goons still stood on the deck of *Godiva* with their Kalashnikovs.

Ho Dung remained at the tiller, but our boat, tethered to *Godiva*, just bobbed along. My stomach had the same dead hollow feeling as the rest of me. I sat by T.K. and clasped my arms around my knees and shivered, waiting for Chuck to erupt again and seal our doom.

Incredibly, I must have dozed off for a moment.

My head jerked up at an ungodly commotion in the cabin. An angry Russian voice shouted and there were the sounds of a scuffle with Chuck yelling, "It's right here! Dammit! It has to be!"

I looked down the companionway. Anatoly had Chuck on his knees again, gun to his head, while Vlad was removing the nautical charts from their locker one by one. He picked up the last chart, and his hand swept across the empty locker.

"Tell where is CD or we kill you." His voice sounded as harsh as his threat. "Then we kill your friends."

Anatoly shoved the gun to Chuck's temple.

I stood at the top of the companionway. "Leave him alone. I have the CD."

They stared up at me.

"The CD is in my duffel bag."

"You bitch!" yelled Chuck. "You conniving bitch."

"Ah, Zara!" Anatoly's sorrowful voice.

Zombie-like, I climbed down into the cabin and went forward to fetch my duffel bag. Anatoly stood by while I unzipped the duffel and groped for the CD. For one worrisome moment, I couldn't find it, and then my fingers found the round disk. When I handed it to Anatoly I said, "This software has caused more trouble and grief than it could possibly be worth!"

Anatoly didn't respond, but removed the CD from its sleeve and examined it. He handed it to Vlad who gave it a cursory glance. They took Chuck's word that the CD was the real McCoy.

I climbed up to the deck to check on T.K. who was still out cold. The fresh air smelled almost life sustaining, and if I could just breathe enough of it, this numb distance from the rest of the world would disappear.

Anatoly motioned me down into the cabin again. Vlad pointed a glowering Chuck to the table. He ordered, "You also sit!" and I sat on the bench next to Chuck, but as far away as I could get. The two Russians sat across from us. Anatoly took off his windbreaker. He wore a navy commando sweater with patches on the shoulder and elbows.

"Now we finish business."

The Aristotle CD-ROM lay on the table with a pile of papers and plastic glasses and Chuck's binoculars.

"If Edgar signed this horse shit, it was without my knowledge or agreement." Chuck, unchastened by his encounter with Anatoly's pistol, pointed to the page he was holding. "I'd never agree to go to Russia. You bozos must have rocks in your heads."

Their faces told me something got lost in translation. "He doesn't want to go to the Soviet Union," I explained.

Vlad crossed his arms and narrowed his eyes. He looked like a disgruntled Buddha. "Sorry, that is deal." He said something to Anatoly, who passed the pistol across the table. Vlad took the pistol, then opened the chamber and removed all the rounds.

"We have little game you have perhaps heard of." He paused and selected one of the rounds that he returned to the pistol. "Named after our motherland and French game of chance." He smiled at Chuck. "You want to play now? Better odds than casino."

My pulse was warming up to run another marathon. Under my sweatshirt, perspiration coursed down my ribs and between my breasts. Chuck sat in a defensive posture, arms crossed in front, staring at the Russians with a scowl that would have curdled milk.

"Look," I said, to Anatoly. "How much quality work will he do if you force him to come along?"

Chuck turned his head and regarded me with suspicious eyes.

Under my breath I said, "It might not be prudent for you to go back to Germany right now."

He continued to give me the stink eye.

"Give the business with Andrea time to cool down, and let the authorities investigate Wulf's death."

He chewed his upper lip.

"You can't return to the States," I reminded him, *sotto voce.* "The I.R.S. and all that."

The Russians watched us but didn't speak.

"You finagled all that money out of old Edgar and his friends. Sweet talk these guys into paying you a bundle."

Chuck licked his lips.

"Can you describe the conditions under which Mr. Goodborn would work?" I asked Vlad, "And how long would he have to stay?"

No answer as Vlad stared from me to Chuck. Now I could feel the sweat beading on my back

"Of course you would pay him generously. He's very talented. And what about the rest of the money for the software?"

"That is what we now speak of," Vlad said stiffly.

"You might as well listen to what they have to offer," I told Chuck as I got to my feet. "I'm going back to T.K."

Anatoly jumped up and placed his hand on my arm. "You stay at table." His sad Slavic eyes met mine. I had stopped watching the parade and had joined the marching band.

"What do you want Mr. Goodborn to do?" I asked Vlad, plopping down again next to Chuck. Being the go-between would be a lose-lose situation. Why hadn't I kept my mouth shut?

"He must order hardware." Vlad frowned. "Install and test data warehouse software."

"Would that be so hard?" I asked Chuck.

"No, dammit, but…"

"Tell them you want to bring Romy." I spoke low and quickly so the Russians couldn't catch what I was saying. "Ask if you can bring your boat. Make them jump through hoops!"

"Where would he live?" I turned to Vlad. "How many technical people are available to assist? Do they speak English? What is their skill set?"

Chuck stared at me as if I had just deplaned from a space ship. Anatoly brought my laptop to the table and commanded, "Write agreement."

And so I put together what I always thought of as the *Klintholm Agreement*. Chuck turned on his considerable charm and bargained for a decent apartment in Leningrad, a salary, Romy and his boat.

I nudged Chuck again. "Turn up the techno-babble. Geek out a little.

"You mean blah-blah equipment purchases and yada-yada customer acceptance testing." Chuck grinned at me. "The lady with the laptop isn't half as dumb as she acted."

The Russians stared across the table with wary eyes. It would be hard for an English-as-a-not-very-proficient second language speaker to pick up our fast and slangy conversation.

"Very difficult to order U.S. computer parts in Soviet Union." Anatoly, having honed in on "equipment purchases," spoke up.

"That is where the German connections will come in handy," I said, looking at Chuck again. He gave a curt nod. His eyes held a glimmer of admiration.

"I'll need project planning tools," said Chuck, "and an administrative assistant who speaks English—" He paused and looked at me. "All right! I have a great idea!" His grin was a mile wide. "Zara comes too. As my project manager."

"Oh no! I can't." My heart stopped beating.

Vlad nodded emphatically. "Project stays on time. Doesn't turn into five year plan." He and Anatoly roared with laughter. "I like idea."

"You come!" insisted Vlad. "Good technical manager hard to find."

"Oh please!" I said in a strangled voice. "I'm a single parent with a small daughter who needs her mother." With an effort I kept my tears dammed up. "I don't know any details of this software. Chuck will do a terrific job."

Anatoly and Vlad argued in Russian for a few moments, their voices raised, their gestures extravagant, but I couldn't tell who had taken what stance. The last thing I wanted was to be hauled off to Leningrad to work on Chuck's data warehouse. Every time I tried to stifle a sob, I hiccupped.

Anatoly directed a question at me. "Little daughter?" His eyebrows knitted into a puzzled frown.

"Not adventuress?" This from Vlad.

"No," I snuffled, still trying to hold back my tears. "Not adventuress."

"Then only to write agreement." Vlad's voice had assumed its former authority.

My world became whole again. I blew my nose and settled my trembling fingers on the keyboard.

It took forever to hammer out the details. Calmer, I read the draft aloud for everyone, and copied it onto a diskette. While I was digging around in the laptop case for a blank diskette, I found the demo copy of the CD-ROM in one of the many Velcro-closed pockets slipped inside the laptop's reference manual. I put the manual on the table under Chuck's old contract.

"We should have a hard copy of the agreement signed by everyone," I told them, "but I don't have a printer."

"Not to worry." Vlad took the diskette back to *Godiva.*

Chuck went into the head.

Anatoly remained at the table. I liked his sad face and his navy commando sweater and the fact that he was a little in love with me, but I hated his violent unpredictable world.

He pointed at the laptop. "Two things on computer without password." So they *had* snooped in my files.

"*Koteleti Pojarski.*" He smiled and his eye twitched ever so slightly.

"I collect recipes."

His smile grew broader. "And little essay. I like little essay."

"Little essay?" I didn't know what he was talking about.

"What I Did On Summer Vacation."

Shit. The journal. I felt myself blushing, because I had written personal stuff about T.K. and me, words only meant for our eyes.

Anatoly quoted, "'we made love in *Strandkorb,* in woods by nude beach, and in bathroom on pile of damp towels.' When I read of making love, I wish to be man in essay."

He gazed at me with his weary eyes. "Zara, come with me. Bring little daughter."

"No, Anatoly. Thanks, but no. I have to go home." I forced a feeble smile. "Can you check on T.K.? I'm worried about him."

"Anything for Zara." He climbed the companionway stairs up to the deck.

I swapped the demo copy of the CD-ROM for the real copy. They looked identical. My fingers shook like aspen leaves, and my sweat ran in rivers.

Vlad returned with copies of the agreement and a bottle of vodka. Anatoly climbed into the cabin behind him.

"You've a printer on board?" I asked, "and a computer?"

"We are not backward. I keep diskette. Please to delete your copy."

He looked over my shoulder as I erased the document, trying to control my trembling fingers.

Chuck came out of the head smiling so broadly I wondered if he had a secret stash of coke.

"Hey, thanks for your help, Zara. Maybe you can come to Leningrad and whip up a skillet of roast pork fried rice."

I forced another smile. The three of them signed the agreement, and I signed as a witness, then Anatoly and Vlad each made a toast with the peppery vodka. Just what a nervous stomach needed. T.K. woke, joined us in the cabin and drank the rest of this morning's tea. He told an East German joke that made the Russians roar with laughter. I zipped up my laptop and shoved it over the bunk. The Russians gathered up the paperwork and the demo CD-ROM. I tried not to look at it.

When we said our good-byes, Chuck seemed pretty up beat. Anatoly and Vlad, gesturing and jovial, couldn't be the same men who had held the gun to Chuck's head, but I knew circumstances change in an instant.

Chuck and his keepers climbed onto *Godiva*, and the unsmiling men with Kalashnikovs went below deck. T.K. felt well enough to take the tiller while I removed the fenders. Ho Dung went below for a well-earned break.

As *Godiva* pulled away, I took a deep breath and looked up at the sky, ready to thank whoever was keeping an eye on us. The bank of dark thunderheads had rolled off toward the east, leaving the clouds above us rimmed with a gold lining, probably fool's gold, but I didn't care.

I wanted to scream and laugh and cry. Giddy with relief, and still a little drunk, tired to the marrow of my bones, I climbed up on the eel box and pulled my damp sweatshirt over my head. "Chuck!" I yelled, after them. "The legend is true. Here comes the sun!" I waved the sweatshirt over my head and pointed at the sky.

Aboard *Godiva*, necks swiveled.

"I think I'm in love," Chuck bellowed over the sound of the engine.

"Zara, I think I'm in love!" Anatoly's heavily accented words echoed Chuck's.

Their engines rumbled as *Godiva* accelerated. I watched them go, and then I jumped off the eel box and put on my shirt. Ho Dung, ever discrete, remained below. T.K. sat at the tiller, a faint smile on his lips, amused but unfazed by my antics. The color had returned to his face, and his old insouciance was back. Without a word, he pointed behind me in the direction we were heading. A solid contour broke the flat watery horizon. Land!

"Your chalk cliffs behind Klintholm," said T.K.

I stuck my head into the companionway. "Ho Dung! Come and look. We can see Denmark!"

Pointing and grinning at the Danish horizon, Ho Dung made his way to the bow.

I climbed around the eel box and flopped down in the cockpit next to T.K. *"Di di Mau!"* I ordered.

"Aye, aye, captain," he responded, turning the tiller until the compass pointed three hundred ten degrees. Straight across the Baltic to Denmark.

~ * ~

We said goodbye to Ho Dung in Klintholm. I offered to sponsor him if he decided to come to the United States. He said he would consider living in the country of "people with big white shoe," his term for Americans.

Epilogue

The next day, T.K. and I arrived in Berlin via Copenhagen, with new passports and some cash. We checked into a quiet hotel by the Kaiserdamm, and my wish for hours of dreamless sleep in a clean bed was granted.

At breakfast the next morning T.K. left the table before his second cup of coffee, saying he had to "see a man about a dog."

Wanting to forget the last three days, I treated myself to a be-nice-to-Zara day. I started with a trip to the hairdresser, picked up my old passport, caught a noontime Bach organ concert, and ended with a new suitcase and enough clothes and accessories to test its capacity. I ran up an enormous telephone bill talking to Jody and Chloe. I even called the office to report the good news.

T.K. waited for me at our late afternoon rendezvous at the bustling Hotel Kempinski sidewalk café with the pink cloth and the pale umbrella. He read the *Herald-Tribune* and sipped a Campari Orange. Wearing a summer sport coat, with his legs stretched out in front of him, feet crossed at the ankles, he looked like an elegant man about town. Then he took off his sunglasses, revealing bruises and black eyes.

He spotted me, jumped up, kissed my cheek then looked me over with exaggerated interest.

"What happened to the lady with Nantucket hair and a worn out sweat shirt?"

"She has spent an ungodly amount of money to erase all traces of a very bad weekend," I said.

"You won't believe the coup I've pulled off," he said with a smug little smile, just itching to tell me something.

"What?"

"The wall dog we rescued will get a new home. Krista and Heinz are en route to Rügen."

Berliners Krista and Heinz Renneberg T.K.'s oldest friends.

"They're driving to Stralsund to bail the fearsome creature out of the clinic." T.K smiled like a Cheshire cat. "According to the vet, the beast has become rather docile, practically a pussycat in Rottweiler clothing."

"You're kidding."

"The best is still to come. They're taking the dog to Old Mundhenk. Uncle is delighted."

Some stories have a good ending.

T.K. signaled to the waiter and ordered a Campari Orange for me. He hesitated, and then asked, "When are you going back to Chicago?" He lit a cigarette, and waited for my answer.

Saying goodbye would be harder than I had imagined, bonded as we were by adventures, survival and sex.

"Did I ask a particularly difficult question?" he asked, squinting at me.

"I'm leaving for Denver tomorrow."

"Denver?"

"To pick up my daughter."

The waiter set a Campari Orange in front of me. I took a sip.

"I've got something to tell you that I hope will be good news," I said.

"Tell."

Why did I feel hesitant to share the secret?

"I swapped a demo copy for the authentic copy of Aristotle. The Russians and Chuck went off with software that will expire at the end of this month."

"You are shittin' me." His man-about-town look had vanished as he stared at me with wide disbelieving eyes.

"Our friends will be SOL."

"I can't believe it." He didn't seem overjoyed. "Where's the CD? Why didn't you tell me?"

"As of yesterday, the legitimate software is en route to Portland, Maine via the Danish post office. Air Mail, of course."

"Zara, why didn't you tell me? I thought we were partners."

"It just seemed better if no one knew."

He lit a cigarette, leaned back in his chair and exhaled a cloud of smoke. "Holy shit!"

I wanted to say, "There were always so many things you didn't tell me," but I held my tongue.

We sat in silence. He stared at the crowds crossing the Ku'damm then beckoned the waiter and ordered a Cognac.

"Aren't you pleased?"

"Yeah, I'm just in shock."

"I've got more news," I said. "Mostly good."

"I don't know if I can take another dose of your 'good news.'"

"You could have ordered a premium brand of cognac." I smiled, but T.K. still looked miffed. "When I called my office this afternoon, the finance guy told me the second payment from Edgar has finally hit the escrow account." I hesitated. "With Edgar dead, I don't know if we'll ever get the last installment. Probably not."

"That money is most welcome."

The waiter brought the Cognac and T.K. took a long sip.

Again, we sat without speaking. This is what I had feared. What did his silence mean?

"What about you? What are your plans?" I tried to sound bright and interested, but it came out rushed and awkward.

"Berlin for a few more days, and then," his voice trailed off. The look in his eyes was as bruised as his eye sockets.

"And then?"

"I'm going to head back to Rügen. Remember Herr Altmann, the man who wanted us to invest in those windmills?"

"You're going back?"

"And take another look at the windmills. Maybe investigate buying one of those old Baltic villas. Bail the Beemer out of the garage. Pay our hotel bill."

He stubbed his cigarette into the ashtray. "You know the rest. My son is coming over in mid-July. We'll do our annual hike in the Alps."

"That sounds nice."

Nice. Such a gutless, wimpy word. Nice.

I sipped my drink, afraid that if I looked at his battered face again, I would start to howl.

The light at the intersection changed and I watched a herd of Americans crossing the street wearing windbreakers and sneakers. *The people with big white shoe.*

~ * ~

That evening we took a long walk to a neighborhood of large shade trees and substantial villas where many of the consulates were located: a peaceful, ordered world a million miles away from shipping lanes and Kalashnikovs.

We found an Italian restaurant T.K. knew about. Brick walls, trellises and in the background, arias from Italian operas. The fashionable clientele stared covertly at the tall man with two black eyes who looked a little dangerous, and the stylish woman who just picked at her pasta.

We ate without much conversation, aware this was our last night, and that words didn't matter. After dinner, as we tasted various *Grappas*, I thought about asking the hard questions, like what T.K. had known when we set out on this misadventure, and why he had really invited me along, and about his long relationship with Putnam, but those topics would surely ruin the evening. We had no tomorrows ahead of us, and the answers now seemed unimportant.

We caught a taxi back to the hotel. The sky was a confection of dark pink and baby blue as the long midsummer twilight, always reluctant to fade into darkness, lingered another half hour.

"The last time we shared a cab you kissed me," I said, glancing at him.

"Do you want me to?" His voice was gruff, ready for a rebuff.

I turned to him. "Very much."

The weather changed overnight, and Tuesday morning Tegel Airport sulked again in the rain, another world of mirrors with glistening gray images, and watery metallic reflections. With a lump in my throat that felt like a golf ball, I said goodbye to T.K. in the passenger lounge. We both knew it would never work out.

The walk through the jetway seemed long, a procession from the past into the uncertain future, to Chloe and my new life, with the rain the only constant.

~ * ~

I found a great new job with minimum travel, and Chloe thrived in first grade, so why was I feeling down and out? The truth was, I missed T.K. more than I would have thought possible. I had departed so blithely and now I felt like a dull knife was removing my heart, sliver by sliver. We had exchanged a few emails, so I knew T.K. had found his villa in Binz. He also mentioned a temporary position at a university teaching a workshop on the changes in East Europe.

On a Friday evening in October when Chloe was at her father's, I was playing solitaire on my laptop in my pajamas when the phone rang. Not a number I recognized, but right away I knew T.K.'s voice.

"Zara, remember that teaching job I mentioned? Er... the position is in Chicago, actually. How do you like them apples? Just fell into my lap. I'm downtown at the Drake."

He sounded both a little tentative and a little guilty.

"Can you, ah...join me for a drink?"

I donned my best jeans, high heels and a fancy top, grabbed my jacket and locked the door behind me. The old ghosts had slipped into the shadows and life beckoned again.

For an author, nothing beats firsthand visits and interviews, but steeping myself in the background and history of the period were also of prime importance and will, I hope, inform the writing in *World of Mirrors*.

Bibliography:

Childers, Erskine, *The Riddle of the Sands*, New York, Dover Publications, 1976

Dodds, Dina and Allen-Thompson, Pam, editors. *The Wall in My Backyard, East German Women in Transition,* Amherst, University of Massachusetts Press, 1994

Ellis, William S., *Germany—The Morning After*, National Geographic, Vol. 180. No. 3, September 1991, 2 – 41.

Garton Ash, Timothy, *The Magic Lantern*, New York, Vintage Books, 1990

Garton Ash, Timothy, The File, A Personal History, New York, Random House, 1997

Kramer, Jane, *The Politics of Memory, Looking for Germany in the New Germany*, New York, Randon House,

Köhlers Flotten-Kalendar 1994, Das deutsche Jahrbuch der Seefahrt, Herford, Koehlers Verlaggesellschaft, 1994

Markovits, Inge, *Impefect Justic, An East-West German Diary*, Oxford, Clarendon Press, 1995

Müller, Christine & Bodo, *Über Die Ostsee In Die Feiheit*, Bielefeld, Delius Klasing Verlag, 1996

Philipsen, Dirk, *We Were the People, Voices From East German's Revolutionary Autumn of 1989*, Durham, Duke University Press, 1993

Schneider.Peter, *The German Comedy, Scenes of Life After the Wall*, New York, Farrar Straus Giroux, 1991

Vesilind, Priit J., *The Baltic: Area of Power*, National Geographic, Vol. 175, No. 5, May, 1989, 602- 635.

Von Der Porten, Edward, The Hanseatic League, Europe's First Common Market, National Geographic, Vol. 186, No. 4, October, 1994, 56 –79.

Winkler, Hermann, *Zeesboote*, Rostok, Hinstorff, 1990

Wolf, Christa, *The Author's Dimension, Selected Essays*, Chicago, University of Chicago Press, 1993

Wolf, Christa, What Remains & Other Stories, Chicago, University of Chicago Press, 1993

Wolf, Marcus *Man Without A Face, The Autobiography of Communism's Greatest Spymaster,* New York, Random House, 1997

A bit about the CD-ROM and its history: **C**omputer **D**isc **R**ead-**o**nly **M**emory
CD-ROM: Digital information that cannot be changed.
read-only memory – computer memory whose contents can be accessed and read but cannot be changed

1985: CD-ROM, invented by Phillips, produced in collaboration with Sony.

1989: Advanced controllers support an interface that is used by most CD-ROM drives, increasing ease of data transfer and storage.

1993: A CD-ROM drive becomes essential for video gaming

1995: First laptop PC incorporating a CD-ROM drive

Meet Judith Copek

When she's not gardening, travelling or puttering about the kitchen, she's researching her next novel at Burning Man or in the Northwoods of Wisconsin. Judith is a member of Sisters in Crime, Mystery Writers of America and New England Pen. She has published poems, short stories and memoir as well as an earlier novel.

Works From The Pen of Judith Copek

<u>**World of Mirrors**</u> - A failed spy and a clueless techie confront ex-Stasis, conniving Soviets and treacherous colleagues to retrieve bleeding edge stolen software.

<u>**Chased By Death**</u> - A conflicted woman sets out to find her long-missing sister, not expecting her ex-husband's killer to come after her. The perilous chase is on, from South Florida to Northern Nevada in a motorhome with her boyfriend, the boyfriend's daughter, and a cat

Letter to Our Readers

Enjoy this book?

You can make a difference

As an independent publisher, Wings ePress, Inc. does not have the financial clout of the large New York Publishers. We can't afford large magazine spreads or subway posters to tell people about our quality books.

But, we do have something much more effective and powerful than ads. We have a large base of loyal readers.

Honest Reviews help bring the attention of new readers to our books.

If you enjoyed this book, we would appreciate it if you would spend a few minutes posting a review on the site where you purchased this book or on the Wings ePress, Inc. webpages at: https://wingsepress. com/

Visit Our Website

For The Full Inventory
Of Quality Books:

Wings ePress.Inc
https://wingsepress.com/

Quality trade paperbacks and downloads
in multiple formats,
in genres ranging from light romantic comedy
to general fiction and horror.
Wings has something for every reader's taste.
Visit the website, then bookmark it.
We add new titles each month!

Wings ePress Inc.

3000 N. Rock Road

Newton, KS 67114

www.ingramcontent.com/pod-product-compliance
Lightning Source LLC
Chambersburg PA
CBHW061012120726

47910CB00006B/1889